LOUIS DE BERNIÈRES

Louis de Bernières is the bestselling author of *Captain Corelli's Mandolin*, which won the Commonwealth Writers' Prize Best Book in 1995. His most recent books are the short story collection *Labels*, the poetry collection *The Cat in the Treble Clef* and the novels *The Dust That Falls From Dreams* and *So Much Life Left Over*, which also feature characters who appear in *The Autumn of the Ace*.

ALSO BY LOUIS DE BERNIÈRES

FICTION

Station Jim
Labels and Other Stories
So Much Life Left Over
Blue Dog
The Dust that Falls from Dreams
Notwithstanding: Stories from an English Village
A Partisan's Daughter
Birds Without Wings
Red Dog
Sunday Morning at the Centre of the World
Captain Corelli's Mandolin
The Troublesome Offspring of Cardinal Guzman
Señor Vivo and the Coca Lord
The War of Don Emmanuel's Nether Parts

NON-FICTION

The Book of Job: An Introduction

POETRY

The Cat in the Treble Clef
Of Love and Desire
Imagining Alexandria
A Walberswick Goodnight Story

LOUIS DE BERNIÈRES

The Autumn of the Ace

VINTAGE

1 3 5 7 9 10 8 6 4 2

Vintage is part of the Penguin Random House
group of companies whose addresses can be found at
global.penguinrandomhouse.com

Penguin
Random House
UK

Copyright © Louis de Bernières 2020

Illustrations © Nicholas John Frith

Louis de Bernières has asserted his right to be identified as
the author of this Work in accordance with the Copyright,
Designs and Patents Act 1988

First published in Vintage in 2021
First published in hardback by Harvill Secker in 2020

penguin.co.uk/vintage

A CIP catalogue record for this book is available from the
British Library

ISBN 9781529110753 (B format)

Printed and bound in Great Britain by Clays Ltd, Elcograf S.p.A.

The authorised representative in the EEA is Penguin Random House
Ireland, Morrison Chambers, 32 Nassau Street, Dublin D02 YH68.

Penguin Random House is committed to a sustainable future for our
business, our readers and our planet. This book is made from Forest
Stewardship Council® certified paper.

This book is dedicated with infinite gratitude to Lavinia Trevor, whose years of hard work on my behalf made all the difference.

Since this unity means happiness, the individual is thus sent forth into the world by his own spirit to seek his happiness.

Georg Wilhelm Friedrich Hegel

Contents

Dramatis Personae

First generation, the four sisters:

Rosie Pitt, VAD in both world wars, wife of Daniel Pitt, mother of Bertie and Esther.

Christabel, photographer, bisexual lover of both Daniel and Gaskell, mother of Felix and Felicity.

Sophie, mechanic in First World War I, head of a dame school, wife of Fairhead, childless.

Ottilie, VAD in First World War, wife of Frederick, mother of Nora.

First generation, the two brothers:

Daniel Pitt, fighter pilot in First World War, SOE operative in the Second, husband of Rosie, father of Esther, Bertie, Felix and Felicity.

Archie Pitt, formerly of the Indian Army, childless.

First generation, the partners:

Gaskell, painter, lover of Christabel.

Fairhead, sceptical chaplain, husband of Sophie, best friend to Daniel Pitt.

Frederick, former naval officer and official of the Indian Civil Service, husband of Ottilie, father of Nora.

Ashbridge Pendennis (Ash), Rosie's first fiancé, American volunteer, killed in 1915.

The second generation:

Bertie Pitt, former cavalry officer, son of Daniel and Rosie, husband of Kate, father of Theodore, Jemima, Molly and Phoebe.

Kate Pitt, wife of Bertie, mother of Theodore, Jemima, Molly and Phoebe.

Esther Pitt, Wren officer, killed at sea during Second World War, daughter of Daniel and Rosie.

Felix McCosh, architect, son of Daniel Pitt and Christabel McCosh.

Felicity McCosh, daughter of Daniel Pitt and Christabel McCosh.

The third generation:

Theodore Pitt, son of Bertie and Kate.

Molly Pitt, daughter of Bertie and Kate.

Jemima, daughter of Bertie and Kate

Phoebe, daughter of Bertie and Kate.

1

Empty Holster

He paused in the middle of the airfield and thought about his lover. She came to his mind unprompted, a warm, golden image, and almost immediately he heard her voice repeating what she had said to him on the telephone just the evening before: 'Well, darling, we can't keep having wars just to keep you interested, can we? When are you coming up to see us? I'm going to spoil you rotten.'

The war was over, and in its own way it had been as exciting and interesting as the one before, but considerably stranger. This war had taken place by moonlight. The weeks of the dark of the moon had always been time off, as were the nights when there was a moon, but it was too cloudy or tempestuous, or there was no mission. In the last war he had never had the opportunity to become bored, the stress and excitement had been continuous, but in this one he had filled the empty hours with range practice, long walks on the South Downs with borrowed dogs, tinkering with his motorcycle, books and music. He had fulfilled a lifelong ambition by reading all of Balzac's *Comédie Humaine*. He had read all of Thomas Hardy twice, most of Ian Hay's very silly novels, the *Essais* of Montaigne, Sapper's *Bulldog Drummond* novels, in which our patriotic and intrepid hero usually 'shook off his chains and in one bound he was free', hundreds of back issues of *Punch, or The London Charivari*, all of Flaubert and most of P. G. Wodehouse. During his escapades in France he had even borrowed books from farmers and partisans. He had read a great deal of Mauriac and Duhamel, and even tried *Das Kapital* in French, on the insistence of a communist colleague, but it was appallingly dry. He had read the words whilst thinking of something else.

Ever since seeing the enchanting and exquisite Lily Pons performing in Paris a few years before, he had been in love with her, and in his tiny room on the perimeter of the airfield, in what was not much more than a wooden shed, he listened to her records on his wind-up gramophone until they were completely worn out and he had to buy them again.

Apart from that, he had taught French lessons twice a week to whomever on the airfield either wanted or needed to attend. It had occurred to most aircrew that if they were shot down over France, it might indeed be useful to know the language. Daniel's lessons were popular because they included contemporary slang, and comic renditions of regional accents.

It was true that there couldn't be wars just to keep him interested, but nonetheless, up to that moment when Christabel had popped into his mind, Daniel Pitt had been angry and resentful, limping away from the armoury with an empty leather holster at his left hip. He had tried every rhetorical trick he knew to avoid handing in his revolver, but in the end had been defeated by the victory. The moment the war had ended, the forces had reverted to their standard peacetime procedures. Everything was bogged down once more in the old wearisome, stifling clag of regulation and doing things by numbers. Every airman knows it; the moment a war ends the desk pilots are back in the cockpit.

Daniel had argued and prevaricated. He had said that although he was technically in the RAF he was actually working for SOE, and he might well be a flight commander shortly to be promoted to squadron leader, but he was really a soldier, and he was waiting for orders from elsewhere, and in the meantime why couldn't he keep the revolver and ammunition in the locked chest under his bed, just as he always had?

He loved his revolver. It was a Webley Mark VI, and the heft of it in his hand was like that of an instrument in the hands of a musician. It had seen him through his four years of adventures in occupied France as he flew his Lysander in and out by moonlight, dropping off and picking up spies and partisans. It must have saved his life half a dozen times. Now all he had was this empty leather holster, never again to hang from his belt on the left hip.

In the last war Daniel had been a fighter pilot with numerous kills to his credit, but in the spring of 1918 it had been decided that fighter aircraft should be used for ground attack. The chivalrous days of jousting in the clouds suddenly disappeared. Instead he was mowing down soldiers and horses by the hundred, flying his Camel through tempests of answering fire and miraculously surviving them. Since then he had regularly woken up suddenly from vivid dreams in which he flew at hedge height over vast puddles of muddy waters reddening with the blood of the floundering wounded and dying, lolling corpses spilling out of overturned staff cars.

In this second war Daniel, armed only with his Webley Mark VI, had always aimed for the right shoulder. He was a good snapshot, and he had chosen to defeat his enemies only by disarming them. No more machine guns, no more massacre.

During his training, all those years ago before the last war, the Sergeant used to say, 'Remember, lads, your rifle's your best friend,' but this revolver had been more than that. He liked to dismantle it for cleaning and see how long he could make the chamber spin. He would peer up the breech and see the rifling coiling towards the silver sixpence of light at the muzzle. He enjoyed the ritual of the copper brush and the pull-through. Above all he loved firing it at the range, always aspiring to a tighter group. On a good day, firing his revolver at paper targets, feeling the weapon leap in his hands, and seeing the sand spurt up in the bank behind it was all the catharsis that his troubled soul required.

He had finally agreed to hand it in to the armoury on condition that he could get it out again whenever he wanted to do firing practice, that no one else would be allowed to use it, and that he would never be told to make do with another one.

Just as it had in 1918, the peace of 1945 weighed heavily on Daniel's mind. In wartime there is no sense in thinking of one's future, and to have had one in prospect was disturbing and surprising. In late 1918, however, he had had a marriage to look forward to, and a life of doing something interesting somewhere in the colonies. Now he was fifty-three years old, and his mother and one of his daughters were dead. His marriage to Rosie had withered away and he had conceived two children by her bohemian sister, Christabel, who was still his lover even now. It had been a long and happy affair, made more poignant and magical by their long periods of separation, and their joyful reunions.

3

Daniel was staying in the RAF for the time being at least, because he was disinclined to set up a motorcycle dealership again, and could think of nothing else that he might want to do. He was relatively secure because of his high rank, his distinguished service and the decorations he had accumulated. He had been given a safe billet. The only alternative was to become a French teacher in a school somewhere.

Now, at the end of the war, there were too many lacunae in Daniel's heart. The first emptiness was his daughter's death, the second was the recent death of his mother, and the third was having been rejected by his son almost from the day of his birth. 'One of my sons is missing,' he often repeated to himself, 'but where the hell is he?'

These days he felt doubly diminished. As he had said to Christabel, 'I've gone from being a fighter pilot to an SOE operative, to a bloody transport officer, and Bertie doesn't give a tuppenny damn whether I'm dead or alive.' Limping angrily away across the silent airfield, without his beloved revolver, he had felt forsaken, and resolved that he must find Bertie. He would try to explain himself, they would come to an understanding, and at last all would be well.

Halfway back to his billet, he stopped and looked around at the sky now empty of Spitfires and Hudsons. There were no more Messerschmidts, Stukas or Focke-Wulfs coming at you out of the sun. There were flights of ducks and seagulls on the runway. You could hear the birds singing, and in the distance there were village bells ringing the changes. The war really was over; it was time for empty holsters, for commonplace but beautiful things like gluttony and love. He longed suddenly to be in Christabel's arms again. He must go up to Hexham and stay with Gaskell and Christabel.

2

Gaskell Back in Hexham

When Gaskell came home to Hexham, she found that every-thing had fallen into ruin, and that life was suddenly duller than had ever seemed possible.

The first thing she did when she returned was to go down to the barn that served as a hangar for the three biplanes she shared with Daniel Pitt, and which he had bought for a song after the last war, from the Aircraft Disposal Board. She had struggled to free the bolts of the barn door, having to resort, in the end, to releasing fluid and a hammer. The aircraft had suffered six years of disastrous neglect, and she knew just by looking at them in the dusty light that making them airworthy would be either impossible or preposterously expensive. The canvas was rotten, the wires were rusted, the engines seized, the seats had been eaten out by mice, and there was worm in the struts. There were swal-lows' nests under the upper ailerons, and pigeons had been nesting in the rafters above. She wondered where you would find an old-fashioned rigger in these days of steel and aluminium. It was all too damn depressing to contemplate, so she closed the barn doors and walked back to the house, resolving to speak to Daniel about it.

She paused by the redwood that grew on the great lawn before the house, and saw that the house was crumbling. Some of the sashes were rotten, and buddleia grew out of the cracks in the brickwork. The gutters were overflowing with moss, and there were slates missing from the roof. All around her the estate was reverting to nature, its pastures overwhelmed with nettles and brambles, its machinery rusted and seized, its woodlands over-crowded with slender poles competing for the light. Mr Wragge was all that held it together.

This was, she knew, the work of two world wars. In February of 1915 the gamekeepers and labourers had marched away with a Pals regiment, to die together in Flanders on a single day the following summer. The timber mill had not been used since then, and the vast circular saw with its six-foot blade had become accustomed to repose, the thick leather drive belts fragile and crumbling, the waterwheel outside in the stream forever locked, its paddles hung with weed and encrusted with lichen.

She and Christabel had kept the estate working between the wars by subsidising it from their artistic success, but when her parents died the duties had been an almost lethal blow. They had worked flat out for years to pay them off, and then another war had intervened.

Thank God for Oily Wragge. After the Home Guard had stood down in 1944, he had left the Norfolk Regiment to take up a new campaign, one man against the forces of nature on an estate of hundreds of acres and a house with a hundred windows. Thanks to his knowing how to turn a shotgun into a musket, the household had had venison, and firewood over which to roast it. Oily Wragge was sunburned and brawny, all year round it seemed, and his manner was ever-cheerful, but he suffered an inner agitation that would not let him rest. He had been captured by the Ottomans at Kut al Amara in 1915, with all that that entailed.

The interior of the house had changed almost completely. Lock, stock and barrel, Christabel's sister Sophie had moved her dame school up from Blackheath, and installed fifteen small children who had been allowed to run wild in the long corridors and empty rooms, daubing the walls with primitive art and constructing elaborate dens out of rugs and beds, tapestries and chairs. Fifteen land girls, accompanied by an agricultural supervisor, had settled into the outhouses and stables, bringing their high spirits and mischief with them. Then a dozen refugee children had arrived from Liverpool. It had been mayhem, but a beautiful one, and most of the children would remember their parentless war years as the finest of their lives. They would think of Sophie, with her great halo of silver hair, as an angel of delight. Christabel, who devoted much time to photographing them as if they were wild animals she had spotted on safari, they would remember as a kind tall lady with a camera who made them grow potatoes, and always gave away her share of the chocolate.

6

During all that time Gaskell had served in the Air Transport Auxiliary. She had flown every type of aircraft, from Hurricanes to Defiants to Lancaster bombers, to every airfield in Britain. She had slept in tents, in sheds and barns, in the backs of three-tonners. She had returned by train, by ship, by cadging lifts. She had been attacked by German fighters numerous times, and been unable to retaliate because her aircraft were armed on arrival and not on despatch. Through gritted teeth, with perspiration coursing down her face, she had learned to use cloud, to fake a lethal spin, to turn and threaten to ram, to bail out and pray that she would not be machine-gunned as she swayed helplessly beneath the canopy. She had learned to do forced landings in fields, she had crash-landed through trees. She had learned to do almost everything that Daniel Pitt had learned in the Great War.

Gaskell loved Daniel Pitt, even though he was Christabel's other lover, and had had two children by her. She and Christabel had brought Felix and Felicity up, and nothing could have made her happier. She loved Daniel for giving them the children, and because she loved him anyway. She had seldom been jealous, as she was when Christabel went astray with other women. Of course she lay alone at night wondering exactly what Daniel and Christabel were doing when he was in the house, but nearly always, in the early hours, Christabel would slip back into bed beside her, smelling of his cologne, cuddle up, and whisper, 'You know I love you just as much, don't you, darling? Probably more.'

Gaskell had seen Daniel Pitt many more times in the war than Christabel, because she had frequently delivered to Tangmere, and Daniel had always been free during the dark of the moon. As he was adept at swapping his cigarette ration for petrol they had gone to Brighton on his combination, and on jaunts to Winchester and Salisbury. Daniel let her drive the combination, something he trusted no one else but Oily Wragge to do, but she and Daniel were friends in the way that men are, and never discussed his relationship with Christabel.

Now it was September 1945 and all those years had gone. The children were back in Blackheath and Liverpool, there would be no more flying and no more wild excitement. The land girls had left behind nothing but bare truckle beds and broken hearts.

Gaskell was back with her lover, wondering if it could ever be the same, and even if she still loved her at all. Gaskell had looked at herself in the mirror and noted the changes. Before the war she had dressed in a Norfolk jacket and plus fours, with a smart tie and a high-collared shirt. She had worn a green tarboosh on her head, sported a monocle, smoked Black Russians through a preposterously long cigarette holder. She had slicked her short black hair with brilliantine, and affected a languid Bloomsbury drawl.

Now she dressed in brogues and the practical tweeds of a middle-aged man, and her grey hair was too short for slicking back. Smoking just made her cough, and there had been no Abdullas or Black Russians for years, just cheap cigarettes whose tobacco sometimes slid out if you pointed them downwards. Her face was redder and her features were slowly collapsing into imprecision. The meagre diet and frantic activity of the war had pinched her features. She realised that she had once been beautiful in her own singular way, just as Christabel had. All that she recognised, looking back out at herself, were her captivatingly green eyes.

She had talked with Christabel last night, and they had made a decision. The only way to recreate their life together was to get back to work. Gaskell must take up her palette again, and Christabel must restock her darkroom. A mutual life requires a plan. They would aim for their first full post-war exhibition. It would be in September 1946, and they would take it to London, Edinburgh and Dublin. It would be their salvation through Art.

3

Oily Wragge (1)

When the second war ended, it was a bit like when the first one did, with all of us old soldiers wondering what was going to happen next, and what would become of us. I had a whale of a war in the Norfolks, my old regiment in the last scrap, mostly messing about in Thetford Forest, and I was sort of all right because when they wound up the Home Guard I went to work for Miss Gaskell and Miss Christabel up in Hexham, and that compared pretty damn well with what I went through in Mespot in 1915 and then in the Turkish camps.

It didn't turn out so good for Captain Pitt, though. I say 'Captain', because he wanted to keep his old army rank from the Royal Flying Corps, but he went into the second war as a flight lieutenant, and later on they made him a squadron leader. He also came out with a limp because he lost two of his toes doing very hush-hush stuff in France, flying spooks in and out in Lysanders, which he's not allowed to talk about, but I happen to know he's got a bar on his Military Cross, and a Legion of Honour and a *Croix de Guerre*.

He also got a broken heart because his daughter Esther was sunk, torpedoed, and gone down in five minutes flat. I'd say it took him a good five years to get his smile back, because no amount of medals and stripes and derring-do ever makes up for something like that.

I was out in Dortmund with him before the war, and we had a motorcycle business we'd set up with a couple of Kraut friends of his he'd captured in the Great War. Of course we'd had to come home when the slurry hit the spreader, and that was why I'd had to leave behind my German missus. Baldhart and me weren't married, but we might just as well have been. She didn't even have a passport, and we didn't think we'd be apart that long. She was my landlady to begin with, in a big house that used to

9

be posh before her husband got killed at Verdun. In my day it was full of a nice gaggle of naughty girls, some of them getting paid, and some not.

I had great times with Baldhart, and I really and truly loved her. Back in Blighty for the years of the war I couldn't stop thinking about her, and it was eating at me, and I knew I had to go back afterwards and pick it up with her again. It was early in 1946, I asked Miss Christabel and Miss Gaskell if I could have two weeks off, and they said yes, so I borrowed one of the Broughs from the Captain, and drove it all the way back to Dortmund to see if she was still there.

Let's face it, Dortmund always was a shithole, with its thick yellow smog, and everything covered in wet smuts, and the stink of sulphur and burning coke, but even though it was truly a shithole I still loved it because I had the happiest years of my life there, working with the Captain on the motorcycle business, and getting pissed in bed with Baldhart, and shagging each other silly in a house full of sluts.

But when I went back, there wan't no Dortmund. There was just thousands of acres of rubble and burned timbers. There was no houses and no shops and no smog and no Hoelsch Steel-works and not even any pigeons or rats or cats. I couldn't find where Willy and Fritzl's business used to be, and I couldn't find where Baldhart's house was, because there wasn't nothing anywhere, there weren't even streets or anything with an address. And this is what you do with twenty-one thousand tons of high explosives and incendiaries when you're getting revenge for the Blitz and you've got to get rid of the factories.

Well, there *was* a few people about the place. *Trümmerfrauen*. Women in rags, they was everywhere you looked, so thin you could see the bones. They reminded me of those wrecked Armenian women back in Mespot in 1915, with horseshoes nailed to their feet, but these women had their feet wrapped in rags or paper, and they was working ever so slowly but never giving up. They were sifting through the rubble finding anything that wasn't broken, and making neat little rows of them. I asked one of them if she knew where Baldhart's street had been, but she just looked at me with big mad eyes and shook her head. She was filthy. I could just about see the stink coming off of her.

And this other woman comes towards me, and I suppose she'd be about Baldhart's age, and she's stumbling through the rubble and falling over at every step, and she's got bleeding hands, and she comes up to me and kneels in front of me and holds out her hand, with the palm up all covered with cuts, and her face is all smeared and her hair is all matted. And she looks up and offers herself for a few marks.

Well, I had this half-eaten jam sandwich in my pocket and I got it out and I gave it to her, and she wolfed it down and then she licked the paper, like a dog, and then she held out her hand again, like before, and asked me if I wanted something. *Was kann ich für Sie tun? Wollen Sie etwas?* And she started scrabbling at my flies, but I backed off. I had two half-crowns in my pocket and I put them in her hand, and she knelt back on her ankles and held up the coins and just stared at them. Just knelt there, staring at the coins. I don't know where she could have spent them. There wasn't no bank to change them in.

I went and sat on some steps that must have once led to a door. I didn't have a clue where I was. And I looked out over that fucking great desert of wreckage, going on and on forever, and all those skeletal *Trümmerfrauen,* scarecrows in rags picking through the ruins, and I put my elbows on my knees and hung my head, and I just knew what had happened to Baldhart back in 1943.

Even so I looked around for two more days, but then I got back on the Brough and came home, and after that I considered that my last chance was gone, and I was just going to go on from day to day until there was no more days.

4

Puss

The unorthodox *ménage à trois* of Christabel, Daniel and Gaskell resumed its natural course during his visit to Hexham in late 1945. All of them had feared that it would go badly, that it would be impossible to re-establish their old *convivencia*, but their happiness at being back together for the first time in years, assisted by venison and burgundy, had been exhilarating. They had sat before the fire in the dilapidated drawing room, with its rotting velvet curtains, crumbling carpet and scarred wallpaper, and it was as if it was 1939 again. They had drunk a little too much, because all of them believed in moderate excess, while Gaskell and Christabel had talked about art and related sad and ribald stories of the sexual escapades of their set of bohemian friends.

That night, it had been silently acknowledged that Christabel would spend the night with Daniel, just as in the old days, and so it was that at half past midnight, Gaskell had taken Daniel in her arms and hugged him warmly. 'Have fun,' she had said. 'I think I'm too tired and happy to be jealous.' Christabel had kissed her on the cheek, saying, 'Goodnight, darling, we do love you,' and Gaskell had gone alone to her bed and slept in peace.

Their lives became as they had been before, with Daniel appearing in Hexham on his motorcycle every month or so, and Christabel occasionally travelling down to stay in Chichester, so as to be near the airfield at Tangmere. She and Gaskell resumed their work, because work was becoming ever more important the older they grew. In April of 1949 Gaskell and Christabel had such a successful exhibition that they celebrated the sudden windfall by fulfilling a very old ambition. They had been talking about it ever since the 1920s, and now they finally got around to it.

Whereas it had been easy to bring Daniel back into their lives, it had not been easy for the two lovers to rebuild their own relationship after the war. They had spent almost all of it apart, and a relationship only survives when the two concerned are growing together in common project. Christabel had kept up her photography, in the sense that she had kept a record of the bedlam that the house had become during the conflict, but Gaskell had not put brush to canvas once, making do with filling her sketchbooks with charcoal drawings. Their artistic life had fallen into abeyance, and both were all too aware that a new and much younger generation with different attitudes and values was snapping at their heels. It almost felt as though it was time to hand on the baton and get out of the way. In any event, their band of bohemian and sexually omnivorous brothers and sisters, who 'lived in squares, painted in circles, and loved in triangles', was steadily being whittled away; Lytton in 1932, Dora by suicide in 1932, then Roger fell downstairs in 1934, and Julian was killed in Spain in 1937. JMK's heart gave out in 1946, and of course, in 1941, Virginia filled her pockets with stones and waded into a river. Those that were left seemed to have scattered. Gaskell and Christabel felt like remnants.

They were both in their fifties, and felt as if their golden days had passed. They had been revolutionaries in their time, and now their revolution had grown stale. The thought of learning new ways and abandoning long-cherished standards was too much to bear. They both wished to continue as they had been, working to the same ideals, living for the sake of pleasure and art, even if it meant becoming like the standard bearer who advances into battle, only to look around and discover that all the troops have gone.

To make everything gloomier still, quite apart from the fact that the estate and the house were in terrible condition, their children had grown up. Gaskell had hardly seen Felix since he was twelve, and Felicity since she was ten. Now she was learning Pitman Shorthand at a college in London, and he was filling in time teaching French at a Dickensian prep school with a culture of cold showers, constipation and flogging. He was wondering whether or not to go to university, or go abroad. For both Christabel and Gaskell, the absence of the children, the passing of the wonderful years of their infancy and childhood, had left a devastating void in their lives.

They had walked the estate together, mulling things over, reflecting that it would be pointless to part at this time of their lives, thinking of things that might pull them back together now that their beauty had faded, everything that could be said had already been said, and their physical passion had largely died away. They decided that Gaskell must experiment with every painting style she could think of, in the hope of finding a new direction that might fire her up, and that she should also work on her drawing technique. Christabel told her that she should do something with her charcoals. She herself was to work up to an exhibition of her photographs of the house and estate as they had been during the war, with a view to publishing them as a book. She was going to ask Tom Eliot if he would perhaps write a few lines as captions.

For years now, ever since the 1920s, despite the doubts of their friends, Gaskell and Christabel had had the idea that it would be great fun to have a pet lion, and now that their exhibition had sold well, they finally bought one from the Pet Kingdom department in Harrods.

This was not any ordinary lion, but a white lion from Timbavati in South Africa, a rare and precious creature, sacred in his native land. He had been born the only male in a litter of four cubs, which had been found abandoned and starving in the bush near Acornhoek, and raised by a farmer who quickly realised that he had a valuable asset on his hands. By the time he reached Harrods he was twelve weeks old, and although he would have to be fed milk until he was ten months, he was just beginning to take meat. Thanks to being tended by humans, he was completely tame.

Gaskell and Christabel had heard about it from a friend, and driven down in their Bentley Speed Six, which they parked outside the shop in Knightsbridge as they went in to enquire. They were tempted by the tigers and leopards, and even the alligators, but this white kitten was playful, friendly and enchanting. They bought it, and three days later it arrived by train at Hexham, where Oily Wragge and the floor manager who had accompanied it on its journey unloaded the crate and heaved it into the back of a van.

By the time the lion arrived at the estate, so had Felix, Felicity and Daniel. They gathered together on the lawn for the prising open of the crate, and peered inside at the animal which was already quite large, although tiny by comparison with what it would be in three years' time. It gazed back up at them with the most beautiful and innocent golden eyes that Africa had ever conjured from the earth.

'It's so adorable!' whispered Christabel reverently, and Gaskell said, 'Who's going to lift it out?'

'I will,' said Felicity. She bent down and gathered it under the armpits, heaving it out and gathering it to her chest. Her black hair fell about her face as she buried her nose in its fur. 'He smells so sweet!' she said, adding, 'My gosh, he's terribly heavy.'

Daniel looked at his unacknowledged daughter cuddling the cub, and a pang shot through his chest and took him by the throat. How painful it is to have to love so much. It had been the same with Esther; loving too much lays you wide open for that fatal stab under the ribs. The cub licked Felicity's chin, and she exclaimed, 'His tongue's like sandpaper!'

They took turns to carry the cub, each exclaiming at its weight, and then Felix put it down on the grass, saying, 'I expect he could do with a scamper.'

The cub stood for a second, then suddenly skipped and shot up the redwood tree, clinging to the thick bark about seven feet up. 'Oh gawd,' said Oily Wragge, suspecting that it would be him who would have to get it down.

'He's stuck,' said Daniel. Back in the mid-twenties he had advised Christabel and Gaskell not to get one, and he had been getting ready to say 'I told you so'. But now, even he was captivated.

The cub looked around wild-eyed, and Felix, who was tallest of all of them, went up and lifted him off the tree, a substantial amount of bark coming away with the claws. Daniel watched his son wistfully; Felix was very much as he had been when he was that age, black-haired, pale-skinned and blue-eyed; but he was taller and probably stronger. It occurred to Daniel that perhaps the whole point of death was so that every generation might be an improvement on the last. Felix put the cub down, rolled it over, and ruffled its stomach and chest. The cat clamped his arm with forepaws and teeth, and began to scrabble away at it with his hind claws.

'Lucky I had a coat on,' said Felix, after he had managed to disentangle himself. 'Look, he's disembowelled my sleeve. I think we'd better clip his nails.'

'Imagine what he'll do to the furniture,' said Felicity brightly. 'It's lucky it's all wrecked already.'

'It's the stair carpet and curtains I'm worried about,' said Daniel.

That evening after supper, Oily Wragge went straight to bed. He was never entirely sure what his place was in this strange household, whether he was expected to stay and chat about subjects that did not interest him and people of whom he had never heard, or whether he was expected to disappear. He was unclear as to whether he was an employee, or an honorary member of the family, and he was puzzled as to what the nature of all the relationships really was. In any event, he felt more comfortable in bed reading magazines about motorcycles than he did sitting with the others as they talked about G. E. Moore or Lady Ottoline Morrell. The only one he felt at home with was Daniel Pitt, who seemed indifferently to straddle both worlds. Mr Wragge had been a kind of uncle to Felix and Felicity for a couple of years, but they had grown up so quickly that sometimes he looked at them and wondered who they were.

Downstairs Felicity sat on Daniel's knee with one arm around his neck, as she always had since she was a little girl, and Felix sat between his two mothers on the sofa. Daniel, Felix and Gaskell were nursing a dram of whisky each, and Felicity and Christabel were sipping crème de menthe. The enormous white kitten lay on its back on the rug in front of the fire, fast asleep with its paws in the air.

'What are we going to call him?' asked Felicity. 'It has to be Simba, doesn't it?'

'Darling,' said Gaskell, 'everybody's pet lion is called Simba.'

'How about Leontari?' suggested Christabel. 'It means "Little Lion" in Greek.'

'How on earth do you know that?' asked Felix, raising an eyebrow.

'Oh, you know, as you go through life, you pick things up. Either one is naturally scholarly and learned or one isn't.' She raised an eyebrow archly and looked at Felix with a knowing air. 'Actually my father had a Greek dictionary that I snaffled after he died, so I looked it up.'

'I don't have any suggestions,' said Daniel. 'In my experience cats end up with some sort of name anyway, and it's never the one you gave them at the outset.'

'Well,' said Felicity, 'I like the idea of Leontari. It's very original and very nice, and it suits him.'

'Anything but Simba, darling,' said Gaskell. 'Leontari it is.'

In the morning Wragge came down when they were at breakfast, made himself a triple-decker strawberry jam sandwich from slices of toast, waved it at the lion who was being fed slices of bacon by Felicity, and said, 'Has anyone taken him out yet? He must be just about ready to squirt.'

'It's raining,' said Felix.

'S'all right with me. I'll put a coat and cap on and he won't care anyway. I'll take him out for a stroll. Come on, Puss.'

5

A Letter to Felix

Hendon Aerodrome
North London

4 May 1949

My dear boy,

  Thank you for your note, which arrived yesterday, with its request for advice and its news of the latest antics of the good Puss. I did expect that he would try to climb the curtains one of these days, and I am not a bit surprised that he has done so. They were done for, in any case, were they not? I am also not at all surprised that your football did not survive his attentions. I suggest you get an old-fashioned medicine ball, as they are quite solid, and would take very much longer to destroy.

  As for advice about national service, well, I dare say that any of the services would lead to travel. If you join the Royal Armoured Corps you will almost certainly be sent to Germany. If you manage to wangle your way into an elite regiment, such as the Blues, or the Coldstreams, you would make a lot of useful connections should you want, for example, to be 'something in the City' afterwards. If you join the infantry you may find yourself in some ghastly tropical hellhole looking for communists. If you join the RAF I doubt if they would bother to teach you to fly if you are only to be doing eighteen months' service. I don't know much about the navy, but I imagine that being confined to a very small space with a great many other men for weeks at a time would only suit a certain kind of person. Submarines would be even worse.

  If I had to do national service I would try to get myself into the Royal Engineers or the Signals, because there is so much scope for learning things that will be of practical use all through life. For example, one could end up as anything from an architect to a motor engineer. However, as you are not altogether very like me, I don't know what to advise, except to look at their lists of options and see what takes your fancy.

  What do you want to do afterwards? Go to university?

I would say three things. Firstly, in the services you never get what you volunteered for. Secondly, there is a surprising amount of empty time to get through, and I strongly advise you to learn a musical instrument, or get into the habit of extensive reading, or take up some sort of time-consuming activity such as ornithology. Thirdly, you will be treated so badly that you will not possibly survive without a very good sense of humour.

I have seen quite a lot of Felicity recently, as she lives not far away, in a flat with two other girls from her college. Recently she came to a mess dinner with me, and I am flattered to say, some of my brother officers actually believed her to be my mistress! Such is my undeserved reputation.

Good news about Ireland, eh?

All the best, your loving sort-of-uncle,

Daniel P.

6

Frederick and Ottilie in 1947

Almost all of their friends had decided to stay on in India, some remaining in their jobs on short contracts, and others retiring to their bungalows in the hills to live off whatever pensions or private incomes they had. Many were from families that had lived and served in India for three or four generations, to whom Britain was no longer in any real sense a home, and it was surely better to keep up the old way of life as long as possible, hoping that the money did not run out before their lives did. Younger officers in the army made enquiries as to whether it was possible to retain their commands, or some kind of role in the armed forces, and it usually was. The tea planters found no reason to leave, as yet, but nonetheless made enquiries about moving to Ceylon, if the worst came to the worst.

The Europeans who were living in the Punjab or Kashmir, or Bengal, regions on the new borders between India and the two Pakistans, necessarily left within days of the holocaust that whipped up within a few hours of independence. They made their way to Bombay or Delhi, most of them shipping home, passing through the Gateway to India for the last time with tears in their eyes, but also with relief in their hearts. After Port Said, the men followed the time-honoured custom of throwing their tropical topis into the Mediterranean. That was how you gave up on India; you let it float away.

Frederick and Ottilie thought hard about leaving. In Madras there had been no anti-Muslim riots, and British colonial officers and administrators continued to share their offices with their Indian colleagues, who had been brought in in ever greater numbers for many years now, after the Indianisation Act of 1919, and ever since the rules had been changed, so that Indians no longer had to go to Cambridge to qualify for the ICS. It had all been surprisingly smooth and gentlemanly, because the British had been planning the transfer for years, and only recently, because of Mountbatten's lightning decisions, had had to get round to finishing off the job, perhaps too hastily, but expeditiously at the very least. Everybody realised that if you create an educated native elite, it is only natural and inevitable that one day it will step into your shoes and oblige you to step into your slippers.

Frederick was Secretary to the Judicial Department, and Remembrancer of Legal Affairs. He came home one night, settled himself on the veranda with a chota peg and said, 'Well, Ottilie, my darling. They've asked me to stay on. The usual three-year contract. What do you think? Shall we give India-for-the-Indians a chance?'

Ottilie had become ever more like herself over the years. Her breasts had become heavier, her pear-shaped body more pear-shaped, her abundant hair still framing her large brown eyes, but now entirely silver. She still loved Frederick with all her heart, even though he was stooped, and very much weakened by occasional bouts of malaria.

'You're fifty-four now,' she said. 'If we stay another three years, you'll be fifty-seven, and then what will you do in the last seven before you retire?'

'They might renew again,' he said.

'But what if they don't?'

'What worries me is that I may not be treated very well. I mean, the boot's on the other foot now, isn't it?'

'Are there any signs of that?'

'Well, no, but you can't help but be a little anxious. We have rather lorded it over them, haven't we?'

'But we've had Indian staff senior to junior Europeans for ages now, and *chee-chees* too. And you haven't been personally lording, as far as I know.'

'Other people have,' said Frederick. 'You get damned by association, if you know what I mean. The temptation to get your own back would be pretty much irresistible, don't you think? I'd be desperately sorry to leave. This place has got under my skin. You know what they say: you can take the man out of India, but you can't take India out of the man. Can you really imagine living somewhere like Woking?'

'It doesn't have to be Woking, darling. Of course it's harder for you. You've been here much longer than I have.'

'What would we do back in Blighty? I can ask for a transfer to the BHCS, and I'd certainly get one, but it would all be preposterously dull, wouldn't it?'

'We'd just have to bite the bullet, and go back and see.'

'I absolutely don't want to end up teaching history in a prep school.'

'And I don't want to be matron in a prep school.'

'Actually it wouldn't be so bad, would it? Long holidays and masses of cricket. Anyway, it's horrifying what's been happening since August, isn't it? Muslims against Hindus, Muslims against Sikhs, massacres and atrocities. Trains arriving in stations laden with nothing but corpses. I hear the Muslims have left Delhi, and it's filled up with Hindus and Sikhs coming the other way. They're all in tents. Millions of them. Everything's gone to the dogs already. I suppose it should have been obvious after the Great Killing.'

'But that's all been up north, darling. It's still lovely here.' She looked out over the twilit garden, and sighed. 'It's still so beautiful, just as it was before. Everything's so normal it's as if nothing has happened. Maybe it's all been a dream, a beautiful dream, but it's not over yet. We don't have to wake up until we get woken, do we? I mean, we're not in any danger, are we? No one's going to come after us, it'll just be Indians against Indians.'

'What if the violence spreads? It's bound to.'

'But is anyone turning against us? I mean, is anyone rounding up Europeans? Anywhere?'

'No. Not yet. But they've had to empty out of Simla and Peshawar and Lahore. And Bengal's a mess too. And would you like to be here when they start killing each other? Your clinic would never cope, you can be sure of that. India for the Indians. Hooray.'

'But wouldn't we miss it terribly? I mean, just think how fond we are of everybody. Just the thought of abandoning the servants is heartbreaking. What would they do?'

'I doubt we'd have any in Blighty, would we? It might be a relief. It drives me doolally that you have to have half a dozen more servants than you need, just because one servant's caste means he can't fetch hay for the horses and another's means that he can fetch it but he can't give it to the horse. The sheer madness of it's infuriating.'

'Is it any more doolally than the Warrant of Precedence?'

Frederick laughed. 'No, I suppose it can't be. In some ways we're no better than they are, are we, really?'

She watched a tiny squirrel with a brown stripe along its back, bustling up a neem tree. 'You'll have your pension, won't you? You've done your twenty-five years. What's it going to be worth?'

'Somewhere around one thousand a year. And the compensation would be something like £4,500.'

'But that's simply enormous. We could easily live off that at home. And we could have a char woman.'

'Yes, we could, but we'd have to buy a house too, unless I get a job at a school, with accommodation thrown in, or we rent somewhere. But I'd really rather not. I think I'd go for a job in Whitehall, or just retire and eat lotus.'

'Think of the competition,' said Ottilie doubtfully. 'There'll be hundreds of people back from India. Practically all the Europeans in *Thacker's Directory*, I should think.'

'Well, I know I couldn't be a box-wallah. I've got no commercial sense at all.'

'How much is a house, do you think?'

'A nice little place in the Cotswolds would set us back a couple of thousand. And we'd need a car. That's another five hundred.'

'We could get a second-hand one. I've heard you can get just about anything on hire purchase, these days. What about this house? What would we do with it?'

'Well, you know Ali Khan? My golf partner? The tea and jute and spice and everything else wallah who comes here for dinner just about every month? Well, he's made an offer. More than we could expect, given that so many people are selling up. He says he's always loved this house ever since he came in '32 and we served him a *gurrum* he'd never had before.'

'Well, the view is gorgeous,' said Ottilie.

'And he said he'd keep on the servants.'

'What if we left?' said Ottilie. 'What about Sir Barkalot? I couldn't bear for him to be in quarantine for six months in some dreadful kennel. He couldn't bear it either. And we can't possibly put him down.'

'Hmm, well, he's eight years old, isn't he? Labradors never get past twelve.'

'A three-year contract might see him out,' said Ottilie. 'Then we can go home. And Nora will be nineteen. That's still lovely and young. She can go to art college, or do a secretarial course, or go to Paris and fall in love with a *deuxieme dragon* and inherit a chateau on the Loire. The trouble is, she doesn't really have any interests, does she? She seems to have no vocation whatsoever.'

'None at all. She only likes mooning about and playing tennis and eating chocolate eclairs before they melt. Maybe she's just marriage fodder.'

Ottilie laughed. 'Oh no, we'll have to send her to a finishing school in Switzerland, to brighten her up! Anyway, it doesn't seem to matter with girls, does it? Almost all of us end up having babies anyway. If you're plumbed up like a girl, you end up doing what girls do. Look at me. I was a VAD in the Great War. I did great things. I worked my socks off for four years, and then ended up with a baby. Two babies, counting you.'

Frederick stabbed her playfully with his elbow and she stabbed him back with hers. He said, 'I think you might be forgetting that you've been supervising a very busy clinic all this time. I did ask Nora if she would mind moving back home, and she said she wouldn't.' He paused. 'Are we really going to stay in India because of a potty old Labrador with asthma?'

'It looks like it,' she replied. 'And because we still love it here. Perhaps we'll have had enough by 1950.'

'When and if we do go, I think we should retire to Bosham,' said Frederick. 'We could get a little dinghy and sail on the Solent, and I could gaze longingly at HMS *Howe* going in and out of Portsmouth, and think about Jutland.'

'If we went home,' said Ottilie, 'you'd have to learn to cook. Remember, I've been spoiled, and don't know a colander from a lemon squeezer.'

'Rock-hard mutton chops, rock-hard potatoes, and rock-hard peas,' said Frederick. 'I'm sure I could manage that. That's all we've lived off for decades, apart from the *gurrum*.'

'Oh my goodness, we couldn't possibly live without that. Where would we get all the spices in England? Would I have to go up to Fortnum & Mason's every month? Are there trains from Chichester? I'm going to have to get the cooks to teach you before we go.'

She turned and looked at him, her round eyes shining. 'Maybe we could live in France and have real, wonderful food for the rest of our lives. Mutton that's actually sheep, and not scabby old goat.'

'We'd better start at home, don't you think? We can branch out from there.'

'Do you still love me?' asked Ottilie, taking his hand. 'You haven't said it for ages.'

Taken by surprise, Frederick said, 'Of course I do. Marrying you was the best wheeze I ever pulled off. I love your round eyes and your round face, and your quirks, and your lovely voice. Always have.'

'And my round backside?'

'And your round backside.'

'It's getting rounder now that I'm on the turn.'

'I'm on the turn too,' said Frederick. 'Do you still love me?'

'Best wheeze I ever pulled off. Thank God for broken wrists. I look back and can't think how deft and clever I was, rescuing you like that.'

'Thank God for wet steps and smooth leather soles, and public lectures on Fabian Socialism.'

'And now India's got Nehru in charge and he's a Fabian! I do so wonder how it'll all turn out.'

'Well, at least he can't nationalise us,' said Frederick. 'The ICS already is. Let's see what the next three years have in store for us.'

7

Daniel Pitt's Second Dream

It is raining and soon there will be lightning. Violet flames are shooting forward from the windscreen de-icer tubes, and then, magically, they spread over the black Lysander until it has become a beautiful luminous ghost, bucking and lurching in the storm.

Daniel removes a flying gauntlet and spreads his fingers five inches from the windscreen. A steady stream of blue sparks crackles from his fingertips to the Perspex. He is a sorcerer, playing with St Elmo's fire.

'If I die today I have lived long enough,' he thinks, 'but I have to get *Armandine* home.'

He is trying to get back to Tangmere, a wounded SOE agent in the back, but a massive cold front has intervened. The Lysander cannot fly high enough to go over it, but he climbs to ten thousand feet anyway. The cumulonimbus is boiling upwards to thirty thousand, seething and rolling. Inside it the lightning is crackling back and forth. Down at seven hundred feet, an apocalyptic rain is drowning Normandy.

He flies ten minutes east and then twenty minutes west to try to find a break, but there is none. He dives practically to ground level in order to fly beneath it in the rain, but it is too low, and the deluge forces him even lower. He puts his gloved hand out of the window for a few seconds, and it is just as he suspected. When he brings his hand back in, it is coated with a thick film. Ice is forming on the windscreen, on all the flying surfaces. No wonder the plane is sinking. Soon the carburettor may begin to freeze.

He retreats southwards and thinks over the situation. He feels he has no choice but to fly straight through the cold front, because soon there will not be enough fuel to get him home and he will be forced to land in France. He climbs to ten thousand feet, adjusts the carburettor heat, turns up the cabin lights, and flies into the centre of the storm.

The direction indicator spins. There is too much static for the compass to be trusted. He tightens his safety harness. The air speed indicator gets stuck on 170 knots, frozen solid. The black Lysander is thrown about like a leaf in autumn. He fights with the controls, all his muscles aching, sweat pouring down his face. He has no moment in which to imagine how Armandine must be suffering in the back.

The altimeter reads twelve thousand feet, but begins steadily to drop. Daniel knows that he is accumulating ice. He puts the propeller onto fine pitch, but it makes no difference. His heart is thumping in his chest, faster and faster. He fights back the panic. The black Lysander bucks and lurches. He remembers that back in the last war you could enter a cloud and not realise that you were flying upside down. That was probably what killed Albert Ball.

The lightning flashes are so blinding and so frequent that it feels as though his thoughts are being deleted.

He pulls the override control and the engine roars with new life, but still the aircraft descends. He is trying to prevent it being flipped onto its back. The engine misfires, cuts out, fires again, runs at such low revs as to be useless. He thinks about bailing out, but how does he tell Armandine, who has apparently forgotten to put on her headset? No pilot bails out leaving a passenger inside. Death before dishonour. A pilot is like the captain of a sinking ship.

The black Lysander is being pitched about like a cork on waves. The violence of it is beyond belief. He drops the nose to gain more control, but the extra speed exaggerates the turbulence. He fears that his Lizzie will lose her wings and fall like a stricken bird.

At nine hundred feet where all is lost, a miraculous updraught lifts the plane to four thousand. He is thrown out of the edge of the tempest. He is almost out of fuel, and he has no choice but to land, no nearer to England than he had been when he entered the front.

He finds a level field, but there is a ditch across the middle of it that the landing light reveals too late. He locks the wheels but the aircraft skids on the frosty ground, they catch in the ditch, and the black Lysander flips smartly onto its nose. Daniel is restrained by his Sutton harness, but badly wrenches his neck.

He is outside in the freezing midnight, stabbing at the tank with a commando knife that Armandine has handed him. But the tank is self-sealing, and there is almost nothing in it in any case. He fires a Very light into the trickle three times. Three times he runs away but the fire goes out.

In his dream a platoon of German soldiers runs across the field as he tries to set fire to the plane for the last time. He takes his revolver from its holster and cocks it. He ducks down and takes aim, but the soldiers metamorphose into his dead daughter Esther, in her Wren's uniform. She takes the revolver from his hand and tucks it fondly back into its holster, fastening the stud. She puts her arms around him and says, 'Daddy, Daddy, don't be ashamed. You're one of the thirty-seven,' and he realises without being told that almost all the British bombers had failed to return that night, destroyed by the storm that has so capriciously ejected him.

8

Back to Blighty

Three years passed, Sir Barkalot died and was buried under the gulmohar tree where he loved to lie in the shade, and two by two, their European friends began to depart, either to go home or to be posted elsewhere in India. The club had more brown faces than white these days, but had, strangely enough, become even more rigid about enforcing the admissions criteria and the rules in general. Frederick and Ottilie had plenty of friends and acquaintances amongst the Anglo-Indians and the higher caste Hindus, but like many of the British they found the more educated Muslims easiest to get along with. There had even been something enjoyable about not assuming precedence any more. Life was more congenial, somehow, when one didn't have to put on airs or assume leadership. Humility was less of a burden.

But Frederick was not particularly strong any more, and even found himself nostalgic for the grey skies of Britain. His friends and colleagues begged him to stay, for friendship's sake, and there were still balls and garden parties, tennis matches, and rounds of golf at the Gymkhana course, quirkily situated in the middle of the racetrack, where he regularly won the foursomes with his partner Ali Khan, who never hit the ball further than 150 yards, but always straight down the middle of the fairway, and rarely needed more than one putt on the green. Frederick teased him that he played golf like an old woman, and Ali Khan would reply, 'And how does he play who always loses to an old woman?'

When his contract expired and, to his surprise, the offer came for its renewal, Ottilie and Frederick decided to leave even so.

'I never was going to be a *burra memsahib*, anyway, was I?' said Ottilie. 'And if I am, I don't want to die as one. And the clinic's in safe hands, and I want to be with my family before they all die off. I want to see Scotland again, and we can go to Gretna Green, and see if the anvil is still there.'

'I feel that the tide is really going out now,' said Frederick mournfully. 'It's like fishing from the beach. When the tide starts to go out, you pack it in.'

They sold the house to Ali Khan, and Frederick gave him his set of golf clubs as a spare.

As they left their bungalow for the last time, handing over the keys to Ali Khan's manager, Ottilie said, 'I've loved it here, every minute of it. But think how lovely it'll be to see Sophie and Fairhead whenever we want, and Daniel, and Archie, and Rosie and Christabel, and our friends from here who've gone home already. We can have reunions and weep nostalgically for the old days over our rock-hard mutton chops.'

'The question is, after all this time, where is home? Is it here, or there? But we need shaking up a bit anyway, don't we? A new start... It might do us good,' said Frederick. 'Do you know, sad as it all is, I feel almost relieved to be off. Let's face it, this country's completely ungovernable. So many races, so many languages, too much bloody religion and superstition. It's not one country, it's dozens, all jostling and scrapping. And to cap it all, their damn stupid caste system, and all the things they won't eat and won't do.'

'Oh, but it's still such a frightful wrench. Saying goodbye to the servants was the worst thing I've ever had to do. I felt like such a heel. You could see how hurt they were. When they put those garlands of marigolds round our necks, and stepped back, and just stood there weeping into their hands. I could hardly bear it. I wish we could have brought them with us.'

'Ali Khan will look after them. We can send photographs and things from home.' He turned and looked down at her. 'But wasn't that a hell of a send-off at the club? Unforgettable. I've never been hoisted up on shoulders like that before. Let alone been paraded round and round the lawns.'

'At least we parted friends. We weren't kicked out. We could have stayed. I'm glad you said *jai hind* like that, at the end of your speech,' she said. 'It was just right. How they cheered!'

When they went to embark at the port of Madras, they found almost all the members of the club, brown and white, waiting for them with garlands, and as the steamer left, they joined hands and sang 'Auld Lang Syne'. Ottilie waved and wept, and Frederick could think of nothing other than to stand ramrod-straight and give the naval salute. *Jai hind*, he thought, *jai hind*.

They had decided not to take the long and elaborate railway journey to Bombay, but to take ship via Colombo instead, so that they could stay in the Grand Old Hotel and see Mount Lavinia and Colombo, and then visit Bombay for the last time. Frederick wanted to take a photograph of Ottilie standing beneath the magnificent arch of the Gateway of India.

The Suez Canal was the usual hellish torment, but once out of Port Said, Frederick threw his tropical topi into the Mediterranean. They watched it bobbing on the surface, until it was caught in the wash of the ship, turned over, and sank. 'Well, that's goodbye then,' said Frederick. 'Let's go to the bow now, and see what's ahead.'

Ottilie put her hand up to shade her eyes, and looked out over the sparkling sea. 'You remember what Gandhiji said, when they told him that independence had come at last? He said, "I have no message to give on independence, because my heart has dried up." That's how I feel. I feel my heart's dried up. How are we supposed to put India behind us? Do you think, if it's dreadful at home, we could come back? They've still got rationing. It might be unbearably dull. Everyone'll be having shoe leather for lunch and we'll just be longing for a pukka tiffin.'

'Poor old Gandhi,' said Frederick. 'I wonder if he ever regretted what he brought about, before he was killed.'

'I do have faith in Nehru,' said Ottilie.

'Yes, so have I. But he has an impossible job.'

They stopped in Malta to see Valletta, where they ate rabbit for the first time in years, and in Gibraltar where they did not go up the mountain to see the Barbary apes, because in India they had already been plagued by *jungli* monkeys for two decades, and never wanted to see another.

Frederick, Ottilie and Nora disembarked at Southampton to find some of the country hopping about, waving imaginary umbrellas, pretending to be Gene Kelly in *Singing in the Rain*, and others fiercely arguing about whether or not Derek Bentley deserved to be hanged. Soon they were all back in The Grampians at Eltham, so that suddenly the big empty, cobwebbed house was once again a family home. Ottilie's sister Sophie and her husband Fairhead motored over from Blackheath to have dinner and stay the night, and Rosie cooked a proper meal for the first time in years. Everybody had been asked to bring their meat ration with them, so she could make an enormous cottage pie, padded out with baked beans, chopped turnips, carrots and peas, followed by baked apples with custard. In the cellar she found four bottles of burgundy that had been there since before the war, and when she decanted them she found that none we're corked.

She had worked flat out for a week to make the house presentable, beating the carpets outdoors on the lawn, washing and ironing the sheets, airing the bedrooms, and wiping away several years' worth of dust from all the horizontal surfaces. The frantic activity energised her, and her heart was thrilling with the pleasure of having her sweet-natured, long-lost sister back again. The one thing she could not do was reduce her colony of cats, or entirely get rid of the stench of her toms' markings, so that the house smelled strangely of tainted disinfectant.

At supper that night they toasted the new young Queen, and Frederick made a speech thanking Rosie for 'putting us up and putting up with us'. Rosie looked around the table and hardly knew what to feel. There was Fairhead, much too thin, with his bright eyes set in a grey face and his toothbrush moustache orange yellow at the centre after so many years of compulsive smoking; her sister Sophie, her halo of frizzy hair now perfectly white, but unchanged in body or face, still talking the same kind of curiously intelligent nonsense as she always had; her sister Ottilie, much dumpier now, with her heavy sagging breasts and round-eyed good humour; Frederick, still very much the naval officer who had fought at Jutland in one war, and in the Indian Ocean in another, but now stooped at the shoulder and hollow in the chest; her niece Nora, almost twenty, whom she barely knew at all, the very image of Ottilie at the same age, with her bob of shiny black hair and her creamy skin, and the same low soft voice. Her third sister, Christabel, had sent a telegram of apology from Hexham, and Archie in Brighton had not turned up because he was too drunk and confused to get to the station, and too indigent to buy a ticket even if he had.

Rosie wondered what the others saw when they looked at her. She realised that she had not aged well, and never perceived it more sharply than when reunited with her relatives. Her lardy diet of fried eggs, fried bread and sausages had done her no good, she knew that, but for years now she had lacked the motivation to feed herself properly, as if she had decided that she did not deserve life and health. Her brush with breast cancer had left her fearful, and her arduous years caring for the wounded at Netley had left her permanently exhausted. How everything had changed; here she was, in her father's house, in his place at the head of the table, and at the opposite end, in her mother's place, was Frederick, a man she hardly knew.

'Rosie, why are you crying?' asked Ottilie.

'Oh, I'm just so happy to see you all. It's … it's … and I keep thinking of everybody who isn't here.'

'Here's to Esther, and Mother and Father, and the Pendennises and the Pals, and Christabel and Gaskell, and Cookie,' said Ottilie, raising her glass. 'Everyone who's gone, and everyone who's still here.'

'Absent friends,' proposed Frederick.

Rosie instinctively tried to think of Ashbridge, but was perplexed to find herself thinking of Daniel. She froze in a kind of guilty horror, as if she had failed in her duty.

'And new beginnings,' said Fairhead, raising his glass. 'Rosie, my dear, really, whatever is the matter?'

'What new beginnings?' she asked. 'Where are my new beginnings?'

She put her head in her hands and wept.

9

Daniel Pitt's Third Dream

It begins with the chronic aching in his toes that he has learned to incorporate into his dreams so that he does not have to wake up every time the throbbing and stinging attacks him. He sees the smug smile of the Gestapo officer as he stands with his hands behind his back, at ease as he demands code names. He feels the cold edge of the chisel across the joint of his fourth toe, and watches as the kneeling torturer raises the mallet. He shuts his eyes and winces in advance.

Then the scene switches and he hears the screams of *Odette* as, one by one, her toenails are wrenched out with pliers. He sees her writhing in the chair where she has been strapped down. The same Nazi officer is there, still smiling smugly with his hands behind his back, standing at ease as he demands the names of agents. She tells him lies, lies and ever more desperate lies.

Odette becomes Violette, she of half a dozen names, Louisa, Vicky Taylor, La Petite Anglaise, Mme Villeret, the tiny widow with her infant daughter. Daniel remembers how adorable and beautiful she was, how his heart leapt whenever he knew that it was he that was to fly her, or meet her for briefing and debriefing in the derelict cottage on the perimeter at Tangmere. He hears her Parisian accent in French, her cockney one in English, how she would switch from one to the other when they talked. He remembers her ringing laughter. Now he knows that she was tortured by the *Sicherheitsdienst*, and then worked almost to death in Ravensbrück, until one day she had to kneel so that SS-Rottenführer Schult could put a bullet through the back of her head in the presence of the *Kommandant* and the Chief Medical Officer.

They swim before his eyes, in and out of focus; Pickard, Cocky Dundas, Hugh Verity, Peter Churchill, Felix, Armandine, La Doucette, Whippy Nesbitt-Dufort, so many of them, half of them dead.

He dreams of his Lizzie. He loved her possibly even more than the Camels, Pups and Snipes he had flown in the previous war.

Lizzie has been painted black, with a ladder permanently fixed to the side. She can take off in thirty-six yards and fly for ten hours with armaments removed and extra fuel tanks. She can land, pick up an agent, and take off in four minutes flat. She is the ideal last love of the middle-aged pilot, much more fun than the Hudsons from which he dropped the parachutists. After the war he has his Lizzie's serial number tattooed on his upper arm, and commissions an artist to paint a picture of her, flying out of a storm.

This Lizzie, his last, is the one that picks him up when he is rescued from that field in Brittany, dressed as a peasant, hobbling on crutches, his left foot bleeding into its bandage, an unlit Gauloise hanging from a corner of his mouth for authenticity. He inherited this Lizzie when its pilot was moved to a reconnaissance squadron.

He dreams of how, during the two weeks of every month when there was no moon, he flew his obsolete Hurricane by day, above the cliffs of Sussex, looking for trouble, stunting for the troops on Beachy Head. Wherever he moves he has a photograph of his aeroplane that hangs beneath his painting of the black Lysander.

He dreams of stunting, of Nazi officers and torturers, helpful peasants, the crunch of blade through bone, of Armandine, and Violette.

10

Sophie and Fairhead

It was Saturday morning, and Sophie and Fairhead were lying naked in bed with nothing to do but talk nonsense. He lay on his back with his head on the pillow, and she lay across the bed, playing with his body, drawing circles round his nipples with a wet forefinger. Then she moved her hand further down.

'What on earth are you doing?' he asked. 'Are you trying to wrench it off?'

'I'm driving to Bromley.'

'Truly?'

'Yes, this is the gearstick. First gear, and we're off! Second gear, third gear! Forty miles an hour and we're on Lee Road. Oh no, there's an omnibus, down to second! Zoom, overtake, back into third!'

'My darling, a great many cars have four gears these days.'

'Oh yes, so they do. Into fourth! A clear run down Burnt Ash Hill! My darling?'

'Yes?'

'Something funny's happening to your gearstick. Methinks it's getting longer and renitent. It is rigidifying. What can be wrong with it?'

'Can't think. Should we stop for maintenance?'

'But you don't like maintenance in the mornings. You are not a matitudinal sensualist. You are a pip-emma parson person, preferably post-prandial, after the port and cheese.'

'Seems a shame to waste it.'

'How will we ever get to Bromley?'

'Bugger Bromley.'

'I want to get to Bromley by changing gear with my feet,' she said, altering her position. 'What does it feel like?'

'Strangely the same as your hands. All cool and delicate and a little bit dry and scrapy, but in a delicious way.'

'I think we're in Bromley,' she said. 'Your gear lever seems to have become more or less stuck in neutral.'

Afterwards she toyed with him and said, 'I don't think I'll ever get used to what strange things these are.'

'I'm assuming that this may be the only one whose acquaintance you may have made. Other examples may not be so strange.'

'I've seen the one on Michelangelo's *David*. This is far more prodigious. That is a mere cocktail sausage, little more than an *hors d'oeuvres*. This is a proper *wurst*.'

'How civil of you to say so. Anyway, what I've got isn't as strange as what you've got, I don't think.'

'Mine's all tucked away. It is most discreet and modest. It is in purdah. It is the very soul of feminine discretion. The acme of tuckedawayness.'

'It's lucky we're a good fit,' said Fairhead, kissing her on the forehead as they lay face-to-face. 'Fancy still being at it after all these years. Can you believe it's thirty years? You've only got one eye now.'

'*O miserere mei*, I am waxing cyclopean,' said Sophie. 'Ooh, now you have four.'

'Won't it be wonderful to visit Ottilie and Frederick? Frederick says he has a little dinghy, and we can go out fishing.'

'If we leave after lunch we'll get there by teatime. We can have dabs for supper.'

'They seem very happy in Bosham.'

'Frederick says they miss the sunshine, but it's lovely and peaceful without all the servants. I think Daniel will be there too. He's still at Tangmere, so he'll pop over on his combination. Apparently they've adopted an enormous French mastiff, called Boomer. Did I tell you? Ottilie told me on the phone. It has a scrumpled-up face and runs more slowly than it walks. I hope it gets on with Crusty.'

Sophie turned on her front and said, 'Scratch me. With your chin. Right in the middle.'

Fairhead supported himself on his arms and ran his chin up and down her spine, then back and forth between her shoulder blades, just as she liked, whilst she issued little exclamations and instructions. 'Further up! Further left! Down a bit! Ooh, that's so lovely! A bit harder! Now do it with your nails!'

After she was satisfied she rolled over and put her arm around his neck. 'Do you suppose that the Good Lord specifically designed stubble for scratching ladies' backs?'

'For that reason and no other,' replied Fairhead.

There was a brief silence, and then Sophie said, 'My darling?'

'Yes?'

'Do you think that Frederick and Ottilie are still, you know, at it? Like us?'

Fairhead looked out of the window. 'I've no idea,' he said at length. 'I have the impression that with most couples it wears off quite quickly. I think we might be different. I think we might just be very lucky, or perhaps not at all normal. It didn't last for Daniel and Rosie.'

'Just think how different our lives would have been if you hadn't come to The Grampians to talk to Rosie about Ash. Poor old Ash. Poor old Rosie.'

'But lucky old us.'

11

Poor Old Archie

Archie Pitt has not eaten for five days. He has become too weak and dejected to go out and riffle through the litter bins on the promenade, or walk up and down looking for dropped pennies. In the pocket of his jacket he has only thruppence ha'penny, because he spends his pension on cheap blended whisky, and there will be no more money for two weeks.

He takes the coins out of his pocket, and notes that one of the pennies is black, very worn out, and has the plump outline of the elderly Queen Victoria shadowed on one side. The other penny is a King George V, and the halfpenny is a King Edward VII. He has four shiny farthings from the reign of the new Queen.

'I've lived through four reigns, and now I'm on the fifth,' he says aloud. He stands up, but feels extremely faint, and sits down again. 'Bugger it,' he says.

This month Archie has spent his last few shillings on a half-gallon can of methylated spirit, which he has poured into some empty whisky bottles, before going outside to find a dustbin for the can. One has to preserve a certain dignity, even after one has departed.

Archie feels a strange excitement, the same as his brother Daniel had once felt when standing in despair above the abyss at Beachy Head, during the war, a combination of physical fear and the joy of imminent liberation.

'You've always been your own worst enemy, old boy,' says Archie. 'It's time to take up the sword.'

The urge to leave some words behind becomes irresistible, and he reaches into the breast pocket of his jacket to take out his fountain pen. His father had given it to him on his tenth birthday. He unscrews the cap and taps the nib on the blotter to make the ink flow. He makes several beginnings. Really there is only one person that he wishes to address at this point, although he feels guilty about not also writing a note to Daniel.

He gives up. His hand is too tremulous, and there is nothing he might write that could encapsulate the universe of love and sorrow which he has inhabited for so many bleak decades. Then he turns to a new sheet and writes:

For some people it is right to be born, but for me it was not right. I was mistaken to be born, and unwise to linger so long. I think it is better to stop whilst I am still able to make the decision to do so, and although I am afraid, I feel light at heart now that the decision has been made. *Amavi, et non amandus sum, et judicatus sum.*

Archie wonders whether to smoke whilst he drinks, but decides against it. This is a serious business, not an evening at the club. He pours himself a glass of methylated spirit, and tosses it down in one. The taste is repulsive, because it has been denatured, but he detaches his judgement, and tries to be disgusted with it from outside himself. He feels the same deliberately induced indifference that he once used to summon quite often, when dealing with the remains of comrades who had been disembowelled and castrated by Afghan tribesmen.

He is unsure how fast things will happen, and soon realises that they will be unconscionably slow. It is irritating to have to wait, when there is liberty in attendance. Then he thinks that perhaps it is a good thing that the intoxication is delayed, because he will be able to drink that much more of it, and so be sure of its beneficial effect. He sets himself the target of drinking all the bottles before he falls into unconsciousness, and resolves to spend his last morsel of time thinking about what his life might have meant.

It is unbearably, disappointingly slow, but then he begins to feel cold, and shivers. He stands up carefully and goes out into the backyard, because he does not want to be found with urine stains on the front of his trousers. One has a certain dignity to conserve. When he returns, he feels suddenly very weak as he makes his way back towards his desk, and sinks to his knees in the middle of the floor. He lies face down, but stretches out his hand and turns himself over, so that he will not have to inhale the rank, greasy stench of the carpet. As the cold comes over him, he looks up at the ceiling and sees there is a crack that is exactly like the shape of the road to Peshawar, if you are approaching from Kohat, after you have left the Khyber Pass.

His pupils dilate until they are as large as a cat's in the dark, and he begins to convulse, repeatedly, but it does not seem too painful or disconcerting, because the dose has been so overwhelming that it is impossible to be aware of what is happening to his body. He turns on his side half an hour later, and vomits.

Twenty-four hours later, Archie is still convulsing, and completely blind, but this means nothing to him at all. He has travelled up to the road from Kohat and is now walking away from the mountains beside a train of camels that includes three elephants carrying howdahs. At the side of the road a Pathan in a white turban is selling rifles that he has brought from the Adam Khel factory. In the distance Archie can see the town ramparts, and the minaret of the Jama Masjid. The muezzin is calling the azan, and above him two vultures circle on the updraught.

As he comes through the gate to the Qissa Khwani Bazaar, a group of men haggles over a mare, and a scribe is taking the thumbprint of one who cannot write. A flamboyant storyteller with a long tail at the back of his turban sits on a mat with his back against the flank of a sleeping camel, and recounts the romance of Layla and Majnun, whilst his brother a few yards away recites the quatrains of Kushal to a small knot of listeners.

Archie suddenly has the urge to go to the Shabqakar Fort, in case any of his old comrades are still there, but first he falls to his knees and leans down for a long moment to touch his forehead to the earth. Then he sits on a low wall, and realises without surprise that he is thirty years old again, and dressed not as a soldier but as a Pathan. He puts his hand on the hilt of his sword, and adjusts the heft of the rifle on his back. He tries to look at the sky, and squints against the sun. He waggles his toes in his chappals, and inhales the toasted aroma of hot dust. He leans down, picks up a handful of dust, and pours it from one hand to the other, and is content. For so many years he has dreamed of this dust.

Archie Pitt is home.

12

Rosie Pitt's Dream

There is a full moon shining through the window so intensely that it almost radiates heat. Silver lines of light shine brilliantly up and down the wall where it has slanted through the chinks in the curtain. Rosie has been waking and sleeping, waking and sleeping.

She dreams that she is standing on the peak of a mountain in Palestine, looking out over the kingdoms of this world. The world is not round or flat, but convex, so that the kingdoms and principalities are easier to perceive. She is dressed in her bridal clothes, and the veil covers her face. Everything looks gauzy and indistinct.

Next to her stands her bridegroom, much taller than she is, and out of the corner of her eye she sees his chest rise and fall as he breathes. He smells of frankincense, and a palpable warmth pulses out of him.

She feels neither joy nor sorrow, but a deep, calm resignation. She feels his hand in hers, firm but detached and unresponsive. He has long fingers.

A deep baritone voice that she takes to be from God says, 'You may kiss the bride.'

She lifts her veil, closes her eyes and raises her face. She feels the softness of his lips briefly on hers, and the tickle of a moustache. 'Oh,' she thinks, happiness surging through her.

But then she opens her eyes and finds herself looking into the steady brown eyes of Jesus. His gaze burns her brain, to the centre of her head.

She cries out, wakes suddenly, sits up, her right hand clasped to her chest, hardly able to breathe.

13

Bones

It is with a terrible foreboding in his heart that Daniel motors down to Brighton in the autumn of 1954. At about the same time Bertie's wife produces their first son, without Daniel even knowing that she is pregnant and that he is to be a grandfather. Ever since Esther drowned, and despite his efforts and good intentions, Daniel has steadily drifted ever further away from his son, through no choice of his own. Since his own mother's death, his source of news about his son has dried up, as Rosie never replies to his letters, and, Daniel suspects, never passes on any of his greetings either, intercepting any letters or parcels that he sends care of The Grampians. In any case, Bertie is in Germany with his armoured regiment now, practising for the Soviet invasion on Lüneburg Heath, and is not often home on leave.

Archie normally writes to Daniel once a fortnight, although never with any real information. He mainly mentions the weather, or quotes Livy, or Horace, or Suetonius. In addition, Archie, if he has the coins, sometimes telephones him from one of the boxes by West Pier, usually when he is drunk. On a windy day, with the racket of the traffic and the tumultuous waves crashing in the background, it is damnably difficult to have any kind of decent conversation at all.

In April, after fourteen years, rationing was finally lifted, and housewives tossed their ration books onto the fire, so that now everybody who can afford it can look forward to guzzling whatever they like at Christmas. Daniel is thinking of proposing to Archie that they should go away and spend the holiday in Trouville. Daniel is able to live reasonably well these days. Not only does he have plenty of work at Tangmere, but he has a military pension from two world wars, plus a pension awarded to him on account of the injury to his foot. He is by no means rich, but he can afford the occasional frivolity. Archie is not as keen on motorcycling as his brother, and suffers from cramp if he is in the sidecar, from cold if he rides pillion, so Daniel is thinking that they should go to France on the boat train.

The slum where Archie lives has not changed. The cobbles are still slimy and haphazard, the pavement slabs still broken, and there is still washing hanging across the street from house to house even though there is little chance of it drying or remaining clean in an atmosphere that is hung with wet coal smoke.

He cuts the engine of the Brough, and leaves it in gear so it will not be tempted to roll away. He raises his goggles, and climbs off, stiff from cold. Now that he is sixty-two he finds that, cold or not, he stiffens up after any length of time in one position, and this has been a thirty-mile drive. He dismounts and claps his gauntleted hands together. These days he has flying gloves from the Second World War, because his beloved gauntlets from the Great War have finally fallen to pieces. They were yellow, with stiff hairs on the back. He hasn't thrown them away, but has wrapped them tenderly in tissue and put them away in a drawer.

He limps down the steps to Archie's door and knocks, and when there is no response, he climbs back up and knocks on the front door of the people above.

It is Grace who comes to the door, with a baby tucked into the crook of her elbow. She has grown up slight and flat-chested, but is undeniably a pretty girl. She has the butt end of a Woodbine stuck in the middle of her mouth, and is blinking against the smoke. Daniel remembers when he first saw her, as a child herself, being borne about in the arms of her brother. 'Oh, hello,' she says. 'It's you. Bloody awful weather.'

'How are you?' asks Daniel.

'Got a baby,' says Grace.

'So I see. And how's your brother?'

'On the bins with Dad. It ain't much but we don't starve.'

'You must have got married,' says Daniel brightly.

'Bloody didn't,' says Grace. 'Just got knocked up. Hold on a mo.' She removes the cigarette from her mouth, throws it down, and stubs it out with her foot. 'I'm glad you've turned up,' she says, ''cause we didn't have no idea where you was. We ain't seen poor Archie for weeks, and there's been an effing stink like you wouldn't believe. And the rats are something chronic. Makes you want to puke. We was going to fetch the bobbies. We thought he'd gone away. He did, you know, go away sometimes, for a long time and then come back. Never told nobody nothing. You don't want to be a nosy bugger, though, do you?'

Daniel looks at her for a moment, dread rising up in him. 'Thank you,' he says, and goes back down the steps, where he puts all his weight against the door, and cracks it open, the rotting timber breaking away at the lock.

What he beholds will never leave him for the rest of his life, and he often wishes that he had simply gone for the police.

The nightmare will return just as it happened. It is not simply the rich sweet vile stink of putrefaction that will come back and make him retch, but also the vision of his brother's body in the state to which it has been reduced. The floor is thick with a carpet of glistening dead beetles and flies, because once they had hatched, they had been unable to leave. There is a wide dark thick circle stained and dried into the rug around the body, where the fluids of decomposition have spread and congealed.

The skeleton lies fully clothed in trousers, jacket and tie. The shoes have been eaten away and so have the socks. There is no meat, even of the blackened and dried kind, left on the bones, because the rats have been as efficient as the flies and beetles. They have even eaten the cartilage and tendons. When Daniel looks at the skull he sees no resemblance to his brother's face, but only the exiguous scaffolding on which that face had been constructed.

Dumb with horror, regret and guilt, Daniel stands still with his hands in his pockets, his fists folding and unfolding. He kneels down and runs his fingers across the forehead and round the empty eye sockets.

Then a strange calm comes over him, and, with a kind of detached curiosity he stands up and walks around the little room looking at the relics of his brother's life. There is very little to show for it. Rows of whisky bottles stand in ranks like soldiers against one wall, twenty to a platoon, three platoons to a company, and it seems that every dish has been used for cigarette ends, piled up in heaps that could not have been raised any higher.

A pack of Gitanes lies unopened on the bedside table. The ceiling is yellow from nicotine. On the wall is a stained print of Alfred Crowdy Lovett's *Soldiers of the 45th Rattray's Sikhs, 'The Drums' Jat Sikhs, 1911*, with its proud drum major facing the artist, his drummers behind him.

Daniel opens the drawers of the chest and finds Archie's CMG and his Webley revolver, the one he had used to beat off an attack by tribesmen, single-handedly, in Waziristan. It is the WG Army model of 1899, which officers used to buy privately for use in their campaigns. Daniel suddenly remembers that it had originally belonged to his brother Arthur, who had been killed in South Africa. One of his comrades had brought it home and returned it to the family, along with his sword, its blade so much sharpened that it was six inches shorter than its scabbard. Daniel hefts the pistol in his hand. It is almost identical in appearance to the revolver he had had to hand in to the armourer at Tangmere, the one that had seen him through the war in France. He opens it up and spins the chamber. He looks up the breech to see the condition of the bore. Archie has cared for it well. Its barrel is six inches long, and he has just the empty holster for it. He puts it into the pocket of his flying jacket, along with four small boxes of ammunition. He had always liked that gun, it was a part of Archie's essence. It was Archie's pistol, and before that it been Arthur's. He was damned if he was going to hand it in.

In a large round box he finds Archie's striped turban, with its badge of a quoit transfixed by a vertical sword, and in another is a heavy skull that Daniel concludes must be that of a tiger. Neatly wrapped in tissues in a tin trunk is the magnificent uniform of the 45th Rattray's Sikhs. There is the scarlet tunic with gold brocade, blue service trousers, knee-length blancoed spats, a red sash, and a belt with its snake buckle. Daniel still has his own uniform from back then, before he ran off to join the Royal Flying Corps, but Archie's seems like an antique, forcing Daniel to concede to himself that that is what his own is too. There is the similar uniform of the 11th Sikhs, of which Rattray's had become the 3rd Battalion in 1922. In more tissue is wrapped the very practical officer's service dress of a Frontier Scout.

There is a home-made Afghan rifle with an absurdly long barrel. Daniel remembers the story of its capture. There is a Pathan sword, like a lethally attenuated scalene triangle, a Puratan sword with a Damascus blade and beautiful red leather scabbard, and there is a three-foot khanda. In an oilskin Daniel finds a formal sabre, beautifully polished, and in another the very practical infantry sword that Archie had used on campaign. It has nicks in the blade, and some dark stains. It is still as sharp as a scalpel. Archie has several knives and Sikh daggers, the gifts or legacies of his comrades. Daniel remembers Archie showing them to him once, fondling them with his hands, explaining, 'This one's a kabaz, it has a straight blade, d'you see? And this one's a kirpan, lion-headed, don't you know.' He had talked to his brother as if he had not known what all these things were, even though he had the same weapons himself, similarly stored in tin trunks with peeling and yellowing cabin labels stuck on them at careless angles.

In the old cigar box containing his row of campaign medals, there is a small box with a George Cross in it, and Daniel wonders why on earth it is there. He is astonished to see, upon close inspection, that it has been engraved with Archie's name. His brother's few clothes are all neat and in order, folded into their own compartments, and Daniel realises that Archie had only had two pairs of socks and two pairs of underpants. There are a few books, mostly about India, including the monumental history by James Mill. Daniel picks one volume out, and finds it carefully annotated in the precise and elegant hand of Archie's youth, overlaid with the wobbling script of his alcoholic middle age. He sees that Archie also has *The Greek Anthology*, and has taken Virgil's *Eclogues* out of Brighton Library. It is now long overdue, and he wonders if the library will insist upon the fine.

On the table is a notepad, and Daniel flicks it open. On the first page, Archie has written, 'De duobus malis minus est semper eligendum. Plures crapula quam gladius. Acta est fabula.' On the second page it says, '*Death is the twin brother of sleep.*' He flicks through the pad. '*My dear Rosie*', '*My darling Rosie*', '*I have tried . . .*', '*I know that . . .*', '*Whatever happens, I'll always . . .*', '*Beloved girl, please forgive me for these words which you must find unwelcome . . .*' Then he finds Archie's final, dignified note. '*For some people it was right to be born, but for me it was not right …*'

'Oh, Archie,' sighs Daniel. 'Oh, Archie, you preposterous fool …' He decides to take the pad with him, to preserve his brother's privacy.

He goes back up the stairs and tucks the revolver and the notepad down into the pocket of his sidecar. Grace comes to the door, this time holding a mop, and Daniel says, 'Don't go in there.'

'Oh gawd,' says Gracie tearfully, putting her hands to her face. 'Poor old Archie.'

Daniel walks briskly down towards the front, fighting the pain from his foot. He curses the ingratitude and carelessness of this country that abandons its faithful servants and old soldiers to rot in ignominy. He stops the first policeman he encounters on the beat.

14

The Funeral

It proves relatively easy to tidy up the remnants of his brother's existence. There is hardly any probate to prove, and everything in Archie's will has been left to him. Daniel tells Gracie that she and her neighbours can do what they like with the bed, table and chairs. The rest of Archie's possessions fit easily into his sidecar. He pays the landlord for the repair of the door, and cleans out the place himself, having bought a mop, disinfectant, bucket and scrubbing brush at the ironmonger's three streets away. He feels it is the least he can do for Archie, who had so much wanted to be erased.

The funeral is unconventional, in that Daniel has put the bones in a large hinged box, along with a copy of *Sport and Life in the Further Himalaya* by Major R. L. Kennion, and Charles Chenevix Trench's *The Frontier Scouts*. The box of bones is arranged at the centre of a plinth at the front of the chancel. Daniel has dutifully put a notice of death in *The Times* and the *Telegraph*, but has no idea if anyone will come. He has engaged the choir of the church to sing 'Abide With Me' and the Nunc Dimittis, and has demanded of them that they conclude with 'Onward Christian Soldiers', as rousingly as they can manage, because that was what Archie had been, and that is what he would have liked.

On the morning of the funeral Daniel arrives early with the box, and finds himself astounded by the number of people who have come, considering that it is January, and there are five degrees of frost. There are about fifteen gentlemen who had served with him at one time or another, accompanied by their scarfed, muffed and behatted wives, their breath steaming as they exchange small talk. They all seem to know each other, and shake hands across the pews.

At the rear of the church sit Archie's neighbours, dressed in old army greatcoats, mittens and woolly hats, about twenty of them. Daniel greets them, saying, 'Please, do move to the front. You don't have to sit back here,' but Gracie says, 'Begging your pardon, sir, but that lot in the front's too posh for us. We're all right where we are.' Daniel shakes their hands in turn, realising that he knows or recognises almost none of them. They are part of Archie's hidden life.

Rosie and her three sisters are there, and Felix and Felicity, and Frederick, Gaskell and Fairhead. When he sees Rosie enter the church, he feels a strange emotion enter into him, compounded of anger, fear, longing and regret. He moves to kiss her cheek, as is his wont, but she holds out her hand to him. There is little left of the woman he had loved in his youth. The other sisters put a hand on his shoulder and kiss him fondly, as they naturally would, and Fairhead pumps his hand vigorously, saying, 'So sorry, old boy, such a perfectly dreadful thing to have happened.' Daniel sees Fairhead consulting with the clergyman who is to conduct the service, and that some kind of agreement is being arrived at. Felicity and Felix wave to him discreetly, and he feels that familiar sensation of sadness combined with delight. It is a delight, but also a deep pain, to have children who do not know you as their father.

Daniel struggles with himself all through the service. The part of him that is an officer and a gentleman, trained to be Spartan and Stoic, knows that it is strictly required of him that he should restrain his emotions, but his whole nature rebels against it. Eventually, during the singing of 'Abide With Me', he gets up from his place at the front, and goes to sit at the back, behind a pillar, so that he can grieve as he lists.

Most of what he feels is rage. He notices that Ottilie is sitting next to her husband Frederick, with her face buried in her hands, and that her shoulders are heaving. Poor Ottilie, he thinks. However happy you are, it is hard to lose the first person with whom you were ever deeply in love.

At the conclusion of the service Fairhead goes to the front, stands in the transept, and faces the congregation.

'Archie was a fine fellow,' he says. 'He was a childhood friend of my wife and her sisters, always ready to give, and never asking anything for himself. He served his King and Emperor in India and in France, and was frequently decorated. His courage was legendary. It was not the kind of courage that comes from bravado or from being unimaginative, which is perhaps the most common kind of courage. It was the courage which comes naturally from greatness of soul, the courage that comes from selflessness. It was also a philosophical courage, or – may I say it? – a religious courage, that understands that one's own life is a very little and unimportant thing, but that the lives of others have supreme value. Those of you who have read his obituary in *The Times* may by now be aware for the first time that he won a Military Cross with bar, in the first case for single-handedly silencing a machine gun that was threatening the safety of his platoon, and in the second for carrying a wounded comrade to safety whilst in the open and under heavy fire. It appears that during the last war he entered a burning old people's home here in Brighton, and brought out several of the bedbound. For this he was awarded the George Cross, and apparently told no one at all. Somehow we all missed it when it was gazetted in *The Times*.

'I was personally very fond of Archie, and admired him tremendously. It is a matter of great regret to me that I did not see him for too many years, and that I was never aware that he had so undeservedly fallen on such hard times. It is for this reason, as the last thing that I can do for him, and with the kind permission of the rector here, that I now pronounce the blessing, a blessing that perforce has passed my lips an uncountable number of times when I have been in attendance to the dying during the Great War, and to those dying in hospital a great many times since. Nonetheless, these words never lose their power to reassure and to console.' Fairhead pauses, and then intones, 'The Lord bless you and keep you …' he begins, and Daniel's mind immediately strays in its usual direction, the direction of wondering why God refuses to do a better job of keeping his flock.

At the church door afterwards, Daniel bids farewell to Archie's neighbours, realising that he will never see any of them again. Gracie's older brother says, 'I always wanted to thank you again, sir.'

'Really? What for?

'The first time I ever saw you, sir, when you came and I looked after your combination, you gave me a new football, and a shilling, and you bought my knackered football for sixpence. It was very kind of you, sir, you're a gentleman, sir.'

'It's good of you to say so,' says Daniel.

'My dad bought some ox liver with the sixpence. Never forgot it, sir.'

'You kept the effin shilling,' says his father.

Daniel turns to Gracie. 'How's the baby?' he asks.

'Gone,' says Gracie matter-of-factly. 'Whooping cough, sir.'

'Oh God,' says Daniel. 'I'm so sorry.'

'Better off dead anyway, sir,' says Gracie. 'Reckon we all are. Lucky old Posher. I mean lucky old Mr Archie, sir.'

'Yes,' says Daniel, 'lucky old Mr Archie.'

The neighbours decline to come to the Grand Hotel for tea, rightly assuming that they would have been turned away by the doorman, and unattracted in any case by the kind of effete items that posh people like to eat, such as anchovy paste sandwiches. They are going to go in a gaggle to get saveloy and chips and eat it together in Posher's memory, and then Gracie's father will go out for three pipkins of cider.

At the hotel, Gaskell sits silently, smoking her Abdullas from a long holder, as she always used to, and, now that she is once again prosperous and well fed, looking very much as she always did, except that her short hair is now perfectly white. She has resumed her old style of dress, in Norfolk jacket, monocle and tie. She has recently had a successful exhibition of somewhat Fauvist paintings in Vauxhall, at the same time as Christabel has had one in Edinburgh, of a sequence of photographs called *Hebridean Storms*. Christabel is still tall and elegant, very much the same, but also white-haired, and these days Sophie has an immense halo of brilliant snowy hair that is marvellous to see when the sun shines through it. Ottilie has become plump, but is much more poised than she ever was in youth. Her life of emotional focus and common sense has lent her the serenity of a sage.

'You look splendidly well,' says Daniel to Fairhead.

'I am indeed very well. Gave up smoking, you know. I read all this stuff they're just coming out with, about cancer and so on, and I thought "What the hell? Might as well knock it on the head." I feel ten years younger, and Sophie says my face has gone from grey to rosy pink. I'm damnably hungry, though, getting fat as a porker, and every other thought is about having a gasper. I'm not going to give in though. I'm going on long walks to take advantage of the extra puff. Sophie and I are thinking of walking in the Lakes in spring, doing a Wordsworth. Do you like Wordsworth? "Lines Written a Few Miles Above Tintern Abbey"...sublime.'

'I've never read Wordsworth,' says Daniel. 'I'm a philistine. I read books about engineering mainly.'

'Each to his own,' says Fairhead. 'I'd read engineering books too, if I was bright enough to understand them. Anyway, you're a liar. Your French half is highly cultured. It's your British half that's in need of improvement. I've heard you quote Montaigne. I've never once heard you quote Shakespeare.'

'I often quote Shakespeare! I'm full of wise saws and modern instances, I'll have you know! Oh, and I've been meaning to ask you for years, and I was reminded when you mentioned Archie's MC. What did you get yours for?'

'Didn't know you knew,' says Fairhead, looking away.

'When we first knew each other you were always in uniform. Naturally I recognised the ribbon. I had one myself.'

'Don't really like to talk about it,' says Fairhead.

'I'll just ask Sophie,' threatens Daniel, and to his astonishment Fairhead replies, 'She doesn't know either. She's never asked and I've never told her.'

'Go on, old chap, tell me.'

'Oh well...if you must...I was up in the front line and the company officers were having a last-minute briefing just before an attack when they got blown to smithereens. There was nobody else, so I led the company attack.'

'You led a company attack? You went over the top? A chaplain? Fairhead, that's extraordinary. How did it go?'

'We took the salient. Thirty-five men lost though.'

'That was a long way beyond the call of duty,' exclaims Daniel. 'Good God, Fairhead, I had no idea. What a man you are! I'm lost in admiration. And you've never told Sophie? Gracious! I'm going to tell her myself.'

'I was a captain, and there wasn't anyone else,' says Fairhead. 'The poor buggers had no choice but to do as I said. Lucky it worked out, really.' Fairhead looks into the middle distance, as if at a memory, and says, 'I didn't have to kill anybody, thank God. I didn't even have a pistol. I went out with a wooden cross on my chest, a dog collar round my neck, the Soldiers' New Testament in my pocket, a swagger stick in one hand, and a Book of Common Prayer in the other, and that was about it. Lucky I didn't get shot. My theory is that even the Bosch didn't like to shoot a priest.'

'You were saved by the breastplate of righteousness,' says Daniel, and the two old friends laugh.

Ottilie comes over, her eyes and the tip of her nose red, and she puts her right hand softly on Daniel's shoulder, and kisses him gently on the cheek. She says, 'I'm so very sorry. He was such a lovely man. I was so desperately fond of him.'

'I often told him that he should have married you,' says Daniel.

Ottilie looks away, and says in a pained voice, 'Yes, well. It was not to be. And I was all right in the end, wasn't I? I don't think that anyone could have been an improvement on Frederick. Archie was a lost soul, really, wasn't he? If you think about it, he got married to the bottle. I don't think he was capable of happiness. With anyone, let alone me.' She hesitates, and then says, 'Is it too late for you to try again with Rosie? Forgive me, but I am a sort of sister to you, aren't I? And sisters have privileges, don't they? Over their brothers? It's just that I've always thought, I really have, that you two do love each other after all.'

Daniel does not know what to say. The truth is that he is so angry with Rosie in so many ways that no amount of still loving her can conciliate him. And there is Christabel to think of. He says, a little curtly, 'It's probably your sister to whom you should be talking.'

'Who are you two going to grow old with?' asks Ottilie, and Daniel smiles and shrugs. He feels a shaft of spiritual pain brought on by the prospect of a desert of loneliness.

Gaskell and Christabel come over to him and kiss him on the cheek. 'It's so awful,' says Christabel, 'to die like that.'

Daniel shrugs again. 'What can you do? You carry on. How's Puss?'

'He's completely destroyed an enormous Scots pine by using it as a scratching post. All the bark's come off, and it's died. We still have him in the house sometimes, but mostly he's out in a paddock. Wragge's made him a sort of small mountain to sit on top of, and a shed to sleep in. And, would you believe it, some local people got up a petition to have him confined, even though he wouldn't hurt a fly. Stupid busybodies.'

'We told them to bugger off,' says Gaskell. 'Bloody peasants.'

'Even so, we have put a proper chain-link fence around his patch.'

'We took him into Hexham in the back of the Bentley,' says Gaskell, 'and we got stopped by the police for going too fast, and then Puss suddenly sat up in the back seat, and yawned, and the policeman took one look and fled.'

'It was priceless!'

'Good old Puss,' said Daniel. 'I must come up and see you all. It's been a couple of months.'

'You really must go and speak to Rosie,' says Christabel. 'She keeps looking in your direction.'

Rosie is the only one of the company who seems greatly diminished by time. Her hair has thinned and turned storm-cloud grey, and her face bears a troubled but defiant expression.

'I'm surprised you had a Christian ceremony,' she says, during an awkward moment when they find themselves side by side and alone at one end of the tea room.

'It was for Archie,' replies Daniel. 'He was a Christian gentleman without a doubt. He would have been horrified at the thought of not having a proper funeral. I would have been horrified on his behalf, sceptic that I am. When I die they can just put me in the ground and empty a bottle of burgundy over my grave, but Archie needed a pukka send-off.'

'Why did you do it the wrong way round? I mean, why have him cremated first? And why's the box so big?'

'I didn't. He hasn't been cremated. When I found him he was just a skeleton, and I had the bones disarticulated. There was no flesh to speak of. That's why the box is rather bigger than an urn. Anyway, he always said he wanted to be buried in Peshawar. And I thought he might like to come to his own funeral. He was dead set on going back to India one day. He loved it, and it was far enough from you. I'm going to take his bones to Peshawar. I'll go to the Indian High Commission and see what I can arrange. I mean the Pakistani one. I'll never get used to the partition. Bloody Jinna! What a damned stupid idea! You realise that Archie adored you all his life?'

'Of course I knew. Everybody kept pointing it out. It was very painful, but it couldn't be helped, could it? I married his brother.'

'If you'd divorced me, maybe he would have stood a chance.'

'What? Me marry Archie? I am sure you're not allowed to. Doesn't it say in the Bible that you can't marry your brother's wife?'

'I don't know. I see you don't change, Rosie.'

'I never for one moment thought of marrying Archie, even if I could have done,' says Rosie. 'I never had the right kind of love. And Ottilie was hopelessly in love with him. It would have been unspeakably cruel to her, wouldn't it?

'I know it's not your fault. Of course it isn't. But being in love with you and not being able to break away spoiled his whole life. He lived loving you and he died loving you. The Pathans have a saying, you know: "Patience is bitter, but its fruits are sweet." It never paid off for Archie.'

'Poor old Archie,' says Rosie, 'he was such a sweet man. Do we know how he died?'

'Impossible to tell, I'm afraid. Open verdict.'

'If it was suicide, he would go to hell,' says Rosie. 'I do hope it wasn't suicide. I'd hate to think of poor Archie in hell.'

'Oh, Rosie, for God's sake! Won't you ever think for yourself?'

'I always have,' says Rosie indignantly. 'It's just that you've never liked what I think.'

'Any God who'd consign Archie to hell can go there Himself, in my opinion.' Rosie bridles, and he adds, 'Oh, no, I am sorry, I didn't mean to offend you. Again. Anyway, could you possibly do me a favour?'

'A favour? What kind of favour?'

'Well, Archie left me a few things, and I've nowhere to put them. As The Grampians must be practically empty, could you find a corner for them somewhere? There are several swords and knives, uniforms, a sheaf of arrows and a bow, an assegai, a Zulu shield, a large brass telescope, a skull, and quite a few books about India.'

'Why can't you look after them?'

Daniel pauses, and replies, 'I'm going to Canada.'

'Canada? But, Daniel, you're sixty-two! You can't go to Canada.'

'Why not? My mother is dead, even my favourite aunt is dead, my brother is dead, my daughter is dead, you have made a point of standing in the way of my happiness since the day we married, and you have been turning my son against me since the day he was born. Why isn't he here today? Is he in Germany? I have absolutely nothing to stay for. I had a very exciting war and now I'm just a transport officer who has to fret about tyres and anti-freeze. I'm as energetic as I ever was, I still have a flying licence, and I am just like my great-uncle, the mysterious colonel, who got to a hundred and three. I'm going to take the combination to New York, and drive to Vancouver. I've always wanted to drive across America.'

'But how long will you go for?'

'I don't know. About six months, I suppose.'

'What will you do when you get back?'

'What I always do. Something to do with motorcycles.'

'Isn't it time you grew out of roaring around on motorcycles?' Rosie looks away and feels a chasm open up in her stomach. 'You can't leave the RAF again! You can't go, Daniel. Please don't go.'

'No, I am going. Definitely. I have already resigned my commission. After I get back from Peshawar. I might come back via South Africa, because I've never seen the graves of my other brothers. I'd like to be in their presence again, so to speak. And I may be sixty-two, but I'm not showing too many signs of decay. Even so, I don't feel I have very much time left to have adventures in. I've been to the subcontinent and Africa, but I've never been to the Americas.' He pauses, and says, 'I'm very much looking forward to going back to Peshawar. After partition... well, I'm expecting it to be ruined, to be frank, but somehow still the same. Anyway, there's absolutely nothing for me here any more.'

Rosie wants to reach out a hand to restrain him. She says, 'What about me? There's me.'

'What do you mean, there's you?'

Rosie clutches her handbag a little tighter, and says feebly, 'I'm still here. You're still my husband.'

'I'm hardly your husband any more, am I?'

'You made a promise to God.'

'It was you who made a promise to God. As far as I am concerned, I made my promise to you, personally. You didn't keep your promise, so I'm released from mine. It's simple.'

'But I did keep my promise!'

'To love, honour and obey? Well, I never expected you to obey me. You could have left that out. It's plain from your behaviour that you didn't honour me, or love me.'

'But, Daniel, I did! I do.'

'No, you don't. I'm sorry, but it's quite obvious. And why would you say this now, when it's decades too late, and can't make any difference?'

Rosie sits down heavily and takes a handkerchief from her bag, which she kneads between her fingers. 'I know I've done terrible things. I don't know why, but I couldn't help myself.' She looks up at him and smiles weakly. 'Whatever I did, whatever went wrong, I always did love you, in my heart.'

'Rosie, there's something you haven't learned about love.'

'Is there?' She looks up tearfully. 'Is there really?'

'Yes. You think love is about what you say and what you feel. How easy it is to say "I love you" and have warm feelings in your heart! And that misses the essence of it altogether.'

'So what's this essence, then?'

'Love isn't about what you say. Oratory … rhetoric … have nothing to do with it. And it isn't what you feel. It's about what you do. I don't trust words, and I can never know exactly what's hidden in your heart. It might be an ocean or it might be a songbird or it might be a thorn bush. But I could tell how much you loved me by what you did and didn't do. Love is what love does. It's as simple as that. You can read it as clearly as the neon on the front of a theatre. I never listened to what you said, I just suffered what you did.'

Protest rises up in Rosie's throat, but she can think of no riposte. Instead she says, 'What about all your possessions?'

'I hardly have any. I had to leave a large amount behind in Germany, if you remember. I'll sell what I can live without, and, as I say, I'm hoping you'll have some of it in your cellar. The little I need I'll put in the combination. I'm going to take my tennis racket, my gramophone, and my favourite books and records. The Brough will come with me in a crate, and I'll ride it across to Vancouver.'

'Just as we took the Henley to Ceylon,' says Rosie.

'Well, I'd better be going,' says Daniel. 'I want to take a walk on Beachy Head.'

'In this weather? You're not going to jump off, are you?'

'No, that would prevent me from going to Canada. I went to Beachy Head after Esther died, and I had a slightly strange encounter there that I still don't entirely understand. It's where I go and reflect if I'm in the area. Then I'll go to Partridge Green and take a look at my mother's old cottage.'

Rosie takes the train back to Victoria that evening, and then the branch line to Mottingham. As she walks the length of Court Road, in dense fog, it seems to be crowded with ghosts. She is appalled that the box in the church had contained disarticulated bones. She remembers the day at Christmas when Archie and Daniel and Fluke had terrified them all with their Afghan dances. It is too stark, to think that Archie has been reduced to bones in a box.

The house is freezing and dark, and there is a frost forming exquisitely delicate lacework on the insides of the windowpanes. It would be cruelly empty but for her tribe of cats. As they rub themselves against her ankles and miaow, clawing at her legs for food, Rosie wonders at her own deliberate meanness in not telling Daniel that he has just become a grandfather. She wonders if any of the others have mentioned it. She wonders, indeed, if she has told any of them either.

She makes herself a pot of tea, and sits at the kitchen table. It is tea from Ceylon, and she thinks about the distant time when she and Daniel and Esther had gone there to make a new start. The names of the estates begin to come back to her. It had all been truly wonderful until the stillbirth, and back then, of course, she was writing poetry. Back then it had seemed as if an infinity of time stretched before her; there were so many possibilities remaining.

She lifts the quilted cosy from the teapot and puts her hands inside it to warm them up. Then she puts it on her head, feeling the delicious warmth at her temples and forehead. It is a good fit, and very comforting.

She is still wearing it when she goes to bed at half past nine, for lack of anything to stay up for. As she turns at the top of the stairs, labouring for breath, she sees herself in the long mirror, and stands still with shock. She looks very much like her mother who, in old age, had become eccentric to the point of madness. Rosie sees a lonely old madwoman with a tea cosy on her head, who has made a mess of everything, and been too proud to backtrack or apologise, or even to follow her own heart.

She sits on her bed, feeling all over again the familiar pangs of guilt, self-hatred and helplessness. One of her cats is curled up on the eiderdown, and she lies next to it with her face in its warm sweet-smelling fur. She weeps.

After a while she gets up, and wipes her nose with a lacy handkerchief that is now thirty years old and worn through in one corner. She goes back out into the freezing corridor and confronts herself in the mirror. She glares at her own eyes that glare back. She raises a finger and points it accusingly, touching its tip to the tip of the reflection that accuses her in its turn.

'You stupid woman,' she says contemptuously. 'Look at you. You were going to be a poet.'

15

The Tablet

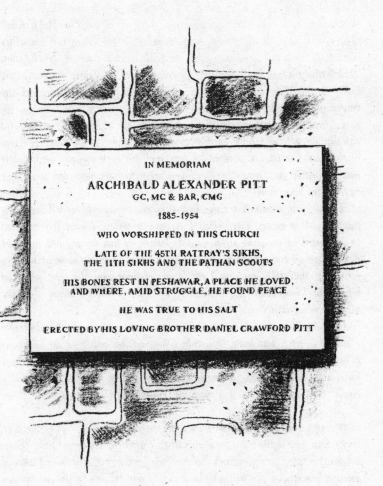

IN MEMORIAM

ARCHIBALD ALEXANDER PITT
GC, MC & BAR, CMG

1885-1954

WHO WORSHIPPED IN THIS CHURCH

LATE OF THE 45TH RATTRAY'S SIKHS,
THE 11TH SIKHS AND THE PATHAN SCOUTS

HIS BONES REST IN PESHAWAR, A PLACE HE LOVED,
AND WHERE, AMID STRUGGLE, HE FOUND PEACE

HE WAS TRUE TO HIS SALT

ERECTED BY HIS LOVING BROTHER DANIEL CRAWFORD PITT

16

A Note to Gaskell

The RAF Club
128 Piccadilly
London

14 February 1955

My dear Green-Eyed Monster,

I am so sorry that we had little chance to talk at Archie's funeral, and equally sorry that I have seen not nearly enough of you since the end of the war. I must say, you and Christabel did look awfully well. Silver hair definitely suits you both, and you seem to have perfected your style beyond improvement.

Thank you so much for the beautiful photograph of us all last year, flat out asleep on the lawn with Puss as our pillow. I have never ceased to be surprised at what an admirable fellow he has turned out to be. A pet lion could have been a catastrophic mistake. I know it must be very annoying that tradesmen will no longer deliver, and that the postman refuses to come down the drive, but for Puss I should think that the inconvenience is definitely worth it.

I would like to come up to Hexham to see you (and the admirable Puss, of course), not least to decide what we are going to do with our poor old aeroplanes. If we could get Felix and Felicity there at the same time, well, that would be a bonus. I do hope you've still got your Bentley Speed Six, and didn't sell it after all. I have been longing to take it for a spin again.

It seems strange now, how I used to see you so often during the war, every time you delivered a new aircraft to Tangmere. You must have flown so many types; you wouldn't believe how envious I still am. I always knew when it was you bringing in a new plane because of the marvellous panache of your landings. How you would have loved to do Gosport landings in a Camel! I often think I should have joined the ATA instead of 661 Squadron. I am still somewhat troubled by what I had to do, and

*what happened both to me and to many of my charges. I have recurrent
nightmares that I won't bore you with.*

*As you know, I am going to Peshawar with Archie's bones. Do you
think, therefore, that I could come up and join you for a week or two?
I also want to discuss with you and Christabel a plan I have to go to
Canada, at least for a few months. I feel that she should be in agreement
with whatever I do, and of course we have Felix and Felicity to take
into account.*

*I assure you both of my deepest and fondest love,
Your very own Daniel P.*

17

To Be Buried in Peshawar

In order to avoid the hellish temperatures of summer, Daniel travelled in the spring of 1955, enduring the Suez Canal for the fifth time in his life. The journey was replete with memories, and he wondered what had happened to the young Greek doctor he had met when returning last time. There had been a cataclysmic earthquake in Cephallonia in 1953, and Daniel had often found himself hoping that the doctor and his daughter had survived it.

On the first voyage, to Ceylon, he had made friends with an Egyptian gentleman whose name he now struggled to recall. He mostly thought about how seasick Rosie had been, and of how he had had Esther to himself. It was deeply painful to think of her as a little girl, charming the Greek doctor, and asking wonderful questions, such as 'Where does the Tooth Fairy get her money from?' Daniel remembered telling her that she sold the teeth. Thinking of Esther gave him a deep ache in the guts, that of irremediable absence.

It took Daniel four days to travel the one thousand miles from Karachi to Peshawar on the train, because he broke his journey in Rohri and Lahore, to have a look around, for old times' sake. In Rohri he wanted to stroll by the great waters of the Indus, and in Lahore he just wanted to walk around remembering. Even though this was Pakistan, he still could not prevent himself from thinking of it as India. It was all so familiar, yet there was so much that was different. The chaos and noise were worse than ever, there seemed to be many more people, and the stink of clapped-out engines burning oil overwhelmed the more lovely aroma of spices that he had always recalled so fondly. There were more beggars and lepers than before, squatting outside the mosques, waiting for the faithful to fill their bowls with rice.

It was impossible not to notice that there were no white faces, no Hindus, and no Sikhs. The womenfolk seemed to have vanished almost altogether, leaving only a few figures so completely draped that they seemed reduced to their own silhouette. This was a country that had quite deliberately and self-consciously diminished itself, withdrawn like a snail into its shell.

He was travelling as lightly as he had as a Frontier Scout, with nothing but a change of clothing in his scrip, a washbag, a hussif, and a very closely printed French translation of *War and Peace*, which he thought would probably see him through the empty hours of travel. There would be no trunk or suitcase, and no hiring of aggressively desperate porters. In another knapsack that rattled as he limped, he carried the bones of his brother.

It had greatly amused him, the horror and amazement of the customs officers at Karachi, who had riffled through his few possessions in the hope of something valuable that they could confiscate, or pass over in return for a bribe. 'This is my brother,' he had told them, 'and it was his wish to be buried in Peshawar.'

'Go! Go! Go!' they exclaimed, shrinking back and waving him away. 'God be with you, and with your brother's bones.'

Daniel knew that he was an anomaly, a strange foreign creature in a place where such as himself no longer fitted in. To be the one white man in a sea of dark faces and darker eyes was to be both common property, and to be alone. But the solitude was not something he felt at all deeply. He had his brother after all, he had a mission, and he was back in a place where he had once belonged, had experienced hair-raising adventures, and picked up the elements of the languages. He had known enough Urdu for pleasantries and practicalities, and it was coming back surprisingly quickly. He knew that when he reached Peshawar the Pashto would return, but not the Hindko, because that was probably still only really spoken in the city centre, and he had never needed to learn it at all thoroughly. In any case, enough people spoke English, and he was being forever accosted by eager men wishing to practise it upon him. 'English sahib! English sahib! I speak! I speak!'

In the train the passengers solemnly shared between them whatever food they had, and at stations Daniel would get out and buy snacks from the hawkers on the platforms. He had decided that in his demeanour he should be quiet, modest, generous and courteous, instinctively knowing that one could not play the white man in a country whence the white man had departed. He would gaze around and think, 'So this is what it is like without us.' It was now an ancient country that was reverting to being itself.

Everyone would ask him 'Why sahib here?' and he would say 'To bury my brother,' and they would ask 'Where sahib brother?' and he would pat his bag of bones. 'He was a Frontier Scout. He wanted to be buried in Peshawar.' The fact that his journey was a kind of pilgrimage, a sacred undertaking, a pledge of honour, elicited respect and reverence from his interlocutors. 'Good man, sahib,' they would say seriously, patting the back of his hand, and adding, 'Watch out, Peshawar very fierce place.'

Daniel suspected that being a man in his sixties made him both more respectable and less threatening than if he had been as young as he was the last time he was here. He had been only sixteen when he had been shipped out to Ceylon and then almost immediately to India. He wondered if his Sikh regiment had survived partition and independence, and tried to remember what it had been like to have that wonderful turban on his head. Of course, the Frontier Scouts had been a different kettle of fish altogether. When he reached Peshawar he would have to try to find out if they had been assimilated into the Pakistan Army. Presumably the North-West Frontier was as wild and tribal as ever, and you would still need soldiers who could trudge for days up and down mountains and along nullahs, carrying rifles, ammunition and iron rations, ready at any time to be ambushed and have their testicles thrust down their own throats by fanatics with hennaed beards, high on bhang.

Peshawar when he first had known it had been a walled city of sixteen gates, one of which led out to the Khyber Pass. It was a city drenched in history, and one could feel it, omnipresent, hanging in the air. It had been taken by the White Huns, the Mughals, the Persians, the Mongols, the Sikhs and then the British. Daniel had sometimes felt spooked by the thought that he was walking the same earth as Alexander the Great. Peshawar was a city that had seen everything, lost everything, fallen often, and always risen up. It had no choice, because it was on the caravan route. But it was exclusively a Muslim city now.

66

On 7 September 1947 the Sikhs had been herded into their quarter and incinerated, along with a great many Hindus. Tribesmen had poured in in lorries and tongas, and the slaughter had continued for a week. The Jews had left for Israel. The remains of gurdwaras, churches, Hindu temples and Buddhist monasteries were now decaying in silent witness to the ephemerality of all greatness, prosperity and conviviality. Who would there be, after the Muslims?

When Daniel arrived at the station not long after dawn, he planned to go straight to the Qissa Khwani Bazaar to find a tailor who could make him some local clothes, and to seek accommodation. It was in this bazaar that, long after his time here, the British had killed several hundred peaceful followers of Ghaffar Khan, Peshawar's version of Mahatma Gandhi, but the blood of those martyrs had left neither stains nor monument, and neither did anyone make a point of commemorating the massacre.

If Daniel had reckoned upon simply walking to the bazaar, it was because he had forgotten about the semi-feral hordes of little boys who were always waiting for something notable to happen. Imitating his limp and pretending to have knapsacks on their backs, a gaggle of sweet-faced, grubby little urchins marched along behind him, chanting '*Parangay! Parangay! Parangay!*' From time to time he would turn round suddenly, pretending to be a tiger, with his teeth bared and his fingers outstretched like claws, so that they would scatter, shrieking in mock terror, laughing and tripping over each other.

His arrival at the bazaar necessarily became a public event, more like a parade than anything else, and he was soon surrounded by a knot of curious men, who were astonished to see a white man again, after eight years without them. They ringed him at a respectful and attentive distance, reminding him of what happened to members of the royal family at garden parties.

'*Assalamu alaykum*,' he said, and '*Alaykum assalam*,' they responded in surprise, looking at one another as if to confirm that they really had heard this white man greeting them so formally according to the old formula. Daniel put his hands together as if in prayer, and delivered the little speech he had prepared and practised over and over again in the train, until the words had naturalised themselves in his mouth. '*Zma num Daniel Pitt day. Ze de Bartaniya aw Farans yam* … My name is Daniel Pitt. I have come from England and from France. In this bag I have the bones of my brother. I have come to bury these bones, because he loved this place. *Khayat ghwaram* … I need a tailor to make me some clothes … a carpenter … a pickaxe, a spade … and a place to sleep the night. *Rasara mrasta kawalay shey?* I ask your help.'

There was a short silence whilst the men looked at each other, and then a distinguished-looking gentleman stepped forward and said, 'You speak Pashto.'

'I was here when I was young,' said Daniel, waving his hand towards the Khyber Gate. 'I remember there used to be a Sikh with two performing bears in this bazaar, and a snake charmer who used a gramophone instead of a pipe. I was out there in the mountains with my sepoys, my Pathans. I am a soldier. My brother was here too. His last wish was to be buried here.'

'You speak Pashto quite well, with some mistakes,' said the man. 'You must have a good memory. I speak English.'

'If you help me, I will pay you,' said Daniel.

'Hospitality is a matter of honour, sir.'

'I will not pay for hospitality. But I will pay for work.'

The man held out his right hand, which was much stained with ink, and Daniel shook it. It felt dry and hard in his grip. 'My name is *Ostaz* Yaqub. I am a letter writer. I know more than most of these men.'

'Yes, he is a scholar,' said a man behind him.

Ostaz Yaqub was tall and lean, with a greying moustache. He wore white salwar kameez, and a white turban. Daniel noted that his expression spoke of sorrow, resignation and dignity. He still had all his teeth, but they were brown and disarrayed. The chappals on his feet were very nearly worn down to nothing, and the skin of his heels was hard and dry, the wide cracks in the skin filled with dust.

'I worked for the British when they were here,' said *Ostaz* Yaqub. 'I was a translator in the courtroom, in four languages. Sir, I was an important man, a man of honour. But God who gives also takes away, and now there is almost no translation, and so I write letters for the illiterate.'

'I was a soldier,' said Daniel.

'As you said. Sometimes a soldier can also be a scholar,' said Yaqub. 'I remember officers who would recite in Latin and Greek. Perhaps we shall have things to discuss. First of all we shall go to my house. You can sleep there. You will sleep with me, and my wife will sleep with our daughters, so that there is no disturbance to the women.'

'Do you have sons?'

'I have a son, but he has gone to Hyderabad. There is work in Hyderabad. I mean the one in this country, and not the one in India. I have another son in Quetta. This place is almost dead. Allah no longer smiles on Peshawar.'

'Peshawar has died many times,' said Daniel. 'It always rises again.'

'*Inshallah*,' said Yaqub. 'Come, sir. Perhaps we could speak English. I am forgetting it, and you could help me to remember.'

'I am hoping to bring back my Pashto,' said Daniel.

Yaqub clicked his tongue impatiently, and Daniel said, 'We shall speak Pashto in the morning and English in the afternoon,' whereupon Yaqub smiled brightly, put one finger in the air, and said in English, 'Ah, a compromise!' Daniel felt a warm glow of recognition. He had always liked the local pronunciation of English, with its musical emplacement of stress.

Accompanied by a slightly smaller gaggle of little boys, they left the bazaar, which was just as he remembered it, a frenzy of hawkers, bullock carts, refractory camels, Afghans with heavy beards and home-made rifles, and yelling natives in white turbans, with the long tail at the back. There were a few women in pale blue burkas, walking close to walls, leading children by the hand.

'Sir, I would like to carry one of your burdens,' said *Ostaz* Yaqub, knowing that this was a test of Daniel's trust.

Aware of this, Daniel handed over the scrip containing his clothes, saying, 'My burden is not great. I would like to carry the bones of my brother myself.'

'Sir, the bones of your brother should not be carried by anyone else.'

Ostaz Yaqub lived in a small house near the jewellers' quarter. It was made of painted, unbaked mud bricks, held together here and there with timber, and above the door an ornately carved balcony projected over the street. This was the kind of house that was safest in an earthquake; lightly built, flexible, and not too difficult to rebuild. Outside the door Yaqub stopped and spread his hands. 'My house is humble, sir,' he said. 'It used to be much more clean and well painted, when I was a translator, but it is a house full of happiness. My children were born here, and, God willing, this is the house where I will die.'

'But, *Ostaz*, not for many years, I hope,' said Daniel.

'I too hope for more years, but nobody knows what God's plan is. The angel writes the day of your death in a book, on the day that you are born, and no one else may read it.'

Daniel resisted the temptation to dispute that there might be any God with a plan, and said, 'Indeed, *Ostaz,* the future is not always in our own hands.'

'You will meet my wife,' said Yaqub. 'She is a good woman but she has no education, and she has never seen any need of it. I have taught my daughters to read a little because I saw the light of intelligence. But I may have done a bad thing. Why train a hound to hunt where there is no game? Why train a horse to race when there is no racing?'

'The reason is for their own satisfaction,' said Daniel, 'and for the sake of their children. They can teach them to read.'

'After we have eaten, my daughters will recite the poetry of Khushal Khan Khattak, and they compose verses themselves in two or four lines. Some of them are very beautiful. They will recite you their own lines.'

'When I was here, my sepoys loved to tell stories.'

'I collect stories and write them down,' said Yaqub, 'otherwise they change too much, or become lost. I go to the Street of the Storytellers, and make notes. But you know, there are not so many stories. What have we got? Love and hate, good and evil, honour and revenge, heroism and cowardice, loyalty and betrayal, warring and stealing, stories in which great kings and chieftains are brought down, and others in which they are raised up, stories of trickery, and stories where people are caught in their own traps, and there are stories of calamity and disaster, such as earthquakes, and long stories about families. The stories are all the same. Only the details are different.'

'Fortunately, *Ostaz,* it is only the details that matter.'

'Still, poetry is better, when one finds a new way of saying something so old that it has been said since the beginning of time. Tell me, what is the news from England? How is the new Queen?'

'The new Queen seems to be doing very well. She is very beautiful, as you probably know, and hmm, well, Winston Churchill has resigned and now we have a new Prime Minister called Anthony Eden. He wants more people to have their own house, instead of paying rent, and he has a smart moustache. What is the news in Pakistan?'

'We are poorer and more corrupt than ever, but apart from that, we are in Paradise. Shall we go into my house? I will enter first, and tell the women. Then I shall return and invite you in.'

Daniel waited at the door and could just hear Yaqub's wife's complaints. 'What? Are you a madman? You're bringing a *parangay* who isn't even a cousin of a cousin of a cousin, and you want me to feed him when we have nothing at all in the house but the stains on the big plate from last night that I haven't washed yet? And what happens when all the neighbours and our cousins hear about it and they come in to sit and to ogle, and I have to feed them as well? And what about me and our poor girls, that we have to cover ourselves in our own house when it's dark enough in here already? And where will he sleep? And have I got to bed down in the shithouse, husband?'

'Hush, woman,' Yaqub was saying, 'hush, he understands Pashto. He will hear you.'

'What do I care? What do you care? I'm only your wife. How much do you care about the extra work, the cutting and cooking, and scrubbing vegetables, and picking the little stones out of the rice so that nobody breaks their teeth, and me having to sleep squatting down all night in the shithouse so that I daren't fall asleep at all for fear of falling in?'

'You will sleep with the girls, woman. Now hush. I'll give you money. Go and fetch a chicken and you and the girls make a *palaw.* A good one, a proper *qabuli* with sultanas and carrots, and make some *bolani* ...'

'We will make a feast fit for a chieftain, husband, and then when he departs we will starve for a week! And me having to bed down with the girls, with their farting and snoring even worse than you.'

'Keep your voice down, woman! Now go and tell the girls to cover up, and I'll bring him in.'

When Yaqub emerged back into the sunlight, Daniel laughed wryly and said, 'Your wife is not very pleased.'

Yaqub blew out his cheeks and shrugged with resignation, saying 'Wives' as if that explained everything. 'She does everything I ask,' he said, adding, 'She is very like a cow that bellows when you push her into a field, but still she goes into the field.'

'I think I will be gone in two or three days, *Ostaz*. If your wife is annoyed, I will find somewhere else tomorrow.'

'You will find another place only if I also become annoyed,' said Yaqub, 'and perhaps not even then.'

When Daniel was led in to meet the women it was to be greeted by four shapes of different heights and widths, standing side by side in a row, all concealed beneath burkas, with barely a glittering of eyes discernible behind their grids. '*Staray me she!*' they all said together, and Daniel said, '*Salamat osey!*'

'*Pe khayr raghle* ... Welcome!'

The women were Aadila, Madiha, Sabiha and Wafiya, and Daniel knew straight away that he would never remember which was which, realising that it hardly mattered, since he could address all of the daughters as *peghla*. It was already clear that Aadila, the short plump figure that exuded indignation even through her robes, was the mistress of the house, and she could be addressed as *merman*.

'*Khayre Ose*. Thank you for having me in your house.'

The house had two rooms on the ground floor, the smaller of which served as a kitchen, where ingredients were prepared on the floor, the women sitting on their heels about the pans. The cooking was done outside, with charcoal, under a crude lean-to. The larger room was dark and comfortable, with low divans arranged around the walls, and overlapping rugs laid upon the floor. At night this room accommodated the girls, and Yaqub and Aadila slept upstairs, climbing a ladder that went up through the floor. If, for some reason, the girls were to be concealed from visitors, then they would ascend the ladder, and occupy themselves up there until the coast was clear.

Whilst the women attended to the imminent *palaw*, Daniel and Yaqub sat cross-legged on the floor with their backs to a divan, drinking light sweet tea from brass cups. Yaqub stroked his moustache with his forefinger, and cut straight to the chase.

'What is your religion?'

'I am not religious. I was a Christian, but now I have no belief.'

Yaqub was stunned. 'How is this possible? Is this not very bad? Is this common with your people? How can a man live without God? How can a man be trusted who has no God?'

'You can trust me,' said Daniel, 'because even if I have no God, I do have my honour. And amongst Europeans it is becoming more common to find people who say that you cannot know whether there is a God or not.'

'So you do not say that there is no God?'

'No, I don't say that. I say that I cannot know.'

Yaqub was still pained and perplexed. 'I am very sorry for you. This is a terrible fate, to have no belief. There is no one here like that, not one person.'

'Perhaps when I die I will find out the truth.'

'I pray that God will have the patience to forgive an understanding that comes so late. But God is merciful and compassionate. Let me think about this, because it seems to me a very great mystery, this business of unbelief. We will speak again later, when I have thought about it. *Tsu kalan yast?*'

'I am almost sixty-three years old.'

'You seem very well, very strong, for such an old man.'

'In my family a few of the men have lived very long.'

'Perhaps they are frightened to die because of their unbelief.'

'I am the only one like that. The others are Christians.'

'*Tsumra mashuman lare?*'

'I have two sons and two daughters, but one of my daughters was killed in the war.'

'May God give her peace. I also lost a daughter. She was taken by a fever. I know what it is to lose a daughter. *Tsu wruna aw khwandi lare?*'

'I had three brothers, and all of them are dead. Two of them died in South Africa, one of enteric fever and one in an ambush. I don't have sisters. This brother who I bring with me ... I found him dead, and already nothing but bones, so I don't know exactly why or when he died. I am very much afraid that he killed himself.'

'That would be a very great sin.'

'I am glad that I will never know. After I have buried him I will go to South Africa to find the graves of my other brothers. I hardly remember them. They were much older than me.'

'And your mother, your father?'

'My mother died, towards the end of the war, and my father died when I was a boy. He was killed in a fight...A duel.'

'Ah,' said Yaqub, 'this is the best kind of death for a man. Alas, it is not the kind of death that awaits a translator.'

'Your wife and your daughters would find things very hard if you were to die in a fight, my friend.'

'My sons would come,' said Yaqub. 'But, as I said, the time and manner of your death is written by an angel in a book even as you are born. But of course, death always comes as a surprise.'

'I very much hope to die by surprise,' said Daniel. 'I've always believed and hoped that I would die by falling to earth. I was a pilot in both wars.'

'From your lips to the ear of God,' said Yaqub. 'Tell me about being a soldier. This I will be very interested to hear.'

'I joined Rattray's Sikhs before I was twenty, and then was sent to the Frontier Scouts. When the Great War broke out I went home on leave and joined the Royal Flying Corps, so I was technically a deserter. I flew scouts...fighter planes...And then in the last war I was in the Royal Air Force, but I was going in and out of France on secret missions. I am still not permitted to talk about it.'

'Even so far from home?'

'Even so far from home.'

'And why do you limp? Were you injured?'

'I have lost two toes.'

'A man can live well without two toes. I trust you have lived well without them?'

'I don't even notice any more.'

'God be thanked. If I were to lose my right hand, I would learn to write with my left, and if I was to lose that hand I would

74

write with a pen in my toes. And of course I could dictate to one of my daughters, and she could write. Have you ever been shot?'

'Yes, in the Great War, but it did little damage. I had some time off, and then I was back in the air.'

'I have never been shot,' said Yaqub mournfully, 'but I have been cut with a sword. By the way, I have nothing to smoke. I was very ill once, and when I recovered, I found I could no longer smoke. My friends would laugh at me and say I was no longer a man, but one day I became enraged, and that is why I was cut with the sword. But ever since then, it has been accepted.'

'The same happened to me!' exclaimed Daniel. 'I was very ill with a fever, and then, when I recovered, I couldn't smoke. In Europe we are beginning to believe that it is very bad for you. '

'And you were insulted for it? For not smoking?'

'Not insulted. Mocked. But there was never a fight.'

There was a low yowl and a scratching at the door, and Yaqub stood up to let in a long, tall, slender, brindled cat with yellow eyes and torn ears. It came confidently up to Daniel, and arched its body as he was stroked, purring loudly.

'This is Pisho,' said Yaqub. 'He is a very fine cat. As you see, he has the biggest balls on any cat ever seen.'

'They are indeed most impressive.'

'He makes good use of them. All of the kittens in this part of Peshawar are his. He fights every night and comes in bleeding but victorious. He has four wives, and a hundred concubines, like a sultan. Male cats are more sweet-natured than the females. Sometimes Pisho walks through the streets behind me, calling to me. The Prophet, peace be upon him, is said to have loved cats, so if one wants to be like him, one must also be gentle with cats.'

'When I was here all those years ago, a mullah told me that the Prophet had a disciple who loved cats so much that he was known as "father of kittens".'

'This is a good story. I pray it might be true. I believe that it is a *hadith* from the collection of Bukhari.'

'In my family we have a pet lion,' said Daniel. 'He is completely white, with beautiful golden eyes.'

'You come from a family of kings?'

'No. A family of eccentrics. I have a photograph.' Daniel reached into his jacket pocket and took out his wallet. From it he withdrew a small photograph, and handed it to Yaqub.

'This is my son Felix,' he said, 'and this is my daughter Felicity. This woman is their mother, and this woman is her friend. This is the lion. Obviously.'

'Your son is a soldier?'

'Temporarily. He's doing national service.'

'And this is your wife?'

Daniel hesitated, embarrassed. 'She is a wife. Not the wife I married, but still a kind of wife.'

'Ah,' said Yaqub imperturbably, 'a concubine. The lion is exceedingly large. Your family must have a great sense of fate, of being resigned to it, to live with a creature like that. Or great faith in God. The sultans used to keep leopards and cheetahs, for hunting. It must have been a fine sight.' He handed the photograph back to Daniel, sighed, and said, 'This is the first time in eight years I have seen even a picture of a woman with an uncovered head.'

'It must seem strange to you.'

'To every nation its own prophet,' quoted Yaqub, 'and its own customs.'

A large metal plate was borne into the room by two of the sisters, and set on the low table in front of them. It was a most beautiful mound of *palaw*, the rice a light golden colour, studded with sultanas and morsels of vegetables, with nuggets of mutton and chicken that had been torn rather than sliced. The smell was delicate and delightful. Around the edge was arranged flat bread.

'*Mehrebani wakrey,*' said the girls together, and Daniel thanked them with '*Tashakor! Takashor!*'

Yaqub waved them away, and indicated to Daniel that he should help himself, taking a piece of bread to use as a scoop.

'In my country we eat with the women,' said Daniel. 'This is one of the differences between us. To me it seems strange to eat only with men.'

'I remember,' said Yaqub, tossing a piece of chicken to Pisho. 'We saw the women eat with the men, and we talked of it, but you know, this is much better for the women. It is very difficult to eat when the face is covered, and in any case they eat all the best things before they bring the plate out. We men are left with the toughest and leanest meat. When you go out, and you see a woman in the street, even though she is covered up, you can see that she is fat. She waddles like a duck or a goose. Have you ever seen a fat man in this province? No! We men are all thin.'

'In my country they also eat the best things before they bring the rest in, and then we men have to share even that with them.'

'Life is very unjust,' said Yaqub, contentedly shovelling another mouthful. 'After this we will eat *ferni*. My girls make it very well. You will enjoy it, if they have left any.'

'Is that a Snider?' asked Daniel, gesturing towards a long antique rifle that stood propped against a corner of the room.

'It is a Snider. A very good one. The bore is immaculate, but I have no ammunition. It was taken from a British soldier by my great-grandfather, at Kohat, in the Pass. You see that long knife leaning next to it? That's the one he used to cut off the soldier's head.'

That night, in the upper room, with Pisho vibrating on his chest and the bulbuls setting up an operetta nearby, Daniel lay on the floor next to Yaqub, too happy and too excited to sleep. The one thing he dreaded about old age was the prospect of no more adventure; but now he was here, and before long he would be back at sea, and then in South Africa, out in the veld, and then he would be in Canada, motorcycling across the continent to British Columbia, and then, one day, before he was too old, perhaps he would take the Brough to Mexico and back. He felt a mild sense of panic that, whereas in 1919 he had wondered what he would do with so much life left over, now there may not be enough.

18

Out on the Water

Frederick and Ottilie had bought a battered little sailing dinghy and joined the sailing club, but since neither of them really knew how to sail, they had bought a small outboard engine to clamp onto the back of it. It was a guilty pleasure to creep out onto the Solent under power, in the hope of not being caught cheating by the sail snobs.

In India their social life had revolved around the Gymkhana Club, and here their sailing club also provided an instant society, of people who were happy to spend hours scraping off varnish, getting wet and filthy, and living more outdoors than in. It did not take long before they had worked out which ones were going to be their friends. Frederick enjoyed instant credibility as a sailor because of his service at the Battle of Jutland, and later in the RIN, so his inadequacy with sail was politely overlooked. Ottilie's joy at being able to live by the sea, just as she had in Madras, made her a naturally popular companion for those indefatigably organising treasure hunts, beetle drives and charity cake stalls. She had bought the cheapest new car there was, a Ford Popular, for £390, so that she would not be stranded when Frederick was off in the huge, antiquated old Rover 16 that he had saved from a scrapyard, and rebuilt with Daniel's help.

Ottilie was a common sight, bowling along the lanes of Fishbourne, grinding the gears, never losing that peculiar smile of delight that comes to the faces of those who have fallen in love with their first car. It was almost impossible to drive it in the rain, because the wiper worked on a vacuum from the exhaust manifold, and worked more slowly the faster one accelerated. That aside, it had bought her a most wonderful freedom.

In August of 1954, there was an evening that seemed to go on forever. Rationing had ended, and Ottilie had cooked an enormous leg of lamb, intending that the leftovers would keep them going for a day or two, reheated in gravy, or chopped up in a hash. She was increasingly realising that it was much more fun to cook for yourself than to be cooked for by servants, because then you had everything exactly as you liked it. They had drunk a bottle of claret with it, out on the terrace, and were sitting side by side, hand in hand for the first time in weeks, helping themselves to a box of sugared almonds that sat on the table before them.

'Let's take the boat out,' said Frederick. 'The tide's almost in. We can have an hour or two on the water.'

'But it's so peaceful!'

'Think how lovely it'll be when the lights go on in Chichester. Why don't we potter down to Thorney Island? We can take a handline and catch a fish.'

'I don't really want to,' said Ottilie. 'It's so blissful here on the terrace. I hardly want to move at all. But I know I'll like it when I'm out there. Come on then! I'll just go and scruff up. You'd better too. No point in going out in cavalry twills, blazer and cravat.'

'Better put on something warm; it'll be colder out on the water.'

Twenty minutes later they were puttering out of Bosham harbour, southwards along the creek. On one side of the boat sat Boomer, their gargantuan French mastiff, with his sad crumpled face, and his boxer-like brindled markings in brown and black. Frederick sat on the other side to counterbalance him, and Ottilie took the helm, it having been decided that she would navigate them out and he would navigate their return.

The twilight was very still, and the owls screeched and hooted. Frederick trailed his hand in the water, governing the handline that had a simple mackerel spinner on the other end, even though there were seldom any mackerel this far up the creek. He had no expectation of catching anything, and was enjoying what he liked to call 'a bit of *dolce far niente*'.

'Isn't this lovely?' said Ottilie.

'It couldn't be lovelier, really, could it?'

'On evenings like this, I don't miss India at all.'

'India was a dream; a beautiful one, but even so, it was a dream. I'm glad we had it, but now I suppose we've woken up.'

'Isn't it funny, how we dreamed of home when we were out there, and now we're home, we dream of India?'

'We can go back and visit if we want. It's not as if India has sunk into the sea. We've still got friends there.'

'What about Boomer?'

'Hmm, dogs and children. Always a complication.'

At that moment there was a violent strike on Frederick's line, and he exclaimed 'Oh good Lord!' as a loop of braid streaked through his hand. 'We've caught something absolutely enormous,' he said. 'Can you stop the engine?'

Twenty minutes later Frederick managed to land the largest sea bass that either of them had ever seen. It was thirty inches long, a solid, struggling creature, athletic and barbarous, with its spined fins and elegantly curved lateral line. Boomer nearly upset the boat in his efforts to inspect it, but Frederick held him off with his shoulder as he strove to unhook it.

'This'll feed, I don't know, six people, perhaps,' he said. 'It's an absolute bloody prize.'

'How are we going to kill it, though?'

'I haven't got a priest. What can we whack it with?'

'I suppose we could just let it drown in air.'

'Oh no, that's too cruel.'

They looked down at the heroic, aristocratic fish, gulping and feebly flicking its tail, until eventually Frederick sighed and said, 'It's too beautiful to kill.'

'Let's put it back,' said Ottilie.

'Yes, let's do that. Let's let it go.'

He lifted the fish carefully and lowered it into the water, cradling it as you would a returning salmon. Suddenly it thrashed, and darted off.

'Damn,' said Frederick, holding up his right hand, which had blood streaming from a cut in the palm. 'I completely forgot about the gills.'

That night they lay side by side in bed, hand in hand, sleepy and happy. 'You know,' said Ottilie, 'this evening was such a glorious one, I mean, I was so happy, it was worth leaving India for. Out on the water with you and Boomer, and nothing to worry about, and the spire of the cathedral against the sky, it was pure bliss.'

'We could have had the same evening in India, except the fish would have been a *bhetki* or a butterfish. The lights would have been Madras instead of Chichester. It would have been warmer but the sun would have set much earlier.'

Ottilie thought for a while, and eventually said, 'My darling?'

'Yes?'

'We can't keep going on and on about India. We should do with India what we did with the fish. We should just let it go.'

19

The Cross

At dawn they breakfasted on hard-boiled eggs, yogurt and some remains of the *palaw*, and then set out to visit Yaqub's wife's great-uncle's wife's second cousin's grandson, who was a joiner and carpenter.

It proved to be a delicate mission. Zarif was a serious young man with a strongly developed sense of probity, who worked in the small courtyard behind his house near the bazaar. The muscles and tendons of his arms were the most clearly defined that Daniel could remember ever having seen, and his ragged work clothes were delicately hung with sawdust. A long spill from a plane had attached itself to the tip of his beard, and he wore a grubby bandage around one forefinger, where he had accidentally sliced himself with a chisel two days before. The constant stinging and aching had not improved his temper.

'No, *webakhsha*, I am sorry, I will not make a cross, even for all the gold of Persia.'

'But, cousin, it is only a cross. What could be more easy?'

'*Webakhsha.*'

'But it is for the grave of a Christian sahib who used to live amongst us.'

'I am a Muslim. I do not make crosses. And the cross is a terrible thing. It is an instrument of torture and execution. It is madness to kneel down before a cross and pray to it. This is idolatry. I will not make you a cross.'

'Nobody prays to a cross,' said Daniel.

'I have seen it with my own eyes! People kneeling before a cross and praying to it!'

'They are not praying to the cross, they are just praying in front of it. They are praying to Allah.'

'Do you think I am ignorant? I'm not deceived. I also know that they pray to Jesus Son of Mary, and say that he too is God, and they pray to three gods who are one god, and they are God, and Jesus, and Mary the Virgin, his mother. This is all blasphemy and madness.'

'He is very confused,' said Daniel to Yaqub, in English.

'The Christians are confused,' replied Yaqub. 'They are so used to all these strange ideas that they don't see the strangeness of them. Is it any wonder if they confuse us with their own confusions?'

'And everybody knows,' said Zarif, 'that Jesus Son of Mary was not killed on the cross. It was someone who looked like him. This is stated by the Prophet himself, peace be upon him.'

'I am not a Christian,' said Daniel, 'but my brother was. He would have liked a cross on his grave.'

'I have said what I have said.'

Daniel looked around at Zarif's small collection of tools, and asked, 'What if I buy a billet of wood from you, and hire these tools and your workplace for one hour, and make the cross myself?'

'You know how to do this?'

'Yes.'

'But you are a soldier. *Ostaz* Yaqub has told me.'

'I am many things. I also know how to fly an aircraft and repair a motorcycle.'

'What do you think of this idea, cousin?' asked Yaqub.

'I will have to go into the house, so that no blasphemy is committed under my eyes.'

Zarif rummaged in a pile of scraps, throwing timbers aside until he found what he was looking for, a solid length of teak. 'This is proof against the weather,' he said, 'something made of this is very good for the outside. It is used for ships. Now I will go.'

As Daniel worked with the unfamiliar but efficient tools, cutting and chiselling out two mortises, Yaqub watched him with interest, his hands behind his back.

'You know, sir, I have been wondering why this is such a curious thing to behold, and I have just understood it is because this is the very first time in my life that I have ever seen a white man working with his hands.'

Daniel laughed softly, and said, 'If you were to come to Britain or France you would see that most of us are working with our hands. We are not the same at home as we were here.'

Daniel wondered how he was going to join the two pieces together, as he could see no screws anywhere, but then he realised that he should peg it with two of the dowels that Zafir had made and left in a neat bundle at the back of his bench. Nearby there was an old press drill set up, operated under its own weight, with a bit of the correct size already installed. On the casting it said 'Edward Preston & Sons, Birmingham'.

'Look, *Ostaz*,' said Daniel to Yaqub, pointing to the nameplate. 'We left something useful behind us.'

'*Mashallah*,' said Yaqub.

When the cross was completed and Daniel had shaved off the stubs of the dowels, he took from his pocket a small brass plate, on which was engraved:

Archibald Alexander Pitt

1885–1954

A beloved son and brother

He was true to his salt.

'I need to pin this to the cross, and then we are done,' said Daniel. 'All I need is four nails.'

Afterwards, Daniel took off his jacket, and wrapped the cross so that Zarif would not have to see it, whereupon Yaqub put his head into the house and called, 'Cousin, the terrible deed is done, and there has been no divine punishment yet.'

Zarif was obviously twitching to see whether the infidel had done a good job, and kept glancing down at the jacket where it lay on the bench concealing its dreadful secret. Daniel said, 'Your press drill is a wonderful machine.'

'Yes,' replied Zarif, 'without it life would be harder. And I have a saw. Come, see. This is also from Britain, but it stopped working, and now I don't know what to do with it.'

At the back of the yard was a circular saw with a fifteen-inch blade and a movable fence. 'This was my father's,' said Zarif, 'and a man could make planks with it. I have kept it clean and sharp and well oiled in his memory, but it no longer moves.'

Daniel inspected it, running his fingers over the cogs, and trying to turn the long handle that made them spin.

'Has this ever been taken apart?'

'It was taken apart to be cleaned, and regreased inside, and then when it was put back together it no longer worked, even though it was put back exactly the same.'

'Do you have a … ?' He stopped and asked Yaqub. '*Ostaz*, do you know the Pashto for "spanner"?' He pointed to a large nut, and made a wrenching motion with his hands.

'Ah,' said Yaqub, 'you mean *wrinch*.'

Zafir trotted away down the road to a cousin who, he was sure, had a large adjustable spanner. Whilst he was away, Daniel took out his wad of rupees, and said to Yaqub, 'How much should I pay him?'

Yaqub frowned seriously and extracted some notes, giving them back to Daniel. 'This pays for the wood, and this pays for the hire of the tools. I have taken enough to show that you are generous, but not so much as to show that you are a foolish and conceited man who throws his money about. You should leave them on the bench, with a hammer to weight them down, and Zarif will count them when we have gone, and he will sigh and say, "Thanks be to God, this infidel has judged well."'

When Zafir returned somewhat breathless, Daniel took the spanner from him and noted that it also said 'Made in Birmingham'. It bore the arrow of British government property, and somebody had punched into it the letters 'KDG'. He remembered that the King's Dragoon Guards had once been stationed here.

Daniel pointed to the large double nuts at each end of the spindle, and realised that he had no idea how to say 'bearing' in Pashto. '*Mohtaram* Zarif, I believe these are done up too tightly. They are not tightened to make things strong, but only enough to keep them together. The outer nut locks the inner one.'

He loosened all four nuts, and then turned the handle, causing the blade to spin into life. He tightened the nuts up a fraction, until there was the barest song of friction. Zafir was wide-eyed with delight, clapping his hands and exclaiming, '*Alhamdulilla! Alhamdulilla!*'

He collected a plank and fed it through the blade whilst Daniel worked the long crank handle.

'I am very happy, I am very happy,' he was singing as the plank emerged, neatly cut into two lengths. He held them up for Daniel to admire, and then put them down on the bench, where he saw the notes under the hammer. He resisted the temptation to pick them up and count them, and turned back to Daniel, clasping his shoulders and kissing him on each cheek. '*Yusulmak, yusulmak,*' he cried.

'*Ze ham injinyar yam,*' said Daniel, as if explaining that he was also an engineer might somehow make his feat of prestidigitation seem more modest.

20

Plans for an Exhibition

Since the war Christabel and Gaskell had felt as if they were being steadily pushed to the margins by the younger people coming up behind them, who, more often than not, were only achieving recognition through some sort of gimmickry, or having a particular axe to grind.

In the life of an artist there are usually three stages; when you are young you are a prodigy, when you are almost dead you are a 'grand old man', or 'dame' in their case, and in the interim you are just another part of the scenery.

Gaskell and Christabel had worked hard to remain original without falling behind the times, only mounting their trademark joint exhibitions when their subject matter seemed to coincide for such a collaboration to make artistic sense. Their *War at Home in Two Hundred Frames* had done exceptionally well, Gaskell working up her charcoal sketches of the daily life of aerodromes into a hundred highly detailed and atmospheric oil paintings, all executed on imperial-size canvas with plain brown frames, and Christabel printing out her pictures of land girls at work and the implausible chaos of their house full of children on photographic paper of exactly the same size. These they compiled into a large book that the public could buy at the gallery. It had been an expensive exhibition to mount, but they had made money from it. What was most noticeable about it was that, as usual, the general public liked exactly those things of which the critics were most scornful. Gaskell had sold almost all her paintings to old RAF types.

The hostility of the critics caused them some heartache and self-doubt, for an artist is far more wounded by negativity than gratified by praise.

One night they were in bed after turning out the light, when Gaskell murmured, 'Darling?'

'Yes?'

'What are we going to do next?'

Christabel turned and lay on her back, as if talking to the ceiling. 'I don't know. It's strange to do so well and end up so demoralised, isn't it? They're making us feel out of date and left behind when really we're not. It almost makes you want to give up.'

'That man in *The Times* was so scathing. It made me want to track him down and give him two barrels.'

'I know. But he's only a year out of Oxford. What does he know really? He's just trying to make his mark. You know, I think we've got to give up trying so hard. I think from now on we should do what we bloody well like and not give a damn about what the papers say.'

'That might be the best way of staying original,' said Gaskell.

'Let's do a show all about Puss. He's the most extraordinary subject we're ever likely to have. And let's make it as strange as we like. Completely bonkers, if that's what we fancy. We'll call it "The FTBC Show" and not tell anyone what it means, but everybody will just call it the White Lion Exhibition. We can do it in a year and put it on at the Dulwich Picture Gallery. That's such a special place for us.'

'But, darling, what does "FTBC" stand for?'

'Fuck the Bloody Critics. Where is Puss anyway?'

Gaskell said, 'The last time I saw him he was downstairs, sprawled upside down on the sofa in the library, with his paws in the air.'

'Thank God for that. It's impossible to sleep with him taking up the whole bed. You're either completely squished or forced into contortions.'

'We really ought to shut him out of the bedroom at night.'

'But we're too soft, aren't we? We don't have the heart. And he'd just rear up and spring the door open anyway.'

'We've turned into a couple of mad old coots,' said Gaskell.

'Who cares?' said Christabel. 'From now on it's FTBC.'

21

The Cemetery

Daniel and Yaqub arrived at the cemetery on Jamrud Road in two rickshaws, drawn by barefoot men so skeletally thin, sun-blacked, and malnourished that Daniel could not understand how they were able to run at all. He started to hatch a fantasy in his head, of fixing a two-stroke motor to each rickshaw, and an extra front wheel with a handlebar, so that all the sheer exhausting brutality could be taken out of the whole enterprise.

The wall of the cemetery was already showing signs of disrepair, and it was clear that people had been taking advantage of a crumbled section to take shortcuts. The lychgate was draped in a glorious raiment of varicoloured bougainvillea, and behind it, amongst the twenty acres of tilting stones, the grid of footpaths and the rough grass, stood palm trees, peepal and sheesham. Yaqub said, 'Well, here we are at the *ghora cabrestan*. This is a terrible place for mosquitoes.' He waved his left hand. 'Nearly all the graves are in this half, and over there –' waving his right hand – 'there are hardly any graves, apart from the new ones.'

'There are new ones? There are still white people here?'

'No, sir, there are no white people. The new graves are those of the Christians you left behind. Apostates. The bones of the white men have new neighbours now, which are the bones of brown men, and the bones are all turning yellow together. So it is that death laughs at us and makes us all the same race.'

'I think my brother would be content to lie amongst the new graves,' said Daniel. 'He was not at home with his own people.'

'We should turn right at the water tank, then,' said Yaqub. 'Come, let me carry the pick and the spade, so that you can carry the bones and the cross.'

The two men stopped in Zone D, where there were few graves in the northern part, and were momentarily confused by such a generous choice of location. 'Away from these trees,' said Yaqub. 'They will make it impossible to dig, because of the roots.'

In what Daniel judged to be the centre, he put down the bag of Archie's bones, and set to work first with the pick, to loosen the soil, and then the spade, to lever the hard earth out. 'Let me fetch water,' said Yaqub. 'I will pour it over the ground to make it softer.'

He returned from the tank with an old bucket whose handle had long been missing, poured it tenderly over the ground where Daniel had disturbed the surface, and went away to fetch more.

'Your idea was a very intelligent one,' said Daniel, when he had dug down a couple of feet. 'It's made it much easier.'

'You know, sir,' said Yaqub as he sat on his haunches and played with a bent of grass, 'I would offer to help, except that I am a scholar, and, as I said before, this is the first time I have ever seen a white man working with his hands. I am too overwhelmed with wonder to help at present.'

'You are mocking me, *Ostaz* Yaqub,' said Daniel. 'I am glad that Pathans still have their sense of humour. And anyway, this hole is too small for both of us. This is the last thing that can be done for my brother, and so I wish to do it myself.'

'I will wave away the mosquitoes,' said Yaqub, 'so that I do not have to experience the shame and humiliation of uselessness.'

When the hole was too deep to dig any further, Daniel scrambled out, and wiped his brow with the back of his hand. 'It's time to bury the bones,' he said.

He set them out at the side of the grave, and then lay down on his stomach to place them neatly at the bottom of the pit, beginning with the larger ones. They clinked together softly. Lastly he took the skull, and stood up to look at it, trying to see his brother's flesh upon it. Yaqub pointed with his forefinger and said, 'This is where the soul lives, in the skull; I have no doubt of it.'

Daniel put the forehead of the skull to his lips, and held his breath in order not to have to inhale its musty smell. He kissed it twice and said, '*Au revoir, mon brave. À la prochaine. Tu es chez toi maintenant.*' He knelt down and placed it in the centre of the arrangement of bones. At its side he put the two books, and an envelope containing the sheets of paper upon which Archie had written his final messages.

'May I have the honour, sir,' asked Yaqub, 'of putting in the first earth?'

'Of course you can, *Ostaz*,' said Daniel. 'He would have liked the idea of being buried by a Pathan. If you wish, you can put all the earth in.'

'Some of it must be yours,' said Yaqub. 'I will do the first half.' He bent down, took up the spade, and dribbled the dampened soil from it very gently, so that it pattered down like rain. 'I think that you should hold the cross in place, so that it is well planted, and also so that I don't have to touch it myself.'

Afterwards they gazed down at the heap of soil with its cross in the centre, and Daniel said, 'I buried my little son in Ceylon in a grave the same size as this.'

'Who knows why Allah does what He does?' said Yaqub.

'You are lucky to have a God to believe in,' said Daniel. 'I'm envious of you.'

'I don't know why you have no God. For me He is like the air that I breathe and the water I drink.'

Daniel was well acquainted with the impossibility of building a philosophical bridge between believers and himself. He said, 'I remember what it was like, when God was like the air and the water.' It had always been a wonder to him that Muslims managed to mention God in every sentence.

'The mosquitoes are terrible,' said Yaqub, slapping at the back of his hand. 'We should move from here or we'll be made into pincushions.'

'I'd like to wander around the graves,' said Daniel.

It was a sombre experience. The monuments were beautiful, with their carvings and Celtic crosses, but they told tales of unendurable suffering and misfortune. Died of Burns. Killed by his Chokidar who Mistook him for an Intruder. Stabbed to Death. Shot by Tribesmen. Died from Wounds Incurred in a Dacoity. Fell from a Horse. Killed in the Afghan War. Assassinated by a Ghazi. Shot by Accident. Diphtheria. Hereditary Syphilis. Influenza. Enteric Fever. Malaria. Died of Heat Apoplexy. Died of Heat Exhaustion. Assassinated in the Khyber Pass. Fell Victim to the

Dreadful Distemper of Smallpox. Sank Exhausted by the United Effects of the Climate and his Labours. Hornet Stings. Polo Accident. Alcoholic Poisoning. Earthquake. Rabies. Plague. Hysterical Mania. Dropsy. Fatty Heart. Scalding. Concussion. Abdominal Injuries. Cerebral Embolism. Intestinal Obstruction. Nephritis. Remittent Fever. Convulsions. Premature Labour. Cholera. Bronchitis. Typhoid. Peritonitis. Perforated Gastric Ulcer. Killed in Action at Shabqadar in an Engagement with the Hill Tribes. Smallpox. Puerperal Septicaemia. Uraemia. Asphyxia. Tetanus. Killed in a Flying Accident. Bullet Wound to the Head. He Died that Others Might Live. Gunshot Wound One Evening whilst out Riding with his Sister. Shot at Peshawar. Shot in the Abdomen. Fractured Skull. Tyalaria. Gunshot Wound to the Head, Self-Inflicted. Meningitis. Septicaemia. Pyelitis. Thrown from his Horse. Drowned in the Swat River. Multiple Injuries. Murdered by a Pathan. Found Dead. He Was Shot during an Incident near Charsadda which is on the Road to Mardan from Peshawar. Delirium Tremens. Assassinated by an Afghan. Killed in action at Gandad Kotal Aged 22 Years. Haemorrhage of the Womb. Dislocation of the Spine. Gunshot Wounds to the Elbow and Buttocks. Suicide by Hanging whilst of Unsound Mind. Killed in Action in the Bara Valley. Killed in Action Kajuri Plain. Burns Received in Gallantly Fighting a Fire. Childbirth; Thy Will Be Done Aged 17 Years and 8 Months. Be Still and Know that I am God.

Then there were the graves of the children. Whooping Cough. Measles. Dysentery. Died Aged 3 Months of Debility. In Memory of Our Loving Babe Percival. In Loving Memory of Nelly Winifred Beloved Daughter. Diarrhoea Aged 1 Month and 13 Days. Convulsions Aged 9 Months. Bronchitis Aged 13 Weeks. Malaria Aged 2 Years and 9 Months. Teething. Croup. He Died Aged 1 Hour. Shock Aged 9 Months. Smallpox aged 12 Days. Wasted Away after only 26 Days of Life. Polio Encephalitis. *How We Loved You Girlie Darling. How We Miss and Want You Still, But God Wanted You Our Treasure. Rest in Peace, It is His Will. Just As Our Bud Was Opening, In Glory to the Day, Down Came the Heavenly Gardener and Plucked Our Bud Away. To See in One Short Hour Decayed the Hope of Future Years, To Feel How Vain a Father's Prayers, How Warm a Mother's Tears.* Uraemic Coma aged 8 Months. The Babe Died Aged Half an Hour from Asphyxia. *Suffer little children to come unto me for such is the Kingdom of Heaven.*

Daniel and Yaqub wandered from headstone to headstone, reading the epitaphs, and then stood before the regimental memorials of the Black Watch, the King's Royal Rifles, the King's Dragoon Guards, the Royal Garrison Artillery, the Royal Horse Artillery, the Royal Irish Fusiliers, the Royal Irish Regiment, the Royal Welch Fusiliers, the 61st and the 87th Infantries, with their long lists of young men gone.

Daniel stopped before the memorial to Lieutenant Colonel Irvine Walter, and said, 'I knew this man when I was here.'

They read the inscription. 'Chief Medical Officer NWFP who lost his life in the Nagoman River when leading the Peshawar Vale Hunt of which he was the master. 26 January 1919. Ever faithful to duty, ever loyal to friendship. Drowned near Abazai Camp, aged 54 years.'

Daniel gazed at it for a long time, waved his left hand impatiently, and said, 'What a bloody stupid way to go.'

'To be killed hunting is a man's death,' protested Yaqub.

'Hunting a deer, perhaps. The Peshawar Vale Hunt used to hunt jackals, because there weren't any foxes. I remember them. A bunch of good-humoured and gallant horsemen who tried to pretend against all the evidence that this was England. What could be more futile than to get yourself killed whilst hunting something you're not even going to eat?'

'This place depresses you,' said Yaqub.

'It makes me bloody angry,' said Daniel. 'There's hardly a soul over forty in this cemetery. It was the same in Ceylon.'

Yaqub gestured to take in the entire necropolis, and said, 'All these young soldiers and their wives, and these little children, and these doctors and clergymen, they were the coin with which you bought your dominion. They came here thinking they were human beings, full of hope and courage and a sense of duty, but they were only coins. And now the currency has changed and all these coins are worth nothing any more, and they corrode down to nothing under this unhappy soil and these disintegrating stones, and what was bought by means of their flesh and their actions has been abandoned, and it is as if they were never here at all, and now everything is as it was before. The tribesmen still kill each other, the *ghazis* dream of holy wars, and the caravans loaded with opium and rifles come in from Afghanistan.'

'I was thinking exactly the same thing,' said Daniel, 'but without such poetry. Come, let's sit for a while under this tree. Tell me some more verses composed by your daughters.'

They sat under a sheesham tree, and Yaqub said, 'This one is by my eldest daughter, Madiha:

> Nightingale, is it any wonder
> That if you sing so sweetly
> People will come
> And lock you in a cage?

'And this one is by Sabiha:

> A stream cannot be a river, nor a mound a mountain.
> A lamp cannot be the moon, nor a planet the sun.
> A worm may look like a snake,
> But still it is only a worm.

'And this one is by my youngest daughter Wafiya:

> Angels are made of light
> And the jinns are made of fire,
> But we are made of four things,
> And so we are confused,
> And that is why our lives are hard.'

'I like the one about the nightingales best,' said Daniel. 'Do you compose verses yourself?'

'I thought of one when we were looking at the graves,' answered Yaqub, 'and they were making me think about the passing of time. The verse is this:

> O Yaqub, you are getting old,
> And still you think of stupid things.

You are only a scribe, but
You dream of wars and honour,
And you dream of pretty girls.'

'Does a man ever stop dreaming of pretty girls?' asked Daniel.
'I pray to Allah that I will still be thinking of them as I lie
dying. There is a verse of Kushal which goes:

If you go to the graveyard
And dig in the grave of a pretty girl,
You will not find the girl, but white bones
And the black dust of her womb.

'Do you have verses?'
'There is a verse I like very much, about death, but I didn't
compose it. I was made to memorise it at school, and I have
never forgotten it.'
'Recite,' said Yaqub.
Daniel gathered his recollection together for a moment and recited:

'Under the wide and starry sky,
Dig the grave and let me lie:
Glad did I live and gladly die
And I laid me down with a will.

This be the verse you grave for me:
Here he lies where he longed to be;
Home is the sailor home from the sea,
And the hunter home from the hill.'

A profound silence fell between the two men, and eventually
Yaqub sighed and said, 'If two peoples were to love each other's
poetry, do you think they could ever be enemies?'
'I'm afraid so,' said Daniel.
'Yes, you are right. It was a stupid question.'
'It wasn't so stupid. But you know, we had two wars against
Germany, even though we admired their philosophers and loved
their music more than any other. Can we go and listen to a

95

storyteller? I haven't heard one since I was here as a young man. We can find one in the bazaar.'

'What story would you like?'

'Layla and Majnun. I last heard it in 1914.'

'Ah, I know exactly the right storyteller for this. Every time he tells it, it becomes more elaborate. This may take an hour.'

'We have an hour,' said Daniel. 'But first I want to stand over my brother's grave for the last time.'

'God willing, it may not be the last time. You will always have friends if you return.'

'I don't know how much time I still have,' said Daniel.

'But perhaps you will have enough, *inshallah*.'

'I would very much like to walk around the place and see all the old sights; Edwardes College, the Mohabbat Khan Mosque, the Cunningham Clock Tower, the Hastings Memorial, all these things. But mostly I want to go out and look at the Jamrud Fort on the Pass, for the last time.'

'We should also see some cricket at the Peshawar Club ground,' said Yaqub, 'if you want to return to the old days. Cricket is one great thing for which we continue to thank you. The energy and skill of our young men is a wonderful thing to see.'

Before Daniel left Peshawar, he went to the jewellers' quarter and bought a gold fountain pen and a watch as a farewell present for Yaqub. On the pen was engraved 'Mrs Susan Brooks'. On the back of the watch was engraved 'Lt. Col. John Haughton 36th Sikhs'. Yaqub saw him off from the station, the two men holding a long handshake, and unable to say much to each other. Daniel left Peshawar feeling peculiarly empty, and Yaqub returned to his family feeling peculiarly alone.

Two days after Daniel Pitt had left Peshawar, Zarif the Joiner slipped into the cemetery of the European dead, and wandered about until he found Archie's grave. He was surprised to find it amongst the new graves of the apostates, rather than amongst the old graves of the Europeans. He wrapped a cloth round the top of the cross so that his hand would not have to touch it directly, worked it out of the grave by pushing it back and forth whilst pulling it upward. It came out with a small jerk, and he wound it in a kameez, and stole it.

It seemed to him that it was no sin to steal from the grave of a Christian, and that such a fine piece of teak was wasted there, being left to weather and turn grey in the implacable sun and winds of the frontier.

For ten days after that he suffered prolonged, arduous nights of insomnia, punctuated by dreams in which he was followed by an invisible avenger with a swagger stick in his left hand, who beat him across the back with the flat of an infantry sword, crying out in a sepulchral voice, '*Melmastia! Nang! Khegara!*' On the eleventh day, understanding that he had infringed the Pashtunwali, he returned the cross to the grave, unable to bear the ignominy and humiliation of having stolen from a dead man, even though the latter had only been an infidel.

To atone for the infamy of what he had done, he planted the infidel's mound with flowers and came at the end of every blazing day to water them.

22

The FTBC Exhibition

The Dulwich Picture Gallery was packed for a month, not least because Gaskell and Christabel staunchly refused to tell a living soul what FTBC might possibly stand for. The rumours were plentiful and gratifying, but not one speculation came anywhere near the mark. The mystery of it caused people to come who otherwise would have stayed at home and listened to the wireless, or walked their dogs on Clapham Common. The papers reported it, just as the two women had expected, as the 'FTBC (White Lion) Exhibition'.

Christabel had taken many dozens of pictures of Puss simply being a cat. There was one of him sitting bolt upright in a wheelbarrow, and another of him in a large cardboard box. One, called *The Lion of Judah*, had him sitting exactly in the middle of a Star of David that Christabel had chalked on the lawn. In another he was in his characteristic panicked pose, attached to the trunk, all his muscles straining against gravity, halfway up the redwood tree. There was one of him prettily chasing a butterfly, another of him on his back, a football between his forepaws, and another of him perched precariously on top of a stack of paving slabs.

There were photographs of him with the family, lying across the laps of Felix, Felicity and Gaskell, and of the family lying side by side on the lawn using his flank as a pillow as he slept. There was one of Puss up on his hind legs, being teased with a peacock feather. There was a very charming one of Felicity gazing soulfully at the camera as he slumbered with his head in her lap, and another of Felix grimacing as he was being embraced, the lion towering over him, his forelegs across the young man's shoulders as he licked the side of his head. There were several of Puss in his favoured sleeping positions, draped over beds, sofas, piles of logs, or flat on his back. There was one very remarkable close-up of the inside of his mouth as he yawned, and a whole series of him roaring. It was as if the roars could be heard just in the act of looking. There was a powerful speaker set up next to these pictures, and every now and then Christabel would startle the viewer with a real roar that she had enregistered on a tape recorder. Mostly she waited for those distinctively supercilious people with wire-framed spectacles and notebooks that she knew to be critics.

It was generally agreed that Gaskell's contribution was the more remarkable, however. She chose this occasion to reveal her extraordinary talent for forgery, by painting portraits of Puss in the styles of Great Masters. There was a Puss in the manner of Rembrandt, a Puss lying on his side on a chaise longue in the manner of Goya's *Naked Maja*, another of him in Stuart costume, like a Van Dyck. There was Puss as Goya's *Marchioness of Santa Cruz*, there was a pointillist Seurat, another in thickly laid blues and yellows, in a patch of sunflowers. There was one of Puss sitting dejectedly at a table in front of an empty glass, as in a Degas. There was one of him with the family, all naked in the woods, in the form of a *Déjeuner sur l'herbe*, so that he looked like the only one who was clothed. In honour of Picasso there was a *Demoiselles d'Avignon* with his head in place of those of the sinister-looking women, another in the manner of the Blue period, and yet another in the manner of the Rose. There was a cubist Puss that looked exactly like a Braque. There was one painting, a completely abstract, gawdy mess that took Gaskell only ten minutes to execute, entitled *White Lion in the Robes of a Philosopher*, and another of Puss with a beret and fantastic moustache, simply entitled *Surrealist*. There was a very elegant and sophisticated Puss in the manner of John Singer Sargent, and most popular of all, and the first to sell, were the naive realist portraits after Douanier Rousseau, all worked up from pictures taken by Christabel whilst out walking with Puss on the estate.

Almost all the photographs and portraits sold within a month, and once again Gaskell and Christabel went home and weighed up this commercial success against their critical failure. Gaskell was most pleased that she had sold all the pictures she had done as recapitulations of her former styles, and Christabel was delighted that she had managed to capture the cat's natural domesticity.

Even the critics agreed that the white lion was an extraordinarily beautiful creature, and that its unblinking innocent golden eyes were possibly the most remarkable they had ever seen portrayed in oils or captured on film.

'It makes a change,' remarked Gaskell drily, 'from people, going on and on about my green ones.'

23

Daniel in Colombo

I left Peshawar without the weight of my brother's bones upon my back.

Leaving was hard. Yaqub and I had become fast friends even though we might as well have been different species. We both knew that we would never see each other again, and at the station we stood shaking each other's hands until we heard the last blast of the whistle and the doors were beginning to slam. I was repeating '*Tashakor, tashakor*' and he was saying '*Melgere! Melgere! Khuday pe man, khuday pe aman!*' He embraced me and kissed me on both cheeks. As the train departed he ran along the platform clutching at my extended hand, '*Khuday pe man! Khuday pe aman!*' until the platform ran out. I saw him standing there alone with his hands at his side, giving out a palpable air of sadness, and I waved to him until he turned on his heel and walked back the way he had run. A man like him must have endured terrible loneliness, a scholar in a land where the only others are clerics. As for me, I was waving goodbye not only to my brother's bones, but to the first adventurous scenes of my youth, out there to play the Great Game on behalf of the Empire.

I remember how invulnerable I felt, how it was impossible not to be young forever, how the future would always be before me, how death could only befall another. I suppose that the sheer hell of Westminster School had been a perfect preparation for the North-West Frontier. It certainly filled us with a confident Christianity that assured us of our righteousness and our civilising mission. What we actually did was pay the tribesmen not to kill us or each other, and no doubt the Pakistanis still do.

Even so, we are so constituted that we are capable of improbable loves. A man might love his horse, or his rifle, or a supremely ugly woman, or his favourite spade, or a cat, or, like Archie, he can even learn to love the bearded and hennaed fanatics of those inhospitable hills, and the hills themselves. Certainly I remember how blissful it was to lie at night in a nullah, pistol in my right hand and sword in my left, sleepless with admiration for the stars. And I remember the faultless hospitality and good manners of the chiefs who would not dream of harming you if you were in their tents, but, if they were to capture you in the wilderness, would flay the skin from your body whilst you were yet alive. If there were a blood feud, the only way to save yourself was to seek sanctuary with those who were sworn to kill you, and never step outside their house again.

During the Great War I loved my comrades and my aeroplanes, sometimes even my enemies, and only when that was over was there time and opportunity for the love of women. Sometimes I am glad that everything went wrong in that respect, because now I have so much more to remember.

I wonder if there will be any more; perhaps I might find the last and greatest love of all, or perhaps there will be one or two fond flirtations. I sometimes think that I might still possess the physical energy for love, but lack the enthusiasm, and sometimes I forget that I am really still with Christabel, and likely to be so until I die.

I often thought of Samadara, and never more so than during the days I spent in Colombo.

I arrived in Ceylon in April of 1955. It was during that strange hiatus when General Sir John Kotelawala was Prime Minister, before Solomon Bandaranaike won the election that led to the establishment of Sinhala as the official language, and thereby set in train his own assassination and the permanent insurrection of the Tamils.

The island was a dominion at the time, and still buzzing with chatter about the beautiful young Queen's visit exactly a year before. Apparently the Hill Club had preserved all the dishes from her banquet there inside glass cases. We'd retained our military bases in Ceylon, I was told, but I saw almost no personnel in Colombo, and I had no time or inclination to visit Trincomalee.

In the fantastic humidity and raucous chaos of Colombo I felt nothing but melancholy. I wanted more than anything to take the road or the train up to Kandy and Nuwara Eliya, to go to the highlands, to enquire after my old friends the Bassetts, and perhaps to find Samadara.

I knew that she was most likely to be dead, and that if I found her she would certainly be at the heart of a family that would not be glad to see me. I confess that, much as I yearned for her, and had never stopped yearning for her, the most part of me wanted to remember her as an exquisite young woman with faultless, glowing skin, black hair that caught the light, and a lithe body that swayed with sensuality as she walked. I thought that if she were to see me as a man in his sixties, she too would feel the same desperate sense of loss and decline. We would look at each other and ache for all the children we never had, the meals we had never eaten, the evenings not spent on a terrace beneath the stars.

I longed more than anything to visit the grave of my child at Christ Church, to reflect upon what other things might have come to pass. I visit graves to reflect upon what my life has meant, and what it will come to. I often sit in the graveyard of St Peter's Church in Notwithstanding. I have visited many graves in the latter years of my life, but that one, of my dead child in Ceylon, is the one to which I should have returned, above all others. How I wish that I had.

I wondered what had happened to the Reverend Williams, who had helped me bury my child, and I wondered what had happened to Ali Bey, the Egyptian gentleman who had befriended us on the voyage out, and to Hugh Bassett, who had sat with me on my first night in the GOH, and, when Rosie left the room, advised me as to the protocols of taking a native mistress. I remembered how Hugh and I had played gun snap in the evenings, climbed Adam's Peak from every possible angle, and talked for hours about setting up some kind of business involving aeroplanes. Where do our words go, and what happens to yesterday's dreams? It is as if somewhere Hugh and I are still young, still making plans, still amazed at having survived, still bright-eyed with possibility.

Colombo was almost empty of Europeans. I found one or two in H. W. Cave & Co., where Rosie used to go and buy books, and there were a few on the Galle Face Promenade. There were some in the Grand Old Hotel, and some at Mount Lavinia, but you could see that the people we had trained up to become the elite had already taken over. We had educated them to be like us, and then banned them from our clubs, and so they had prised us out and sent us home. Then they became the same as us, and set themselves up in our place.

In Colombo I ate alone, or went out and bought street food. The pungency of the curry leaves brought Samadara back to me. I felt more alone and regretful than I had ever felt in my life, until a strange thing happened to me as I was walking through the Victoria Arcade, one of only two great coincidences that have occurred in my life.

A powerfully built, dapper man of about my age suddenly stepped in front of me and looked intently into my face, stopping me in my tracks. He was a smartly dressed Sikh, with a grey turban on his head, and a generous but well-trimmed beard with its moustache jauntily waxed into two upwards crescents at either end. I think he was the only Sikh I had ever seen in Ceylon, and yet he looked completely familiar.

'I am believing that it really is you,' he said, in an accent that was redolent of the Punjab.

I held up my hands and said, 'You seem very familiar.'

He stood there smiling, and put his hands together. 'You are Lieutenant Pitt, Rattray's Sikhs,' he said, grinning broadly, 'and I am Daljit Singh.'

'Sepoy Daljit Singh Bittu Khalistan?'

'The very same. But one day I became a subedar major. No more sepoy!'

'My God,' I said.

'My God, indeed,' said Daljit.

'I became a squadron leader in the RAF,' I said, 'but I still think of myself as a captain in the army.'

'Do you remember, sir, how once you saved my life? On the side of that mountain whose name I am forgetting?'

'And do you remember how you saved mine? At the river?'

'It was all long time ago. Shall we shake hands?'

I felt my eyes prickling, and said 'No', because there seemed nothing more fitting than to clasp the old soldier to my chest.

When I released him and stepped back, both of us had tears in our eyes.

'All our youth has gone, isn't it?' said Daljit. 'Such a long time. I have fifteen grandchildren now.'

'Where are you staying?'

'At the GOH, sahib.'

'What are you doing here? Such a long way from home?'

'General merchandise, sahib. Tea, trinkets, cinnamon. I've become almost an Arab or a Parsee. But now I am living in Delhi.'

'I never heard of a Sikh who became a merchant,' I said.

'I also have weapons,' said Daljit,' and that is most suitable for a Sikh to trade, I am thinking.'

'Daljit Singh, will you do me the honour of dining with me at the GOH tonight?'

'We will talk about the old days, sir. I have too much to tell you.'

And that is how I remade the acquaintance of the soldier who as a sepoy had been my batman, who had once saved my life on a mountain when a Pathan was holding a knife to my throat. Now I had almost nothing, and he was a rich man with a big house full of servants, but he still wanted to call me 'sir' and 'sahib'. We laughed about that, but it was too late to change. We were to remain in touch until the day, twenty years later, when one of his sons sent me the letter to inform me of his death, enclosing the three stripes from the upper arm of his old uniform as a memento. He also sent me his father's priceless kirpan, with its embroidered gatra, because the old man had requested him to do so.

24

Daniel in South Africa

I stayed only a few days in Ceylon because it was eighteen days by sea from Colombo to Durban, and I wished to avoid the Yala Monsoon, which arrives in May or June, and can make the voyage very unpleasant indeed. I wanted to travel in the sunshine.

As soon as I got to Durban, however, I wished I had stayed in Ceylon. I did admire the fabulous coaling facilities at the harbour, but I was appalled by the whaling slips where the giant beasts were being flensed in the open air, in a welter of gore, surrounded by a wild maelstrom of wheeling and shrieking gulls.

I hated South Africa from the very start. It wasn't just the oppressive humidity of Durban; the weather was on the turn for winter anyway, and a light rain fell, washing the air a little cooler from time to time. After Ceylon, it had the atmosphere of a place that had been poisoned. Smuts had been defeated and died, and now the Boers were obsessed by their pet bogeyman, the *svart gevaar*, and invoking God's election of themselves as the chosen race, justified by all sorts of tendentious allusions to the Old Testament. It was pointless even trying to have a sensible conversation with a Boer. I gave up on my first night in the hotel. What I was witnessing was the same collective lunacy that had perplexed me in Germany before the war. The place had the same sinister feel to it.

At the bar of the hotel there was a solitary man I recognised instantly as the kind of dislocated Briton who has nothing to leave or stay for. He was sitting alone drinking gin and tonic at a small round table by the window in a melancholy reverie, whilst pretending to read a newspaper. Before him on the table was a tin ashtray piled high with half-smoked cigarettes. His whole atmosphere and demeanour reminded me strongly of Archie. Our eyes met, and I felt obliged to ask if I could join him. He was a man of about my age, with watery blue eyes, and a body much run to corpulence. I introduced myself and held out a hand for him to shake.

He asked me what I was doing here and I told him about the quest to find the graves of my brothers. 'Well,' he said, 'that was all for nothing, wasn't it?'

I asked him what he meant, and for the next hour I listened to his monologue about how the country had gone to the dogs, and how he would leave if only he knew where to go. He told me that he had been a public prosecutor, but the Boer government had purged the police, the courts and the civil service of British whites. It was awarding contracts only to Afrikaner businesses. It had gerrymandered the constituencies and even made new constituencies so as to make itself electorally invulnerable. Anyone could be arrested for being a communist, even if they had never heard of Marx and thought that socialism was a card game. He told me that just before I arrived the Boers had destroyed an entire suburb of Johannesburg and moved 60,000 black people out, to turn it into a white city. 'You'll notice,' he said, 'there's something going on with the *kaffirs*. They're giving each other thumbs-up signs when they pass in the street, and muttering some kind of slogan. They can't spend more than seventy-two hours in a city, before they're carted off out into the countryside. There's going to be a revolution, and I'll be strung up the same as the bloody Boers, won't I? We're all going to end up dangling from the bloody trees. As soon as the *kaffirs* get a decent leader, and realise there's more of them than there is of us. We're buggered. I wish I could go back to Blighty.'

I said I'd seen the signs everywhere, '*slegs vir blankes*' and '*nie blankes*', and I didn't know which counters to go to, where I was allowed to piss, or even sit down.

'We're fucked, old boy,' he said. 'I hate to say it, but we're fucked. The *kaffirs* despise you a little less when they realise that you're British, but the Boers are always going to despise you for being the wrong kind of white, and they'll never forgive us for winning the war.'

I listened to his complaints and predictions, and thought about how I had recently spent several hours with my old Indian batman, relaxing together in the GOH, talking about old times. In this country, that would have been a criminal offence.

As if he were reading my mind, he said, 'What unites people is being in the shit together. The reason there's no hope for us here is that everyone's in the shit except for the Boers. The Brits are in up to their knees, the coloureds are in it up to their ribs, the Bantus are in it up to their necks, and the Boers are strutting around being called *baas*, and thinking they're the heirs of the earth and God's chosen people. If you're not all in it together, sooner or later the ones in the shit turn on the ones who aren't. There's millions of Bantus; one day they'll hang us all.'

'I'm going to Canada,' I said. 'What about thinking of going there?'

'If I could afford to leave, I would. There's about to be a bloody massacre.' He paused, and then said, 'I was in North Africa and Italy. That's how I know about being together in the shit. By the way, if you're going exploring, do you want to buy a car? It's no good to me any more, and I could do with the cash. I could use it for the passage home. In steerage.'

I gave up on my plan to explore Durban for a few days and bought the redundant lawyer's saloon. He had become tipsy, it seems, left the road, and turned it over. Now that he had no salary there was no prospect of repairing it.

It was horribly bashed up along the driver's side, and one had to get in through the passenger door, but the engine purred sweetly, the brakes worked, and it seemed mechanically sound. I bought a few tools, a foot pump and a tool roll from an iron-monger near the harbour, a spare tyre from a scrapyard, two five-gallon jerrycans for petrol, and another for water. The following morning I set off early.

The road ran in parallel to the railway track, and I realised too late that if I had had any sense, I would have taken the train, as it passed by every place that I wanted to be, all the way to Ladysmith and beyond. Even so, I enjoyed the independence of being my own driver, and not having to cope with the irksome business of trying to determine where I was allowed to sit or buy myself a cup of tea. I was condemned to travel alone, for I soon discovered that the Bantus either couldn't or wouldn't accept lifts from a white man.

I drove through a landscape of scrubby dark green trees, yellowed grass, undulating veld and symmetrical rocky knolls. From time to time I saw herds of impala, and I think I might have seen a leopard. The road had few motor vehicles on it, but a great deal of small drawn carts, and entire families of Africans on foot. I was in no great hurry, so I stopped for the night in Pietermaritzburg. I went to see the church that had been built by Italian POWs in the war, and the city hall, and then sat in the botanic gardens until the darkness set in.

I set off early the next day to find the grave of my brother in Estcourt. It lay amongst others, by the banks of the Bloukrans River, not far from the railway cutting, the place where the track turns sharply left after crossing the water. This was where an armoured train was stopped by rocks on the line, and one of the trucks derailed. It was at this ambush that Winston Churchill was captured by the Boers.

Every man in the overgrown graveyard had his own white cross. Most were Dublin Fusiliers and Durban Light Infantry, and there was one grave where the inscription was made entirely with .303 cartridge cases.

My brother was there because he had been shot in the back by a sniper a few days later, whilst relieving himself against a tree. He'd been in the Durban Light Infantry.

I hardly remember my two oldest brothers. Archie and I had been, as it were, an afterthought, and they were much bigger than me. I remember their game of picking me up and slinging me across the room so that I landed plumb on the sofa, and how they used to stand me on their shoulders so that I could pick the apples out of one of our trees. I remember their manly scent of fresh sweat, and their mad games of football, competing with each other to send the ball flying past me as I stood in front of the chalked rectangle on the garden wall that separated us from the McCosh family. I was tiny and terrified, a completely inef-fectual goalkeeper, but I suppose it was good practice for being under fire, and I realised years later that my real job had been to return the ball.

What is a man in his sixties supposed to feel when he stands in a foreign land, over the grave of a brother of whom he remembers almost nothing, except that he loved him? I had tears in my eyes, but also a certain rage in my heart. He came to South Africa by the same means as I was sent abroad, through the Public Schools Emigration Scheme. There was little for us at home and so we were sent to man the outposts of the Empire. Some of us truly loved the adventure. Some found absolute fulfilment, and some were lost even to themselves. None of us questioned it. We all believed in our mission, and, in the last analysis, it was better to be somebody with servants in the colonies than a nobody at home. Looking back on it, home could be a pretty stifling billet, and going abroad could turn you into an optimist.

My brother came all this way to die pissing against a tree. I had travelled thousands of miles to visit this grave, but I stood there in the sharp sunlight for not much more than half an hour, feeling not very much at all, except a little bewildered. I read and reread his name: Arthur John Groombridge Raoul Pitt. Died of Wounds. We used to call him Artie. My mother would dress in smoky grey on the anniversary of his death, and sit by the window looking out over the lawn where he had played as a boy. I remember once she turned and looked at me, when I was about twelve years old, dabbed at her eyes with a small handkerchief, and said, '*Oh la peine, quelle douleur, quelle tristesse! Viens, mon petit. Embrasse-moi.*' She held me and stroked my head, her chest heaving with little sobs. I thought at the time that my brother had died a hero, and I was proud of him. It said on his tombstone that he had been one of the many who had saved South Africa for the Empire.

But down in that grave lay the crumbling bones of a young man who had been shot pissing against a tree, who might as well have never lived.

All around I could hear the bustle and scraping of insects, the calls of birds that I did not recognise. I felt the declining heat of the sun gently toasting my skin and soaking through the fibres of my shirt. I wandered about looking for something to leave on the grave, but found nothing except a long speckled feather, which I stuck upright into the soil of the mound. I wanted to say something, but I never speak to God because He never speaks to me. I went down on my haunches, balancing myself with one hand on the headstone. I put the other on the turf and whispered, 'Artie, I've got your Webley. Archie had it. Now it's mine. Archie's gone. I expect you know.' I paused, feeling foolish and ineffectual, and added, 'And I've got your sword that you practically honed to death, with the hunting horn on the basket.'

I turned and went back to the car. I had one more brother to visit, but I decided that first I had to stop at Colenso and Spioenkop, and walk the battlefields.

At Spioenkop I stood on that hillside reading the inscriptions on the mass graves that had been made out of the hopelessly shallow, makeshift British trenches, filled with the stones from their improvised breastworks. I wondered what it must have been like to have been trapped there in the open, being fired at and shelled from above, from all directions, in extreme heat, for hours on end, without shelter or water. Beneath these stones lay men from Lancashire, Middlesex and Scotland.

An old soldier often feels like an anomaly that has been accidentally left over, a remnant. I lived, but those beneath my feet had not. Nobody grieves for them now. One day there will be nobody left to weep for me, and then nobody left to weep for those who did.

I wish I knew what it all means, and if it means nothing at all, I would like to know that too.

The stones around the perimeter of those long rectangular graves had been whitewashed. The army has always loved its blanco and its whitewash. We used to whitewash the trunks of trees at the barracks, and the boulders beside the driveways. We give sparkling whitewashed stones to our dead soldiers whilst their bones become ochre and crumble beneath, because this is all we can do for them now that we've used up their lives. The truth is that we do it not for them, but for ourselves. If I had died in battle I would have wished it to be in a wild place where the birds could pick me clean and the wild dogs break my bones for marrow. I wouldn't want to make do with whitewashed stones.

I remember Archie saying to me once, after too many whiskies, '*Mon brave*, life is entirely a battle. Everyone, in the end, dies in battle.'

I drove over the Bulwer Bridge into Colenso, and stayed for two days, partly because I liked the town. It had wide streets, with some tall palm trees dotted about, and low buildings that gave it a feeling of spaciousness. It was in truth a company town, because down on the Tugela River was a vast coal-fired power station with four chimneys, and three of those cooling towers that resemble pepper pots. It reminded me of a battleship, or an ocean liner. The company employed virtually everybody, and even supplied the townspeople with hot water. It was an impressive sight. Rather than go to all the bother of looking around for a 'whites only' hotel or boarding house, I made myself as comfortable as I could in the car, and slept there, curled up on the back seat.

On my second day I set out early and walked the battlefield. I wanted to see the Boer positions on Hart's Hill, where the stones were still heaped into defensive positions. Then I went to Wynne's Hill, and down to the loop in the river where the Irish Brigade was entrapped and almost wiped out. I wandered about Ambleside Cemetery nearby, where the Irish were buried. Those Irish dead are doubly forgotten. Their compatriots have chosen to forget their loyal service in the construction of the Empire, and its defence in the Great War, and like to think that they were the colonised.

I began to ask myself why I was spending so much time in cemeteries now that I was getting older; after all, I too would be a permanent resident in one of them sooner or later. I was often made thoughtful by civilian cemeteries, particularly when I found the graves of children, but I suffered a profound melancholy in military cemeteries. Perhaps it was because what was won by all these deaths was always ephemeral. In Afghanistan we fought for decades to quell the anarchy and brutality of the tribes, and then we left, and everything was as it was before. In South Africa the Boers attacked us, and we defeated them. We lost 21,000 men, and perhaps 300,000 horses. Then, a few decades later, the Boers got the country anyway. When, finally, I go to Flanders to visit the grave of Ashbridge Pendennis, my boyhood friend and my wife's first fiancé, I expect to find him amongst hundreds of thousands of dead, and I know what I am going to think. In 1919 we all believed the war was over, and no more men would have to die; and then, in 1939, we discovered that the war had not ended at all. There had merely been a break. Ash's death from peritonitis, with his abdomen pierced by shrapnel, had bought nothing, not even time. Time was all that had been bought by the actions of Artie and Ernest in South Africa.

There is a lot to be said for dying in one's prime. Even so, if I had died over the skies of France in the Great War, I would have had no children and no lovers. I would never have flown a Lysander or a Hurricane. On the other hand I wouldn't have been captured and tortured in the second war, and I would not have had to live to see my daughter killed by a submarine, or endure the hostility of a son who hates me.

After Colenso, my legs aching from climbing so many hills, and my skin tingling with sunburn, I drove the short distance to Ladysmith, to pay my last act of homage in South Africa. In Murchison Street I found the Royal Hotel, and was grateful for a good wash, something to eat, a creaky but comfortable bed, and in the morning I went out to find flowers.

Ernest was with the Natal Carbineers. He survived the whole campaign – Colenso, Spioenkop, Vaal Krantz and Tugela Heights – and was one of the men who rode with the Imperial Light Horse into Ladysmith when Lord Dundonald entered it with Winston Churchill at his side, when it was relieved after 118 days of siege, on 27 February 1900.

Ernest Newton Edward Pitt is buried in the war cemetery even though he died of enteric fever in the epidemic that struck the town after the victory. He was, at the end, deaf, delirious and shitting blood. Apparently the disease ulcerated his intestines, and the contents of his guts leaked into his abdomen. It is more soldierly to have been shot pissing against a tree, but at least he died after a victory.

I found his grave easily, because the cemetery is well laid out, and not particularly crowded. I put my flowers on his grave, looked down at it for a few minutes, and then went and sat on the low brick wall. The earth was pink and the grass was ragged and worn. It was a pleasant day, with just the right amount of warmth in the air, but I felt empty, and extremely tired. I hardly knew what to say or do, so I just looked down and said, 'Well, Ernie, here I am at last.' I had done what I had travelled so far to do, and laid all three of my brothers to rest in my own mind. Now I could go home and think about leaving for Canada.

I drove slowly back to Durban, enjoying the hills and then the veld because I knew I would never see them again, and parked the car outside the house of the forlorn lawyer from whom I had bought it. I posted the keys through his letter box, hitched up my knapsack, and walked to the harbour to see about finding a passage home, away from that vile place where the whales were being flensed.

25

Felicity and Daniel in the Corner House

Daniel and Felicity faced each other across the table in a Lyons Corner House, pouring tea from the heavy fake silver teapot, and working their way through a pile of very buttery teacakes. The nippies in their white aprons and mob caps scurried about, delivering toast and top-up pots steaming with scalding water.

Felicity was twenty-five years old now, exactly on the cusp between girlhood and womanhood, as velvety and alluring as she would ever be. She wore her black hair long, waved in the manner of some actress that she admired, and knew how to look askance at her interlocutors in the most fetching way. Her eyes were bright blue, like Daniel's, and her pale skin and dark hair gave her the air of an Irish colleen. Ever since her secretarial course had begun, and then finding her first job at an accountant's in Hayes, she and Daniel had seen a great deal of each other, as he was now based at Hendon.

Their meetings at the Corner House had become a regular thing, but this time Felicity was in the mood for a confrontation.

'I think you should know,' she said suddenly, wiping her lips with her napkin, 'that I am going to get married and move to Hong Kong. And I want you to give me away, as I don't have a *proper* father.'

Daniel perceived the peculiar emphasis on the word 'proper' and felt a pang of nervousness strike him in the chest and throat. 'Oh,' he said feebly. 'Who is he? What does he do?'

'He's called Robert Quarton and he's from an old family in Northamptonshire, but they've almost run out of money, and he's the second son. They've got an enormous Gothic house that's falling to pieces and a great big deer park that they've turned into a potato patch.'

'Not many prospects then?'

'He's very successful. He's keeping the whole caboodle going almost on his own. He's fantastically clever and he works in banking. He's with the Hong Kong and Shanghai Bank.'

'In Hong Kong there's nothing to do except play tennis,' said Daniel. 'You'd be bored to death in no time. And it's extremely humid.'

'I like tennis. I just want to be normal.'

'Normal?'

'Yes. Be a wife and have babies, and look after a house and, actually, I love tennis and I'm very good at it. I beat you last time.'

'Yes, but I'm an old man. When I was thirty you wouldn't have stood a chance. You don't have any ambitions?'

'Those are my ambitions. I don't have any talents, do I? I'm not going to be a sculptor or a film star, am I? I want a nice life with people I love who can love me back and don't want me to be something I'm not. I want to be normal. And don't say "What's normal anyway?" because you do know perfectly well what I mean.'

'Does "normal" mean that you don't have any demons snapping at your heels?'

'It means not being forced into a mould that doesn't fit. I mean, look at my family! I've got two mothers, one of whom, much as I adore her, is virtually a man. She plays cricket and shoots pheasants with a twelve-bore, and wears a monocle, and drives a huge old Bentley at breakneck speed, terrifying the locals. My other mother is a tall and languid English rose who sees the world not with her own eyes, but through a lens. They sleep together and always have, and have never tried to hide it. They have affairs with each other's friends and squabble about it late at night when they think we're asleep, and then Gaskell storms out and drives off into the night. And their friends have nervous breakdowns, and die by falling downstairs or walking into rivers with their pockets full of stones. Their house is the most unbelievable chaos. Imagine what it was like during the war! Full of mad grubby children climbing up the curtains, and land girls with big thighs getting up to high jinks with each other and the younger members of the Home Guard, and Oily Wragge going out and coming back with a deer draped across his shoulders because he'd shot it with a musket.

'And why did Felix and I get sent to Bedales instead of a proper school? It was all champagne socialists who read the Harold Laski edition of *The Communist Manifesto* and little books by Bertrand Russell, who'd never done a day's work in their lives. You know … their mothers were all potters with inherited wealth, and their fathers were all "something in the City" who wanted to be poets and were actually only remotely socialist at weekends. And now, do we have an Alsatian or a tabby? No, we have an enormous white lion who sleeps on our beds, and smells really quite strong, and we have to collect up his manure and spread it on the garden to keep the deer away from the roses. And the other day he pinned me down by sleeping across my lap, and I couldn't move an inch, and then he started doing the most rank cushion-creepers you've ever smelled in your life. I was totally trapped and it was completely appalling.'

'To me it all sounds like fantastic fun,' said Daniel.

'It's fantastic fun to remember,' said Felicity, 'but the fun of living it has worn off. It's too chaotic. I've had enough of all the eccentricity and the self-indulgence.'

'You just want to be normal.'

'Yes. And look at my relatives! I mean, Sophie is adorable, but she's bats. Ottilie and Frederick are in mourning for India, like a couple of forlorn ghosts who can't escape from their previous lives. Fairhead is obsessed with raising the dead so he can find out what the afterlife is like, and he's actually devoted his whole life to attending the dying, as if he can't live with the living. He's like the shy person at a party who stands by the door all the way through, just waiting for it to be late enough to leave decently. And poor old humiliated Rosie, who obviously loves you to bits but is completely hamstrung by guilt and religion, and she's just waiting to die, alone in that great big house with a colony of cats.'

'And what about Felix? What does he feel about it?'

'You'd better ask him. Luckily for him, he's a bit strange. He fits in with the family better than I do. I mean, he's quite flamboyant, and you'd think he was an invert until you see him surrounded by adoring girls whose hearts he breaks one after the other. This idea of his, to become an architect, seems to suit him very well. It's sociable and creative, and it pays well. He's got a talent for drawing, and he understands money. He's started to talk like somebody from a Jane Austen novel, by the way, I don't know if you've noticed. Felix is fine, though. He doesn't mind what anyone thinks of him. It's a huge strength.'

'You've left me out of your list of oddities,' said Daniel, avoiding her gaze by pouring her another cup of tea.

'Hmm, well, what can I say? You're a war hero twice over. You've been a fabulous father *substitute*, ha ha, who's always had plenty of time for us.'

'But?'

'You're in your sixties and you're still roaring around on a vast old motorcycle when most people like you are in a Humber Super Snipe, getting fat and reactionary. You could have been pretty much anything but you got stuck in the RAF even though you hate the forces in peacetime and don't see the point of it. You're actually a bohemian like Gaskell and Christabel, but you've given years to an institution that is about as unbohemian as one can possibly imagine. And you and Gaskell and Christabel are stuck in the middle of a huge great lie that you can't wriggle out of and nobody dares speak about. How do you think it's been for Felix and me, not being able to be truthful even with each other? Do you think we didn't notice who was sleeping with who when you were up there? Do you think we haven't noticed some obvious resemblances?'

Daniel flushed and leaned back in his chair. 'You know I can't talk about that. Banquo is at the table, and everyone can see him, but we have to act as if we don't. Otherwise the consequences are too awful to contemplate. The point is that you are surrounded by people who love you, very original people with strange morals, perhaps, but who you love in return. If I've loved you *as if* you were a daughter, it's been exactly the same love as I had for Esther. I think you'd find it oppressive being "normal".'

Felicity looked away and smoothed her hair from her face. 'Well, I'd like to try it for a while, and then I'll find out. And I'll be back from HK every year for a month or two, if I want to dip back into the loony bin.'

'You know I would miss you terribly. It would be almost like losing you.'

'Wait 'til you meet my fiancé. You'll like him. He did his national service in the RAF, so you'll have something in common. And he is extremely good at tennis.'

'And how do you know he's normal? It takes months to find out what a person is really like. The honeymoon wears off, and then it's too late. You're done for. What if he turns out to be one of those people who dresses up in rubber and wants to be whipped with a brassiere?'

'Well,' said Felicity, 'if I've learned one thing from you it's that if you're going to do something, you've got to plunge in and do it thoroughly. Then if it's a disaster, you've done your best, and you don't have yourself to blame.'

'In Hong Kong you'd have a team of servants. Is that normal? Is that how you want to live? There's nothing more fatally boring than not having enough to do.'

'It's completely normal in Hong Kong. And what's wrong with idling about so that lots of other people can have jobs?'

'Perhaps I could come out to Hong Kong and visit you,' said Daniel.

Felicity smiled and took his hand across the table. She wrinkled her nose and said, 'I knew you'd say that. Knowing you, you'd come on your motorcycle.'

'First of all I'm probably going to Canada for a little while,' said Daniel. 'I need one last big adventure.'

'Wasn't it enough to go to Pakistan with your brother's bones in a bag?'

'Well, I've always wanted to drive across America.'

'On an obsolete motorcycle?'

Daniel nodded. 'Yes, on a motorcycle.'

26

A Note from Oily Wragge

Daniel received a card from Oily Wragge. It was a small one, with the usual robin on a snowy branch, and inside, on the verso of the 'Christmas Greetings' page, Wragge had written:

> Christmas is coming
> The burglars are about
> Electrify your knockers
> And keep the buggers out.

Folded into it was a note that read:

Dear Captain Pitt, sir,

I am told that you are going to Canada. I have been here longer than ten years, and I have had enough of this lark up here at Hexham.

The thing is that as you know Miss Gaskell and Miss Christabel went and bought Puss from Harrods, but it's me they are expecting to muck him out and take him for walks, and it was all very well when he was little and sweet like a sodding great kitten, but as you know he has grown into a bloody great beast with terrible bad breath and he goes up on his hind legs and puts his paws on my shoulders and licks my face and practicly takes the skin off, and I am thinking what if things turn nasty? We have put in a lot of fencing and he has a few acres to do what he wants in and although he is a lion and not a lioness and therefore not fond of hard work or going hunting, he has already made a proper mess of a goose that landed in front of his eyes when he was snoozing. We keep him well fed from what the slaughterhouse chucks out, and the deer that I shoot but I still think what if he takes a fancy to a bit of human? Sometimes he goes bonkers and tears around for a few seconds like a cat do, but he is a bloody great thing and it is not funny if you are in the way. Every night I have to go out and bring him in with a lead round his neck, and he has been very good so far but I have to tell you it is proper frightening when I call him and he comes bounding along and I do feel just like I did against the Turks back in 1915 when they were charging us with their Alla oo akbars and we were waiting for the order to fire until they were practicly on us except that Abdul didn't want to lick our faces off.

So like I said I have had enough of this lark in Hexham and I have never been to Canada, and I could do with a long ride to blow away the cobwebs, so I am asking can I come too?

Your old mucker,
Oily W.

PS I expec you have seen that advert everywhere, about tea, and so I want to know if Typhoo put the T in Britain, who put the cunt in Scunthorpe? And also, do you answer me this: What is brown and steaming and comes out of Cowes?

Daniel wrote back,

Dear Mr Wragge,

I'm surprised that you no longer feel happy about being Puss's keeper. I have always thought that he is a very affectionate and congenial soul. Still, things only have to go wrong once, I suppose. Perhaps I shouldn't blame you at all for being wary of him. Of course now I have to wonder who would possibly take your place. Intrepid lion keepers would be at a premium, I should think.

My plan is to land at New York, and drive the Brough combination across the USA and Canada, and end up in British Columbia, because it's less frozen than the other provinces in the winter. When I get there I will look around for a temporary occupation.

As you are such a good mechanic, and you ride a Brough as well as any man alive, and we have always got on exceedingly well, you are welcome to come with me and take a hand in the enterprise. I would be terribly pleased not to have to sell George the Second, or put it into storage, and have you ride it across Canada instead. I often think of how we rode back on the two Georges from Germany, with the Wolffs. I sometimes hear from them; they have all done terribly well in America.

I intend to go in the spring, for obvious reasons, so you have until then to make up your mind (and get a passport).

Yours ever,

Daniel Pitt, alias the Captain.

PS The answer to your last question is the Isle of Wight Ferry, and as to who did that terrible thing to Scunthorpe, well, I have enquired about it from my sister-in-law Sophie, who knows everything about words, and she has consulted the Oxford Dictionary of Names. *She tells me that it was originally called Escumetorp, and that it means a place belonging to Skuma. My suspicion is that it was turned into Scunthorpe by some humorist in the early days of literacy, perhaps a scribe with an unclerical turn of mind, or perhaps it became Scuntorpe, and then they put the 'h' in, in an attempt to make it a little more respectable.*

Wragge sent a postcard back saying: '*You're on. I'd better get myself sorted at this end, and help find somebody else to look after Puss. I am going to go to Norwich for a while so that I do be proper at home for a while, afore we go.*'

27

Oily Wragge (2)

Well, that was quite a ride for two old blokes on two old bikes. They were the best bikes ever made, according to the Captain, and I have to admit they hardly let us down once, apart from punctures.

It was bloody boring on the steamship, and I didn't do anything but sit and smoke a pipe and feel sick, but once we got to New York and I saw that Liberty statue all green and massive sticking up into the sky, and that Empire State Building looking like a great long radio set, I did feel a lot better. The Yanks made a pain in the arse of themselves as we tried to get in, there was a damn great queue, and you had to answer a load of stupid questions, like 'Is it your intention to assassinate the president?' but after that all the Yanks we met were as friendly as you like, all the way to BC.

Well, the first thing we did was get on a boat and go and look at that statue, and what you notice is that it's covered all over with chewing gum as high up as you can reach. You wouldn't do that to Nelson's Column, would you? The Captain was disgusted and so was I.

Captain Pitt worked out that it was three thousand miles to BC and about fifty hours of motoring, so he figured it would take about a week to get there. Why he wanted to go to BC I didn't ask, because I didn't much care one way or the other, to be honest, but when I got there I realised it was because there was more climate to choose from. I mean, you can freeze your tits off in the Cascades, or be nice and warm in the Fraser Valley, all in the same day.

The Captain had these laminated maps with rings around the towns in blue chinagraph, and these were where he thought we'd stay after each day's riding, but none of it worked out and it took us three weeks, not least because the Captain was just too bloody friendly and curious. He was still a good-looking man, with those surprising blue eyes, and there wasn't an ounce of fat on him, and he had one of those moustaches which is quite clipped, but it's the right length, not like that stupid little tache that Hitler had. He never did go for one of those handlebar RAF moustaches like Jimmy Edwards either. The Captain looked a lot younger than he was, and he was togged up in all his old flying gear, with a pilot's helmet and goggles, and big fur-lined boots, and a fat furry sheepskin flying jacket, and he wore one of those white silk flying scarves that make you look like a proper war hero even if you're only the dustman, so everywhere we stopped someone looked at the British bikes, and said 'Hey, you look like a Hurricane pilot' or 'Hey, I guess you're a Spitfire pilot', and like that we ended up staying with people I can't even remember now, who filled us up with steaks and waffles and maple syrup and wanted to talk about aeroplanes and motorbikes, and they wanted to prove that theirs were better than ours, which is something that Yanks are always keen on. Out in the boondocks there were types who made their own ammunition and spent the day in the wilderness blasting away at metal cut-outs of charging soldiers. The Captain loved that. And everybody always wanted to talk about the Queen, which is because they haven't got one of their own, and wish they had. If we didn't know whether or not the Queen liked strawberry jam or how many carriages she had, we just made it up. And the Captain spent a lot of time looking at the engines and suspensions of American cars and crawling underneath and being helpful when we should have been riding to Spokane, or whatever. He'd perk up whenever he saw an old flathead Ford, and as for those Yanks, they loved our big shiny Brough Superiors with the Swallow sidecars. The men that is, and they had to say that Harley-Davidsons were even bigger and better of course. The women just got charmed by the Captain, and made doggy eyes at him the same as those Kraut girls in Dortmund before the war. At least every three days the Captain got offered a ride out on a horse, and that was him gone all day. Once he went hunting with this bloke we met in the middle of bloody nowhere for a few days. I didn't fancy it, and when he came back he had a story about meeting a bear on a forest path, and there was a damn great deer draped across the bonnet of that man's truck. One thing you find out about people from Canada and that bit of Yankyland is that every single one of them has got a bear story, and they have to tell it over and over again every time they sit down and open a tin of beer. What I liked was seeing coyotes and raccoons and skunks, and the eagles I had never seen the like of in England.

Those Yanks were so hospitable that we didn't pay for one night's lodging. After a while I even got to like American beer, and that Tennessee whiskey slid down well. Of course it helped that the Captain was a famous ace in the Great War. He got recognised by older men sometimes, and the kind of younger ones who make model aeroplanes.

Sometimes we just bivouacked under the stars in the middle of nowhere. We had them vulcanised army capes that could double up as bivvies. Bloody marvellous things. We used to cook up cans of sausages and beans on little twig fires and talk about all the war we'd seen and the dead people we'd known, and I'd light up, and he'd say, 'They're not called coffin nails for nothing.'

I remember a lot of names and faces and incidents, all in a big jumble, and mile upon endless mile of totally flat land with roads so straight they must have been laid out with one enormous bit of string stretched tight, and lovely forests like the ones at Flathead, and Lolo, and the Little Missouri Grassland was quite something. You wouldn't believe how many places we went through. Cleveland, Toledo, South Bend, Chicago, Rockford, Madison, Eau Claire, St Cloud, Fargo, Bismarck, Coeur d'Alene, it just goes on and on. If I look now at a map of North America, I think, 'Bloody hell, I rode across all that.' The thing I remember best is that Coulee Dam. And the numb bum and the aching shoulders and the tingling in my fingers.

I often got to thinking about how the Captain and me were good mates, even though he was a toff and I was just a mister, but the thing is that if you spend long enough with someone you don't think about all that. When you're mending a puncture out in the forest, you're just old sweats together, aren't you? I wouldn't have respected him if he wasn't tough as old boots, and nor him me neither. It's what happens if you've been in the services, and anyway the RFC and the RAF was never as snobbed up as the army. I was in the Norfolks, so I was probably more snobbed up than he was. We didn't like it when we got given an officer up from the ranks.

I have to tell you that the last bit of that journey, through the Okanagan Forest up into Penticton, was just about the most beautiful ride I ever had, and then you arrive at that lovely little wooden town in the mountains, and that massive enormous lake, and it wasn't bloody surprising that the Captain and I just sat on the banks of it, and he turned and looked at me, with the engines of the Broughs ticking behind us as they cooled down, and he took the words out of my mouth. He said, 'I think we've arrived. Let's not bother with going on to Vancouver.'

'You're right,' I said. 'Bugger Vancouver.'

It was on that very same day, when we were mooching about the town, that I went into a sweetshop on Main Street to get some baccy, and the last great miracle of my life happened, which explains why I ended up a Canadian and never did come home to Blighty when the Captain did.

And you know what? Here's a curious thing. Once I got to BC and started to think about home, the one thing I truly missed was Puss, even though I'd come all this way just to put him behind me.

28

Rosie and Margareta

One Sunday, a tall and dignified woman of about Rosie's age had come unexpectedly to matins in St John's Church, Eltham. She sat alone at one end of a pew, and seemed to be taking her cue from observing the rest of the congregation.

Rosie was also alone, because although she came to services and sometimes helped out with church fetes and flower arranging, she considered her relationship to God to be a private one rather than part of a group enterprise. Apart from her tribe of cats, she was alone even when in company, except when Bertie and Kate came to stay.

Kate had turned out to be a wonderful daughter-in-law. She was still as pretty and lively as a teenager, with coppery hair, plump lips and pale skin. People would ask her if she was Irish, and she would say, 'Isn't everybody?' Her mother was indeed from Donegal, but her father was an English officer in the Irish Guards, who had somehow managed to survive all four years of the Great War, and end up a general, finishing his career as a strategic adviser in the Ministry of War. Kate had either an English or an Irish accent, depending upon who she was with.

Kate's parents approved of Bertie straight away, being exactly the kind of man to whom their daughter ought to be married. He had had a distinguished war, and was a major in a venerable and highly regarded regiment. They chose not to perceive that he was moody and aloof, and drank too much.

Kate knew about all that, but loved and married him anyway. She saw something soft and vulnerable beneath Bertie's bluster, something that could be nurtured and brought to the fore with time. She knew why he drank. It was not just that British officers had a cult of heavy drinking; it was also that two squadrons of his comrades had been annihilated in Italy in twenty minutes of action during the Battle of Coriano Ridge. No one survives such horror without consigning their serenity to oblivion. Kate thought she could pull him back, and she was almost right. After two years of marriage he was no longer drinking a bottle of brandy a day, and became helpless only on mess nights. There was comedy even in this; once he came home stark naked apart from his cavalry boots, and she found him in the morning, curled up fast asleep on the floor of the downstairs lavatory.

On Valentine's Day of 1955 he gave her a book of love poetry, with 'To my salvation, with love and gratitude forever' inscribed on the flyleaf.

Bertie was with the British Army of the Rhine and spent days at a time involved in arduous tank exercises on Lüneberg Heath, in a permanent state of battle readiness for the Soviet invasion. Kate was forced to kick her heels in Fallingbostel, socialising with other officers' spouses, and sorting out the perplexingly complicated problems of the wives of the troopers in Bertie's squadron. As she had not yet conceived, she came home quite often to see her parents, who lived in Gerrards Cross, and to stay with Rosie.

Rosie and Kate developed a special bond. Kate could see how much Rosie suffered. She was no longer the chestnut-haired, freckle-faced poetess of her youth, with a bohemian silver bangle on the bare flesh of her upper arm. She had worked flat out as a VAD in the same hospital at Netley in two world wars, and was still emotionally exhausted, not least by Esther's death on the *Aguila*. Physically she had no confidence any more, because she had lost a breast to cancer in 1939. Every day she woke up amazed by the miracle of having survived, of the cancer not having reappeared elsewhere, but at the same time she had lost any sense of herself as an attractive or interesting woman. Now she lived not for the love she might receive, but for the love she might give.

Bertie was not a responsive soul, but Kate was. She was full of life, laughter and uncomplicated affection. She would link her arm in Rosie's as they strolled down to the Tarn, and Rosie would tell her all over again how it was said that it had no bottom, and that her husband Daniel had once rescued a drowning dog from its waters, and that was what made her realise that she was going to marry him. Together they visited the graves of Rosie's parents in the graveyard of St John's, and Rosie would tell her about how her father had had a dozen mistresses, and how shocking it had been to find out about it at the reading of his will. They went to the golf club, and Rosie showed Kate the green where her father had dropped dead after scoring a hole in one. They took a small posy of flowers with them once, and Kate deposited it in the hole, the pair of them scurrying away afterwards, giggling like schoolgirls.

In the house Kate tidied up behind Rosie and the cats, as subtly as she could, so as not to humiliate her. When Rosie was out shopping Kate would scrub away at the greasy black rings of the bath, and, as a birthday present, had a carpenter install an elegant walnut catflap with a leather hinge in the back door. She made decent meals to replace the heaps of fried eggs and sausages upon which Rosie had become dependent, and would leave a shepherd's pie or a cauliflower cheese in the fridge for Rosie to discover after she had left.

With Kate, Rosie opened up her heart, and so she learned all about the untimely death of Rosie's fiancé Ashbridge in 1915, and how she had never really got over it, and how she had lost a child in Ceylon, and how her husband Daniel had just drifted away until she barely saw him at all, and then finally he'd stayed away altogether, but she couldn't possibly get a divorce, because she had made a promise to God on her wedding day, and she was sorry because Bertie had never really had a proper father, and she hoped that he would know how to be one himself when the grandchildren arrived.

Kate sensed that Rosie would spring back to life the moment she had a grandchild, and so she wanted a baby as much for Rosie's sake as for her own. For her it would mean something positive to do to while away the infernal boredom of garrison life, it would give her things to say in her letters to Rosie, and a feeling that there really was an ever-expanding future.

Rosie and Kate had to wait until 1956 for Theodore to be born, but two years earlier a tall, ungainly, wide-hipped, horse-faced woman walked alone into matins at St John's, and Rosie found the longest and best friendship of her life.

It was raining heavily by the end of the service, and many of the congregation held back inside the church in the hope of its passing. Rosie stood in the porch, her once fashionable cloche hat crammed down over her thinning hair, and beside her stood the tall mysterious woman, with an umbrella.

'Which way are you going?' she asked, in such a strong German accent that it came out as 'Vich vay are you going?'

'Just a few yards,' answered Rosie, pointing down Court Road. 'I live opposite the palace. I can get there without getting very wet, if I walk fast enough.'

'We will share this umbrella,' said Margareta, 'and we will walk as slowly as we like, and breathe in the nice fresh air that is being washed.'

At her door, Rosie invited Margareta in, and gave her tea in the drawing room. Margareta drank it continental style with no milk or sugar, and a slice of lemon, except that Rosie had not had a lemon in the house for years, so she had to drink it without.

'To drink tea with milk and sugar is a crime,' drawled Margareta bluntly. 'I will never understand this English thing.'

'I think we picked up the habit in India,' said Rosie. 'They drink it so dark and strong that you have to put milk and sugar in to make it drinkable at all. They even brew it up with condensed milk.'

'It is still a terrible thing, when tea is such a delicate drink. You must try it. It will change your mind forever.'

Margareta was from Prenzlau, in East Germany, and had joined the stream of those who left before the wall went up in 1961.

'The communists, they are destroying my country,' she said. 'There is no money, there is nothing to buy, they are always trying to catch you thinking and saying the wrong things, and everybody is a spy on everybody else, and most *schlecht* of all there is no fun. And the Russians, they raped every woman in 1945, even the little girls and the old women, and now they want our minds as well.'

'How did you get here?'

'On the boat and the train. How everybody comes.'

'But don't they make it difficult?'

'My cousin is the West German Ambassador. You have a very great number of cats.'

'I had a cat called Caractacus, years and years ago, and then I got another one, and these are their descendants. I just can't bear to part with the kittens.'

'I like dogs,' said Margareta, 'but these cats are very good. They have *so viel* dignity. They are like ornaments, sitting everywhere, like those four on the piano. I will think of them as sculptures, and then I will like them even more.'

As Margareta left, she looked down at Rosie and said, 'You know, I am going to be British. I have decided. I don't like us Germans any more. For me, I have had enough of being German. I like the British, how everything is a mess, but everything works. I will find a way. I think you and I will be friends. I think you like me.'

'Yes,' said Rosie. 'Drop in whenever you're passing.'

'I won't be passing. I will only be coming on purpose.'

'Why did you come into the church?'

'It was going to rain. I like *anthropologie*. I think it is the same word in English. I wanted to see how the English talk with God. It was good. I liked it. It's not so different.'

'Come again next Sunday,' said Rosie.

'Now I am going,' said Margareta. 'Now do I shake your hand like an English, or do I kiss you on the cheek like a French? I would like to be correct.'

Rosie laughed. 'What do Germans do? Shake my hand this time. Next time we meet kiss me once on my right cheek. When you leave you will kiss me on both cheeks, and then when you come back you can kiss me on each cheek, like a Frenchman.' Rosie paused and said quietly, 'My husband was half French.'

'He *was*? He is dead? I am so sorry.'

'Not dead,' replied Rosie. 'Gone. He's gone to Canada.'

'You tell me about it next time,' said Margareta, and Rosie watched her stride away in the direction of Mottingham, her long feet angled outwards, swinging her umbrella in unladylike circles, just like Charlie Chaplin.

She went back inside and tried some tea without milk or sugar, but it had sat on the leaves too long, and was dark and bitter. She suddenly remembered Daniel in Ceylon, lecturing her about how you should drink it black, very hot and weak, and how she had bridled at the implied criticism of her dogged Britishness. She made a new pot with only one spoonful of leaves, and sat with two cats on her lap, savouring the elegant and refreshing taste of it, wondering if Daniel had made it to Canada, and whether he ever thought of her, and what he would think if he knew that she was finally drinking tea in the French manner, as he had always told her that she should.

29

Oily Wragge (3)

We went straight to Main Street because that's what you do. You ride to the middle of a town and then you ask around about a place to stay. We had a lot of money left over because thanks to all the hospitable Yanks on the way we'd spent almost nothing except on petrol, which the Yanks call gas, which is daft if you think about it, because gas isn't a liquid, is it? and I'd say somebody should teach these Yanks proper English, and the Captain'd laugh and say he thought it was nice there was so many ways of saying things the same but different. There was this bloke we stayed with who said 'Gee wollakus' a lot, and after that me and the Captain started saying it too.

Well, anyway, I went into that sweetshop on Main Street, Penticton, and the Captain was hanging about outside looking at the things in the window, probably the card with penknives on it, and behind the counter was this woman a few years younger than me and so she was quite old if you think about it, you know, a bit spread out in the middle and a bit top-heavy, and a bit of a chin under her chops, and her hair must have been grey underneath all that brown dye, and she had a sensible hairstyle and flat heels, but she had a nice smile and flirty eyes, and she says 'What can I do for you then?' and I say 'Got any proper English baccy?'

'It's nearly all English, love.'

She had an accent that was obviously London, but covered over with Canadian, and I say 'Where you from then?' and she says 'I'm from here' and I say 'Before' and she says 'East London, but further out. I'm not a cockney. I'm almost Essex. You're from Norfolk, aren't you? What brings you here?'

'Him outside,' I says. 'I got cheesed off with being a lion keeper, except now I miss the lion quite a lot, and the Captain wanted to come to Canada on a motorbike, so here we are.'

'Well, bother me, a lion keeper,' and she glanced out at the Captain who was looking at those penknives. This startled expression comes over her face, and she opens up the counter and runs out. I go out too, and there she is face-to-face with him saying, 'It's you, isn't it? Don't you recognise me then?'

'Umm,' he says. 'You do seem very familiar. Give me a clue.'

'Batty old Mrs McCosh.'

'Another.'

'You helped me beat the carpet when it wasn't your place. And I married the policeman who stopped you giving someone a beating when he'd run over a couple of kids.'

'Ah,' he says, snapping his fingers, and doing a little dance step. 'I remember! You and the policeman went to Canada, didn't you?'

'I must have,' she says.

He takes her hands in his, kisses her on the cheek like a proper Frog, and says, 'Gracious me, Millicent, how we've changed.'

'Well, you haven't,' she says. 'I'm just a floppy old bag now, but you look like you always did, but grey.'

Well, I looked at that woman and I thought 'She's a fine old girl' and I say, 'How about introducing us?'

'Mr Wragge, this is Millicent, who used to work for the McCosh family at The Grampians. Surely you must remember her?'

She turns her eyes on me and they're big and grey like they'd always been, and she says, 'Oh, Oily, is that really you?'

I say, 'What, I've changed that much that you didn't recognise me, but you did recognise the Captain?' and she says, 'Well, you've changed a lot more than he has, haven't you? When you turned up in Eltham you weren't much more nor a skinny starving little tramp, were you? Sleeping in a wheelbarrow in that poky hole under the conservatory! Look at you now! Almost a gentleman, and your duds fit, and the soles ain't flapping from your shoes, and all your scabs've all gone.'

'Almost! Thanks!'

'We've got some catching up to do,' she says.

30

Exorcism

Rosie left Victoria Station and stopped for a minute to look at Little Ben, an elegant black-and-gilt outdoor grandfather clock that had been presented to Great Britain by France, on an unwontedly friendly impulse. Then she walked up Victoria Street in the direction of the cathedral.

She had never visited it before and was amazed. She had seen no other building like it in England, and it reminded her of the mosques she had seen in Egypt, except that it was made of red brick, with horizontal white stripes, so that it resembled a Viennese cake. It was undeniably magnificent. She wondered at the mosaic of Christ above the door, attended by Saints Peter, Mary, Joseph and Edward, and read the inscription: *Domine Jesu Rex et Redemptor per Sanguinem Tuum Salva Nos.*

Rosie crept in through the great doors, clutching her handbag to her chest with both hands, and found herself in the middle of a Latin Mass. She sat and looked around her at all the colourful, seductive paraphernalia of Catholicism. The air was heavy with incense, and the ceiling was already beginning to blacken from the smoke of so many candles over the few years since the cathedral had been built. Suspended above the end of the nave was the immense elongated great rood, depicting Christ upon the cross, and because of the inclination of his head, it was impossible to tell whether he was dead, or just looking downward to the earth.

She listened to the beautiful voice of the priest, quivering with religious certainty, and became so immersed in the ceremony that when the silvery bell suddenly tinkled, a shiver ran up her spine, and tears prickled in her eyes. She suddenly remembered visiting a Catholic church in Malta, on the journey home from Ceylon. It seemed many lifetimes ago.

After the service, she hardly knew what to do. She walked around the nave, looking at the enormous octagonal font, and the small St Christopher donated by Hilaire Belloc, in gratitude for his son's safe passage to France. She peered into the side chapels, and admired Eric Gill's famous and controversial Stations of the Cross. She was in no doubt herself; she loved them on sight. She noticed that the large bronze statue of St Peter had very clean, untarnished toes, thanks to being kissed so often by the faithful.

In the Chapel of St George and the English Martyrs, she stopped to gaze on the most remarkable thing of all, the body of St John Southworth, his hands and his face concealed behind shining silver simulacra. In 1654 he had been hanged, drawn and quartered, and then his remains had been stitched back together by the faithful, finally finding their resting place here in 1934. Rosie reflected on his great goodness, his philanthropy, his hideous suffering, and began to feel a little less sorry for herself.

She was both determined and uncertain, knowing what had to be done, but not understanding how she was going to set about it. She approached the row of confessionals, and noticed a pair of black shoes behind the curtain of one of them. There was a low murmuring within, and very shortly an elderly woman emerged from the neighbouring one, crossing herself vigorously and avoiding Rosie's eyes as she scurried past. 'I wonder what she did,' thought Rosie. She did not have the appearance of a natural sinner. She'd heard that some people went to confession for the same reason they went to the doctor, for a few minutes of company. Apparently you were supposed to go even when you had done nothing wrong, and you had to come up with things like 'impure thoughts'.

The priest came out of his booth and found Rosie standing in front of him anxiously.

'Good morning, my child,' he said, 'and what can I be doing for you?' He had a soft Dublin accent and large grey eyes that seemed both peaceful and critical. He was a solid man of about fifty years of age.

'I don't…' began Rosie.

'You don't what, my child?'

'Um. It's difficult. But I have a request.'

'A request?'

'Yes.' Rosie hesitated, looked at the floor, summoned up all her courage, and said softly, 'I want to be exorcised.'

'Exorcised? Did you say "exorcised"?'

'I did, Father.'

'Shall we go into the confessional?'

'I'm not sure I'm allowed to.'

'And why not? Are you not a Catholic?'

'Of course I am, Father. But not Roman.'

'How can you be Catholic and not Roman?'

'Anglo-Catholic.' The priest pulled an ironic, sour expression, and Rosie said, 'I am sorry, Father. I've often wanted to become a Roman, but something holds me back. I can't quite put my finger on it. It's to do with fidelity. It can't be helped. And I think you should have some services in English, for people who don't understand Latin. And anyone should be allowed to read the Bible. And if St Peter was married, and he was the original Pope, why can't priests get married? And I don't think that books should be banned.'

'I'm sure your list of objections may be quite a lot longer. But if you're to come to us, the Lord will show you the way,' said the priest.

'I think that if he were going to, he would have done so by now.'

'Have you talked to your own priest? About exorcism?'

'In Eltham? He said that I obviously wasn't possessed and that I would have to go to a special exorcist and get permission from the Bishop. And he said that Romans were much better at it anyway.'

'He said that? Good Lord! Well, that's good to hear, surely.'

'I think it's to do with apostolic succession,' said Rosie. 'Anglicans have a secret worry that they're not the real thing. It isn't very reassuring to know that you're only an Anglican because some dreadful old king wanted to abandon his wife.'

'I see your point. Did you try Our Lady Help of Christians? In Mottingham? Isn't that much nearer?'

'I was afraid of being seen to go in. I mean, all my friends and neighbours are Anglican. It would have been embarrassing.'

'Shall we sit? Perhaps we don't need to be going into the confessional at all.'

They sat side by side in a pew, and the priest asked, 'Do you have your eyes rolling up into your head, when the Devil's on you?'

'No, Father.'

'And do you speak in a strange voice that isn't yours, but seems to come through you?'

'No, Father.'

'And do you rebel and become furious when you see, for example, a church, or a crucifix?'

'No, Father.'

'And when the Devil's on you, do you vomit strange things, like pins?'

'No, Father.'

'Well, I am deeply grieved in having to agree with your own priest, him being an Anglican and all, God forgive him, but it is indeed obvious that you are not possessed, and if you were, I'd have to refer you to the Bishop, the same as your man in Eltham.'

'Oh but I am. I do evil things. I think vile and evil thoughts. I have a devil inside me who pretends to be me and makes me think and do and say things that I hate myself for.'

'If you don't mind telling me, what have you done that's so terrible?'

'I drove Daniel away. My husband.'

'There's many a woman's done that. What did you do?'

'I neglected him. Deliberately. And I refused to move out of my mother's house when he couldn't stand living with her any longer. And I kept the children from him as much as I could. And I know it was a horrible thing to do to him, and to the children.'

'How could you do that? He's the legal guardian, surely? He could have taken them.'

'It wasn't practical. You know, he had to work. He couldn't have afforded a nanny. And he didn't have the heart. He loved me very much. And now there's only my son Bertie left, and he's long flown the nest. And I brought him up to hate his father.'

'That was indeed an evil thing to do.'

'I know it was. I'll always despise myself for it.'

138

'But you didn't love him, this husband of yours?'

'Oh no. I did. I just did everything wrong. Because of this devil inside.'

'Do you know why this all happened?'

'I've thought about it a great deal, and I'm sure it's because I lost Ash, my fiancé, in 1915. Poor Daniel could never live up to him, because Ash was dead and he wasn't. Every time I looked at Daniel, I saw that he wasn't Ash.'

The priest sighed and gazed up at the stained glass of the clerestory. 'I've heard this story so many times,' he said. 'You would truly be amazed. The world is full of women who don't know how to love a living man. I take it that you do love him, after all, as a matter of fact, all things told?'

'Yes.'

She looked at him tearfully, and he said, 'You're not possessed, you know. Every human being on this earth has an angel and a devil at war with each other in the spirit. I do. Even His Holiness does. What you are lamenting is the unavoidable and unchangeable fact that you are human.'

'What should I do, Father?'

'You must find your husband and ask forgiveness. If he forgives you, then everything is possible. You should begin by doing small things together, like going to a Corner House. Have you asked God to forgive you?'

'Yes. Quite often.'

'And?'

'There's no reply. Why should He forgive me? I can't even forgive myself. I don't even understand myself, except...'

'Yes?'

'Father, if I promised faithfully to pray for somebody every night, and then one night I didn't, because I was too tired, and then he's killed the next day... well...'

'Is this what happened? You think it was your fault?'

'My fiancé, Ash, was killed in February of 1915, the day after I forgot to pray for him.'

'I'm very sorry for your trouble.'

'Even when I loved Daniel – my husband – very deeply, it still always felt like infidelity.'

'And you knowing very well that it wasn't? Come now. Let's be having no more of this nonsense, shall we? The first thing to do is approach your husband and ask for forgiveness. And you must resolve to keep your wedding vows.'

'I can't,' said Rosie.

'Why not? It's a question of courage, that's all.'

'He's gone to Canada. We were so estranged that he left me no address. He went to take his brother's bones to Peshawar, and he said something about his brothers in South Africa, about finding their graves. Now I have no idea where he is. He was going to leave all his possessions with me, but he didn't. He left them with Christabel, my sister in Hexham. He's in Canada already. He said he'd be away about six months.'

'Perhaps he'll write.'

'I don't think he will. Father, I've never felt so lonely and desperate. Before, he was still there in a strange sort of way, his absence was a kind of presence, but now he's completely gone. Now it's just me and the cats, rattling around in a huge empty house that used to be full of laughter. Luckily I do have one friend. If it wasn't for Margareta I do believe I'd be desperate.'

The priest looked at her and said, 'Well, at any rate, I don't think I need to give you a penance. You've made one for yourself. You'll find that prayer is better for sorting yourself out than it is for preventing bullets. Pray. And let's hear no more about exorcism and a devil inside. The Devil is one half of what we are, my child, and we fight him by fighting with ourselves.'

'I did two more terrible things,' said Rosie.

'And are you going to tell me?'

She nodded, and looked at the floor. 'Before the war we were going to make a new start in Tanganyika, and just as the ship was about to go I took the children down the gangplank, and he had to leave without us.'

'And the other thing?'

'He has a child by a native woman in Ceylon. It was a long time ago now. I tore up the letter. He doesn't know.'

'Then you must ask his forgiveness for both those things.'

'Even if it was a child of sin?'

'Sure, it's a serious shameful thing to have a child out of wedlock, but God doesn't blame the child, and it may be that your husband could do something for it if he only knew.'

'I'll have to write to him,' said Rosie. 'But I don't know exactly where he is.'

'He will certainly write to his friends.'

'He's bound to write to Fairhead, my brother-in-law. And to my sister Christabel.'

'Well, there you go, then.'

Rosie looked around the cathedral and said, 'You know, Father, I think this may be the holiest place in England.'

'I'm glad you say that. I'm inclined to agree with you, but I've not yet been to Walsingham. Or Lindisfarne. And then there's St Cuthbert buried in Durham. Now, stay here as long as you like, won't you?'

'Thank you, Father.'

He patted her gently on the shoulder, looked intently into her eyes, and left.

Rosie rendezvoused for lunch with Margareta in St Martin's Lane, and then took the train back to Eltham. The big house was cold and dark, and she sat in the kitchen drinking tea, still wearing her hat and scarf and gloves, with the cats sitting on the table before her. She thought about the Pals, her childhood friends, and about how time even robs you of the consolation that ought to come from happy memories.

31

Daniel to Fairhead

127 Ellis Street
Penticton BC
Canada

17 September 1955

My dear Fairhead,

I saw a review of your new book The Other Side of Science *in the* Vancouver Sun, *and have ordered it by post from Vancouver. I felt I had to write to you, first of all to congratulate you on its good reception, but also so that you and dear Sophie can catch up on my doings.*

Wragge and I arrived here in late spring after a somewhat Homeric ride across the continent, which turned out to be a far greater adventure than we had anticipated. I did keep a journal, and perhaps I will show it to you one day, because it was the biggest journey that we and the Broughs have ever undertaken, and was full of incident and interest. I discovered that Wragge is quite the artist, and he contributed many a cartoon.

I am renting a little side-gabled cottage with a red door on the east side of Penticton Creek. They tell me that this is the oldest part of town and was laid out in 1892. It's a long street of residences mixed up with businesses, and there is, for instance, a brewery and a 'funeral home', so, as Wragge says, you can conveniently drink yourself to death. The houses are pretty and homely, and indeed the whole town displays a most happy eclecticism in its architecture. There is Edwardian, and art deco, and art moderne, and Queen Anne Revival, and God knows what else. Almost all houses are single-storeyed, often with a room in the void of the roof, and most are built in a combination of concrete and wood, painted in pretty colours.

The town runs on orchards and timber as far as I can see. They have spectacular methods of transporting the logs on systems of slides and cables and water troughs. It's a joy to see the sheer ingenuity of it. The orchards, mostly of peaches, are like patches of the Garden of Eden. Peach patches. It occurred to me straight away that this would be prime terroir for vineyards, but nobody has ever thought of planting one, it seems.

Most splendid of all are the snowy mountains and the lake, which is vast, and used to be the main transport facility before the roads and railway were finished. There were some fabulous tugs and a paddle steamer that used to ply it, but now they are laid up on shore and kept as monuments. Of course, there is a marina with sailing boats, and I'd say that messing about on the lake is probably the most popular recreation. They even have women's races in war canoes. It raises my heart to see those Amazons going at it like windmills, as you can probably imagine. I hope to find my ideal woman here one day; I don't think one could do better than a fit and energetic Canadienne who isn't afraid of anything, and knows how to cook a moose with one hand whilst lassoing you with the other. They have an annual Peach Festival Queen Pageant in bathing costumes! There are plenty of people still on horses!

Apparently, when Europeans first moved here, it was the local Indians who sold them fish, and straw for their horses, in exchange for things that they wanted for themselves, so there has always been peace and cooperation here between the newcomers and the natives.

The reason I am telling you this is that I was standing on the beach looking out over the water, when I became aware that an Indian was standing next to me. He was a very big man of about forty, much taller and more heavily built than I am. He wasn't at all like the Indians you see in films, with buckskins and warpaint and a feather in his headband. He was dressed much the same as me, but with a huge bush hat on his head. He had coppery skin, black fiery eyes, black hair with flecks of grey, and a big hooked nose with narrow nostrils.

He didn't talk like a movie Indian either, you know the sort of thing, 'pale face speak with forked tongue, heap bad medicine' and all that. He just said, 'You seen it yet?'

I said, 'Seen what?' and he said, 'You seen Oggy? I come here every evening and watch out for him. My name's Davey. Most call me Wavey Davey 'cause I used to be a drunk.'

I introduced myself and we shook hands, and I asked him who Oggy was.

It transpired that Oggy is a monster called Ogopogo that lives in the lake. Wavey Davey said it was about fifty foot long and might be a plesiosaur or a Basilosaurus or a Mosasaurus, and that he'd seen it in 1946 along with a few carloads of other people at the Mission Beach. He said, 'I reckon it might be one heck of a damn great water snake.'

I said, 'How do you know it's still alive?' and he said, 'Because there ain't been no body floated up and washed up.'

Wavey Davey turned out to be an interesting character. We sat side by side looking out over the water until it became dark. He said he was a Syilx of the Okanagan Nation, and descended from a chieftain called Hwistesmetxe'qen (he wrote it down for me, and it means Walking Grizzly Bear) and is also related to the chief of the Penticton Band, Gideon Enneas, who also happens to be a Rocky Mountain Ranger, and he'd spent the war as a mechanical engineer, so naturally my ears pricked up and we got to talking about machinery.

Wragge and I have rented a small workshop and set up a new business on Ellis Street, calling it Motorcycle City. We realised there was quite a lot of competition in town already, but also a lot of demand, so we went to those other businesses and asked them if they'd like to subcontract work to us if they had taken on too much. It has been working rather well, so they see us as helpers rather than competitors, especially as we won't be here very long, but of course we have ended up doing all sorts of odd pieces of work such as repairing mowers, outboard motors, chainsaws and fruit-spraying machines. We get the use of their lathes and mills, which is a huge bonus. You may not know what engineers are like, but we are an arcane brotherhood that communicates in code, so Wragge and I have made a great many friends already.

I was sitting with Wavey Davey as it grew dark, and he said, 'I'm gonna find that monster if I have to put it there myself,' and I said, 'How will you do that?' and he replied, 'I'm gonna build a submarine.'

I said, 'Do you know how to?' and he said, 'I'll figure it out.' I said, 'Do you think you'll need any help?' and he said, 'Reckon I might.'

So, my dear Fairhead, Wragge and I went to eat supper at his house made of logs, where he got a large turkey out of a freezer and sawed off the crown of it with a chainsaw. We drank a great deal of beer, ate the fowl, still a little raw, several hours later, and began to draw up plans for a decent-sized submersible. Wavey Davey insists that it must be white, but otherwise we have very little idea how to pull this stunt off. I will be going to Vancouver shortly to see if I can find out anything in the library.

The best news concerns Wragge, and it involves an extraordinary coincidence. You may remember a young maid at The Grampians called Millicent. She was very pretty and utterly charming, and I was terribly fond of her. She was engaged to a young man called Hutch, who served with Ash in the HAC, but he died in the influenza epidemic after the war. There used to be two policemen who would call by and surreptitiously take tea with Millicent and Cookie in the kitchen at The Grampians. One was called Chalky White and the other was Dusty Miller. It was Dusty who intervened when I was giving that man a drubbing for running into some children in that AC Six when he was three sheets to the wind. Millicent married Dusty and they emigrated to Canada because he had a burning desire to be a Mountie.

Apparently he did become an excellent horseman, and having served in Newfoundland and Ontario, ended up in British Columbia. They had three children who have now all left home and gone to Toronto, and Dusty himself died about ten years ago when his horse was shot from under him by a desperado in the hills above Hedley, so that he fell and struck his head on a boulder. Millicent is desperately proud of him, and seems pleased that he was able to die heroically rather than by the attrition of old age, which 'wouldn't have suited him very much at all, I don't think'.

Millicent, it turned out, was running a tobacconist and sweetshop here in Penticton, and we bumped into her on our first day in town!

I may be old, but I am still vain, and I was fully expecting her to feel the same twinges for me as we had felt for each other all those decades ago before I left for Ceylon with Rosie and Esther.

But not a bit of it! She and Wragge have fallen head over heels in love and they are already living together in a house that was once, apparently, the town's bordello, mainly frequented by the then mayor. It was called the Ideal Rooms, and the girls used to come out and play with the children in the street until a certain Madeleine Beauchamp called them in. There was a bouncer called Gordon Dickson who is still a local legend.

You may remember that in Dortmund before the war Wragge had a paramour called Baldhart who did not survive the bombing, and I do believe this is his first romance since 1939. He is ridiculously happy, and cannot resist regaling me with accounts of their amorous exploits. Yesterday he told me rather thoughtfully that 'Tits bigger than a handful are a waste'. Millicent and Wragge are intending to marry next spring, and if I am still here I shall be the best man. He is unclear as to whether this would make him a bigamist, though, because his first wife ran off with a Gordon Highlander during the Great War, and he has no idea whether or not she is still alive. Millicent says that she doesn't care, so I will just keep quiet about it and be best man with my fingers crossed.

Let me see, what else is there to tell you? Last month we had a rodeo, and I think it was the most exciting and entertaining thing I have ever seen. The courage and expertise of the horsemen (and women) were breathtaking. They put out boards in the arena and did square dancing, which is a lot of fun once you have mastered the steps. If you are not very fit, you soon become exhausted. There are even people who call themselves Aquaducks, who do square dancing in the lake. I would say that eccentricity is the main British export to this part of the world.

It was absurdly hot here in August. Everyone is still talking about the Vancouver Empire and Commonwealth Games where Roger Bannister won the mile, and poor old Jim Peters got to the stadium a quarter of an hour ahead of everyone else, and so nearly won the marathon but collapsed with heat exhaustion half a lap from the finishing line. What a metaphor for so many lives!

Have you heard about the new Boeing 707? I can't wait to see one. I do believe they are developing it in Seattle, so I suppose there might be a fair chance of seeing one day. I don't think it'll be in service for a year or two yet.

My best love to you and Sophie, and of course to Ottilie and Frederick and everyone else you may be in touch with who remembers me with any fondness. I will write to you again soon, and tell you how the submarine is progressing.

Your old friend,
Daniel P.

PS Madeleine Beauchamp was French, I hear, as all good madams should be, but I have been very disappointed to find that not a single person here speaks French. They say that there is a small community of francophones in Calgary, which is of course on the other side of the Rockies, but otherwise I would probably have to go to Quebec. I had always assumed that this was a bilingual country, and the chance of speaking French was one of the attractions of coming here. I suppose I could have gone to France, but then I wouldn't have had the chance to speak English.

There is a Chinese laundry, and some Greeks, some Japanese, plenty of Indians, and one solitary black man who is very well liked and doesn't seem to mind his nickname, which is hardly a complimentary one. I suppose the poor fellow has no say in the matter and has had to get used to it.

PPS I know this is hard to believe, but Millicent and Wragge have a pet skunk that they feed on eggs.

PPPS Rattlesnakes are very popular for making hatbands, and Wavey Davey has given me a raccoon-skin hat.

32

Messages and Conversations

Daniel Pitt to Wavey Davey:
We need to find out how deep the lake is and how long. And how deep would we want the submarine to go? I doubt if any living creature would be far down, because of the water pressure. If we go very deep, we'd need an immensely strong pressure hull, wouldn't we?

WD to DP:
It's 761.15 feet deep at the deepest. About 228 average. The lake is damn long, maybe 85 miles. Oggy's seen at the surface mostly, so we don't need to go deep.

DP to WD:
If it's seen on the surface, why do we need a submarine?

WD to DP:
So we can see the rest of it.

DP to WD:
So do we want a sub that can go at least 190 miles to get there and back? It's a tall order.

WD to DP:
I reckon we can tow it to where we want to explore.

Oily Wragge to WD and DP:
It'll be electric underwater all right? 'Cause otherwise we'll get choked, but is it diesel or petrol for on top?

WD to OW:
Petrol is gas, yes?

OW to WD:
Yes. But petrol isn't a gas, is it?

DP to OW:
Diesel is safer.

WD to OW:
We should use gas, I reckon. We can use a Ford flathead engine, cheap and good. Use the normal starter motor, and the dynamo to charge the batteries. Switch over to electric with a siding pinion on the drive shaft.

DP to WD:
Is it worth using the normal gearbox to save bother?

WD to DP:
Boats don't need gears, I reckon, but it sure would save bother. Easier to start the engine in neutral too. I reckon we'd only use first gear.

DP to WD and OW:
If we use 20 12-volt batteries wired in parallel, we'll get 240 volts. We can use a converter and run lights etc on 12 volts. If we get or build an electric motor that runs on 240 volts pressure, we should get a lot of horsepower. If we make the keel out of three-sided box section, we can put the batteries side by side in that section all along the boat, and they'll double as ballast.

OW to DP and WD:
That's bloody genius. What about using one of them snorkels so we can run the petrol or diesel engine underwater, with another snorkel for exhaust?

DP to OW:
Good idea. It's called a snort.

OW to DP:
If a dog was called a nog it would still be a dog, wouldn't it? Same difference. They'll need some kind of valve to stop the

water getting in. Some kind of float valve. Should be easy. You could even use a soccer ball.

WD to DP and OW:
Saddle tanks or double hull?

DP to WD:
Saddle tanks. It's much easier, and the sub doesn't have to look beautiful anyway.

OW to WD:
Saddle tanks, but they got to fill and empty at the same rate or the boat'll tip if you think about it.

DP to OW and WD:
What about air conditioning? It might get damn stuffy and hot.

OW to DP and WD:
Yes and what if somebody farts? What if one of us has been eating beans?

WD to OW and DP:
We go and get a big old fridge and a fan. Also you can make oxygen with a candle full of sodium chlorate and powdered iron, and you can get rid of CO_2 by passing it through soda lime canisters.

OW to WD:
Bloody hell, how do you know that?

DP to WD:
As we won't be at war, will we ever be submerged long enough to need it?

WD to DP:
We will if we sink.

OW to WD and DP:
Talking of sinking I think we should weld a bloody great hoop on the top to take a shackle and cable, and the first time we go out and dive we should have a boat alongside with a derrick to haul us back up just in case we can't come back up on our own.

WD to OW:
There aren't any tugs on the lake any more or any boats with derricks. It's just sailboats and powerboats.

OW to DP and WD:
I've just thought that as we use up the petrol or diesel the boat will get lighter and harder to keep down.

DP to OW:
You let water into the fuel tanks to make up the weight.

OW to DP:
Sounds wrong to me. We don't want water in the fuel, do we?

DP to OW:
The petrol floats on top of the water.

WD to OW and DP:
What about the steering gear? Cables or hydraulic?

OW to WD:
Mostly rods, like on a Ford Popular braking system. It's bloody good. You rig it up so the rods always pull and not push.

DP to WD:
How about a joystick system, as you have on an aeroplane? I know how to do that.

WD to DP:
Well, you would, wouldn't you?

OW to WD and DP:
I've just thought all right it's easy to let water into the ballast tanks when you want to sink, but what about pumping air back in when you want to come back up? You can't use the air in the hull because we'd end up in a vacuum and our eyes would pop out on us.

WD to OW:
You can get big bottles that you fill up with an air compressor, and you can drive the compressor off the engine when you're on the surface or using the snort.

DP to OW and WD:
One screw or two? I favour one.

WD to DP:
Two is better for steering.

OW to DP:
I like as many screws as I can get.

DP to OW:
I'm past it.

OW to DP:
I thought I was.

WD to DP and OW:
I reckon we should have one screw that sends wash over the hydrovane. I spoke to a navy man who said you need a hydrovane on the front as well, because it works better than the one at the back. The rear one just keeps you level.

OW to DP and WD:
We'll need a depth gauge.

DP to OW:
And an inclinometer.

OW to DP:
Well, that's easy 'cause all you got to do is get two spirit levels and stick them together crossways. In fact you don't even need to stick them together, as long as they're crossways.

DP to OW:
Who's the genius now?

OW to DP:
Can you remember the words to that song the troops used to sing about?

> My Nellie's a whore
> My Nellie's a whore
> Her favourite phrase is bollocks to you
> My Nellie's a whore.

Was there any other words? It's been driving me doolally trying to remember.

DP to OW:
Damn you, now I can't get that stupid song out of my brain.

33

Rosie to Daniel

The Grampians
24 Court Road
Eltham
Kent

17 October 1957

Dear Daniel,

I hope that this reaches you and that it finds you well. I was in WH Smith when I saw the Motoring Annual 1957, *and remembered that it was your birthday. As I feel sorry that I have not given you a birthday present since about 1932, I decided to buy it for you and hope that it finds you in Canada. I glanced at it in the shop, and I thought you might enjoy the articles about continental touring, and about the future development of power plants in vehicles. I couldn't help noticing that the Americans are working on a driverless car, to be controlled by electronic sensors at the sides of the roads, and I thought, 'My goodness, how Daniel would hate that!' Now that you are sixty-five, I can't help but wonder if you are as much of a motorcycle fanatic as you used to be, or whether you are considering finally moving on to four wheels.*

Were you terribly pleased to hear that Stirling Moss won at Monza?

I also enclose a tie that I found rolled up in one of the drawers, which must go back to when we were here at The Grampians after our return from Ceylon. It's the one from Nuwara Eliya Golf Club, with an arm brandishing a golf club, and 'Spero Meliora' embroidered on it. It was the only tie that you regularly wore, apart from your Royal Flying Corps one, and so I thought you might like it back. Don't we all hope for better things?

I found your address by asking Fairhead for it. He and Sophie are very well indeed. Fairhead is writing a book called Mysticism for Infidels, *which is his follow-up to* The Other Side of Science, *and*

Sophie is gathering funds to set up a small hospital for wildlife, of which there is a surprising amount in Blackheath. Recently their dog died, so now they have three graves in their garden to Crusty, Crusty the Second, and Crusty the Third.

Fairhead tells me that you and Wragge and an Indian called 'Wavey Davey' have nearly finished building a submarine, and are going in search of a monster in a lake. I thought to myself, 'That sounds so much like Daniel.'

I know that you are very much in touch with everyone except Bertie and me, so perhaps there is no point in giving you the family news, but you may not know that Bertie is out in Germany with his regiment, and has been made Adjutant. He and Kate and Theodore are all well. Bertie says that fraternisation with the Germans is strongly frowned upon, and he finds this very irritating. He spends much time on exercise. I am sometimes concerned about his behaviour with respect to Kate and the child, and I wonder if I should blame myself somewhat, because, thanks to me, he grew up without knowing what a proper father or husband ought to be like. He drinks too much, and it makes him impatient and surly. His shouting is horrible at times. He couldn't be more different from my own father. As you know, he had a very difficult war, and I am afraid he is taking it out on everybody else around him.

Do you remember what we used to do at Christmas, when we'd leave a florin by the children's plates at mealtimes, and plough through an awful lot of bangers and mash?

Oh, Daniel, I do know how very bad I have sometimes been. I often compare myself to a whited sepulchre. I am sixty-six years old. Why is it that self-knowledge arrives too late? How can I feel, knowing that time is irreversible and I am so far beyond forgiveness? And I have things that I really must tell you, but I can't bear to, not least because they would place me in such a bad light. How I would hate it for you to know how despicable I am!

I am still living here on my own with a great many cats, who are a wonderful comfort to me. You may remember Caractacus, who I found in a sack. The cats I have now are a part of his considerable dynasty, but even so this house that was so bursting with life in 1914 is now a ghost of its former self. Where are Father and Mother, and Cookie, and the Pals, and the Pendennises? I visit some of them in the graveyard in St

John's, and then I go and sit by the Tarn, and remember deciding to marry you when you dived in to save that poor dog that died anyway.

Talking of graves, I have decided to go to France to visit Ash's grave, probably next spring. How I would love it if you were here, and we could go together. I imagine us standing there, our fingers twining together for the first time in thirty years. It was Ash's death that brought us together, and the memory of him alive that kept us apart. I might go with my friend Margareta. She is German, and we have been friends for a while now. I think you would like her. She is tall rather like Christabel, and is very direct, rather like Gaskell. She is ugly and ungainly, but we get on like a house on fire, and do you know, I have never found out what she did in the war. She never mentions it, and I have never dared ask, in case it was something shameful that would put me off.

I imagine that you must be very cold in Canada. I am glad to hear from Fairhead and Sophie that Motorcycle City is going well, and that Mr Wragge continues to be your staunch support. How wonderful that he and Millicent have got married. I am so pleased for him.

I have been very lucky because the cancer has never come back. I don't think that the full impact hit me until after the war was over, when I suddenly had time to think about it. I am often surprised to be yet alive, but not always very thankful. Is your foot all right?

I have been wanting to ask you whether you feel you have achieved everything that you wanted out of life. Is it enough for you, are you satisfied, that you have ended up in Canada running a motorcycle business, after all the wonderfully important things that you did in two world wars?

As for me, the poetry left me, and I never did become a poet. I don't even read it any more. The years left to me grow fewer and fewer, and I can't help but feel that I have been in so many ways a failure. I miss not being a part of anything, and not part of whatever is round the corner for those who are as young as we were, once upon a time.

Oh, Daniel, what I want, more than anything, is just to sit face-to-face and talk and talk and talk with you for weeks and weeks and weeks until there is nothing more to be said, and our millions of words are scattered about our feet on the carpet, and I have forgiven you for not being Ash, and you have forgiven me for ever wishing that you had been.

Happy birthday, very late in the day, and all the other birthdays I ignored, I hope they were happy too, and that there are many more to come. Do remember that you originally intended to stay in Canada for six months. When are you coming back? Everyone is growing ever more forlorn without you.

Your Rosie

34

Daniel to Rosie

127 Ellis Street
Penticton BC
Canada

17 November 1957

Dear Rosie,

Many thanks for your letter and your gift of the Motoring Annual, which I did indeed find extremely interesting. It is a fine book for browsing when one is supposed to be doing something else. Everything changes so quickly these days that it is difficult to keep up with all the developments, but I do know that I will hate it if all cars eventually drive themselves! I don't know why, but I do love motoring. Perhaps it's because it is so much fun to be able to proceed faster than one could ever hope to run.

I am indeed sorry to hear that Bertie is turning out to be a poor father and husband. If you can't deal with it yourself, perhaps you should ask Fairhead or Ottilie to have a frank talk with him, but all the same I think it is down to you as the one parent with whom he has a relationship to set him straight. I know this kind of thing takes great courage, but courage is one thing, dear Rosie, that you have never lacked.

You ask me if my foot is all right. Well, I still get stabs of pain from the bases of my hacked off toes, and I will always have a limp. To be honest, the worst thing is the recurrent nightmares I have to suffer. I had one in particular for years after the Great War, which was of an endless procession of the dead, and now I have new ones from the last. I wake up suddenly just as the chisel cracks through the bones. I dream about what happened to Odette and poor Violette as well, and there is another one about a time when I was caught in a ferocious tempest whilst flying my Lysander over France.

It is clear that you are not contented with the path that your life has taken, and you ask me if I am contented with mine. No, I am not. I am not contented by my past, glorious and exciting as that has sometimes been. I am not contented with what happened to us, and nor am I happy with the fallout from it. However, I only have a few years left to me now, and I am learning to draw the maximum pleasure and interest from what little remains. I don't like to be on my own, because I become melancholy, but when I have company I am as vivacious and good-humoured as I ever was. Wavey Davey and his wife often have me round to their extraordinary cabin, which is in the middle of an orchard, and made of vertical lodge poles, and Wragge and Millicent often have me round to theirs, which used to be a house of ill repute, it is said.

I have no theories about the meaning of life or God's purpose, or whatever. I live for the love between friends, and for the interesting things I find to do, that's all. I am certainly very glad that you have found a new friend in Margareta.

Millicent is quite unlike what she was when she was a servant at The Grampians. You would hardly recognise her, not just because she has aged and filled out, but because in Canada she has learned a sort of confident equality. It's not 'A very good morning, sir' it's 'Hello, you old rascal'. She is full of jollity. She runs a sweetshop and tobacconist and is doing very well for herself. It smells lovely in there, too! How strange it is that unlit tobacco smells so much nicer.

In the two years since I arrived, we have built quite a substantial submarine. It was this project that has delayed my return for so long. I couldn't bear to leave it half constructed. It has involved numerous trips to consult naval engineers and old seadogs, and so much improvisation that it might as well have been designed by Heath Robinson. Inside, it is a positive bird's nest of pipes and rods and cables and levers.

Obviously one cannot just go out and buy seacocks and valves from stalls in Vancouver, so almost everything has to be made from scratch, or improvised out of something else. Fortunately we have a great many excellent engineering shops here that have allowed us to use their lathes and mills. We have put in thousands of hours of plumbing, welding, forging, riveting, testing, and much of our material was originally just old scrap that we found lying about in orchards or on roadsides. At the last we painted it white so that it would be easier to find if it sank.

There are numerous difficulties to overcome, such as making sure that it won't be nose- or tail-heavy. We put separate tanks near the stern and the bow so that we can fill them to different levels for an even trim.

Our biggest problem was thinking how we could transport such a monster to the lake, launch it, and then get it out again if it should prove to need alteration. You may not believe this, and to think about it makes me laugh, but in the end we realised that it would have to have wheels on it. Imagine the hilarity and celebration when we hauled it through the street behind a tractor! It was like a carnival, and the only thing missing was a brass band. By the time we got to the water it was festooned with children.

It's only a two-man submarine, and Wragge and Wavey Davey insisted that I should be captain because I used to be a squadron leader.

They took it in turns to come out with me on the surface trials, but both refused to come with me when we went for the first submersion. I don't think I have ever been more terrified. My heart was leaping in my chest, and I was thinking of all the things I might never get to do if I was to die. What I did was try varying degrees of semi-submersion, until I was sure that it all worked properly, and then, my dear, I went for the real thing.

So it was, dear Rosie, that after all those years of sweat and toil, the Ogapogo slipped beneath the waters of Lake Okanagan for the first time, and I discovered that, even with a powerful searchlight on the bow, visibility was not much more than one yard.

After Wragge and Wavey Davey had come out and seen this for themselves, we sat on the beach in dejected silence, and finally Wavey Davey said, 'Well, I guess we'll just have to build a floatplane. Might get to spot that critter from the air.'

So, that's it. I have taken the whole episode as a lesson in life. We completely forgot to ask ourselves the most obvious question before we got started. What mattered in the end, however, is that we three had the most tremendous fun working together, planning everything, having barbecues, drinking beer, joshing each other, talking about old wars and old comrades. For that reason we are going to build a floatplane. Or rebuild one. I have been thinking that perhaps we could find an old Supermarine Walrus somewhere, strip it down, and rebuild it from scratch. I fear I may be here a few months more.

It turns out that we have transgressed any number of laws and regulations, and we've had several visits from the Mounties. It's obvious that they don't give a damn, however. Beer bottles have been cracked open, toasts to submarines have been proposed, and blind eyes put to telescopes.

There isn't much other news. The Queen generated a flurry of royalist enthusiasm when she opened parliament in Ottawa. I was very glad to hear that Mr Bevan has persuaded the Labour Party not to give up the bomb. British idealists are uniquely lacking in common sense, aren't they? I wonder why that is. I am puzzled as to why somebody of Bertrand Russell's intelligence cannot perceive the sense of being able to negotiate with the Soviet Union as an equal. I have never forgotten a conversation that I once had with him on a train to Cambridge.

What else? Well, the peaches are absolutely lovely this year, and I have grown some grapes on the south side of my little clapboard house. I intend to make some wine, just to show the locals that it can be done. I have dreams of vineyards in place of peach orchards!

I expect you have heard from Christabel that Puss is in the doghouse for frightening the new rector when he came round to enquire as to why she and Gaskell are never to be seen in church. Apparently Puss suddenly reared up from behind the sofa when they were in the drawing room sipping tea and eating scones. I wish I'd been there to see it.

Your letter is full of regret. I too have regrets. But life is a system of ladders; you climb up them, then you kick them away, or they are removed by someone else, and then you can't go back. We will have a long talk when I return, whenever that may be.

Enjoy yourself if you can.

Your old Pal,

Daniel P.

35

Rosie at Bailleul

In the spring of 1958 Rosie and Margareta went to Fallingbostel to stay with Bertie and Kate, and spend some time with the infant Theodore, who had arrived two years before. Like all grandmothers, Rosie was convinced that her daughter-in-law needed special advice and assistance from a properly experienced mother such as herself. Just as Kate had anticipated, the child had brought joy and optimism back into the older woman's life.

Rosie took Margareta with her for three reasons. One was that they had become almost inseparable. They had been to Rome and Florence, at Margareta's expense, and set about learning Italian together, and were already planning that in 1960 they would go and see Oberammergau. The second was that as Margareta was German, it would be nice for her to see a part of Germany where she had never been, and of course she could help Rosie out with any linguistic problems on the journey. She was determined not to go back to Prenzlau, because it was 'my dear, too bloody *deprimierend*' to see what the communists had done with it, and anyway, there was no one still there that she wanted to see, and the only thing she missed was the Unteruckersee. Anyone with any spark of life in them had left. The third reason was that Rosie could not face visiting Ash's grave on her own.

They arrived in Bailleul by train, and booked themselves into the Belle Hotel, a red-brick building in the Rue de Lille that was far from beautiful, but had a certain quirky flair to it. They learned from the receptionist that the whole town had been completely destroyed by 100,000 shells in 1918, and then rebuilt in the Flemish style, in a miracle of dogged reconstruction. There was nothing here that Ash would have recognised.

They had decided to find the grave on the evening of their arrival, and then return in the morning with flowers, simply to stay there for an hour or two in the quiet of the dead, before going to Lille and onward into Germany. Accordingly, having unpacked in their room and taken tea, and armed with a map sketched for them by the same receptionist, they set off to the Grand Place, and thence up the leper road.

'I like it here in the Hauts-de-France,' said Margareta, as they trudged the mile or so to the cemetery, 'All the French and Dutch place names mixed together, all side by side. It gives the feeling that you don't know where you are.'

'I don't know what to feel,' said Rosie, who was wondering what it would be like to stand over the grave of her first fiancé, for the first time, forty-three years after his death. She had made a cult of him for so long that it made her nervous to be visiting his shrine at last.

The original graveyard had been founded by the 12th Battalion, the Royal Scots, following the terrible attrition at Arras, but Ash lay in the extension to the communal cemetery. When Rosie and Margareta reached the gate, they stood appalled at the task that lay ahead of them. Rosie had not asked the Commonwealth War Graves Commission for the number of his plot, because it had not occurred to her that one graveyard might hold over four thousand dead, all laid out in immaculate lawns, in sparkling rows of identical graves. She felt a deep sense of shame in not having been able to imagine how vast this field of the dead might be, even though she remembered perfectly well that it was there because of the casualty clearing stations nearby, where Ash had died of peritonitis. 'Do you think there'll be a list pinned up somewhere?' she asked.

'Oh, I think so,' said Margareta, 'but I like the idea ... Let's each take one corner and walk along, and when one of us sees the name, she calls out. That way we get to feel how many were killed. Let's look for him. I like to look for him, and not be told where he is.'

The two women separated, and twenty minutes later Rosie heard Margareta calling 'I found him, I found him!' She turned and saw her friend signalling.

Rosie came over, heart fluttering in her chest, and there he was, Ashbridge Pendennis, Honourable Artillery Company, Died of Wounds Received at Kemmel, 19/2/15.

She stood staring at the headstone, and then down at the level grass, unable to imagine the state of the corpse that lay buried there, unable to connect it with her vivid memories of the young American that she had kissed so often and so greedily all those years ago.

'Oh, Margareta,' she said, 'I can't ... I don't feel anything.'

'Don't worry,' said Margareta, 'the feelings will come in their own time. Believe me, I know.'

'Who do you think left these flowers?' asked Rosie.

'They are very old, maybe last year, or the year before,' said Margareta, picking up the bedraggled remains of a bouquet inside its fragile wrapping of brittle cellophane. 'And look, there is a little tin box.'

'Who could have left it?'

It was a narrow, cream-and-brown Rubberco puncture repair tin, extremely rusted. Margareta struggled for a minute with the lid, and it popped off quite suddenly, escaping her grip and fluttering to the ground. Inside was a small sheet of writing paper, rolled tightly into a scroll. 'What's it say? Who's it from?' asked Rosie, and Margareta handed it to her.

Rosie unrolled it, and immediately recognised the handwriting. She read it, her hands shaking a little, and then passed it to Margareta, who read:

Dear Ash,

I have always intended to come and visit you here, and now I have done so. Time has carried me along, and I seem to be visiting a great many graves these days. I have buried Archie's bones in Peshawar, and have even made pilgrimage to my dead brothers in South Africa.

I am about to leave for Canada, but I wanted to come here first. Of the Pals, I am the only surviving male, but Rosie and her sisters are still with us. I think back often on the bright golden days before the Great War, when we were young, King Edward was frolicking with his actresses, and the whole world seemed to lie at our feet.

Although you left us in 1915, you have been present in our hearts ever since. Because of your death I have four children, and because Rosie always loved you faithfully, your legacy to me has been that I have been condemned to wander the world like an Odysseus without an Ithaca to which I might return. Of course it's not your fault, and I bear you no animus. I wish simply that you had lived, so that the rest of us could have had the lives we were born for.

If there is a life hereafter, well, what can I say? Perhaps one day we will play tennis together, or I will be flying stunts for you again in a Camel that never crashes, over trenches where songs are sung and bullets are fired but no one ever dies. If there is no life hereafter then one day we will be together in the same abyss of nothingness and oblivion. I have learned, and I believe, that a certain happiness resides in nothingness.

Now I am going to get back on my motorcycle and visit all the aerodromes where I served in the Great War, if I can find them.

Farewell. I hope you are sleeping well, and dreaming of us, as we often dream of you.

Your old Pal,
Daniel Pitt

Rosie took the letter from her friend and read it again. Very slowly she put her hand down and lowered herself onto the grass.

'Oh, don't cry,' said Margareta, putting her hand on Rosie's shoulder.

'It's not as I thought,' sobbed Rosie.

'What isn't as you thought?'

'I thought I'd be weeping over Ash's grave. I thought I'd be crying for Ash.'

'And so?'

Rosie waved the letter. 'Daniel says he has four children. He has two with me, and there's one in Ceylon he doesn't know about. So he has five children. Who are the other two? Where are the other two? What kind of man is he? Why don't I know about them?'

Margareta was quietly perplexed by Rosie's refusal to see the obvious, but she chose to say nothing.

On her knees in the grass at Ash's graveside, Rosie hung her head. 'I can't feel anything,' she said. 'I can't feel anything at all. I feel empty. Let's not come back here tomorrow morning. Let's go straight to the station.'

36

Mr Deakes

Rosie had got into the habit of dozing next to the fire, so that her left leg had become strangely mottled. It was a small coal fire that could be ignited by means of a gas poker mounted on a rubber tube that was fed from a tap next to her armchair, and it generated enough heat to fill just one end of that large drawing room. When she was not dozing, Rosie knitted cardigans and scarves, or read. Mostly she looked forward to when Margareta came to stay, or when they went off together to explore the nooks and crannies of England. They had recently stayed in Ryde, and were soon to go to the New Forest.

On this day in October she had read the Epistle to the Hebrews, and been particularly struck by the passage which reads: 'Let brotherly love continue. Be not forgetful to entertain strangers; for thereby some have entertained angels unawares. Remember them that are in bonds, as bound with them; and them which suffer adversity, as being yourselves also in the body.'

Rosie realised that she cannot ever have entertained an angel unawares, because she had never once taken in a stranger, and on this account she felt a little unworthy. She recalled hearing that there were people who laid an extra place at table, in case by chance Jesus Christ himself should turn up unexpectedly.

After putting the Bible down next to her chair, one of her cats jumped into her lap, and its warmth and resonant purring soon put her to sleep. She dreamed again that she was all decked in bridal white, veiled, bearing a bouquet of flowers, getting married to Jesus Christ. She was feeling confused and anxious, as she had at her own wedding to Daniel all those years ago. She did not seem to be anywhere in particular, but simply floating in a featureless land. She was waiting for her groom to appear, and was wondering whether he would ever come at all.

She looked about, but could see very little through the gauze of her veil.

Very suddenly she was standing next to Jesus on the top of a mountain, with her right hand in his left, and before them, thousands of feet below, was a vast desert thronged with nuns. He looked exactly as he had in the *Illustrated Children's Bible* of her childhood. She said to him, 'I have just remembered that I am already married,' and he laughed and indicated all the women below with a wave of his right arm. 'All these women wear my wedding ring,' he said. 'What is monogamy to me?'

'Is this the same mountain where Satan brought you?' asked Rosie.

If there had been any reply, Rosie did not remember it when she woke up. He had seemed not unpleasantly flippant this time, and had not burned her with his eyes. She knew it was one of those dreams that she would never forget, and felt somewhat relieved that she did not remember having gone ahead and married him.

Two days later it was raining heavily outside, when there was a knock on the front door. Putting down her knitting, and making a point of remembering how many stitches she had made, she went to the door, and then, for some reason, took the precaution of going into the morning room to look through the window to see who it was. Her heart sank, because it was a tramp.

In those days when there were no hostels that would take anyone for more than one night every month, it was the tramp's fate to be permanently on the move, travelling by foot from one spike to another, and for this reason the destitute and homeless were far more visible than they would be in later years. It was common to see whole families of tramps, existing on roadside verges, warming their hands on little fires in truncated petrol cans. If one of them came to the door, it was to ask for odd jobs, because a couple of shillings would buy them another day's accommodation, another day's food, another day's tobacco.

Rosie was frightened of tramps, even though she loved and respected old servicemen, and knew perfectly well that that's what most of these men were. Unwilling to open the front door, she ran upstairs, and opened the sash of what had once been Esther's room. 'Can I help you?' she called down.

'Got any odd jobs, missus?' asked the man. 'I only need another fivepence.'

He was probably in his forties, thin and rachitic, dressed in terrible greasy rags patched together with bailing twine. His boots were bound about with strips of cloth to reduce the flapping of the soles, and his trousers were so short that she could see that he wore no socks. On his head was a peaked cap that must once have belonged to a coalman, because it was shiny with graphite.

Rosie was about to say 'No, I'm terribly sorry, but I have nothing for you to do' when she realised with a pang of shame that she had a very great deal for him to do. The house and garden had gone to pot in many ways.

The tramp had an open and friendly face, albeit extremely dirty, and had managed to have a shave within the last week. His teeth were the colour of antique pine. He had steady blue eyes, and a terrible air of defeat. Despite his outdoor life, his face was grey. When Rosie said nothing at all, he tipped his cap and said, 'Don't worry, missus, don't worry at all. I'll be off. I'm sorry to 'ave troubled you.'

As he went out through the gate, he stopped and petted one of Rosie's cats, who was arching her back on top of a gate pillar. Touched by his tenderness, and almost against her will, she called out, 'I do have some jobs.'

Rosie watched Mr Deakes through the window as he swept the fallen leaves from the lawn. It was clear that he was trying to work hard, but was incapable of it, stopping for breath every minute or so, and leaning on the wire rake. She realised what was most wrong with him.

Rosie went to the kitchen and made a large mug of strong milky tea, into which she stirred three teaspoons of sugar, and then she emptied an entire packet of digestive biscuits onto a plate. These she carried out into the garden on a tray, which she set down on the gravel of the path, noticing suddenly how weedy it was.

'You can have as many of these biscuits as you like,' she said, adding lamely, 'I am not fond of them myself, so they won't be missed.'

Deakes looked down in disbelief, and knelt before the plate, taking one biscuit and nibbling a tiny crescent out of the rim. He chewed very slowly, closed his eyes, and swallowed.

Rosie said, 'What have you been living off?'

'They give us two slices of bread with margarine.'

'That's all?'

'I do walk sixteen miles for that, sometimes,' said Deakes. 'And in the morning they send us back out with a crust and bit of cheese, and then we walk the next sixteen miles for the next two slices.'

'When did you last have a proper meal?'

'What? To sit down to? God knows, missus. Three, four years?'

'You have malnutrition.'

'Do I? I thought I was just starving.'

'Starving is no food. Malnutrition is not enough of the right food. What else is wrong with you, Mr Deakes? You can speak freely, I was a VAD in both wars.'

'Well, I can't hardly breathe sometimes, and my feet hurt like hell, begging your pardon, and in the morning I can't hardly walk at all.'

'Have you got skin conditions? Scabies, for instance?'

'I've got it something terrible. The itching at night...I can't hardly sleep...and all the other blokes can't sleep either, what with all the racket, the getting up to go in the bucket, and the coughing and snoring, and the mad blokes yelling in their dreams.'

'My father is dead,' said Rosie.

'I'm sorry to hear of that, missus, but what're you telling me that for?'

'Many years ago, after the Great War, my husband discovered a vagrant sleeping under the conservatory. It turned out that he was an old soldier...the Norfolk Regiment...He'd been through Kut. He was called Wragge, so everybody knew him as Oily.'

'Yes, missus?'

Rosie took a deep breath and said, 'My father gave him work as a gardener. He let him sleep under the conservatory, and in the end he was with us for absolutely years, until my mother shot him with an air rifle.'

'Did she? What are you saying, missus?'

'I am not a good woman,' said Rosie, 'but I wouldn't want to be less than my father.'

'I see,' said Deakes. 'Or perhaps I don't see.'

'Are you an old soldier?'

'Yes, missus. I was a Royal Engineer, a carpenter really. I was in Greece, then North Africa, and then in Italy, and then I was demobbed, and I came home and I found my wife didn't want me and she had another fellow's kid. There you have it. There was a big fight, and I whacked him on the side of the head with a bit of pipe, and there I was in the nick, and when I came out I had nothing, not even my carpentry tools, and no one would have me because I was a criminal. So that was that. I was on the road.'

He stopped, and said, 'I'm sorry, missus, I don't know why I'm telling you all this. It just all slipped out, like.'

Rosie was unsure. 'Have you ever whacked anyone else?'

'Course I have. But I've never not once whacked a woman, not even my missus when I found out what she'd been up to. I wouldn't have the strength to whack a mouse these days, mind.'

'Don't you have any family, Mr Deakes? Is there no one you can turn to?'

'The Royal Engineers was my family. I'm a Barnardo's boy.'

'Mr Wragge was a Barnardo's boy ... our old gardener. His wife left him when he was away fighting.'

'There's a lot of us about. We're a breed, we are. Chucked away once, then chucked away twice. The only ones worse off than us is borstal boys. Or those boys that get sent to public school, because if you think about it, them schools are really just posh borstal.'

Rosie summoned up her courage, and said, 'Mr Deakes, if you want to sleep ... just for tonight ... under the conservatory, in the barrow room, where Mr Wragge used to ... there's an electric light in there now ... I'll make you a proper meal and I'll wash your clothes. I can bring you a bucket of hot water for a stand-up

wash. I can give you some of my husband's clothes…he left them
behind…'

'Don't give me clothes,' said Deakes, 'I'd only have to sell 'em.
Food's more important, see?'

'What do you like to eat?'

'What do I like to eat? I'm not proud, missus. I've eaten stuff
put out for the birds. I've eaten lard from half a coconut shell, I
have. I've stolen oats from horses' nosebags.'

'In the evenings I usually have sausages and eggs. I can give
you some of those, and I can probably find mushrooms, and fry
up a tomato. And, as you see, we have plenty of windfalls. You
can have as many of those as you like.'

'Why, missus?'

'Why? Why what?'

'Why would you do all this, for a bit of old rubbish like me?'

'Are you at all religious, Mr Deakes? Are you a Christian?'

He narrowed his eyes. 'Oh gawd, you're not Sally Army, are
you? Have I got to sing hymns and pray? Because if I do have
to, I'll do it. But I won't mean it. I do it for bread and margarine
and a mug of tea, that's all.'

'I just wondered,' said Rosie. 'I recently read something in the
Bible about looking after strangers…'

'Just as well for me, then,' said Deakes.

'Let's look under the conservatory. Well, it was a conservatory
until we got bombed. Now it's just a terrace.'

The room under the conservatory was a consequence of the
construction of the house, which had been designed with grandeur in mind. For grandeur one needs steps up to the front door,
and this automatically means that one has vertical space to fill
under the first floor. The Grampians had a network of service
corridors, which were a great boon to plumbers and electricians
who would otherwise have had to lever up the floorboards, and
it had an entire room under the conservatory, which was filled
with garden tools, the cylinder mower, heaps of sacking, a plain
wooden chair, and the long-disused paraphernalia of croquet and
lawn tennis. There was a single braided flex hanging from the
ceiling, with a bare forty-watt bulb in its socket. In his time here,
Mr Wragge had fixed the small broken window and hung up a

curtain contrived from two tea cloths, which now hung limp and ragged on the cup hooks that he had screwed above the window frame.

'Oh,' said Rosie, 'I had no idea how cobwebby it is nowadays.'

'Spiders is good, missus. Spiders means less bugs. What bothers me is rats.'

'I don't think we've got rats. Because of all the cats. You'll get the cats coming in, probably wanting to sleep on you.'

'Very cosy,' said Deakes. 'I can make a bed out of the netting, and all them sacks.'

'Mr Wragge used to doze in the wheelbarrow sometimes. He thought we didn't know.'

'All right for dozing, missus, but a man needs to stretch out for a proper kip.'

That evening, wrapped in a blanket, Deakes ate his plateful of eggs and sausages in the solitude of the barrow room. Rosie made do with Force, bread and butter, and an apple, because her guest was eating her self-imposed ration, and the next delivery would not be until the morning. Afterwards she took a look at his clothing, and was utterly appalled. It was beyond washing, beyond any kind of recall at all. The garments were thin, ripped and patched, so caked with grime that they more resembled a loose coat of varnish than cloth. She went down into the cellar and found the suitcases containing her father's clothes, which she had not been able to bear parting with after his death.

In the morning, Rosie took a bowl of porridge and a mug of tea down to the barrow room, and then brought down the least good set of Hamilton McCosh's clothes. They had been finely cut in their day, were very old-fashioned and ill-fitting, but certainly good enough for a tramp.

'Blimey, missus,' said Deakes. 'Well, thank you, but like I said, I'll only have to sell 'em.'

'If you sell them you'll be naked, because I burned your old clothes.'

'You burned 'em? You burned 'em?'

'Don't be angry, Mr Deakes. I had to burn them. You know I did. And I have some boots for you to try.'

'I don't know about all this,' said Deakes, scratching his head.

'You must let me clip your hair,' said Rosie. 'I can see you've got head lice.'

'Blimey,' said Deakes, 'this is like being back in the army. You should have been a sergeant major.'

'I'm a bossy old woman who's had no one to boss for a very long time.'

Rosie set up a chair in the middle of the lawn, so that the lice would have nowhere to go, and efficiently cut off Deakes's lank and greasy hair with the scissors from her sewing box. He sat there thinking, 'This is the first time that anyone's willingly touched me for years.' It made him feel strange. 'Before I go,' he said, 'if it's all right with you, I'll just finish off raking these leaves off the lawn. Before the wind blows down a whole lot more.'

'How far have you got to go?'

'Only about ten miles.'

'But you don't have to go. Tonight you can sleep under the conservatory.'

'Can I ask you something, missus?'

'Yes, of course, as long as it's a question I can answer.'

'How often can I come back?'

Rosie hesitated, struggling with herself. 'How often do you do the rounds?'

'I come this way about once a month.'

Rosie thought about all the odd jobs that needed doing, and about how little money she had these days, and replied, 'You can come more often if you like. Every fortnight, perhaps.'

'That's not very practical, missus. You only get one night in each place, and you're not allowed to come back until another month. That's why you can't get a job; it's because you got no address.'

'Well, come back when you can,' said Rosie, 'and why don't I let you use my address?'

'Would you do that? Thanks, missus, you're a saint. After all that nosh, I do feel a whole lot stronger. It's a bit funny, though, like being tipsy.'

'I'll give you some sandwiches to take with you,' said Rosie, 'and you must fill your pockets with apples and pears. Don't forget.'

That afternoon, she watched him leave from the morning-room window, looking very much like her father. He clearly did have difficulty with walking. She went to the rear of the house and looked at the immaculately leafless lawn. An invincible and terrible loneliness overcame her, and she ran to the front door and caught up with Deakes just as he was passing St John's Church.

'Oh, hullo again,' he said.

'I've just remembered that Ives needs a delivery boy. I saw the notice in the shop.'

'Ives?'

'The grocer in Eltham. The one in the high street. They're a big shop now.'

'I'm not a boy though, am I?'

'It doesn't literally mean a boy, does it? The last one was older than you. Do you drive? Or ride a bicycle?'

'Yes, missus, but it's been a long time.'

'You could work for Ives until a carpentry job comes up, couldn't you? I'll vouch for you. I'll come with you. Ives has known me for years. He used to tell my father off for not paying his bills on time.'

Deakes scratched the side of his head in perplexity. 'But you don't know me, and I'm just a lump of old rubbish.'

'Well, you don't look it with a haircut and decent clothes. Are you coming to see Mr Ives or not?'

'Don't have much choice, do I? Like I said, you should have been a sergeant major, you should.'

Later that evening she stood in the hallway and gazed at the portrait of her father, wondering if he would have been proud of her for doing as he had once done.

She returned to her fireside, heaped it with coals, and lit the gas poker. Shame and guilt swept through her, as she reminded herself that Deakes did not really need to sleep beneath the conservatory; this was a house with a dozen empty rooms, with fully made-up beds beneath the dustsheets.

She was a woman, though, and there was a natural vulnerability that discouraged her. Perhaps she should arrange for Deakes to be here when Margareta was. It would feel so much safer, and it would be rewarding to have someone with whom to share the fun of being kind to Deakes.

Outside, the wind picked up and it began to rain. A new fall of varicoloured leaves began to skip, and dance, and spiral across the lawn.

37

Letters

26 August 1963

My dear Daniel,

I have the melancholy task of having to inform you that my lovely Sophie died suddenly on Wednesday afternoon last week. You have seen each other only on rare occasions since Archie's funeral, but I know that you were as fond of her as she was of you, and I am certain, therefore, that you would like to be informed of her passing.

She was energetic, lively and funny right up to the end, just as she always was, and I was been beginning to think that she might even be immortal, given how young she looked and how well she seemed. But, alas, a weak heart appears to be a family trait.

She was gathering strawberries in the garden, when her heart apparently gave out, and she pitched forward. I saw it happen from an upstairs window, and by the time I reached her she had already gone. When I turned her over, her eyes and mouth were wide open, as if amazed.

I have attended thousands of deaths, but they never fail to affect me in the same way. You must know it yourself, having been a soldier. When it is one's own beloved wife, it is a different matter, of course, and you can imagine how devastated I have been, how lost and confused, how intimidated by the prospect of the waves of loss which will, I know, come crashing over me when the initial shock has passed.

I have, as you know, devoted my life to the ministry of souls, convinced that it is my vocation and that I have no choice. I have heard the last wishes of the living, prayed with them, blessed them, held them as they died, buried them and spoken eulogies over them. I have said consoling words to their loved ones, and written letters to their relatives.

Not since 1915 have I been secure in my faith, however. I have never reconciled myself to the evil and suffering in the world, and have many times questioned God as to His goodness and wisdom. I have never had a reply, have listened only to infinite silence, and very often I have been seized by the fear that I have anchored my life to an illusion. I tell you this because I know you will understand, having never had any faith yourself. You have anchored yourself to something else, perhaps, I know not what. You were always good at living in the minute. You went out on your motorcycle to blow your cares away, and I envied you that ability.

I am in need of advice, my dear fellow, since my own is no use to me. Sophie was my life's companion. I could have been happy with no one else but her. She was wise and silly, inventive, original, irreverent, impulsive and, to me, entirely beautiful. My dear fellow, apart from our poor old dog who cannot last very much longer, I am alone for the first time in several decades, and I know not what may come of it.

I thought I would tell you what I have told no one else. As I sat on the ground next to her body, I ate the strawberries from her basket, convinced that that was what she would have done if it had been me who had died whilst picking them.

Do write back when you find the time.

Yours ever,

Fairhead

> Victoria Avenue
> Penticton
> British Columbia
> Canada

14 September 1963

My dear Fairhead,

How deeply sorry I am to hear of Sophie's death. We all go back such a long way, and although some of my memories are painful, I have only ever thought of Sophie with the utmost enjoyment and delight. I frequently recall the funny things she said, and, as I once remarked to you, although she liked to appear silly, she was doing so just to entertain herself. She was the wisest and cleverest of us all, and unlike Rosie and me, for example, she possessed the wisdom of the heart. She chose the right man to love, and she stuck with you through thick and thin, never wavering, and never putting the wrong foot forward.

My dear Fairhead, what advice can you be asking for? You don't say.

I have always known of your doubts. Rosie was shocked by them from the moment she met you, and frequently mentioned them to me in the years before we went our separate ways. She thought it indecent in a clergyman, believing that faith was a question of all or nothing.

We are all growing old, our bodies are beginning to let us down, and the end comes on apace. This is what we have to face up to, and of this subject there is no end. What I have to say is various and disconnected, as I am no philosopher. I did meet Bertrand Russell on a train once, though, as you may remember. He wrote a book called The Conquest of Happiness, but he never did conquer it himself. As for me, I have had several very happy periods in my life, and have concluded that there is no such state as continuous happiness; there are only periods of it, whose memory and flavour carry you through the darker times until the light returns.

I have often thought that our survival of the Great War was a sheer bloody miracle, and that after that, every extra day was simply a stroke of luck. When we in the RFC were ground-strafing during the big offensives of 1918, I must have had literally thousands of machine-gun rounds fired at me. By what miracle did I come through? You were under shellfire for months. And what a marvellous stroke of repeated luck it was for you to have spent all those extra days, thousands of them, with a woman who loved you with all her heart, and thought you as beautiful as you thought her.

My second thought is that if we are simply annihilated by death, then we have nothing to fear, because annihilation is what happens to us every night when we are sound asleep, and all of us like a good sleep. I know that I do. What could be nicer?

My third thought is that it may be that we do survive in some way. You must remember Madame Valentine as vividly as I do. She was sure that we carry on, essentially the same, and that our ideas about heaven and hell were simply superstitions. How this is possible, I can only surmise, but if you take an interest in modern science you will know that matter and energy are the same thing, interconvertible, if there is such a word. It is neither created nor destroyed, but forever changing. It seems to me that mind, or the soul, is simply energy/matter in its highest stage of organisation, and that it would be theoretically possible for it to survive death when it is released. Therefore it does seem possible to me, temperamentally atheistic though I may be, that Sophie and you will meet again one day, and perhaps even be able to resume your life together in some manner. You and I have witnessed a great many deaths in our time. You must have noticed, as I always have, that the dead body is not the person. There is always the absolute sense that somebody has left.

My advice, then, is to consider that, either way, you have a good chance of winning. There is hope, my dear Fairhead, and it is in that hope that you must go forward. Your enthusiasm for intellectual enquiry has only grown stronger as you have grown older, and my advice is simply to keep that momentum up. I say this not because a man as intelligently sceptical as you would ever expect to arrive at some destinatory revelation, but because it is always more important to travel than to arrive. To arrive in Ithaca at last would surely be a disappointment. I think that if one ever did arrive at some ultimate philosophical destination, one would just find oneself impelled to set off on a new journey. A philosopher who has at last uncovered the truth would be compelled to go off in search of falsehood.

It is lovely here at this time of year. Why don't you come out? You would love the clapboard houses, the magnificence of the lake and the mountains, and the openness of the good people.

Yours ever,
Daniel

Paleo Periboli
Manor Way
Blackheath
Kent

25 November 1963

My dear Daniel,

Thank you for your letter, and for its amazing promptness too. I remember when it would take two weeks for a letter to get to Canada, and another two weeks for a reply to come back!

I perceive from your letter that you are both a monist and a Heraclitean, perhaps without ever having realised it yourself. This is the first time I have ever come across an explanation of these things that is essentially materialist, although it would seem that according to modern science, matter is not what I thought it was. I think that your views are both interesting and helpful, and have given me much food for thought. I have never been frightened of being dead, but I am fearful of the prospect of dying, if it is protracted and painful. I can only hope to leave as abruptly as Sophie did. She was ever wise, even in the manner of her passing.

You will be interested to know that two nights ago I smelled Sophie's perfume on the landing, and last night I distinctly felt her presence beside me in bed when I woke suddenly in the middle of the night, even to the extent of feeling her breath on my neck, as if she too was sleeping. Even if this was merely 'the dust that falls from dreams', to use one of Sophie's felicitous expressions, I am thankful for it, and feel my heart considerably lightened.

My dear Daniel, I would love to come over and see you, but at present funds simply don't permit. If you can, you should come home. I say this because one of the things that was a constant regret to Sophie and me was that we were childless. You, on the other hand, have a son, with whom you should be urgently reconciled before death calls on you in your turn. You also have no less than four grandchildren that you have never met.

I christened a child this very morning, and that is what put me in mind to speak to you about this. Also, Christabel and Gaskell invited me to stay with them in Hexham, and Ottilie and Frederick came up too. Since you left, Christabel in particular has been very downcast and dejected. Felix and Felicity say that it has been like losing a father. We all agreed that you really should come home. Isn't going into exile a kind of cowardice? What can be your motive for distancing yourself from all those who love you? If it is merely your sense of adventure leading you away on one last quixotic jaunt, then surely you have done it now, there is no need to persist. You did say you would only be gone for six months.

My advice, in return for yours, is that you must have a chasm at the centre of your soul and that you must take steps to overleap it, just as I must find a way to turn mine to good use.

Yours ever,
Fairhead

PS I am wondering if this 'Beatlemania' has reached Canada. It is absolutely rampant here, and it has become like living in an asylum, with all the young girls turning into Bacchantes and the boys affecting

Liverpool accents. These days you have to be 'with it', and if you're not, then you're 'square'. And if you are 'with it' you are deemed to be 'groovy'. It's all as charmingly ridiculous as the argot we used to throw about during the Great War and in the twenties, and I find it most comforting that we humans never run out of new ways to be absurd.

PPS When I was in Hexham Puss fell asleep across my lap and I was quite unable to wake him or move him. I must have been pinned down for two hours, and had time to read almost an entire novel.

The Great Hall
Hexham

27 November 1963

My darling Daniel,

I write to you in the wake of having had Fairhead to stay for a few days. It was the least we could do after the ghastly shock of Sophie's death. We are all still shaken to the core. You will remember that during the Great War she was a driver in France, and many times did such dangerous things as changing tyres under fire, and driving through barrages with important officers on board. She seemed indestructible.

But now my darling, sweet, funny sister is dead. It seems unimaginable, and I am inconsolable, as are Ottilie and Rosie. Who will it be next? The pain of this loss has been so great that I selfishly hope it will be me.

But I am writing mainly to beg you to come home. I know that our companionship has been through many stages, sometimes slipping back into passion, and then back into a calm and enduring understanding. You have written that your life in Canada is wonderful and that Penticton is a perfect paradise, but the fact is that you have cut yourself off from the remaining people who love you. Why have you done this? I can't believe that it was done in order to hurt me; was it, in some obscure way, to spite Rosie?

I can't tell you how much I yearn to see you again, to hold you in my arms, to smell your cologne. As time has gone by I miss you more and more. You said you would be gone for six months or so, which I thought might be a bearable length of time, but you have been gone for eight years! Eight years is a preposterous amount of time to be parted *from the father of your children, and the only man you have truly loved. I always believed that you loved me too. You certainly said that you did, and I remember so well how tender you were on the night before you left.*

Felix misses you too. Felicity has two adorable children you have never met, and she is here only for a month or two every year. I know that you have never got along with Bertie, and he was usually stationed in Germany, but my darling you have loved ones here in England who love you to bits and are as bewildered as I am by your long, seemingly wilful absence. You have many times said how much it agonises you to have children that you love and cannot acknowledge, but doesn't it agonise you even more not to see them at all?

I want to know, my darling, why a man who has been so frequently decorated for heroism in war runs away when the world is at peace, but he has difficulties in his private life or with his feelings. You ran away before the war when you went to Germany, after Mary broke your heart, without thinking how you might have been breaking mine.

This time, when you went to Canada, I thought I could bear it, because, after all, I have Gaskell, and for all of us our most physically passionate days are a long way behind us, and I thought it would only be for half a year.

But, Daniel, my darling, I really can't bear it. I don't see why I should have to bear it. Life is too short for us to be so far apart for such atrocious lengths of time.

> *The grave's a fine and private place,*
> *But none, I think, do there embrace.*

Your everloving and devoted,
Christabel

The Great Hall
Hexham

30 November 1963

My dear Daniel,
I am writing to you behind Christabel's back, so don't tell her about it.

I know she has recently written to you to beg you to return, and the whole family is of one voice on this. Although I am positively dying to have you back, I am writing to ask you not on my own behalf but on Christabel's.

What a strange life we have all had together. You know that when you were here and Christabel was in your bed and not in mine, I always did feel a little forlorn, but I was never jealous. I have always loved both of you, though of course in different ways, and I knew that without you in her bed from time to time and giving her the children she yearned for, I would inevitably have lost her altogether, because she would have been drawn away into a good old conventional marriage with some poor man who would probably always have remained ignorant of her Sapphic side.

I know that I have you to thank for the long and happy years that she and I have had together, and of course I have you to thank for Felix and Felicity, who have been the absolute joy of our lives. You were as wonderful a father to them as you possibly could have been, considering that you have had to masquerade as a kind of 'uncle'. We all remember how you used to motorcycle all the way back from Germany almost every month. What an effort you put in!

But, Daniel darling, you must know how cruel you have been to abandon Christabel for so long, without ever having intimated that your liaison with her is in any way over. She has been as patient as Griselda, and it is really not honourable to keep her waiting or leave her to suffer any more. She sits by the window with tears in her eyes, watching out for the post, and she is frequently drenched in melancholy. If you think for just a moment, you will see that she, of all the women you have been attached to, is the one you have been with the longest. She really is the love of your life, but you have never owned up to it. She is probably your last love too, unless you have been up to no good in Canada.

You said you would be off on an adventure for six months, but you have stretched it out into years. I know that you and Wragge have a successful business, and that you have been having immense fun with your wondrous submarine and your unreliable antique boatplane, but now it is time to put others before yourself.

I ask you to come back even though it means I will have to share Christabel with you again. This is because of course I love her as much as ever, and can't bear to see her suffer.

You will be glad to know that our beloved Puss is very well, and is acquiring a little dignity with age. He too would be glad to see you, I am sure.

Daniel, my darling, this letter is in the form of a request, but you should construe it as an order from your superior officer, who is and always will be, your devoted Green-Eyed Monster, Gaskell.

Victoria Avenue
Penticton
British Columbia
Canada

20 December 1963

My dear Fairhead,

You are, of course, absolutely right. You and I are both old now, and there is very little time to waste, if any. We are of an age when one can be alive and kicking one moment, and dead of pneumonia the next.

I have recently been prompted to think about the nature of courage. You and I, and so many others of our generation, did the most stupidly courageous things imaginable. Speaking for myself, I could only do these things by overcoming my own terror, and I am certain it was the same for all of us. This is not to discount the combined effects of our patriotism, our youthful high spirits, our laughter, our natural gallantry, our love of the King, our determination to 'play up and play the game' and not let our fellows down, and above all, our comradeship. Many also had great trust in God, which, as you know, I never did. When I think of the scrapes I got into on the North-West Frontier, and in the air in both world wars, I am filled with admiration. We were the second to last generation of true Britannic heroes, and Bertie's generation was the last.

This is the thing, Fairhead, old chap. I would love the opportunity to have another scrap with the likes of Voss or Boelcke, and I think at my age I could still throw a Camel around just as well as I could at twenty-six, but I am frightened of having to approach Bertie. This will take a kind of courage that I have never had. Rosie poisoned his mind against me, and after Esther's death there was no one left to take my part. He was never anything but cold towards me. In late 1945, when the war was no longer my chief preoccupation, I remember walking across Tangmere aerodrome in a black cloud because I had been ordered to hand in my favourite revolver, and resolving there and then to bring about a proper reconciliation with him. Now it's 1963 and I still haven't pulled it off. I am seventy-one years old, and time is running out.

I have no idea where he lives, but I am sure that Sophie would have had his address. Do you think you could take a look in her address book? I am thinking of coming over in the summer, and hope to have found some Courage of the Early Morning by then.

In the unlikely event of this reaching you before Christmas, do try to be as happy as you can on the day. I know that Gaskell and Christabel, or Ottilie and Frederick, would be terribly pleased to have you to stay as often as you like. You must forgive me, but I have already written to them about it. Perhaps the admirable Puss will refrain from pinning you down this time. Take him another football as a present, and I will pay you back for it.

I have also heard from Christabel who, like you, begs me to come home. Penticton is a lovely place, and I would guess that Canada must be the best country in the world in which to live, but in the end, isn't it true that the people one loves count for more than any country? I have been delayed here because of the submarine, and then our project to rebuild the boatplane. It's all been wonderfully good fun, and very interesting, and the time has passed very quickly. But sooner or later you are called back to where you belong. Reading Christabel's passionate plea for me to return has made me understand where my heart belongs, and that sooner or later even Daniel Pitt's adventures have to come to an end.

Yours ever,
Daniel

Paleo Periboli
Manor Way
Blackheath
Kent

21 January 1964

My dear Daniel,

I really do have to say to you that Rosie is a sick old woman now-adays, and you must take the opportunity to see her whilst you still can.

She has always loved you deeply, as you must know, but she never did find out how to love you well. I know that you have always loved her in return, but have been too frustrated and angry. She has taken Sophie's death terribly badly, and is visibly declining. I must tell you quite firmly that it is the opinion of all of us that you must get back in time to effect some sort of reconciliation with her, or to arrive at some kind of mutual understanding and, indeed, forgiveness.

Yours ever,
Fairhead

PS The Beatles continue to add to the gaiety of nations, particularly their teenage girls. You don't say if all this has affected Canada yet.

PPS Ottilie and Frederick did indeed invite me for Christmas, and we had a peaceful time in Bosham. I remember you were stationed nearby during the last war. What a lovely place! I missed Gaskell, Christabel and Puss, but I am sure that he will pin me down when next I go up to Hexham.

Victoria Avenue
Penticton
British Columbia
Canada

30 March 1964

My dear Fairhead,

I am so sorry not to have written for a while, but I have been thinking about what you have been saying in your letters. You are, of course, absolutely right. You and I are both very old now, and there is very little time to waste, if any …

I really have resolved to come over this summer, and hope to have found some Courage of the Early Morning by then. I would very much like to visit Sophie's grave with you and leave some flowers on it.

As for Rosie, seeing her would make me feel incomparably sad, but I will of course do as you advise.

Yours ever,
Daniel

PS I enclose a small tome that I found in a second-hand bookshop in Vancouver. I am sorry it is in such terrible condition, and also for its being in French. It is by a German philosopher about whom I know next to nothing, called Arthur Schopenhauer, but my attention was snagged by the title, Essai sur les Fantômes, so I was sure that you would be interested.

Paleo Periboli
Manor Way
Blackheath
Kent

25 May 1964

My dear Daniel,
Thank you for your letter, and most particularly for the little book, which I read with great interest. Schopenhauer's scientific information is somewhat out of date, I presume, but all the same I found the whole thing extremely suggestive. I loved that remark that 'in dreaming, everyone is a Shakespeare', and was very forcibly struck by the idea that when one sees or hears a ghost, one perceives it with the same inner sense that one has during dreams, where things are seen and heard without the use of the eyes or ears. I also find intriguing the idea that there is a substratum to things of which we are all a part, so that we are all, so to speak, connected to each other beneath the surface of appearances. It is exactly what John Donne was saying in his passage about no man being an island.

I have to say that the most entertaining part of the essay is the several pages of excoriating criticism of the Anglican Church. Heretic that I am, I laughed out loud. How wondrous that everything he wrote about it more than a hundred years ago is still true today!

We have two second-hand bookshops in Blackheath, and in one I found an enormous three-volume work of his called The World as Will and Idea *and in the other I found a book of essays. I am determined to master the former, but have already realised that in order to understand Schopenhauer one has to understand Kant, and to understand Kant, one has to understand Leibniz and David Hume. There is a hideous regress, and no doubt I will end up having to read Plato and Lucretius too.*

As you must realise, Sophie's departure left a gap in my life which seemed unbridgeable. One either gives up or finds a new reason to live.

I have decided to switch my attention from theology, about which I know a great deal but believe very little, and take up philosophy.

You may know that Rosie has a friend who practically lives with her now, called Margareta, who is German. She is tall, ugly, very forthright and forceful, and terribly nice, and I am going to have German lessons with her once a week at The Grampians, so that one day I will be able to read Schopenhauer in the original. They say that his prose is absolutely lucid and beautiful, which is most rare in a German philosopher, or any German writer for that matter.

So, what do you think? I have given myself the most enormous everlasting project, which should keep me busy until I reach the very gates of death, and will give me a new journey to undertake now that my darling Sophie has finished hers.

Thank you so very much for your thoughtful gift.

We are so much looking forward to seeing you next month. I do hope the voyage is a pleasant one. Rosie is terribly excited about the prospect of your return, and Gaskell writes that Christabel has gone out and bought three new dresses.

Your old friend,

Fairhead

PS The other day I had the interesting revelation that some infinities are bigger than others. You wouldn't think so, would you? But if you think about it, from now into the past is an infinite amount of time, and from now into the future is an infinite amount of time. But if you add the two infinities together, you get an infinity which is double the size.

38

Rosie's Last Letter to Daniel

For some time Rosie had been suffering from breathlessness, with a deep aching in her left arm. Instead of going to a doctor, she simply set about putting her affairs in order.

She was looking forward to dying, because there was a chance of seeing her father again, and Sophie, and Ash, of course. Given the choice of only one of these three, she would have chosen her father. What would she say to Ash, with him having been killed so young and handsome, and she an old woman with wrinkles in the skin above her knees, and goosewings on her arms? Perhaps one's youth would be restored in heaven, and then she could see Ash again without shame or embarrassment. She could just imagine throwing herself into his arms, and he bending backwards and lifting her off her feet, and whirling her about as he used to, but the awful thing about this image was that whenever it came to her in her dreams at night, she would look up, and the face would be Daniel's. It was Ash, but it was Daniel.

The legal situation was complicated. The Grampians belonged to her and to Christabel and Ottilie, of course, but also to Fairhead, because he would have inherited Sophie's share. Bertie would inherit her own share. It seemed to her that the only solution would be to sell the house and divide the money up equally, but whenever she brought the subject up with the others, they would say, 'Don't worry, we'll sort it all out between ourselves when the time comes.' Fairhead had said, 'There's no point in me inheriting Sophie's share, because I have no children, and I am perfectly all right with the house in Blackheath and the income I have from my books. Just give my share to the others.'

Christabel said that she did not want any money for herself, but that it would be nice to have her share so that she could divide it between Felix and Felicity. Felicity was living like a queen in Hong Kong, but had no private money at all, and Felix was hoping to expand his architectural business.

Rosie did not want to sell The Grampians. To her it was a sacred place, the site of so much happiness and despair, the nursery of her childhood, the sanctuary of her adulthood. It was filled to the eaves with reminiscence, and there was not one room or portrait or stick of furniture that did not resonate with histories. She smiled every time she looked up at the portrait of her great-grandfather, and noticed all over again the small neat hole that Bertie had punched into his shoulder with his grandmother's Britannia air rifle. Sometimes she ran her fingers over the keys of the upright piano, and remembered Ash bawling out the comical songs of their Edwardian youth. He used to sing 'Have a banana' in between the lines, and sometimes 'Thank God I'm normal'. It was too out of tune now even to be a honky-tonk.

The Grampians had fallen into desuetude, and the garden was merely semi-cultivated because Rosie was the only one who went into it, apart from the teenage boy she paid to mow the lawn once a week in summertime, and Mr Deakes, who popped round to do any heavy work. The roses had blackened and died over the years, and the beds she had planted with perennials that needed no attention, and seeded themselves. The spot in the middle of the lawn where the Anderson shelter had been dug out and refilled had never found its level, and was now a marked declivity in the grass. Just in front of it was the exact place where her mother had been struck in an air raid, and her body flung against the wall, next to the blue door.

The blue door in the wall was concealed behind a stand of foxgloves that vibrated with bumblebees, and was half rotten, its hinges rusted almost to nothing. She barely knew any of the neighbours now. The Pendennises were long gone, and in any case she had fallen out with them because of their upbraiding her for keeping Bertie incommunicado with Daniel. She still recalled with a shudder the bitter quarrel she had had with Mrs Pendennis when she had discovered that the latter was acting as a *poste restante* for the children. The sweet woman she had always called 'Mama', the mother of her dead fiancé, had turned against her in disgust, and they had never reconciled.

The one part of the garden that Rosie tended carefully was the animal graveyard at the end of it. Here was Bouncer, the brown dog who had gone mad with energetic delight at King Edward's coronation party, causing such chaos, and here was Caractacus, whose eyes would sometimes light up suddenly before he shot up the curtains and perched on top of the pelmet. Here was Caractacus's lady friend, Calpurnia, and thirteen other graves of their descendants, as Rosie had never had the heart to give away all of each litter, let alone to drown them. At least half of them had been killed by the traffic in Court Road. There was a large pebble on each small mound, with the animal's name painted on it in white enamel. Rosie liked to sit down here in a deckchair on summer evenings, and the present generation of cats would either lounge on the graves of their ancestors or frolic after butterflies. She liked to face the spot where once Daniel and Archie, when they were boys, had vaulted the wall at the same party when Bouncer had disgraced himself.

Sometimes Rosie wandered about the empty house, through the closed-off rooms, dustsheets draped over the furniture. This had been Sophie's room, this one Christabel's. These ones on the top floor, with their small windows and tiny fireplaces, had been the servants'. This was one of the three spare rooms, where she had come to weep secretly and alone in 1915. This had been her parents' room, and in this bed neither of them had died, although it seemed to her as if they had. No one had slept in it since her mother's death in the Blitz.

Here was the kitchen where she fried up her daily ration of fried bread, sausages and eggs, and where Cookie used to reign supreme. Cookie had gone back to Shropshire after Mrs McCosh's death, and there was nothing left of that beautiful intimacy but a Christmas card in ever more shaky handwriting as each year passed.

Here was the morning room, where the huge family Bible was set up on its lectern, and Rosie would sit at the window seat, hoping for visitors. There had been a time when she would open the Bible at random, to use it as an oracle, and that was one of the reasons why she had felt able to marry Daniel. Nowadays a kind of apathy had set in. She knew the Bible so well that it was hardly worth looking at any more. Just as her poetic creativity had dried up, she felt there would be no more revelations, no more direct advice from God.

Here was the cellar, damp and cold, where she stored the coal for the fires, and the meagre possessions left behind and never reclaimed by previous occupants.

Here was the dining room, containing the piano, where there had been so many family Christmases and birthday meals, when her father would jocularly provoke his wife, and she would respond with predictable but ineffective asperity. It was here, too, that her father would sometimes experiment in winter with his golfing inventions, such as the one that registered how far the ball would have gone, and whether or not it was a slice or a hook. He had shattered the chandelier with a driver once.

Under the terrace that used to be a conservatory, before it was destroyed by the same bomb that killed Mrs McCosh, was the room where Mr Wragge used to sleep in the wheelbarrow amongst the gardening tools and the mower. It was just a cavernous darkness now, smelling of petrol and rotting hessian. The window had broken again, and the swallows flew in and out of it in the summer. The return of the swallows in spring was the one thing she most looked forward to.

Short of breath, her left arm aching terribly, Rosie patrolled this museum of poignant memories for the last time, and then went to the dining room, where her father's desk was still set up against the window, and, pumping the small lever at the side, she filled his old fountain pen from the bottle of Quink in the drawer. She removed a cat from its station on the blotter, and began to write.

The Grampians
24 Court Road
Eltham

30 May 1964

My dearest Daniel,

I have sorted a great many things and put them into the crocodile-skin briefcase that used to belong to my father. You will find all sorts of documents and letters, and so on, and I very much hope that one day you will go through them so as to understand me better and, also, some of what happened.

There are so many things I wanted to tell you, and to confess to you. I have in fact been to confession. I went to Westminster Cathedral a long time ago, and spoke to a kindly priest there, even though I am only a Roman in spirit. I was too cowardly to take all his advice, I'm afraid, but I do feel that I have managed to clear things up with God, I very much hope. I know this is all mumbo-jumbo to you, but it means a great deal to me.

However, I have increasingly felt the urgent need to confess to you personally, but this is impossible because you gave up on me and went to Canada. Now I hear from Fairhead that you are returning, and the thought of it fills me with joy.

However, I am not well, and I worry that I will be gone before we have had a chance to make peace with each other.

My life has been quite long enough and it suits me to leave now. I know that my heart is giving out, and that I am to die as my father and Sophie did, although not in quite such a state of happiness. I don't know what it's like to score a hole in one, and the nearest I ever came to it was when we married and had a chance to make something good of our lives, but then it was as if I missed a one-foot putt. My father once told me that my marriage to you could have been an eagle, but that I'd made it into a double bogey. I thought it would amuse you to know that.

Do you remember that when we first arrived at Taprobane Bungalow you found a bird all tangled up with itself? It had a claw stuck over the top of its left pinion. It was like a tiny magpie. You untangled it, and then it sat on your finger and tidied its feathers, and then it flew away across the valley. Well, I was like that bird, except that I had got too used to being tangled, and I couldn't give it up. I had wings, and you were untangling me, but I wouldn't tidy my feathers, and I chose not to fly. I might as well have had no wings.

I have left a separate letter for Bertie, giving him instructions as to what to do with the cats, and so on, but I will try to state here very briefly what I most need to say to you personally.

Firstly, I thank you from the bottom of my heart for the gift of the children. Even though two of them are dead, they were the delight of my life, and I owe them entirely to you.

Secondly, you really did try to take me further on the journey to my heart, and it was me who flunked it. Thank you for trying so hard for so long, and I'm sorry that I chose to wall myself in instead of opening my arms. I would make it up to you if I could, and you will never know how many times I did yearn to do so, but then chose to be a coward and did nothing at all. I suppose I must have thought there was something virtuous and honourable about 'doing a Queen Victoria', even though Ash would have hated me doing it if he had known.

I feel very strange and weak, and so I have to stop, and I think I will not have the time to confess to you as I wanted. Just as you have not had time to confess to me as you should have done. In case I am not here when you arrive, I want you to learn from this letter that my dearest wish would have been to reconcile with you, if only there had been time enough. I am writing this to let you know that in my heart we are reconciled. When you have read these words, I hope you will say, 'Yes, my love, we are reconciled.'

And one further thing: it is my wish that you and Bertie should also be reconciled. I tried to keep him from you out of a possessive selfishness. You know there is something particularly strong about the attachment between a mother and her son. It was the same between you and Esther. No matter how I tried, I could not prevent her from loving you more than she loved me. I couldn't lose Bertie to you in the same way that I lost my daughter.

But everything went further than it should have, and he ended up hating and despising you so much more than I could ever have anticipated. I had sowed the wind, but then such a whirlwind spiralled up from it! He used to tell people that you had not scored all those victories in the air, and that you must have lied about them, even though they are a matter of official record. He told everyone that you had deserted us coldly and cruelly and never even sent me money for the children. How could I disabuse him without admitting that it was me who drove you away and erased you from our lives? There is a box in the attic containing all your letters, and the cheques you sent me that I never cashed. Please find a way to show him those letters and cheques. Also, show him this letter in which I admit how terribly I have behaved. Say that his mother tells him from beyond the grave that it is more important to love well than to love deeply, and that forgiveness follows from understanding.

My own darling, I have four things left to say:

I love you.
I forgive you.
Please forgive me.
Goodbye.
Your very own Rosemary

She stood up very gingerly, feeling that her balance was about to go, and, fighting the pain that was intensifying in her chest and left arm, went to find her sheaf of poetry, with the intention of reading it through to see what could be salvaged or improved. She took a walking stick and, on a sudden impulse, her Book of Common Prayer, and descended the steps into the garden. She walked slowly, preoccupied with the sheer effort of it, hardly able to draw breath. Finally she lowered herself into her deckchair amongst the animals' graves, and accepted with resignation the two cats who immediately jumped into her lap. She looked through the poems for the one that meant the most to her, and, closing her eyes, settled back and tried to befriend the dread that was overwhelming her, coming in waves.

An hour later Margareta let herself in to The Grampians with her own key. She wandered about the house calling for her friend, and then saw from an upper window that although it had been raining for ten minutes, Rosie was slumbering in her usual place, and that there was something strange and ungainly about the manner of her sleep.

39

Angel Hotel

Daniel met Christabel in Guildford late in the afternoon, collecting her from the station in a Ford Corsair that he had hired in Southampton. He was for the moment staying at the RAF Club in London, and had motored through Wandsworth and down the Kingston bypass. Christabel had been to Hampshire.

He had booked two rooms on the cobbled high street at the Angel Hotel, an ancient establishment that had accumulated over the centuries rather than been built, so that it was a labyrinth, and almost impossible to find one's room again, having once left it. For her he had booked a double and for himself a single. He had no idea how this encounter would unravel.

He met her on the platform, and they simply stood face-to-face, smiling. Each saw how much the other had aged, and wondered if the other was thinking the same. She was taller and thinner than he remembered, and he was less broad than she did. She put down her bags, put her arms around his neck, and hugged him tightly to her chest. Eventually she pulled back and wiped her eyes, saying, 'I'm sorry. It's just so wonderful to see you. And I'm so sad.'

'It's all right,' said Daniel. 'I feel the same. I'm ... devastated to hear about Rosie. And so soon after Sophie. It must be awful for you. I wish I'd been here. I'm sorry I missed the funeral. It was just impossible. I wish I'd had the chance to talk to her before she went, I really do.'

'Oh, Daniel,' she said, 'you never should have stayed in Canada. It was wrong of you. And who's next? I do hope it's me. I don't think I could take it if was you or Gaskell. I really couldn't.'

'I'll put your things in the car. Then let's take a walk along the river at Ladymead. It's very beautiful. There are old men and little boys fishing above the waterwheel. I expect you'd like to stretch your legs, wouldn't you?'

'That and a cup of tea. Let's walk first.'

As they strolled along the sward of the riverbank she put her arm in his, and said, 'I've just been to see Puss. He was very happy to see me. Practically bowled me over. It was so sweet. You'd think he hadn't seen me for months.'

'Is he content with his lioness?'

'She wasn't very happy with him at first, I hear. She swiped him across the face, and he was most bemused. Now she's nuzzling him and rubbing her cheek on his. Of course he's got used to being let out for stud, but he never minds coming home again, In fact he goes mad with pleasure the moment we open the crate and let him out. He goes straight up his redwood, clings there for a bit, all wide-eyed, and then has to reverse carefully down again. Always the same! It's very comical. Anyway, these people in Hampshire have a white lioness, so they're hoping for a litter of white cubs. You know, when I haven't seen him for a little while, I start to forget how gigantic he is. I think he's about thirty stone.'

'It's good that Puss worked out so well. It could have been a terrible disaster if he hadn't been so sweet-natured. I'm glad my prognostications were so wide of the mark. How are Felix and Felicity?'

'Dying to see you. Felicity says she's knitted something for you, but I'm not allowed to tell you what it is. She's going to bring it when she comes home for her annual visit. Felix has just been commissioned to design a shopping centre and a small football stadium, and he has yet another new girlfriend he wants you to meet. The last one turned out to be a terrible shrew, if we are to believe his account, but I thought she was rather lovely. You've missed several delightful girlfriends since you've been away. He's very handsome these days. He's grown into himself, if you know what I mean.'

'I'm going to meet him at the RAF Club on Thursday, and we're going to the Haymarket to see something.'

'Give him a big hug from his mother, and tell him to stop neglecting me.'

'I will.'

She stopped and faced him, adjusting the lapels of his coat, and looking down at his shoes. 'And you stop neglecting me too. You are coming home, aren't you? I want it to be like old times. Coming up to Hexham, and going out for drives, and playing cards in the evenings, and laughing over risqué stories. Gaskell wants it too. I know she does.'

'Does she know you're here?

'Of course she does. She's beyond jealousy. She always has been. She loves you as much as I do. There's so little time left, so little life left. Haven't we got to make the most of each other while we still can?'

'I am going to come home. Tomorrow I am going to go and see Bertie. That's why I'm here in Guildford. I'm going to try and straighten things out with him. Then I'll wind things up in Canada. And then I'll be back.'

'Please do it all quickly. When you come back ... will you come and live at Hexham?'

'I don't know ... I can't say ... everything depends on Bertie. Even if I don't come and live in Hexham I'll be up there as often as I can. As often as you want.'

'Promise?'

'Promise.'

Christabel's eyes welled up again. 'Oh, Daniel, it's been eight years!'

'I know, I know. Don't cry. I'm back. I'm back now, I really am.'

'You'll run away again, I know you will.'

'No. I'm going to stand still now. Breathe the air. Gather my thoughts. I'm thinking of writing my memoirs, like Cecil Lewis and Grinnell-Milne.'

'Oh, you should, but you'd have to tell so many lies.'

'Oh God, what an awful thought. I'm not allowed to say anything at all about the SOE. I wouldn't have to lie about what I did in the Great War though.'

'But you would have to lie about what you did in beds.'

'Yes. Only in beds. You lie in beds, and then you lie about them. *Ça, c'est l'amour.*'

That night, they drank champagne before their meal, and Beaujolais with it. After they had eaten, she wiped her mouth with a napkin, took a sip of her wine, and reached out. They held hands across the tabletop, silently looking into each other's faces. Despite the clatter of cutlery and the low drone of conversation at the tables all around them, they felt as if they were disappearing into the distance behind each other's eyes.

When at length they rose from the table, neither of them was sure what would happen next, and neither had the courage to ask; but outside her room, as she cried and clung to him whilst saying goodnight, it became clear.

'I'm not promising anything,' he said.

'That's what you said the first time. All those years ago. Back in Hexham. When you flew up with Gaskell in the Avro.'

'Even so, I'm seventy-two now.'

Christabel kissed him lightly on the lips. 'What does it really matter any more? *Que sera sera*. But just one thing.'

'Yes?'

'Let's turn the lights off. I don't want you to see me. I want you to see me only in the dark. Now that I'm old.'

40

In Notwithstanding

In the early evening of a very hot day, Kate Pitt was surveying the desolation that is the disappointing finale of a summer in which all one's flowers have peaked too early. She was thirty-five years old, still young and attractive, but thickening into sensible motherhood now that she had four children, including a newborn, and no prospect of anything before her but years of nurturing and ferrying. She was happily bogged down in Theodore, aged eight, Molly aged six, Jemima aged four, and Phoebe, an accidental afterthought who was yet a few months old. Phoebe was in a Moses basket in the rose bed as her mother jabbed at weeds with her hoe, knowing perfectly well that it was all somewhat pointless when the clay was baked so hard by the sun. All the same, she loved her garden, and felt a deep need of the exercise.

In their acre and a half, she was responsible for growing, and Bertie was responsible for mowing. He had acquired a very large Suffolk Punch, and almost sprinted behind it as it cut its wonderful parallel stripes into the large lawn that they planned to turn into a grass tennis court, so that the children could spend their time gambolling in bare feet with their friends from the village, who had a habit of simply turning up, so that occasionally there would have to be a succession of phone calls in order to discover whose child was where.

Today was the beginning of the school holidays, and Theodore was indoors making a Hawker Hurricane from an Airfix kit, Molly was swinging in a tyre on an apple tree, and Jemima, her thumb in her mouth, was asleep with the dog in his large wicker basket in the pantry.

Bertie and Kate had settled at the southern end of Surrey, in the village of Notwithstanding. They had chosen it because Bertie had found a job with the Ministry of Defence, and it was on the Portsmouth line to London, within walking distance of the station.

The countryside was very beautiful. These were the Surrey Hills, with Hydon's Ball not far off, and from the top of the common you could see as far as the South Downs. All one could see in between was a vast forest of oak and birch, which gave the impression that the whole region was uninhabited.

Their house had been built in the Surrey farmhouse style, with dark red bricks from the factory at the other end of the village, its upper part clad in red tiles. The facade had almost been lost under a luxuriant invasion of Virginia creeper, and the beds under the windows were packed with hydrangeas. There was a rose bed by the front gate, and a clump of yellow bamboo in a corner that provided both canes for Kate's runner beans and weapons for the children. Behind the house stretched a long garden with an orchard at one end, and, over the fence, a cottage that had once been inhabited by the house's gardener, and now contained an elderly couple who still spoke with the old Surrey accent that had almost vanished from the county, driven out by agricultural mechanisation and the commuting middle classes.

Kate's mother lived nearby, in Abbot's Notwithstanding. There was a kind of pact between them, whereby Kate kept an eye on her mother, and the latter did a great deal of babysitting.

Kate was standing looking at her roses, wondering why some were so sickly, when she detected a movement out of the corner of her eye. It seemed to her that someone had come to the gate, spotted her, and ducked away again.

'Who's there?' she called, but there was no reply. She bent down and peered through the bottom of the laurel hedge. She could see a pair of walking boots with thick socks into which the walker had stuffed the cuffs of his trousers. She went into the house and came out with a stout walking stick. She walked to the bottom of the garden and out through the gate onto the lane, so that she could come up it and peek round the corner of the hedge to see who the intruder was.

Despite her subtlety, she came face-to-face with a tall, slender man of about seventy years of age, who had at exactly that moment lost courage and decided to walk back to Chiddingfold.

'Gracious me,' he said, much surprised, 'an ambush. From behind a bush. Are you going to whack me with that stick? I should warn you, I have been trained in unarmed combat, and my hands are lethal weapons.'

Kate stared at his oddly familiar face and said, 'I know you, don't I?'

'Not me,' he replied, 'but I think you might know my son quite well.'

'Your son?'

'Bertie.'

'Bertie?'

'Yes. Bertie is my son.'

'We thought you were dead.'

'Bertie knows perfectly well that I'm not dead. My wife is dead. His mother is. Of course, you must know that. You must have been at the funeral.'

'You knew Rosie?'

'It's highly probable.'

'I'm sorry, that was a really stupid question. You must be Daniel. The famous ace.'

Phoebe began to wail in her basket, and Daniel said, 'I am sorry to have to put you on the spot...I mean, I know that Bertie doesn't want to see me...has no interest, and so on...but I would be very grateful if you could let me see my grandchildren. It would mean a very great deal. I'd like to hold that one.' He pointed at Phoebe. 'I'm very good at shushing babies. The sweet smell on the tops of their heads, you can just breathe it in, and sigh with happiness.'

'They'd tell their father,' said Kate.

'You don't have to tell them who I am. Tell them I'm a tramp.'

'Where did you walk from?'

'Chiddingfold. Last night I was at the Angel in Guildford, and tonight I'm staying at the Crown.'

'Chiddingfold? That's miles. You must be exhausted.'

'Not a bit. I used to be a Frontier Scout.'

'I've no idea what that is.'

'No, well, why should you? We're a dying breed. Is my son coming home soon?'

'He isn't usually home until about half past seven. Sometimes he misses the last train and stays in London overnight. Come and sit on the terrace and I'll make you a cup of tea. How do you have it?'

'Are you sure? I have it *à la française*. Weak, no milk, no sugar.'

'Lemon?'

'No thank you.'

'Well, let's go in.'

Kate opened the gate, and Daniel went straight to the baby and picked her out of the basket, putting her over his shoulder and patting her back. There was a loud belch, and a glob of thick saliva was projected down the back of his jacket. Phoebe fell quiet. 'It usually works,' said Daniel. 'Do you mind if I sniff the top of her head?'

'I am already getting used to this being a bit strange,' said Kate drily.

Out on the terrace, with a turtle dove calling from an oak tree, and a hot-air balloon from the Godalming Ballooning Club drifting overhead, unleashing a barrage of barking from the neighbourhood dogs, they settled down and sipped at their tea. Kate said suddenly, 'I've never understood Bertie's absolute hatred for you.'

'Absolute hatred? That's very disheartening. I didn't know it was as awful as that.'

'Well, it is. He doesn't have one good thing to say about you.'

'He doesn't, as a matter of fact, know me at all. I did my best, but in the end I had to give up. Rosie turned him against me, right from the moment he was born. It was systematic.'

'Rosie wouldn't do a thing like that! She was a saint.'

'She wasn't entirely a saint. She tried very hard to be one, and failed in one respect. She knew that Esther adored me, and she wanted Bertie all to herself. She wasn't very well ... you know ... psychologically ... in some ways. Looking back, I think I was wrong ... I mean, I think that in reality she might have been ill. She lost her fiancé in 1915, and never got over it. Then she gave birth to a deformed child, who was probably stifled by the midwife, and she never got over that either. Then her father died suddenly and she thought it was her fault that she wasn't there when it happened, and then whenever I landed a good job she refused to leave her mother. After we parted she never cashed my cheques, and whenever I came to visit the children, she often managed to prevent it. I never lost the bond with Esther, but Rosie absolutely prevented me from even beginning one with Bertie. It was all too painful, especially after Esther was killed. In the end, I had to give up and walk away.'

'I really think you should talk to Bertie about all this,' said Kate.

41

Confrontation

Bertie came home hoping to shut himself into the dining room, where his desk was, and knock back a couple of martinis before re-emerging into the light of his family. He was suffering the malaise of having a mistress who was almost certainly unreliable, but who he could not get out of his mind. The fear of being found out made him bad-tempered. He was therefore not in the least delighted to find his wife drinking tea with an elderly stranger out on the patio. 'Damn,' he thought, 'I've bloody well got to be polite and hospitable now, I suppose.'

The older man stood up, and Kate said, 'Darling, you're home early!'

Bertie and Daniel looked at one another, and Bertie blurted out, 'What the bloody hell are you doing here?'

'I have come here to meet my grandchildren. For the first time. And kindly speak to me with respect. I am your father.'

'Who are you to tell me off? Just get out of here before I call the police.'

'The police? Do you seriously think they'd be interested? I was welcomed in by your wife. If you can't embrace me as a son should, you could at least shake my hand and show some common courtesy.'

'I'll never shake your hand. Just get out.'

'I demand the right to know my grandchildren.'

'Just fuck off.'

Kate stood up and very deliberately walked up to her husband. She swung her arm back and slapped him resoundingly across the face.

Bertie was stunned, put his hand to his cheek, and then suddenly raised it. Daniel stepped smartly into his way and pushed him in the chest. 'No. Not ever. No matter what she's done. And I've got a walking stick.'

'Jesus Christ!' exclaimed Bertie. 'What the hell have you turned up for? You wait for your wife to die, and then you suddenly turn up for no good reason a few weeks later. What the hell are you playing at?"

Kate said, 'It's about time you faced up to things. And stop being so foul. It makes you look like a complete yob.'

At that moment, Theodore came out onto the terrace with a model aeroplane in his hand. He held it up and said, 'Look, I've finished. It's a Hurricane. The propeller's a bit wonky and it kept falling off instead of turning, so I had to glue it on, but apart from that, it came out better than the last one.'

'Darling,' said Kate, 'this is your grandfather, whom you've never met before.'

'I really have got two, then?'

'Yes,' said Daniel. 'Can I see your Hurricane? I used to fly these. I had one of my very own for a while.'

Theodore was fabulously impressed; he handed the model over carefully, saying, 'Watch out, because the paint on the tyres takes six hours to dry. I had to use Humbrol for the black because I ran out of Revell.'

Daniel took the plane by the fuselage and held it up. After such a scene it was difficult to keep his hands from trembling. 'This looks like a Mark II. The one I had was a revised Mark I, with metal sheet on the wings instead of linen, and a variable pitch propeller, and eight Browning machine guns.'

'Did you ever fly a Spitfire?'

'Just once. I took it up for a spin.'

'What's better, a Spitfire or a Hurricane?'

'Well, the Hurricane was cheaper and simpler and much easier to repair, and the Spitfire was lighter and stronger but didn't like being damaged, and the Hurricane turned more tightly but caught fire more easily because of the wooden frame, but I always thought I'd rather have a crash in a Hurricane; in the event of having a crash, that is. Have you made lots of models?'

'Tons and tons.'

'Can I see them?'

Theodore took his grandfather's hand and led him indoors. As they went through the French windows, Daniel said, 'But do you know what I honestly think? I'd rather have a Sopwith Camel, any day. Or a Bristol Fighter. Lysanders were wonderful too.'

Bertie looked at the disappearing backs of his father and son, and said nothing. Pointedly ignoring Kate, he strode into the house, shut the door of the dining room, poured himself a stiff martini, and sat at his desk, looking out at the laurel hedge and the small birds that flitted in and out of it. He considered his own churlishness and was surprised by it. Perhaps it was something to do with his mother having died so recently. At the same time, he felt curiosity, excitement and pleasure.

Half an hour later there was a knock at the door, and Daniel came in with Theodore. 'Daddy,' said Theodore, 'this grandfather knows everything about aeroplanes.'

'He ought to. He was an ace in the First World War.'

'I know. Mummy told me ages ago. But you said he wasn't.'

'You and I,' said Daniel, 'are going for a long walk. We might as well take the dog.'

Bertie bridled. 'Are you giving me orders?'

'We have a lot to talk about and a great deal of time to make up. If this opportunity is lost, it might be lost forever. I want to talk to you away from Kate and the children, just you and me, man to man.'

'If you take this grandfather for a walk, will you show him my den in the Bargate quarry?'

'I'd like you to show it to me yourself,' said Daniel. 'Tomorrow perhaps? Today I need to talk to your daddy.'

'I'd like you to leave,' said Bertie. 'I have no interest in getting to know you or hearing what you have to say.'

42

Margareta and Daniel

Daniel met Margareta in Batista's cafe on Tottenham Court Road. She loved it because it was smoky, grubby and crowded, full of people coming to leaf through their haul of second-hand books from the shops on Charing Cross Road, or from Foyles. It had an air of Parisian intellectual ferment, with its clientele of young men smoking Gauloises who wished that they were Jean-Paul Sartre, and young women in berets who wished that they were Simone de Beauvoir.

Daniel recognised her immediately from Fairhead's description. Tall, ugly, ungainly, dressed in drab garments that seemed to have been cobbled together from rectangles.

'You must be Margareta,' he said, approaching her at the table in the far left corner that she had chosen.

'At last! Daniel!' she replied, standing up and shaking his hand as if she were a man. 'What would you like? The coffee is good here because the *patron* is Italian. But you have to go and queue for it. Perhaps you would be being so kind as to bring some croissants. I have already had two, but somehow I made them disappear.'

When they had settled down and were facing each other, Daniel said, 'Fairhead told me that you are staying on at The Grampians as a kind of caretaker, while the family decides what to do with it.'

'That is correct. And you know, Rosie left a great many cats. No one has the heart to destroy them, so I am having them neutered and they will live out their lives, and I won't replace them, until finally they have all gone to the little graveyard at the bottom of the garden.'

'Ah yes, where Bouncer is.'

'Yes. The famous Bouncer who once upset a celebration.'

'The coronation of Edward VII. It was a grand occasion. It was altogether a different world.'

208

'This neutering of cats is a very expensive business,' said Margareta thoughtfully, as if to herself. She looked up. 'But the reason I have asked you to meet me is that I have brought you a letter from Rosie, and a box of your old letters to her. This letter that I am giving you now is the last one, and she wrote it on her final day. I think you should read it. I have kept this and the box of letters for you because I was afraid that Bertie would destroy them. I know all about Bertie.'

She handed it over in a plain unsealed envelope, and Daniel extracted it. It was written in fountain pen, the same wide-nibbed Osmiroid with the side pump that Rosie had used all her life, on the same blue Basildon Bond writing paper that she had always liked to use. It smelled of her familiar perfume. He sniffed at it, and remembered a starlit night in Ceylon, after the monsoon, when her heart had softened and Bertie had been conceived.

It was impossible to read the letter unmoved, and at the end Daniel stood up, and said, 'Excuse me, I have to go out. I'll be back. Don't leave.'

'I understand,' said Margareta softly. 'Take as long as you like.'

Daniel walked rapidly to Soho Square, pacing round and round it until he felt that he could hold himself back. His throat ached. He sat on a bench for a while and watched the ragged pigeons with their mutilated feet, leading their busy, purposeless lives. He felt Rosie's hand on his shoulder and her light kiss on the side of his cheek, as if it were not a memory. He read the letter again, and felt a sense of unworthiness as deep as that which she herself had expressed. All these adventures, these love affairs, these rifts and reconciliations, these moments of bliss or victory, they vanish into memory, and then the memories themselves must vanish into nothingness.

Deeply dejected, Daniel returned to Batista's cafe, where Margareta had passed the time eating four more croissants and smoking two Gitanes. She looked at him without surprise as he sat down opposite her. 'You speak German, don't you?' she asked.

'Yes.'

'Well, I want you to know, I have been Rosie's friend for a long time now. There is nothing she has not told me. We were exceptionally close, like this.' She held up her hands and clasped them together as if in prayer. 'I know everything. *Ich verstehe alles. Alles, ja? Es gibt keine Geheimnisse. Aber es gibt ein Geheimniss das ich Dir nicht sagen kann. Rosie schämte sich zu sehr dafur. Ich kann sie nicht verraten.*'

Daniel walked away from Batista's with Rosie's last letter in his greatcoat pocket, and a string-handled paper carrier bag containing a shoebox full of his letters to his children that Rosie had never passed to them, and the cheques for their maintenance that she had never paid in to Martins Bank.

At Waterloo Station he settled into a second-class carriage. As the train rattled towards Guildford and Portsmouth he could not keep himself from nagging at the terrible question: what had Rosie done that was so terrible that it could not be told, even after she was dead? Of what could she have been so ashamed? It cannot have been anything as banal as infidelity or theft. Rosie had been a kind of saint, after all.

43

Back in Notwithstanding

The two men walked in complete silence past the council houses and the high-walled orphanage at Cherryhurst, with the dog shooting ahead on this well-known and well-loved route. They turned up the long track towards a strangely phallic pink water tower and the solitary white cottage, the banks of blueberries rising high beside them on their sunken road. A squirrel raced and leapt in the immense Scots pines up on their left.

At the cottage at the end of the lane they turned right along the top of the hill, and at the Maclachlan bench, Daniel paused and said, 'I see that your mother failed to bring you up a gentleman.' Bertie looked stunned, and Daniel continued. 'It isn't enough to have been in an elite cavalry regiment and to have had a good war. It isn't enough to have gone to a good school.'

'You're saying I'm not a gentleman?'

'Clearly not. And neither are you a good father.'

'What? Is this coming from you of all people?'

'From me, of all people? You've read the letter your mother wrote to me. You've seen the letters I wrote to you that she never showed you. You've seen the cheques I sent that she didn't pay in. You've read that she asked for us to be reconciled. Don't tell me ever again that I was a bad father.

'I've been here a while now. I've had time to see how you operate. And even if I am a bad father it doesn't follow that my opinions are false. If Adolf Hitler says it is raining when it is in fact raining, it doesn't follow that it can't be raining just because it was Hitler who said it was. I'm telling you, a good father embraces his children when he gets back from work. He asks them what they did. Whether anything interesting has happened. He doesn't go straight to his den and have a stiff drink. Neither does a good husband.'

Bertie raised his hands helplessly in the face of his father's disapproval.

'Let me make one thing perfectly clear to you,' said Daniel, 'something you ought to know without being told, and that is that even if you don't believe what your mother wrote, and you still think I was a bad father and a bad husband, it doesn't confer on you any right to be a bad father and husband yourself.'

'This is too much,' exclaimed Bertie. 'On what possible grounds do you make these accusations?'

'Unlike you, the rest of the family have kept in touch with me. I get letters. I know what's going on. I take an interest. I am very close to Aunt Christabel. I was very close to Sophie. And Fairhead has been my best friend since 1918. All of them tried to tackle your mother and intervene in her bizarre campaign to exclude me from your life. Did you know that I was at your passing out parade, watching from a window in Old College? Did you receive one of the hundreds of letters that I wrote to you? No; because your mother intercepted them. Did you receive any of my Christmas and birthday presents? God knows what your mother did with them. Knowing her, she gave them to a Christian children's home. Do you have any idea how much it cut me that every time I turned up you would run and clasp your mother's legs and try to hide in her skirts? With what dismay I had to listen to Esther telling me what was really going on?'

'Esther was your favourite,' said Bertie.

'Well, of course she was. How could she not be? She was the one who stuck with me through thick and thin. She was the one who told you what was what whilst you refused to believe her, and chose to think I was the Devil incarnate. Of course she was my favourite. I loved you even so, even though your treatment of me and your attitude towards me were completely hateful. I always loved you, even as you pushed me away. I thought of all the things we should have been doing, digging holes, putting up treehouses, shooting tin cans with an airgun, making things in a workshop, and you hurt me the same as if you'd pushed a dagger through my heart. But I loved you even so. I never stopped. I blamed your mother rather than you. Why do you think I'm here?'

'You were a bad husband. A bad husband is a bad father.'

'I was a rejected husband. You know that perfectly well. Your own mother has told you.'

Bertie looked into his father's angry eyes, and hung his head. He looked up, and then looked away. 'How was I supposed to live up to you? The Great Ace? The hero? The one that Esther couldn't stop talking about and worshipping?'

'You had a good war. You did live up to me. I know what happened at Montecieco. I know about your medals, about how you pulled a comrade from a burning tank and carried him across your shoulders back up to the lines. Fairhead and Sophie told me. You won the Military Cross fair and square, the same as Fairhead and me. I always wrote to you to say how proud I was, and you never wrote back. Not once. You didn't invite me to your wedding, and you didn't tell me about the children.'

'I couldn't split my loyalty, the way that Esther could. It was you or her.'

'When your children fall out, do you take sides?'

'No.'

'Exactly. Let's sit on this bench and admire the view.'

They looked across the fading evening towards the south. Daniel pointed his walking stick towards Blackdown and said, 'Tennyson lived there for a while. They called this the Surrey Tyrol in the old days.'

'Why do you walk with a limp?' asked Bertie.

'Because I was captured during the war, in France. The interrogator had the idea of cutting my toes off in succession, and then my fingers, then my nose and ears, and finally my penis. He was quite inventive. I suppose that beating and electrocution weren't quite up to the mark, from his point of view. Rather too conventional. Luckily there was a change of commanding officer, and after only two toes I was taken to hospital to be patched up. The new officer's father had been in the *Luftstreitkräfte* in the Great War, and apparently his father had been an admirer of mine. When he realised who I was, he wouldn't contemplate any further amputation.'

'Christ!' said Bertie. 'How did they cut them off?'

'Mallet and chisel. And a block of wood.'

'What happened?'

'I escaped from the hospital.'

'On crutches?'

'In pyjamas and dressing gown! I did get back home and back to work eventually. I had some pretty narrow squeaks.'

'What on earth were you doing in France?'

'SOE.'

'SOE? I don't believe it. You had two good wars! A hero twice over! I give up.'

'The second doesn't really count, because I'm still bound by the Official Secrets Act. It might as well not have happened from the point of view of getting any credit.'

Bertie shook his head, and Daniel said, 'I hope you speak good French. That would be very important to me.'

'Failed again,' said Bertie. 'My French teachers were all old and mad. One of them used to throw the blackboard rubber at us. Anyway, it's getting cold and dark and I think we've lost the dog. She likes chasing deer. Let's get home. She'll turn up on her own. I've no doubt that Kate's invited you to dinner. You can sit next to Theodore and talk about maximum service ceilings.'

'Are you too English to embrace me as a son embraces his father everywhere else?'

'I'm distressingly English.'

'When we meet I expect to be kissed on each cheek,' said Daniel. 'And you ought to do the same with your own son. Surely you can manage that much Frenchness? And you should teach your children to shake hands like proper French children.'

'Yes, sir, no, sir, three bags full, sir,' said Bertie, and the two men laughed.

Bertie said, 'It's going to take a long time, you know. To think of you more positively.'

'There should be enough time,' said Daniel.

They walked past a shabby low cottage, with an elderly cat perched on the roof of the shed, another on the scraper by the back door, and another on the gatepost. Bertie said, 'Two old spiritualists live here. One of them walks around with the ghost of her husband on her arm, and chats to him, and tries to pay his fare on the bus. They had quite a big circle after the Great War. Everyone trying to get in touch with their lost boys. Then it got smaller and smaller as they all passed to the other side, and now the former members are the ones who come to the séances. So they say.'

Daniel put out a hand to the cat on the gatepost, and it drew its lips back and hissed.

'Spiritualists?' he said, retracting his hand swiftly. 'You must ask Fairhead down. He's always been interested in life after death. Written several books on it. I expect he'd love to meet them.'

He looked wistfully at the old black A35 that was rotting in the garden on deflated and perishing tyres.

'I wouldn't mind buying that off them, and doing it up. I hate to see a perfectly good machine dying of neglect.'

44

At Rosie's Grave

Kate Pitt suggested to the two men that they should visit Rosie's grave together. At first they both demurred, for different reasons, but eventually she wore down their resistance, and, accordingly, they found themselves standing beside it.

It was a cold day, and things were not going well in the world. The pound had just been devalued, the Vietnam War was becoming increasingly bloody and fruitless, and the Welsh Borders were smoking with the stinking pyres of animals that had been slaughtered to prevent the spread of foot-and-mouth disease. Bertie was concerned that his children were going to be corrupted by the Rolling Stones, and it seemed that only Daniel was happy. He had been going back and forth to Hexham, and was excited about the prospect of a new supersonic airliner that was the result of unwonted Anglo-French cooperation. 'One day I'm going to fly in that,' he was saying, 'when I inherit the cash. And even though it's a jet.'

Daniel bought flowers in Eltham, because he wished to make the right impression on Bertie, and because it was the least he could do for his departed wife. He clutched them tightly in his right hand as they stood at the graveside at St John's and gazed down.

'I suppose this is the first time you've seen it,' said Bertie.

'No. I came with Margareta. She is quite a phenomenon.'

'It's funny, but I had been expecting to see you at the funeral.'

'I didn't get the news until it was too late. I was mid-Atlantic.'

'Would you have come? If it had been possible?'

'Yes. But I'd never stopped being angry. Your mother sent my whole life off course. It's funny, this visiting of graves, isn't it? We do it, and it's a ritual that we seem to have to go through, and we look down and we can't help but wonder what the body looks like now.'

'And we think that one day that'll be us. Gently falling to bits six feet down.'

'I know an awful lot of dead people,' said Daniel. 'I've visited so many graves. I buried your Uncle Archie myself, in Peshawar, and then to South Africa to find the graves of my brothers. The odd thing about getting old is that the older you get, the higher the proportion of the people that you love are dead. You become part of a rapidly shrinking minority. When you're my age you are one of the honorary dead. It's made me look forward to moving on. To the last great adventure.'

'When I brought Theodore to see the grave, and I said, "That's Granny down there," he looked up at me and said, "Daddy, why can't we just get her out?"'

'And what did you say?'

'I said, "We can't. She can't move or talk or eat, or do anything at all, and she doesn't even know she's there."'

'You know,' said Daniel, 'I hadn't seen her since the fifties. It was at your Uncle Archie's funeral. She'd aged terribly. But of course I picture her as she was when she was young and vivacious, and writing poetry. She had wavy chestnut hair, and pale skin with freckles, and she had a lovely blue dress, and she had one of those silver bracelets that girls used to wear on their upper arm, and when she was in the sidecar she always wrapped up her hair in a scarf decorated with prints of ponies.'

'She wrote poetry?'

'Didn't you know?'

Bertie shook his head. 'It's news to me.'

'When she was young she was infatuated with poetry. She was convinced that she would be a poet one day. She knew how to write it properly, but she also liked all that obscure modern stuff that doesn't scan or rhyme, and reads like crossword puzzle clues. She was one of the pioneers, really. Didn't you find them after she died?'

'We found a lot of poems that she'd written out, but we thought she'd just copied them. I've got them in a black tin trunk, if you're interested. She'd been reading them when she had that heart attack. We can dig them out later.'

'In Ceylon she wrote me a beautiful poem with a line in it that said, "I'd have you take me further on this journey to my heart." I was very touched. It was when we were making a new start, and everything seemed to be working out for us. We were happy for about two years.'

'My mother once said to me that you'd taken a mistress in Ceylon.'

'Really? She said that?'

'Yes. A native mistress. Is it true? Did you?'

Daniel fell silent, then said, 'I know she can't hear us, but it doesn't feel right, having this kind of conversation at the graveside. Shall we go to the Tarn? That's where she decided to marry me, when I went in and hauled out a dog. Marrying your mother was my reward for an act of compassion.'

'She always adored animals,' said Bertie. 'She loved you for taking pity on an unknown dog.'

At the Tarn they watched the old women throwing crusts to the dogs, and Bertie said, 'So it's true, is it? You did have a mistress in Ceylon.'

'Yes, it's true. I don't want to make excuses, but all the European husbands did. It was par for the course. You know how it is.'

'Do I?'

'How long have you been married? Have you always been faithful?'

Bertie said, 'That's not the kind of question a father asks his son.'

'Well?'

'I think that diplomatic silence is called for.'

'I see you're quite French after all. You still have good relations with Kate, I presume, despite the occasional lapse?'

'You shouldn't ask me that, either. But the answer is "yes". It's what you'd expect after such a long time together. It's comfortable and warm and predictable.'

'Well, I probably shouldn't tell you this at all, since you're my son and your mother is your mother, but she couldn't cope with that side of things. She wanted children, that's all. And after you arrived, that was it.'

'I see,' said Bertie.

'Almost all the masters in Ceylon had mistresses. Samadara was adorable, and I still think about her. I still feel an absolute heel for abandoning her. I only did so because your mother wanted to come home, and left me no choice.'

'Of course you had a choice. You could have sent her home and stayed in Ceylon.'

Daniel looked at him impatiently, and said, 'What? And give up you and Esther? You still don't understand, do you? You don't understand a bloody thing!'

'What am I supposed to understand?'

'I loved Ceylon. I was making a success of it. I adored Samadara, I loved the sport, the coolies, the mountains, the food. Everything! I was going to set up a passenger airline and a postal service. I could have stayed there all my life. I left because I knew I couldn't separate you and Esther from your mother, even though I had the legal right. I didn't come home for your mother's sake! It was because I couldn't bear to give up my children. By then I hardly gave a damn about your mother, to be brutally honest. I was just a ghost in my own bungalow. I came back here because coming home was the only way I could arrange for you to stay with your mother whilst remaining with you myself. I came home because of you and Esther. That's the long and short of it. I loved you too much to take you away from your mother, and I wanted to be with you however rotten my life was with her. And even though it meant leaving Samadara, who was the sweetest girl I've ever known. I still think about her, every day, and wonder how she is.'

Bertie went and sat down on the bench beside the church porch. 'You gave it all up for me and Esther?'

'Yes.'

'Damn. And I've spent all my life kicking you in the teeth.'

'Are you able to tell me why? Esther never did.'

'I only had Mother's version.'

'Don't lie,' said Daniel. 'You had Esther's version. Esther never turned against me. Esther always knew the truth. So did Sophie and Fairhead and all the rest of the family.'

'Esther fought your corner at every turn.'

'So what's the real reason? Why have I been without my son all my life?'

Bertie put his head in his hands, and mumbled, 'I really am so sorry.' He scraped the paving slab with his foot. 'Recently I've thought about it and thought about it. I've even discussed it with Kate. It's got a great deal to do with being loyal to Mother, but there's only one really convincing answer I can come up with.'

'Well, what is it?'

'I've already told you, really,' said Bertie. 'It's bloody impossible to try to live up to a father who's a war hero and a famous fighter ace. How was I supposed to deal with that? All I got at school was everyone going on about it. I felt like an absolute bloody useless failure before I'd even tried to accomplish anything at all.'

Daniel looked down at him sternly. 'You could have tried being proud.'

'Yes. You're right, of course you're right. And you'll be pleased to know that the children have always been thrilled to bits to have you as a grandfather, even though they'd never met you. Now that they do know you, I expect they'll never stop talking about you. Theodore spends all his pocket money on Airfix and Revell models because he wants to make an example of every aircraft you ever flew.'

'You didn't tell me they'd been born, or let me meet them. I only heard anything about them at all because of Fairhead and the others loyally keeping in touch.'

'I'm sorry, Dad. I've cocked things up.'

'You can usually unfuck a snafu,' said Daniel, 'if you try hard enough. It's good to hear you call me "Dad" by the way. You've never called me anything before. Shall we stroll into Eltham and buy flowers? We can put some on your grandparents' grave. They're over against the wall. Then we can go to the pub and have lunch.'

Bertie stood up and put his arms around his father's neck for the first time since he was a tiny boy. He gave a light squeeze and said, 'I think we can unfuck it. I think we are unfucking it. Slowly but surely.'

On the way to the pub, Daniel said, 'I told Theodore that I flew a Lysander in the second war. Has he made a model of one of those yet?'

'Bloody hell, Dad,' said Bertie.

'Well, perhaps I'll tell him about all the tanks you used to be in, and we'll go into Guildford and find him the models at the Model Shop. And have you told him about getting the MC?'

'No. I expect Kate's told him. And how did you know?'

'Fairhead. I was able to follow your exploits through him. He saw it when it was gazetted. That makes four of us in the family with MCs. Archie had a bar on his. Not bad.'

'Let's invite Fairhead down for the weekend, if you don't mind sharing a room with him. There are two singles in the spare room.'

'Yes, he must be pretty bloody lonely. Poor Sophie had a way with words, just like your mother. She was a kind of poet, in her own way. She used to talk about "the dust that falls from dreams". I often didn't know what she meant, but I always knew it was something poetic and profound.'

'I remember she and my mother having rows about you. Sophie always took your part, you'll be glad to know.'

'When we get to the pub, let's drink a toast to Sophie and all the dead people,' said Daniel.

They drove home over the North Downs at Box Hill, arriving in Notwithstanding in the early evening. Bertie said, 'Let's have a dram and then go and look at her poems. If that's what they are.'

'Well, I'll know,' said Daniel. 'Let's have the dram afterwards.'

'There's a lot of other stuff too. There are all her letters from Ashbridge.'

'I don't want to read those,' said Daniel.

'They're very breathless and moving. And we've got Fairhead's letters from the time that he first wrote to Mother about Ashbridge's death, and also Ashbridge's diary from the front. He mentions you in it. He says you went stunting over his lines just to cheer him up.'

'Good Lord! So I did! I'd completely forgotten. A lot of us did that kind of thing. I painted "Long Live the Pals" under the lower wing.'

Up in the dark, dusty attic, Bertie dragged the old tin trunk out beneath the single bare light bulb, and opened it up. Daniel picked up the scuffed and tattered crocodile-skin briefcase, and looked inside. 'This seems to be full of her writing,' he said. 'Let's go downstairs and have a look through.'

They emptied the contents onto the dining-room table.

'These are Ash's letters,' said Bertie, handing over a bundle that had been bound together with a red ribbon. 'For some reason they're charred at the edges.'

'How very curious. I know she used to read them when she thought I wouldn't know. I'd come in and she'd look guilty and hastily put them back in her drawer. It was very hurtful, in a way. You can't compete with a dead man. Was she reading these when she died?'

'No. It was these poems,' said Bertie, handing over another bundle.

'These are definitely hers. Most of them are from Ceylon. She had a burst of writing before her misfortune with the baby. I recognise them. She always wrote on blue Basildon Bond.'

'I really did have no idea that Mother was a poet.'

'She had two poems published in the *Georgian* anthology! Did she never tell you?'

'No. And I've never heard of the *Georgian* anthology.'

'It was extremely important and influential. Everyone who was anyone got into it. It was published every year for about ten years in the teens and twenties. It had all the important poets in it, and in the last two they decided to allow women poets. That's when Rosie got published.'

'There's one I particularly like,' said Bertie. 'Let me find it. Ah, here it is. She was reading this one when she died. It was in her hand when Margareta found her. It's got some truly beautiful lines, like this one you quoted: "I'd have you take me further on this journey to my heart."'

'She wrote that for me,' said Daniel, 'almost as soon as we got there. That line came to her on the terrace. You say she was reading that when she died, and not her letters from Ash?'

'Yes, she was reading that.'

Daniel looked at his son and said, 'That's pretty hard to take. It's fairly clear what she was thinking if she was still reading that in her old age. Look, read it again, all the way through. It's about how she wants to start again, to make a better go of things.'

'She messed it up, though, didn't she?' said Bertie.

'Well, we both did in our own way. We both made a hash of it. Your mother never could bear to backtrack. She was too proud. She couldn't bring herself to meet me halfway, and I ran out of patience. Don't you think these poems are terribly good?'

'Well, yes. I assumed they were by people like Walter de la Mare, or Masefield. The ones we had to learn by heart at school.'

'We should do one last thing for your mother,' said Daniel. 'We should get these printed. Maybe a run of a hundred, just to give them a chance in life.'

'You'd do that?'

'Yes, of course I would. It's a debt. She wrote some of them for me. Not many men get good poems written about them. Most men get lousy ones, if any. Everyone should leave a trace. These poems can be your mother's trace. Then she isn't just bones. And it'll help me to forgive her.'

'I don't understand. How?'

'I don't know. It just would.'

'Did I tell you about Deakes?'

'Deakes?'

'When Mother died, a man came round to The Grampians and insisted that he be allowed to make the coffin, at no charge. Said his name was Deakes. He said she'd saved his life.'

'Saved his life?'

'He said he'd been a tramp, and she tidied him up and found him a job. Then he got himself set up as a carpenter and joiner. That coffin was the finest I've ever seen. It was made of polished American oak, with brass handles.'

Daniel said, 'In her own way, when she was at her best, she was a saint. That was what she always wanted to be. She got more than halfway, it seems.'

'Deakes came to the funeral, and he was the last to leave. He didn't come to the reception. He just stood there looking down at the earth, and then he knelt down and kissed it. She inspired a great many people to love her. You should look through her autograph book from Netley. All the messages from the grateful wounded.'

'I did see them. She showed me after the war; she had it in Ceylon. What happened to your mother's *Madonna and Child*? The one she was so fond of?

'In the attic, wrapped up in an old shirt.'

'Can I have it?'

'I don't see why not.'

45

Point 153, 1967

On 20 September the two men stood at the top of the slopes in Montecieco, in the hills behind Rimini, and looked at the brick war memorial with its white cross and its inscriptions.

'I didn't know that this would be here,' said Bertie. 'Nobody told me about it.'

'It must have been put up by the Italians,' said Daniel. He read: '*In memoria di tutti soldati di molte nazioni I quali nell'adeptimento del loro dovere hanno combattuto sacrifando la vita lontani dalla patria in questa campagna oggi cosi verde e tranquilla.*'

Bertie was looking at the main inscription. 'In memory of the officers and men of the Queen's Bays and the 11th RHA (HAC) who fell in action here on 20 September 1944. "I have fought a good fight, I have finished my course. I have kept the faith."'

'They kept the faith all right,' he said bitterly, 'but it was hardly a good fight. It was a massacre. They didn't stand a bloody chance.'

'Your mother's first fiancé was in the HAC,' said Daniel.

'Ashbridge? Yes, I know about that. But he was in the infantry battalion.'

'He wanted to be a gunner, but they said they had enough of them. I visited his grave a few years ago. We can go again if you like. Next spring perhaps. Then it'll be my turn to show you my war. My first one anyway. I'll show you all the airfields I flew out of.'

The two men turned and looked down the valley. It was a peaceful and beautiful place, with a conical hill rising directly before them in the distance, and lush high ground to their left. Bertie put his hands in his pockets and said, 'I can still see all those burning tanks. This is where I lost all my friends. In one engagement.'

'I almost know how you feel,' said Daniel, 'but I lost my friends in ones and twos. It was just one long, relentless attrition. A lot of them went down in flames.'

'I suppose that might have been worse,' said Bertie.

'It was a hideous strain. We all went mad, really. They called it FSD. Flying sickness disorder. Our version of shell shock. We used to have the most enormous binges. If someone was killed there was a binge. If someone was promoted we had a binge, or if a new recruit arrived. We used to break up the furniture. We played polo using chairs as horses. We played Cardinal Puff and became so drunk that we couldn't stand. Sometimes we were still drunk when we took off in the morning. We'd send out a tender to collect new furniture from all the abandoned houses. Tell me what happened here.'

'Well,' said Bertie, 'this is the end of the Gothic Line. They called this bit the *linea gialla*. We were slowly pushing Kesselring northwards, but he was damned clever and well organised, and he'd constructed a series of fortified lines.'

'You were up against Kesselring?'

'Well, not in person. There was General Baade, and he sent down Kampfgruppe Stollbrock. We liked Baade. He led from the front. He used to send droll messages to us on our radio sets. "OK, Tommy, you can stop firing now. I'm out of range." I heard he died on the last day of the war, and I was actually sorry. We'd been ordered to take Point 153. It's down there and round the corner to the right, where you can't see it.'

'You were told to take an invisible objective? Christ.'

'We could have done it but we got here too late. We were bogged down in mud and heavy weather, and Stollbrock had time to bring in two battalions of *Panzergrenadiers* and put them over there on the left flank. We knew they were there. Colonel Asquith questioned the order and was told "there's no other plan". It was madness. Goodbody never came here to assess the situation. He just sent us to destruction.'

Daniel looked down the valley. 'It's a killing field.'

'Yes. And we'd already been through several kinds of hell. We were almost out of petrol and ammunition. We had to come over this ridge first. I should think the German gunners couldn't believe their luck. We were sitting ducks. The Italians called it the *Balaclava corazzata*.'

'Meaning?'

'The charge of the Light Brigade, in armour. We had an order to capture something we couldn't see, with flanking artillery all the way. For nearly a mile. And our Shermans weren't up to it. They could take a full-frontal hit, but they had light armour on the backs and sides, and we were being pulverised by 88s and 75s from the left. We dreaded the 88s. They started life as anti-aircraft guns, until the Germans realised that if you used them horizontally they were the best anti-tank gun in the world. Once they got your range there was no choice. You piled out or burned. We put down smoke to try to get a retreat under way, but some of us caught fire, and the rest were shot down trying to get back. The sensible ones laid low, and came back after dark. The Germans called our tanks Tommy Cookers.'

'I'm very sorry,' said Daniel. 'I can't tell you how sorry I am.'

Bertie continued to talk mechanically. 'My best friend Christopher was pulled out of a burning tank by one of my brother officers. He slung him over his shoulders and ran back up the slope with him. Then a bullet caught Chris in the head just as they got to the top.

'Anyway, C Squadron was completely annihilated, and only three tanks of B Squadron came back. The regiment lost thirty-four tanks and had only eighteen left. I was spared because I'd been pulled out to command a reconnaissance troop. We had little turretless Stuart tanks that we called Honeys, because they were such a joy. We just had a Bren gun and a good view, and made excellent targets for snipers. All I could do was watch from an OP, and report to HQ on the radio. I was watching the annihilation of my squadron, realising that I should have been down there, dying with them. I've never stopped thinking about it, about how I should have died with them in that little holocaust.

'And that was that. The 9th Lancers arrived, and then the 4th Canadian Highlanders, the Greek Mountain Brigade and Princess Patricia's all turned up at Rimini, and Stollbrock made a tactical retreat in good order. And then the Ghurkhas or the Sherwood Foresters — can't remember which — took Point 153 without opposition.'

'So, in the end, your comrades, they died for nothing,' said Daniel.

'They shall grow not old,' said Bertie. 'I often think that it was all just a senseless and stupid waste, but perhaps it wasn't. Thanks to us keeping the Germans busy, the Canadians took San Fortunato. And do you know a strange thing? When we moved to Notwithstanding, and I went into St Peter's Church for the first time, I found a memorial plaque to Christopher on the wall.'

'That is strange. I had a similar experience. I moved to a town where the church had a plaque to Albert Ball in it.'

'We buried all the men up here, where this memorial is. Christopher's here. There was a driver we couldn't get out of his tank because his boot was caught up in the pedals. He was a young Scottish lad called Jimmy Law, and his twin brother had just been killed in France. After two weeks he was full of maggots, and the padre went down with some men to get him out. Jack Merewood got into the tank and got him out because when he pulled the foot came off in the boot. Oh the stink. They carried him up in a blanket. After all that we needed a new fleet of tanks, and sixty recruits, and when we advanced we found that the Germans had poisoned the wells. They were full of Italian men with their hands tied behind their backs, shot through the head.'

'Well, almost every Italian we've met has thanked you for being here to liberate them. Are you glad that we came? Or do you regret it?'

Bertie turned to his father, his face distorted by the pain he was attempting to suppress. 'I'm glad I came with you. I couldn't have come with anyone who was unable to understand it. And I think that anyone who doesn't know about this will never really know me. Even my wife hardly knows me. Perhaps we should have brought her. I don't know how I will ever explain myself to the children.'

'Old soldiers live in a world that's uninhabitable by anyone else. You know, when you're with me, you are allowed to be yourself,' said Daniel. 'I'm an old soldier, and you are quarter French. And you are my son.'

'I did my weeping the day after,' said Bertie. 'I suspect that we all did. In the end, I really am too damned British though. Big boys don't cry. You put your head down, button up, get on with the job, do your duty.'

'Would you like me to leave you alone for a while? I can walk down into the valley. I want to get the feeling of what it might have been like down there. Why don't you stay here?'

'It's galling for me to have a father who is so much fitter than I am,' said Bertie.

'I've never flown a desk,' said Daniel. 'Thank God. And I stopped smoking. That's something you should think about. I felt ten years younger within a couple of weeks.'

Daniel made his way down the slope, wondering if there was any remnant of scrap in this field, cartridge cases, perhaps, or a buckle. At the bottom he looked up to the left flank and im-agined the 88s and 75s dealing out fire and death, crackling from the top of the ridge. A sick feeling rose up in his throat, and he wanted to sit down and put his head on his knees, but then he caught a movement out of the side of his eye, and turned to see Bertie beginning to make his way down the slope. How strange it was to have acquired a son in old age, who himself seemed to be so old.

As Bertie approached his father, puffing and red-faced, he said, 'Damn this fat. Damn this middle-aged spread. I'm coming with you.'

'With me? Where to?'

'Point 153. I never did see it. Let's take Point 153.'

'*Allons enfants de la patrie*. Point 153; death or glory,' said Daniel, and the two men went down to the end of the field, where it was almost level, and turned right.

'After this,' said Bertie, 'I want to go and see an opera in the old theatre in Vicenza.'

'Vicenza?'

'Yes. Vicenza. We were there after the war. The first thing we did was ship our horses over. It was the time of my life, really. The girls loved us, on our horses.'

'I take it there was a woman, then.'

Bertie laughed softly. 'Yes, there was a woman. In Valdagno. Her family wouldn't let her marry me because I'm not a Catholic. I lost her entirely when we were posted back home to Chester, and then to Germany. I wrote to her for two years and there was never any reply. I expect her mother intercepted the letters.'

'Do you think she's still there?'

'I'm certain she would be, if she's still alive. But I'm not going looking for her. I want to remember her as she was. Why would I want to tamper with my most beautiful memories?'

Daniel thought about this, about Samadara, and Mary, all the others he had lost, and said, 'You're probably right.'

'After Vicenza we must go to Venice and have a meal in the Graspo de Ua, if it's still there, and then stand on the Rialto Bridge and watch the gondolas, and the gondolier must be singing "Torna a Surriento".'

It was a perfectly peaceful day, a pair of crows was harassing a sparrowhawk in the sky above the memorial, and the countryside lay quietly, sleeping off its memories. Point 153 rose before them, and Daniel and his son began to ascend it.

When at last they reached the top, looking out over that sublime, undulating countryside, Bertie stood to attention, facing the slope and the valley. Daniel stood beside him, his hands in his pockets, helplessly feeling his son's immense grief wash over him.

'Do you think,' asked Bertie at last, without turning to look at his father, 'that extreme gallantry... reckless heroism... is ever entirely a waste? Even if it's very soon forgotten, and didn't make any difference?'

Daniel thought back to the mad savagery of the North-West Frontier, and his terrifying and exhilarating days in the skies above France, and worried at a tuft of grass with his foot.

'The worst thing is the fear,' he said eventually. 'Once you've overcome that, it's very beautiful. If there's a God, then God saw the beauty of it.'

'If there's a God,' said Bertie. 'At the time I was a very strong believer. If it wasn't for my faith I don't think I would have got through. Oh well, those of us who were there, we remember it of course. We don't have the choice. And anyway, it's our duty. To remember it as vividly as we can, for as long as we're alive to do so.'

46

Farewell to Penticton

I n the late summer of 1967, the whole of Canada was in uproar over General de Gaulle's undiplomatic and promptly aborted visit to Quebec, but the Okanagan and the Cascade Mountains lay in their usual state of tranquil serenity. At weekends people were bathing in the lake, or fishing, or sailing out of the small marina in their diminutive boats. On the trees the peaches were ripening in their orchards, and in the evenings the rich aroma of chargrilled meat wafted from garden to garden.

Oily Wragge received Daniel's tidings badly.

'You can't bloody leave us, just like that,' he exclaimed. 'You've been away for God knows how long, and now we'll never bloody see you ever again, will we? What'll we do without you? What about our floatplane? Who's going to bloody fly it?'

'You can just motor it round the lake without taking off. You could come back to Blighty too,' said Daniel.

'No I bloody can't. I've got Millicent to stay for, and you've got us to stay for. And what about the business?

'Motorcycle City? You and Wavey can keep it on. And you can hang on to George the Second. I can't ride both the Broughs home, so I'll just take George the First.'

'You'd give me George the Second?' He raised his eyebrows. 'That's a bit generous! But what about the money from the business? How am I supposed to buy you out?'

'I've got my pension from two wars, and a Canadian pension, and the pensions for my war wounds. I'm old. There's nothing I want to buy any more. I've got to the age where having a lot of money is rather pointless.'

'We've got seven thousand in the bank,' said Mr Wragge. 'You can have it. And when I finally pack it in, I'll sell up and send you half.'

'Thank you.' Daniel paused and looked out over Millicent's small garden, with its roses and sunflowers. 'But we can talk about all that when the time comes. Do you think you'd come and visit?'

Wragge looked away. 'Well, I doubt it. I'd like to see Norfolk again though. The old Britannia Barracks. I expect Millicent would like to see The Grampians. But I like it here. This is about as far from stinking Mespot as you can get. This is a bloody paradise, and here I'm staying. I'm done with Blighty.'

'I wouldn't go either, if it wasn't for the family. I've got grandchildren, and old friends who won't be with us very much longer. Otherwise I'd never leave. I did say I'd only be gone for six months. I can't really get away with this any longer.'

'Have you told Wavey?'

'Yes.'

'I suppose he came up with some of that Indian bollocks about native land and the blood of the ancestors.'

'No. He asked me if I'd send him some Cornish fudge when I got back, and said we should go out in the sub and look for Ogopogo one last time, because the Great Spirit might take pity on me, as it'll be my last chance.'

'Did he say that?'

'Yes, but he was joshing as usual. He did say we should go out in the sub for one last time. Also he gave me a sort of net that he's made himself and hung with beads and feathers, and you hang it from the ceiling. I said, "Is that some kind of special tribal ornament?" and he said, "No, it's a dream catcher. Good dreams are small so they go through the mesh, but bad ones are big, so they get caught up." And he put on his pretend Indian voice, and said, "Heap big medicine." I said, "Do you really believe in all that?" and he said, "Pale face heap big stupid. Of course I don't. I'm a fucking engineer, for Chrissake.'''

'You're going to miss Wavey.'

'I'll miss you both. These years in Canada have been amongst the happiest periods of my life, I'd say.'

'Bit of a risk going home then.'

Daniel leaned forward on his chair and said, 'I've reconciled with my son. I don't know how much longer I have to live. My teeth are beginning to break. I want to lay my bones where my son can be laid beside me.'

'Wish I had children,' said Wragge sadly, and then his face brightened. 'Here, what's the difference between a policeman's truncheon and a magic wand?'

'I don't know; what is the difference between a policeman's truncheon and a magic wand?'

'Well, a magic wand is for cunning stunts.'

Daniel laughed.

Oily Wragge looked down at his feet. 'Do you know what my best memory of you is?'

'No. What is?'

'It was when we went to Nanaimo, you in the saddle and me in the chair, and on the ferry we saw those killer whales. They charged the boat line abreast and ducked under at the last moment, remember? And then they came up the other side and laughed at us. And then in Nanaimo I went to have a piss and when I came back you were surrounded by those Hell's Angels, big hairy buggers with all them scars and tattoos and rags round their heads, and their black leathers, about ten of them, and all their ridiculous bikes with the low seats and high handlebars parked up in a row, and I thought "oh bloody hell, he's done for" and I rolled up my sleeves and dived in, and it turned out you were giving them a guided tour of your Brough Superior. I never felt such a pillock in all my life.'

47

Daniel in the Gardener's Cottage

In the autumn of 1967 Daniel disembarked at Southampton for the last time, and waited for his combination to be hoisted out of the hold of the SS *Italia*. He folded his map into the cellophane cover on the tank, and from the docks rode towards Chichester, turning left near Portsmouth to take the tortuous road over the downs. He passed through Petersfield, where his children by Christabel had been sent to school at Bedales, and then through Hindhead and past the Devil's Punchbowl on the left. He remembered picnics there in the distant past, and realised that he still had no idea how that enormous crater had come about. At Milford he telephoned from a phone box, and then took the Petworth Road to Notwithstanding, where the whole family was waiting for him with a Union Jack on the flagpole, and an enormous chocolate cake with 'Welcome Home Grandad' iced onto it in white piping.

Theodore watched his grandfather dismount stiffly and remove his flying helmet and goggles. His hero had come properly into his life at last. He sat on the motorcycle, twisting the throttle grip, growling 'brrm brrm, brrm brrm' as the rest of the family fussed and chattered.

'I've got something to show you,' said Bertie. 'It'll only take a minute.'

Down in the garden of the cottage was Mac's old black A35. 'I got it for nothing,' said Bertie, as Daniel crouched down and attempted to look underneath. 'Mrs Mac just said you've got to take her for a ride when you've got it working. You'll probably have to take Mac's ghost as well.'

Daniel opened up the bonnet and looked at the engine. 'Weslake Series A,' he said 'That's a bonus. How happy I shall be.'

He settled into his quiet life in Gardener's Cottage. He had filled the sidecar of his Brough, bringing home from BC what few possessions he cherished. There was his old wind-up record player that played his 78s of Lily Pons and needed a new needle for each record, his tennis racket, his Louis L'amour novels, his collection of books about the North-West Frontier, those about aviation in the First World War, his militaria, including his Sam Browne and dress sword, his Davey Crockett raccoon-skin hat with its glass eyes and tail, his fur-lined boots and padded shirts, and his many books of photographs, each picture noted and dated in white ink on the thick black paper of the albums. Not least he had Archie's service pistol with the two boxes of rounds left over from his expeditions into the wood with Wavey Davey, which he had guiltlessly smuggled back into the country inside the spare tyre. He wished he had bought more ammunition in the USA on his journey back across America.

Those things he had not wanted he had given away to his friends in Hedley and Penticton, laying them out on a long trestle in the workshop.

For the Brough he and Bertie erected a wooden shed with a corrugated-iron roof, a large window on the south side, and a workbench at one end. On the side of that he made a lean-to for logs and kindling. He took a feed from the house and wired in a light socket and a power point.

One day when out on a jaunt over the Hog's Back, he passed the workshop of the pair of young mechanics who had set up Normandy Motorcycles, thereby making his first new friends in England, and finding the very people who could help him maintain his antiquated bike.

At about the same time, just down the road on the way to Abbott's Notwithstanding, he befriended the two brothers who had inherited their garage from their father, and they permitted him to come and use their machine tools in return for occasional help with particularly puzzling mechanical problems. These brothers maintained Miss Agatha Feakes's 1927 Swift Convertible, and in this way Daniel came to know his neighbour personally. Every night she would gather in her extraordinary menagerie of animals with cries of 'chuffy chuffy chuffy' that echoed across the entire village, reassuring its inhabitants that five o'clock had arrived, and that it was time to put on the kettle.

Somewhat late in life, Daniel Pitt became a fan of the television, although, like almost everybody else, he had first seen one in operation on the occasion of the coronation in 1953. He acquired a small black-and-white television with a heavily convex screen, which could receive both BBC and ITV.

He would switch it on at five o'clock to watch children's programmes such as *Crackerjack*, with Leslie Crowther and Peter Glaze, and he would switch it on to hear Billy Cotton yelling 'Wakey-wakey' at the beginning of the *Billy Cotton Band Show*. He liked the leggy showgirls in *The Black and White Minstrel Show*, and he loved *Mr Pastry*, *The Lone Ranger* and *Bronco*. He watched *Dr Kildare*, and *Z Cars*, and quite often could hardly get the signature tune out of his head for days at a time. Theodore had a terrible habit of whistling it out of tune.

In the school holidays the children would come down and they would settle in front of *Watch with Mother*, which they renamed 'Gawp with Grandad'. Every day you knew what it would be, beginning with *Picture Book* on Mondays. They all heartily despised *Andy Pandy*, but they loved *Tales of the Riverbank* and *The Woodentops*. After *The Flower Pot Men* they would talk Flobalob to each other for the rest of the day. Daniel loved having Jemima and the tiny Phoebe, one on each knee. It took him back to precious times with Esther, and Felix and Felicity.

It was Daniel who eventually taught Phoebe to read, as she sat with her thumb in her mouth following his finger along the text of her Ladybird books, learning to recognise whole words, and then whole phrases at a time, without ever having to learn how to break them down phonetically.

Daniel took to the television not least because he had begun to fall in love, over and over again. Ever since the emergence of the Beatles and the Rolling Stones, the country had come alive with vivacious and beautiful young people. He could not remember anything like it since the flappers of the twenties, except that now the fabulous hedonism had become democratised, and the children of the poor could also become famous and wealthy, throw away their money and behave outrageously.

Daniel fell in love with Julie Felix, and he watched *The Frost Report* not for its satire, but because she was the resident singer.

Subsequently she had her own show, and duetted with all sorts of young people he had never heard of. He had to buy a modern record player in Guildford, and ask Theodore to show him how to use it to play her first four LPs, which he had bought at the same time. He listened to *Changes* over and over again. Julie Felix was beautiful, and her voice was exquisitely pure. In 1968 he went out and bought her single 'Hey, That's No Way to Say Goodbye'. He had never heard a song with such beautiful words. He sang it to himself as he drove his motorcycle about the countryside, thinking of all the loves he had laid aside or lost, and hearing the pattern of the guitar in the back of his mind.

Above all, Daniel loved Jacqueline du Pré, whose playing of Elgar's famous cello concerto transformed it into an intensely exciting erotic experience. He had seen nothing like it since watching Josephine Baker dancing, once upon a night-time, a lifetime ago, in Berlin.

One night, on the Julie Felix show, he watched mesmerised as a handsome gypsy from the south of France, perfectly calm and brimming with arrogant self-confidence and charm, performed miracles of velocity, virtuosity and rhythmic complexity on a flamenco guitar. From then on Daniel was at Record Corner in Godalming, pestering Peter, the young assistant there, to alert him every time a new Manitas de Plata record was issued. At home he would sit bolt upright in his chair with his hands on his knees as Jose Reyes wailed out his Moorish joys and despairs, and Manitas improvised ever more strange variations of tempo and melody.

In the evenings Daniel would usually stroll the one hundred yards to his son's house, and eat with the family. Very often Bertie was not there. 'Working late', or 'At a meeting', Kate would say, with a hint of weary cynicism in her voice, and Daniel began to feel that it was incumbent upon him to have the time for the four children that their father did not.

He took Theodore to the West Surrey Golf Club, where they had lessons with Bob French. Daniel went to the White Elephant shop in Godalming and came back with enough hickory-shafted clubs to approximate to a set. He taught Theodore to play 1920s style, as he had been taught by his own father-in-law all those years ago in Eltham. Mr French tried to persuade him to buy steel shafts, but Daniel refused, eventually buying a short set of Peter Allisses for the boy, but quite comfortable himself with his antiques. One day Miss Agatha Feakes told him that in the cupboard under the stairs she still had a set of her father's clubs, and in the pocket of the crumbling old canvas bag he found some of the practice balls, short range, for use in the garden, which his father-in-law, Hamilton McCosh, had invented and marketed back in the twenties. The clubs, too, were of the kind favoured by the latter, made by Forgan at St Andrews. 'Daddy was mad about golf,' said Agatha. 'I've had all these old hickory-shafted clubs lying about, and I never had the heart to give them to the White Elephant.'

'My father-in-law was an avid golfer too,' said Daniel. 'He had several mistresses, and every one of them lived near to a golf course. I can't remember where they all were now. If you don't mind, I'd like to do these old clubs up and play with them. How much would you like for them?'

Agatha and Daniel sometimes had cups of tea together, and talked about the RAF. She had been engaged to a young pilot stationed at Dunsfold, called Alec, who used to come and do stunts above her house in a Gypsy Moth, throwing down rose stems. Daniel knew without asking that Alec must have been killed, and he talked to her about stunting Snipes, or Pups, or Camels. Aggie was mysterious about her origins, but finally she confided that she had inherited her house from her father, who had taken her mother as a mistress, back in the 1920s.

Daniel and Agatha sometimes went out in her Swift convertible, with her black-and-white goat on the back seat when it was being taken out to stud. Daniel liked to drive the old beast occasionally, and he was a useful man to have on board because he knew how to get it going when it broke down. They used to joke about getting married, if things got desperate, but Agatha was contented with her menagerie of animals that lived in the house, with its newspapers in place of carpets, and Daniel felt no attraction to her whatsoever. 'You're too young for me,' he would say, as they walked in her garden with her arm threaded through his. 'I need someone maturer.' Agatha was a fabulous eccentric, and her enormous breasts, flopping about, loose inside her home-knitted jumpers, were enough to dampen any sexual curiosity that he might have had left. In any case, he was back with Christabel now, contented to have her for his last and most enduring love.

He took Molly and Jemima to tennis lessons at Priorsfield, and to the county championships at Cranleigh, where neither of them ever got beyond the second round, because there was always an infuriating Home Counties tigress with a cut-glass accent who defeated them.

With little Phoebe he walked slowly, hand in hand on the common, making holes in the sand with his stick so that she could plant acorns, and at the Maclachlan bench she would sit on his knee as he pointed out over the birch trees to Blackdown where Tennyson used to live, and to Chanctonbury Ring, where there was a grove of trees frequented by covens of witches, darkened by decades of rumours of human sacrifice. In the autumn they collected blueberries, competing with squirrels and old ladies, and he made up stories about a man who could play tunes and conduct entire conversations by means of farts alone.

It would not be unjust to say that almost all of the children's mathematics homework was done by Daniel for a period of several years. Of the four children he was closest to Phoebe, the youngest, and Theodore, the oldest. To Molly and Jemima he was simply a daily feature of their landscape, but to Phoebe he was someone to love with all her heart, and to Theodore he was an extra father, but a father strangely more in tune with the times than his own.

One November the children decided to make a guy and collect pennies for it in Godalming High Street, but all their attempts at manufacture seemed doomed to failure. In the end they dressed their grandfather in his oldest clothes, stuffed straw up the cuffs, crammed an old straw hat on his head, dirtied his face with charcoal, smeared him with rouge and their mother's lipstick, hung their 'Penny for the Guy' notice round his neck, and made him sit on the pavement outside Woolworths. They collected four pounds eighteen shillings and sixpence, and a photograph made it into the *Surrey Advertiser* under the caption 'Ace Grandad Plays the Bad Guy'. Daniel used the money to buy rockets, Roman candles, firecrackers and jumping jacks, and they set them off on the night of 5th of November, in a light rain, having given up waiting for Bertie to come home.

One Saturday morning in the summer holidays when he was supposed to be babysitting, Daniel summoned the four children, telling them to pile into his A35. 'We're going to have some fun,' he said.

'What are we going to do?' asked Jemima.

'You'll see.'

As they drove up Wormley Hill they passed a cyclist who was struggling terribly against the slope, and Daniel said, 'We're on a mission of mercy. Whoever's in front pushes on this knob here, do you see? You do it just as we're passing someone. Right, Phoebe, are you ready? Just as we're passing. One, two, three, push!'

An arc of water shot out sideways and sprinkled the unsuspecting cyclist, who looked up into the sky.

'They always look up,' said Daniel. 'They never suspect that it's a prank.'

'What have you done, Grandad?' asked Theodore.

'I've turned the windscreen washers sideways.'

'My turn next!' cried Jemima.

'It's Phoebe until we get to Witley, then it's Molly until we get to Milford, and then it's Theo until we get to Godalming, and then it's Jemima. I can't have you scrambling over the seats and fighting with each other when I'm trying to creep up on cyclists.'

Outside King Edward's School Phoebe sprinkled the village bobby, slightly ridiculous in bicycle clips, who looked up with a puzzled expression, and then she caught a teenaged boy who was cycling with no hands on the bars. He too looked up into the sky.

Phoebe began to shake with laughter, and it quickly caught on, first with Molly, then with Theodore and Jemima. Soon they were all so doubled up with mirth that Phoebe cried, 'Oh, oh, I can hardly breathe! Oh! Oh! Oh!'

By the time they had reached Secretts Garden Centre they had scored seven victories, and Daniel had to pull into the side of the road because his own laughter was making it impossible to drive. At the roundabout near the bridge he had to pull in once more, and they all sat in the tiny black car howling and rolling, clutching their stomachs, crying, 'Oh God, oh God, oh God.' Then their last victim overtook them, so Daniel put the car into gear and Theo got him again. At that point they ran out of water, and Daniel had to refill the washer bottle in the public conveniences in the car park behind Waitrose. On the way home they scored twelve more cyclists, all of whom looked up into the sky.

Back in the driveway at Notwithstanding they had to remain in the car for five minutes, too exhausted to get out, their stomachs aching.

'Don't tell your mum and dad,' said Daniel.

When, in their forties, the children brought their families together for Christmas, they agreed that this was not only the best memory they had of their grandfather, but the best of all their memories. Daniel would probably have agreed.

In 1976 Concorde flew over the house for the first time, with a stupendous, apocalyptic roar. Daniel hastened outside, thinking that it was the end of the world, and was mesmerised. Every time he heard it in the coming years he would dash outside and gaze up. It was an inexhaustible wonder, and he longed to fly in it one day.

Bertie would not allow the children to watch *Top of the Pops* on Thursday evenings, because Jimmy Savile, with his hair half white and half black, and his nasal voice, seemed to him too unbearably creepy. He thought the pop bands were ridiculous in their costumes, their lyrics banal beyond belief, and their exhibitionist antics, gleefully recorded by the popular press, positively subversive. Daniel told him, 'If you think about it, ninety nine per cent of popular music has always been rubbish, and ninety-nine per cent of the stars mayflies. You need them just for the one per cent.'

'Well, they can watch it in your house, then,' said Bertie, 'you can put up with all that finger-snapping and those ridiculous yeah yeah yeahs and baby baby babies.' And so all five of them packed onto a sofa, with Phoebe on her grandfather's knee. His irrepressible chortling and his mockery of the absurdity of the whole show would irritate them to the point where the children would cry 'Gramps, you're spoiling it!' and Molly would go behind him and put her hands over his eyes, whilst Jemima put her hands over his ears. He would say, 'Just take them away when Pan's People come on. I love those girls. All this rubbish is worth it just for them.'

'You love all girls,' said Jemima.

'And it's right that I should,' said Daniel. 'It's my duty as an old soldier, an officer and a gentleman. And I'm half French.'

Jemima reached her teens when Theodore was seventeen, Molly was fifteen, and only Phoebe, at eight, was still sweet and un-troubled. It was at this time that Daniel's cottage became a refuge for the teenagers and their friends, who hijacked his record player and played Cream or Led Zeppelin because these were considered 'an infernal racket' and were not tolerated at home. He would limp home from a walk and find that his radio set had been retuned to Radio Caroline, London or Luxembourg. Theodore and his bell-bottomed, long-haired friends drank cider late at night in his motorcycle shed, and once he came home in the A35 to find a familiar smell wafting into his nostrils. He opened the door and said, 'Someone's smoking kif.' Four startled faces looked up at him, and he said, 'Haven't smelled that for years. Lovely smell. Are you sure it's allowed?'

'What's kif, man?' asked Theodore.

'It's what you're smoking,' said Daniel. 'We used to smoke it on the North–West Frontier in our time off. Everyone did. Makes you giggle and then makes you peckish. Is that the stuff?'

Theodore said, 'Please don't tell Mum and Dad.'

'What's it worth?' asked Daniel.

'I'll mow the lawn.'

'You don't have to smoke it, you know,' said Daniel. 'It's prob-ably better if you eat it. Then you don't wreck your lungs. It's no joke, emphysema. I know somebody who got emphysema and had to shoot himself. Why are you wearing that dishcloth round your head? You look like Geronimo.'

'It's not a dishcloth, Grandad, it's a bandanna.'

'Well, I suppose it would be useful if you need a rag quickly. Haven't you got any pockets?'

After Daniel had gone, one of Theodore's friends said, 'Your grandad's so cool and groovy. I thought he would have blown his lid. I kinda dig that he didn't.'

'Man, he's hip, he's the coolest,' said Theodore, in his new transatlantic drawl, 'but Dad, he's so uptight, it's unbelievable.'

In the autumn of that year Theodore was brought in by the police. Someone had altered the sign for the local swimming pool to 'Swim in Poo', and a giant poster for a Clint Eastwood film in Godalming had been cleverly altered so that the bottom line of the L was extended to the bottom of the I in order to form a U. Theodore had been spotted by a bobby on a bicycle, kneeling before the sign for CLINTERGATE, pulling off the same transformation with a wide felt tip.

As Bertie was at work, and Kate was going out for a WI meeting, it was Daniel who fetched Theodore from the police station. The latter was shaking, pale-faced and cowed, having been threatened not only with prosecution, but with shaming in the local press. Mostly he was terrified by the prospect of his father's inevitable, incandescent rage.

When Daniel arrived the policeman who had arrested him and brought him in took Daniel to one side and said, 'Quite the humorist, your little grandson, eh?'

'Are you going to charge him?'

'I'd rather not, sir. I quite enjoyed the joke, to tell the truth. We've all had a bit of a giggle, including the Super.'

'Even so …What shall we do then?'

'I suggest it's a matter for the family to deal with, sir. He's only a boy, and he's hardly a villain.'

Daniel said, 'What if he spends Saturday morning giving your cars a wash. How many have you got?'

'I dunno. About six or seven, sir. Sounds like a good idea to me.'

'Who needs magistrates?'

'You can say that again. Bloody magistrates.'

So it was that Daniel brought Theodore into Godalming on the following Saturday, armed with a bucket, a soft brush, some detergent and a chamois leather. The blue-and-white Morris Minors were sparkled up whilst Daniel went and had a cup of tea in Fleur's and did some early Christmas shopping. That afternoon they went fishing on the Wey, and as they sat side by side catching nothing whatsoever, they were able to converse freely without having to look each other in the eye, as men often do.

'I hope you realise you've made an idiot of yourself.'

'Yes, Grandad.'

'If you want to pull off stunts like that you should either have a lookout or do it under cover of darkness. And leave the engine of your motorcycle running. You could easily have escaped a constable on a bicycle if you'd had any forethought.'

'Oh,' said Theodore, who had been expecting to be upbraided yet again for his act of vandalism.

'And it wasn't very impressive, was it? It didn't amount to much, did it? Hardly on a par with flying upside down under a bridge in London on Empire Day.'

'No, Grandad. Grandad?'

'Yes?'

'Dad wants me to join the army.'

'Well, he would. He's that kind of man. He wants to make a man of you. And you and your friends do all seem to be dressed in military cast-offs. You've sewn proficiency badges and upside-down corporal's stripes onto your jeans. I take it that's just to annoy your father.'

'They're not cast-offs. It's called "army surplus", and it's swords into ploughshares. I don't want to kill anyone, Grandad. All that shouting and marching around...'

'And polishing things. If it moves, salute it, if it doesn't, polish it. What do you really want to do?'

'I want to be in a band.'

'You want to be a pop star? But you don't play anything.'

'I could be the singer.'

'But you can't sing in tune. And you're not pretty. And you've got muscles.'

'I could learn to sing. I could learn drums or something.'

'Well, you'd better get started soon or you'll end up in an office.'

'I don't want to work in an office, Grandad. I don't want to wear a suit and tie. It's so...you know...uncool.'

'Anyway, there's no point joining up in peacetime. It's a horrible dry run. It's all bull and pettiness. Only join up if there's a war on. Even then, you have to face up to certain things. One goes off to war full of romantic ideas about dying a hero's death.

244

Especially when young. Old soldiers know differently. I'd say, without knowing the actual numbers, that almost all the casualties of the Great War were from shellfire. Men just blown to bits. Old soldiers go to war knowing that their death is likely to be inglorious and ignominious. What if I teach you the fun things about being a soldier, like shooting a rifle and bivouacking in the mountains, and cooking up stews on a hexamine stove? You'd have to drop all this sitting about smoking kif and nodding your head in front of the gramophone, and talking bollocks about Buddha, that you hippies are so fond of. You need to get a knapsack on your back and learn to stride out.'

'I'm not a hippy, Grandad.'

'You all look like hippies to me. I had a terrible disappointment the other day. I was walking behind a slender blonde with lovely shining hair, and when I managed to pass her and look back, it was a gormless-looking boy with an overbite, and a failed beard, and bright red acne. It was even more of a disappointment than when I overtook a blonde in the passenger seat of an Austin Westminster, and when I looked back, it was an Afghan hound with a long black nose.'

'Grandad, if I dared you, would you grow sideburns? Just to wind up Mum and Dad. It'd be so far out, it'd be a gas.'

'You want me to look like that Engelbert Humperdinck that your mother's so in love with?'

'I dare you, Grandad.'

'Only if I can shave them off after a month. And on condition that you let me teach you soldierly things. You never know, there might be another war.'

'I'd refuse to fight, Grandad. I'm a pacifist.'

'No you're not. You only think you are. When a soldier comes through your door with the intention of cutting your balls off and raping your sisters, believe me, you suddenly stop being a pacifist.'

From the date of that conversation, Theodore and Daniel took to disappearing into various wildernesses in the school holidays, Theodore always struggling to keep up, but never giving in, inadvertently being prepared for the mountainous future that awaited him.

In the absence of a proper rifle, Daniel bought a BSA Airsporter in Jeffrey's of Guildford, and Theodore became such a good shot with it that he could hit a tin can tossed into the air. He was the only one in the family who knew that Daniel had an illicit revolver, and its heft became familiar to his hand. All his life he would remember going with his grandfather to the centre of the Hurst, and being allowed to fire one shot with it. He would never forget the shock of the recoil as it leapt in his hand, the sliver of bark flying off the oak tree he had skimmed, the whine of the ricochet, and his grandfather saying, 'That's probably the last time this gun will ever fire a shot, unless I have no choice.'

In the summer Theodore would come down with his father's lawnmower and be paid to cut the lawn around the house. Daniel took him bivouacking in the woods, trekking for miles with a backpack, cooking up compo rations on hexamine, in mess tins. When Theodore was old enough, Daniel took him to Normandy Motorcycles beneath the Hog's Back, and helped him choose an old 175cc BSA Bantam that was being sold for fifteen pounds. It was only a stopgap until the boy passed his test, and could move up to a 250, and it was not a great success. At least once a week Theodore would find himself wheeling it down the lane for his grandfather to deal with when it broke down.

It was a terrible machine, copied from a pre-war German model, pitifully underpowered, with an electrical system carefully designed to go wrong as often as possible. Theodore would spend hours kicking it over and failing to start it, raging with frustration. Daniel would remove the spark plug and clean it, and more often than not it would start up, throwing out clouds of aromatic blue smoke. One day Theodore tried it himself and overtightened the spark plug, stripping the thread, so that the cylinder lost compression and would hardly go at all. When Theodore finally graduated to cars, it was in Mac's restored A35 that he passed his test in Guildford.

One summer evening, having sworn him to secrecy, Daniel showed Theodore how to construct a bomb out of sugar and fertiliser, and then they hacked their way through the brambles to the centre of the Hurst, excavated a hole, and blew a dead oak tree out of the ground. It was the most spectacular thing that

246

Theodore had ever seen. They came home, a couple of outlaws, exhilarated and gleeful, but they never repeated the exploit, as if one such transcendent illegality were sufficient for a lifetime.

Daniel kept himself fit by walking immense distances every day, as if he was incapable of renouncing the habits of his days on the North-West Frontier. He would call in at the house and collect Calypso, the family's collie bitch, ever desperate for exercise, otherwise condemned to frustrated hours of attempting to round up the cat. By walking the dog he came to know all the surrounding countryside, from the Hurst, where Polly Wantage, the heroine of English ladies' cricket, dressed as a man in plus fours, liked to go and shoot squirrels with a twelve-bore, to Sweetwater, the silent and lifeless double lake near Witley, fringed with rhododendrons, where he would exhaust Calypso by throwing sticks into the water for her to fetch. He became a common sight, swinging his walking stick as he strode briskly past the council houses in Cherryhurst in his walking boots.

In the summer he dressed like a Pathan tribesman, and in the winter like a Canadian backwoodsman. He would tuck the cuffs of his trousers into his chequered socks, and was invariably in corduroys and padded shirts, the raccoon-skin hat on his head, the tail hanging down behind his back. He had never felt fitter or happier in his life, and nobody thought him eccentric, because in the English countryside you may be as eccentric as you like, and everybody else is as odd as you are. Besides, if you are a famous fighter ace, you have earned the right to dress as a Canadian in winter, and have gypsy music rattling your windows in the summer.

Daniel's cottage was at the end of a dirt track that led to a field, and on most days a herd of Friesians came lowing by, going either in or out of it. He loved their dungy smell, and the way that in cold weather they breathed great clouds of steam. He was not so keen on what their leavings did to the wheels and mudguards of his motorcycle, however, and he kept a hose permanently attached to the outside tap by the front door.

Every now and then Daniel would make an Indian buffet for the family and for his friends. It was the only cuisine that truly interested him, because it took him back to his days in India, but even at the turn of the seventies it was very hard to obtain many of the spices and main ingredients, and there were no Indian cookery books either. Even in his precious *Je Sais Cuisiner* that he had bought in Caen, the sole advice for making curry was to use curry powder. Accordingly, he was regularly sent bags of spices and lentils from Delhi by his old comrade Daljit Singh Bittu Khalistan, and then, after his death, by one of his sons. One year, in celebration of the festival of Hola Mohalla, Daljit sent him a proper housewives' cookbook in parallel text, whose English was so preposterously garbled and picturesque that he would spend happy hours in his armchair chortling over it. Daniel's *tour de force* was a duck hyderabadi so fiery with chilli that he would dare people to have more than one mouthful, and then to the astonishment of those spluttering and flushing from its cumulative effect, he would polish it all off himself. The only people who truly appreciated it were Frederick and Ottilie, who liked to compare it unfavourably to the milder fare in Madras.

48

Christabel and Daniel

Towards the middle of June 1970, whilst the country was in the throes of a general election that would unexpectedly bring Edward Heath to power, Daniel received a mysterious letter from Christabel, asking to meet him in London, so he rang her immediately at her house in Hexham. All she would say was: 'I have to talk to you.'

Daniel and Christabel loved each other as only old lovers can, old lovers who have been prevented by circumstance from being together too much or too little. Daniel was still occasionally pricked by the shame of having had two children by his wife's sister, but it was a shame that he was certain was undeserved, borne in upon him only by the knowledge of what the world would think of him if it knew. In his heart he was convinced he had done nothing wrong. He often thought back to the time when he had flown north with Gaskell in an Avro 504, only to be told after dinner that she and Christabel were desperate for children and wanted him to be the father, because they loved him and could ask no one else. His marriage had been dead on its feet for years, in any case.

He had resisted at first, but now what did he have to regret? He and Christabel had remained lovers intermittently for decades, always knowing that they could turn to each other. She had been able to continue her life with Gaskell, who was the lodestar of her life, and the two children, Felix and Felicity, had brought joy to all three of them. Only Daniel had come out of it with any sorrow, because the children had been told that they had been adopted in France and that he was only their godfather. When he thought of the delightful times with them when they were tiny, before the war, and he was returning every month from Germany on his motorcycle, he still felt the pangs of pain in his gut as he left them once more to return to Dortmund. How strange it was now to reflect that Felix was forty-two years old, Felicity forty, and he hardly ever saw either of them. Felix was still 'playing the field' as he liked to put it, and Felicity was still in Hong Kong. In her most recent letter she had said that they might be posted to Singapore.

Daniel met Christabel for tea in the RAF Club, in Piccadilly. He remembered the early twenties, when it had been the Royal Flying Corps Club, in Bruton Street, and he had baulked at the three guineas membership fee. Christabel was already there when he arrived. She was sitting very upright in one of the comfortable chairs in the foyer, and rose to her feet when he entered. She was still ageing well, a tall and elegant English rose, albeit a grey-haired one, with a slight stoop, but recently she had become much too thin.

He said, 'My dear, you're looking marvellous, as ever,' but he knew by the way that she clung to him that something was terribly wrong. She clasped him too tightly, and her hands were trembling as they pressed against the small of his back.

'Can we ask for a private room, to talk in?' she asked.

In a small office whose walls were hung with hyperrealistic paintings of Bristol Beauforts and de Havilland Mosquitoes with anti-aircraft fire bursting about them, Christabel asked him to pour the tea, and looked at him sorrowfully.

'I'm afraid I've got nothing but bad news.'

'Oh dear, I am sorry.'

Christabel sipped at her tea, and her eyes welled up. 'First of all Puss has just died. We've buried him under the redwood, and there's going to be a big slab on it, and we've commissioned a sculptor to make a full-size bronze of him, to sit on it.'

'But what did he die of?'

'Well, you know, he was getting terribly old. He just got thinner and thinner and weaker and weaker, and he almost stopped eating altogether. In the end he could hardly heave himself upright.'

'He did look rather ragged when I was there last month. Poor old Puss, he'd lost quite a few teeth, hadn't he?'

'Anyway, we were thinking we would have to have him put down. In fact I was thinking of asking you to come up and shoot him.'

'I certainly wouldn't have. It would bring back too many horrible memories.'

'Really? What of?'

'We used to have to shoot airmen who were burning to death in a crash. We called them "flamerinos". No choice. I even had to shoot a friend once. I still dream about it, and wake up in a sweat.'

'Well, anyway, Puss died on his own, during the night. Gaskell and I are devastated, as you can imagine. He made up for the children leaving home.'

'You didn't think of making him into a rug, or having him mounted?'

'We used to joke about doing that, but when it came down to it we loved him too much for that. We just laid him to rest.

'I've been wondering,' she continued, 'what it would have been like for us to have spent our lives together. You know, if you hadn't married Rosie, and if Gaskell hadn't come along when she did.'

'Obviously, I've often wondered the same thing,' he replied.

'I think we both missed out,' said Christabel.

'Of course we did, but we had other things instead, some of them well worth having, don't you think? I mean, haven't you had a wonderful life with Gaskell?'

'Oh, Daniel, it's all going to be over soon. After she's gone I just don't know what I'll do.'

'After she's gone?'

'It's the Parkinson's. We used to get long periods when nothing much seemed to be happening, but recently it's been getting worse and worse. It's accelerating. Every day is more awful than the day before. There's no mistaking it. We're getting to the end, and I'm absolutely helpless and don't know what to do next.'

'Have the shakes got worse?'

Christabel nodded. 'Everything has. Her face has lost all expression, and her eyebrows have gone up her forehead and stayed there. It's like a strange mask, one of those Greek ones from a chorus. Her hands shake all the time, and you know, she can't stop rolling her thumbs and forefingers together, as if she's playing with a dried pea. She can't paint at all now the brush isn't going where she wants it to. You know how precise her painting's always been; she never gave up on being a meticulous draughtsman even when it fell out of fashion and people just started sloshing paint about.'

'She must have been devastated to be forced to give up painting,' said Daniel. 'I had no idea it had got so bad.'

'Her head nods up and down, and her hands jerk…like this. And she's started to walk in a very strange way, all cramped up and hurried, her head bent forwards, and her arms out sideways. It looks as if she's trying to catch her balance all the time. Now she can't sit peacefully because her legs keep kicking out. It's so violent, you'd think she was mad, but she's not. She's completely sane, and she's suffering unbearably. She has not a shred of dignity left.'

'Is it fatal? I suppose it must be.'

'The doctor says that it causes you to die of something else, or you just die of exhaustion. Anyway, she's completely given up. She's utterly miserable and hopeless, and just wants to pack it in. I've never known anyone to be so depressed. There's no cure for it. There's no treatment even. We tried something called hyoscine, but it made no difference. I've had to hide the key to the gun cupboard. Not that she'd stand a chance of loading a gun, in her state. She's obviously going to die soon anyway.'

Daniel leaned forward and took her hand. 'Poor old Green-Eyed Monster,' he said softly. 'Do you remember how your father adored her green eyes?'

'Her eyes are still beautiful,' said Christabel. 'Her eyes are still green.' She began to weep silently, her shoulders heaving. 'Oh, Daniel,' she said. 'Daniel, Daniel, Daniel.'

After a while she lifted her head and fumbled in her handbag for a handkerchief. She wiped her eyes and dabbed at her nose. She looked at him gravely. 'I want to talk to you about the children.'

'Felix and Felicity?'

'Mmm, yes. We've decided that we're going to leave the house to the National Trust. It's in a ghastly state of repair. It's going to cost a fortune to restore it. All the window frames and sashes are rotten, and the lead on the roof needs replacing, and the beams in the cellar have been shredded by death-watch beetle. Even the chimney pots are loose. And paying the inheritance tax in any other way would be a complete impossibility. And there's another thing; as you know, the house was built on the proceeds of slavery all those years ago. We think we should just give it away. We've always thought so.'

'Atonement?'

'Yes, atonement.'

'What about Felix and Felicity?'

'We're asking the National Trust to let them continue to live there, if they ever want to. But of course Felix has his company in Harrogate, and I rather doubt that Felicity will ever come home. They'll get our money and our photographs and our paintings. They'll have plenty to get along with. Gaskell and I did very well for an awful long time, you know.'

'I know you did. You deserved to. You were the best of your generation.'

'We weren't. But we weren't bad either. Now we're just old hat.'

'You'll come back into fashion. Of course you will.'

'Oh, I do have just one tiny bit of good news. You know the three biplanes in the barn, the ones you bought when you came back from Ceylon?'

'Yes, I feel so sorry for them. They've been past redemption for years.'

'But they're not. The Imperial War Museum actually wants to buy them from us. They're going to restore them. They were terribly impressed by the fact that they belonged to you and Gaskell. It makes them doubly "historic" apparently.'

'Good Lord! Once upon a time they were two a penny and seemed so modern, and now they're museum pieces, just like us.'

'About Felix and Felicity . . .'

'Yes?'

'After I'm gone I leave it to you as to whether or not you tell them about us. That you're their father. They suspect anyway. They always have. The questions they used to ask! "Why do we look like Uncle Daniel, and Bertie and Esther?"'

'What do you mean, after you've gone? After Gaskell dies, would you like me to move up to Hexham? For the companionship, if nothing else?'

Christabel looked at him, her eyes brimming with tears, and said 'Oh, Daniel, darling, I would have loved it. I did ask you years ago, but now it's too late.'

'Too late?'

'I'm ill too.' She put her hand to her diaphragm, and said, 'Cancer, just like poor Rosie. But it's gone inside.'

'But Rosie got through it.'

'I won't though. I didn't even know I was ill until it was much too late.'

'How long have you got?'

'Months.'

'Why didn't you tell me before?'

'I felt perfectly well until a month ago, and now it's too late.'

'I'll come up and look after you. You can't possibly manage on your own.'

'But you're down here. We're all in our seventies. You've made up with Bertie, and you've got your grandchildren practically living with you.'

'I may be seventy-eight,' said Daniel, 'but I'm still perfectly well and fit. I'm probably fitter than Bertie is. And I can spare a few months for someone I love.'

'You're so sweet,' said Christabel. 'I was right to love you as I did. In the end, the love is all one has left. Sometimes only the memory of it.'

He said, 'I always found you very beautiful.'

She shook her head. 'I've never been beautiful. Only attractive.'

He stood and went to the window. 'When you love someone they become beautiful. To be loved for your beauty in advance of being known is to be loved in ignorance. But in the end I don't mind whether I loved you for your beauty, or you became beautiful because I loved you. I'll come up and stay, just to help you keep things ticking over. A couple of weeks at a time, perhaps? But when the time comes … if I'm not there … if you know it's any minute...please try to let me know, because I would like to be with you.'

'Yes, come up and stay. It'll be too depressing for you, but Gaskell and I would love it, and it's just impossible coping with her on my own now that I'm ill myself. I haven't got the energy, and it's too miserable for words. But you know, being with us, with me, at the end, may not be possible. Sometimes all I can do is sit and weep. We'll see when the time comes.'

49

Shetland

Gaskell had occasionally flown aircraft into Sumburgh airfield when she was an Attagirl in the Air Transport Auxiliary. The first one had been a Gloster Gladiator, the second had been a Blenheim for No. 254 Squadron, and the last had been a Hurricane for No. 3. She had often stayed there for days at a time, either trapped by foul weather or waiting for transport back to England, and so she knew the mainland very well indeed. She had spent happy hours in the reconnaissance photography hut, learning the ropes out of sheer curiosity, and had travelled all over Shetland in borrowed vehicles. She loved the vivid banks of fiery crocosmia that grew so abundantly in defiance of the weather, seemingly the only flower that could thrive, just as the stunted and bent sycamore was the only tree.

She had once driven up to the lighthouse at Eshaness, and wondered at the stupendous chasm nearby, a great gash cut into the land by the sea. She was told that it had been a gigantic cave in the volcanic rock, whose roof had collapsed due to the pressure of the surging seawater. About its vertical walls flew the fulmar, and out at sea the porpoises and seals dipped in the waves. It was the vertiginous verticality of the drop, as well as its great height, that had most impressed Gaskell back in 1942, and she had always wanted to return.

It was difficult for the two women to travel at all these days. Gaskell's movements were so spasmodic and unpredictable, and her face so strange, that people assumed she was either drunk or a freak. Christabel was gravely weakened, ashen-faced from the lancinating pains that shot through her body and sometimes made her double over, leaving her unable to breathe.

It was September, Daniel had gone back home for a few days, and they had taken the opportunity to come on the ferry to Lerwick from Aberdeen, because, although it took very much longer than flying, it seemed easier, and Gaskell had said, 'I've always wanted to see Fair Isle from a boat rather than from the air.'

A solitary gannet had accompanied the ship all the way from Aberdeen, riding its wake and enjoying the warmth of the air from its funnel. They joked that it was their own modest version of the albatross in *The Rime of the Ancient Mariner*. Now that they had made their minds up, they felt very much more light-hearted.

They had booked for two nights into the Queen's Hotel on Charlotte Street, anticipating that they would need only one of them. They stayed entirely in their room, so as not to embarrass the other guests, and in the morning Christabel dressed Gaskell in her trademark plus fours, tie and Norfolk shooting jacket, and put her favourite brogues on her feet. She brushed her short white hair, slicking it with pomade, as Gaskell liked, and lighting a Black Russian, she offered it up to Gaskell's lips until it had burned down to the filter. 'There,' she said. 'You look quite your old self.'

They hired a Ford Escort saloon from the car hire by the docks, and made a point of telling the owner that they were going to Eshaness Lighthouse. At a letter box along the way Christabel posted him a cheque for fifty pounds, to 'cover the inconvenience'.

As Christabel drove, Gaskell looked once again at the wild and bare landscape that had thrilled her in wartime, and tried not to let her uncontrollable gestures throw Christabel's concentration. Even so, they had to stop in Brae, where Christabel gently tied Gaskell's right wrist to a cord that she attached with a loop to the left-hand door handle, because otherwise it was too difficult to change gear.

At Eshaness Lighthouse Christabel stopped the car, but left the keys in the ignition. She turned to Gaskell and said, 'Well, darling, are we sure that we are doing the right thing?'

Gaskell said nothing, because there was nothing to be said, and in any case she was unable to say it, so Christabel got out and helped disentangle her from the vehicle and from her own limbs. She took Gaskell's arm and said, 'It's not far. Just across the turf. I'm sure we can manage it.'

It had been raining earlier that day, with a vicious horizontal east wind, but now it had calmed to a stiff breeze. The clouds had drifted apart, and the sky had brightened.

Leaning upon each other, the two elderly women faltered and stumbled their way across the wet sward to the edge of the abyss. Gaskell could only shuffle four inches at a time, and during the long, painful progress to the cliff edge, the thought occurred to her that this would be her last flight. She remembered the three old aeroplanes she had shared with Daniel, still rotting in a barn at her estate in Hexham, and told herself that she was perhaps more airworthy these days than they were. Every few seconds, she fell into a paroxysm of flailing and shaking, and Christabel was struck frequently, and hard. 'I'm sorry, I'm sorry, I'm sorry' was all that Gaskell could mutter as her body disobeyed her.

As they stood on the clifftop Christabel watched the fulmar for a little while, and said, 'What a beautiful day this is. Thank God the tide's in.'

She turned and embraced Gaskell, whispering urgently in her ear. 'I love you, my darling. I've loved living with you. What fun we've had. Thank you for my beautiful life. Thank you for everything.' She drew back and kissed her softly on the lips. She remembered when their lips had been not dry and cracked as they were now, but moist, and warm, and passionate.

Gaskell returned her gaze, her huge green eyes brimming with tears. 'It's a pity we couldn't have been married,' she said.

'It wouldn't have made any difference,' said Christabel. She looked at Gaskell's beloved face, frozen into its strange mask by the terrible disease, and in turn Gaskell looked at Christabel, much too thin, with the frightened face of someone who suffers excruciating pains that arrive without warning. She knew that inside the clothing that hung loosely about her, the flesh bore the wide, livid scars of operations upon cancers that had proved inoperable.

'I loved your body so much,' she said.

'And I yours,' said Christabel.

'Now they've turned against us.'

'Well, my darling, we don't need them any more.'

'It's a shame we couldn't tell Daniel. Or the children.'

'They would have tried to stop us.'

Gaskell coughed, and choked. The wind gusted, and she went into spasm, stepping violently sideways, her arms pumping like pistons. This accident meant that no final decision had to be made. They fell together, perfectly parallel, in an ecstasy of terror and regret, until, moments later, their lives were snuffed by an impact so unimaginably violent that their extinction was instantaneous.

After two days the man from Lerwick came to look for his car and found the note on the driver's seat, in which Christabel had laid out details of why they had done as they had, and who to contact, with a request that no attempt be made to search for their bodies. 'We are content to be swallowed by the sea and by the creatures in it,' she had written.

He went to the edge of the chasm and gazed down into it for a few moments. Then he reached into the breast pocket of his jacket and drew out his wallet. He took Christabel's cheque from it, read it, and then held it aloft before releasing it into the east wind. Like a small flimsy bird it twisted and rose out over the ocean, soaring ever higher into the darkening western sky.

Back in Surrey, Daniel received a long, heavy parcel on the same day. It contained two twelve-bore shotguns and a note from Christabel, written in a shaky discursive hand.

My darling,

I am so sorry to have deceived you. We had no choice but to take advantage of your absence. You would have tried to stop us.

Gaskell wanted you to have her Purdeys. She thinks you are probably the one person who would appreciate them the most, being an old warrior. I expect it's illegal to send shotguns through the post, and I don't even know if you have a licence, but honestly, in my condition everything is permitted, isn't it? Who is going to haul me up before a magistrate, after all?

You and I were lovers, on and off, for so many years, and I do think that if it had not been for Gaskell and Rosie we would have made a happy married couple. As it is, I have you to thank for our two beautiful children, and Felicity's children too, and for them I do thank you with every fibre of my being. Watch over them, as I know you always have, and I know I don't even have to ask. Thank you too for so many days and nights of fun and pleasure, such that it is hard to imagine that anyone else has ever known the like. Of course they must have, but all the same I know that, during my patches of good luck, I have been more than lucky.

Death is the fulfilment of life, is it not? Didn't we all learn that when we Pals went off to war? We who survived had so much time to fill out with life. It was all a wonderful bonus if you think about it, and we did use our time well. I am trying not to be bitter about this dreadful unravelling that concludes it.

I have loved you all my life, and if I can I will love you after it as well. Gaskell loved you too. All three of us, we loved so well, didn't we?

Farewell, my old love,
Your Christabel

Kate was eventually to find this letter in Daniel's desk when she was sorting out his affairs for probate, along with many more of Christabel's letters, going back six decades. She hesitated for a few weeks, before deciding to tell Felix and Felicity that, just as everyone had always suspected, they had never been orphans, abandoned in France before the war.

50

Theodore Leaves Home

There seemed to be a general assumption that Theodore would go to university, even though no one else in the family had done so within living memory, and he fell in with this without questioning it, because he was mainly interested in not having to settle down to a proper job. In 1975 it was still not obvious that young people's ideas about 'the alternative society' were a will-o'-the-wisp, and it was yet possible to think that all you needed was to grow your hair long, wear scruffy clothes, go and lie in mud at free rock festivals for days at a time, and then the world would be blissful and peaceful, and no one would have to knuckle down and earn a living. Theodore, full of bourgeois shame in this new era when one's heroes had to be working class, affected a London accent, and obtained a job with the council, emptying the bins, whilst continuing to live with his prosperous family in their large house in Notwithstanding. Bertie was proud that his son was showing himself capable of such heavy labour, but appalled by the lowliness of the job and his workmates.

The latter spotted his fraudulence immediately, and gently mocked him for it. 'Seeing how the other half lives, are you?' they would say. 'Slumming it for a bit?' He asked his mother to stop putting prawns or cress in his sandwiches, and tried to acquire the habit of using 'fuckin'' as his only adjective. When he came home in the evenings, exhausted and stinking of rotten food, Jemima and Molly would dance round him singing, 'My old man's a dustman, he wears a dustman's hat, he wears cor-blimey trousers and he lives in a council flat.'

After he was fired for persistent lateness for work at the depot in Godalming, caused by the terrible ignition system on his fourth-hand BSA Bantam, he worked for Freemantles, delivering sacks of coal which he poured with a satisfyingly thunderous rumble down the wooden chutes into coal bunkers and cellars. If the Bantam broke down, it was still not too far to cycle to the coal yard, which was conveniently next to the pub.

This pub took great pride in having no pride. On the Petworth Road it had mounted a small hoarding advertising Warm Beer and Lousy Food. On its ceiling it had pinned a varicoloured collection of lacy panties donated by inebriated lady customers who had lost bets with the landlord or exchanged them for alcohol. In the garden was a pyramid of large rounded pebbles, the collection of a huge Alsatian dog with blunted teeth, who had become so obsessed with accumulating them that sometimes customers would bring them to him as presents. The landlord was the only Labour voter in the village, and was considered to be either mad or evil by the village's Conservatives and its one family of Liberals. In the public bar old men would sip pints with their shotguns leaned up against the wall, their dogs sighing with boredom under the tables.

But Theodore and his workmates had to drink their pints out in the yard; even the Merry Harriers could not allow folk in who gleamed with coal dust from head to foot.

Thereafter he found work on a pig farm, and would come home each evening smelling so appalling that Kate would make him undress outside before she would allow him into the house, even when it was raining.

After a few months the family considered that Theodore was squandering his gap year, and he himself was questioning his commitment to being working class. Then, one day, his father spotted an advertisement in the small print of the *Daily Telegraph*.

Wanted: schoolteacher for remote Andean town. Vacancy owing to earthquake and sudden increase in population. Numerous children of all ages. No qualifications necessary, but must be able to teach every subject to a high standard. Wage minimal. Board and lodging free. Contract renewable annually. Must be tough and resourceful with good sense of humour. Must be educated. Must learn to speak Castilian PDQ.

Bertie, who was by now thoroughly alarmed and irritated by his son's futurelessness and woolly Marxism, showed the advertisement to Theodore, and said, 'Just what you need. Travel broadens the mind, and all that.'

'I don't speak Spanish,' said Theodore.

'You can bloody well learn it, then,' said Bertie.

Three weeks later Theodore found himself in Aldeburgh on the Suffolk coast, having taken eight hours to get there on his reluctant motorcycle. He was three hours late, and by the time he found the cottage he was looking for, he was thoroughly demoralised, and shaking from fatigue.

He was met at the door by a bearded ginger-haired man in his forties, with bandy legs, salacious eyes and capacious pot belly, whose greeting, in a very slow Cambridge University drawl, was 'Not exactly *a la hora británica*, are you?'

'I'm sorry?'

'I mean you're damned late. You should fit in well in the Andes. How tough are you?'

'I don't know,' said Theodore.

'Ever been in a war? Can you use a revolver?'

'I've got an air rifle. I've shot a revolver once.'

'Piffle piffle air riffle. You're quite good-looking. I dare say the girls would like you. How are you with girls?'

'Well, I don't know. I mean . . .'

'Well, let's go down to the beach. I'll fetch you a towel.'

'We're going swimming? But it's November. And it's raining.'

'You have to be tough for Cochadebajo. It's no picnic.'

'But isn't it tropical? Won't it be hot?'

'Not at that altitude. At ten thousand feet you have be tough. At fifteen thousand feet you have to be even tougher.'

Down on the windswept beach the ginger-haired man stripped completely naked. His circumcised penis was at least eight inches long, even in that cold, and Theodore felt mortally ashamed by the obvious comparison with his own. The owner of this hyperbolical appendage waded out into the terrifying surf, and then plunged through an oncoming wave. Theodore felt that somehow he had no will to resist.

Appalled by the bone-breaking, freezing temperature of the sea, Theodore waded and then swam out to join his prospective employer. 'This'll get the dingleberries out,' said the latter, his eyes swivelling.

'Dingleberries?'

'Dingleberries are the little balls of fluff that that appear in one's underwear, and sometimes entwine themselves in one's pubic hair. Frequently they are of a grey colour and woolly texture. Shall we get out now? You seem to be tough enough, but it worries me that you don't know how to use a revolver.'

'I'm a pacifist,' said Theodore feebly. 'As I said, I have fired one once.'

'No one's a pacifist when someone's about to bugger their goat. My name is Emmanuel, by the way. Everybody calls me Don Emmanuel. When you get to Cochadebajo de los Gatos everyone will call you Don Teodoro, probably. Do you like cats?'

'Yes. Mostly. We've got two, and my grandmother used to have hundreds.'

'What about huge cats? The size of a mastiff? Would you be all right with them? It wouldn't give you asthma or anything?'

'Are they friendly?'

'Exceptionally. And they smell of strawberries. Are you a limp-wristed, molly-coddled feebleton mother's boy, or do you want the job?'

'Yes,' said Theodore doubtfully. 'I mean yes, I want the job.'

'You're the only one who's applied,' said Don Emmanuel.

And so it was that two weeks later Theodore returned from the embassy in London with a polyaetic, flamboyant visa in red and gold, glued into the back pages of his passport, and a fortnight after that found himself in Barranquilla Airport trying to use a telephone box whose instructions were in Castilian, and for which he had no coins.

He had never flown before, and had spent the entire flight gazing with rapture at the clouds below, effulgent with reflected sunlight. Before leaving, Daniel had given him an Agfa 126 that made an impressive clopping noise when the red button was pressed, and by the time that he arrived he had filled an entire film cassette with pictures of clouds. It was unknown to him that once upon a time the vista of sunlit clouds from above had enraptured his grandfather in the early years of aerial war.

In Barranquilla the wet heat came down on him like a blanket of steam, and he thought that somehow he must find his way home even if he had to swim the Caribbean and the Atlantic. He stood in the telephone booth with his head against the partition, sweating torrentially in the unimaginable heat, and began to weep.

Somebody tapped him on the shoulder, and he turned to see a small brown man in a colourful printed shirt, wide belt and tight trousers, looking up at him anxiously. '*Hey, gringo,*' he said. '*Que tal? Te puedo ayudar?*'

So it was that he found himself being looked after by a complete stranger with a Welsh name who spoke no English at all, who put him next morning onto a plane to Valledupar. It was an antique Avianca Dakota that wended its way between the sierras because it lacked the horsepower to fly above them. He was served orange juice in a foam cup that began to dissolve as he drank, by an air hostess in bright red uniform, even down to her lipstick, who tottered about on high heels as the turbulence of the mountain draughts threw her from one side of the cabin to the other.

In Valledupar he was collected by another stranger who took him to a dusty suburb where they watched a television whose programming consisted solely of gradually ascending parallel grey bars, interspersed with sudden fragments of rapid speech. His genial host laughed uproariously at what he must have taken to be a comedy.

In the morning he was sent to a small settlement at the foot of the Sierra Nevada de Santa Martha on an over-engineered Russian jeep with a dozen people hanging off the sides. Amongst the cargo of stocky Indians and black campesinos with their broad-brimmed straw hats and sparkling gold teeth was a pale-skinned black woman with large freckles and ginger hair, a *Zamba*, such as he would never have imagined to exist.

Caught up in this vivid dream, without any possibility of escape or understanding, Theodore gave in and swam with the hypnogogic, fantastical flow of an alternative reality.

In Attanques, a tiny village of howler monkeys and stray dogs in the Andean foothills, he slept in a hammock under an open straw shelter and ate dried salted fish for the first time. In the morning he awoke to the sound of running water and the fanatic cries of tropical birds. Then he walked uphill for three days with a party of wispy-bearded Kogi with Asiatic faces, apparelled in white linen, whose calf muscles bulged like thighs. They wore sandals cut from car tyres, and bore long muskets left behind by conquistadors. They carried coca leaves in the white bags that the women made for them, and pounded them with snail shells in *poporo* gourds, sucking the paste off the pestles. Their mules and donkeys plodded beside them companionably, laden with slaughtered sheep, ammunition and prodigious bunches of green bananas. Theodore ate yams with the texture of cotton wool that tasted of nothing, and guinea pigs roasted on spits. At five thousand feet they came across a demented dog, stumbling in circles. One of the Kogi made great ceremony of loading his musket with powder, ball and wad, took easy aim and shot it.

They passed through a village of straw huts arranged around a flat green, and Theodore caught a glimpse of what life might have been like in the original Garden of Eden. There was one large round hut, and in the exact epicentre of this hut, unbeknown to him, sat a holy man on a stool. This sage had trained in the darkness of a cave for nine years when he was child, and now that he was attuned to the universe, was altruistically devoting his life to maintaining its equilibrium.

At first the vegetation was tropical, alive with butterflies and iridescent with hummingbirds. At greater altitude it became sparse, until it resembled a Japanese garden constructed of stones, and only vast sinister condors wheeled overhead, ever watchful for a useful death. At the side of the stony path stood the remains of ancient buildings, their stones of strangely various sizes, but all perfectly keyed to each other, as though they had once been malleable, slotted together, and later set hard.

After two days' ascent, it became icy; Theodore felt his head pounding, and nausea rising in his guts and throat. He struggled to breathe, frequently clutching at the side of his head, pressing the heels of his hands into his temples. *Soroche*, said the Kogi to each other. The younger brothers always get *soroche*. They don't know that to get rid of it, all you have to do is fuck. Jagged white peaks rose above him into brilliant blue skies that would suddenly cloud over until it was so foggy that he might as well have been on Dartmoor.

During this extraordinary journey, Theodore saw not one woman or child, even in the villages of circular huts. Not once did any of the Kogi say a word to him. What might they have said? What can one say to the younger brothers who do not know that their elder brothers, the Jaguar People, are the survivors of a great civilisation that used to hang gold artefacts upon themselves and upon trees, just for the prettiness of it? What would be the point of telling a younger brother that this is the centre of the universe, and that the mountain he calls Cristobal Colon is really Gonawandua, the very epicentre of the nine-layered world which is both a uterus and an egg? The younger brother does not know that he is the estranged child of Aluna, and that she is the Great Earth Mother, and how will he ever understand that the universe is a system of complementary opposites whose dualisms resolve into systems of fours? The younger brother is a poor, ignorant, pitiable creature who is frightened of death, because he does not know that he will be reborn nine days after it. In the few days of this expedition, there will not be enough time to educate him, so there is no point in talking. He will receive only the same kindness that one might bestow upon a donkey.

At last, when Theodore was beginning to think that this protracted, alien dream could not become more mysterious, they came over a crest of scree, and in the valley a thousand feet below them he beheld an ancient stone city with smoke rising up from its fires. Coming up the slope towards them on a small bay horse was Don Emmanuel. Behind him, with a detached but purposeful air, padded the largest pair of yellow-eyed black cats he had ever seen.

'Welcome to Cochadebajo de los Gatos,' drawled Don Emmanuel as he drew level, 'our wondrous city of unmitigated fornication.'

As Theodore descended the slope into that reclaimed and regenerated stone metropolis of fugitives from the savannah, his heart rose up inside him, and sang with all the beatitude of coming home at last.

51

Bertie and Rosa (1)

S he lived in a flat on the second floor of a house in a sleazy street in Soho, at the centre of London's film industry. There were restaurants and strip clubs, many of them in basements, and small apartments and bedsits containing girls in singles or in pairs, or in brothels. Most of them were enslaved by heroin or alcohol, their lives so chaotic that no other profession was either feasible or practicable. Almost all of them were working for pimps who gave them back just enough to get by on.

One evening, instead of going home, Bertie ate by himself in the Gay Hussar, in Greek Street. Michael Foot was there, eating goulash with Ian Mikardo, the vice president of the Socialist International. Mikardo was banging on about Israel, and Foot was talking across him about how dreadful the Common Market was. Bertie was a staunch Conservative, still glowing with pleasure because of the recent election of Margaret Thatcher, but he thought himself broad-minded enough to hobnob with the luminati of the Opposition. He liked to eavesdrop on socialist conversations, but they were nearly always House of Commons tittle-tattle. Any Conservative spy who ate there would have come out with little information of any importance, but a plausibly sound knowledge of who was fondling whom, in which cupboard.

Afterwards Bertie walked the streets of Soho alone, simply following his feet, round the square, up and down Dean Street, Frith Street, Old Compton Street. He had no intention of going home from Waterloo before the last train. He was discontented and angry. He had been married for twenty-six years and was being driven mad by the thought of all the women he had never been to bed with. It was terrible; his wife Kate had been exemplary, but now she was fifty years old and the menopause had hit her like a falling wall. She was bleeding and exhausted all the time, it seemed, and every now and then her face and neck would glow dark red in the perspiration of her own personal sauna. Her copper hair had become completely white, she had lost her figure, and every month in the week before her period she would meta-morphose into an aggressive monster who would snap at him with contempt the moment he opened his mouth. If he mowed the lawn, she would be angry with him for not spending the time with her, and if he spent the time with her, she would nag at him about all the jobs that needed to be done outside. She would revert to her formerly sweet self in the days that followed, but somehow each month the damage seemed worse, and more difficult to repair. All she could say was, 'I'm so sorry, I'm so sorry, darling, it's the change of life,' and he was supposed to forgive her the humiliation and nastiness over and over again.

Bertie had a great deal to be thankful for, but even the happiness and liberty of his children embittered him. Only Phoebe was still at home, barefoot, dressed in rags and feathers, the heritor of both her great-grandmother's violin and her great-grandmother's talent on it, dancing in her room as she improvised classical versions of the rock songs that she loved, and which seemed to him to be complete rubbish. At the moment it was a song called 'Refugee', which she sang at the top of her voice when she was in the bathroom. Sometimes she sat on his lap and told him that she loved him, but all he could do was sit unmoving, inhaling the freshness of the scent of her hair and patting her back as if she were a pet animal. 'I love you too,' he would say, but he could never make it sound sincere, even though it was. He suffered not from *rigor mortis* but from *rigor vitae*. Throughout the teenage years of his children he had been open-mouthed with longing as a succession of fabulously pretty and vivacious girls came and went. To them he was invisible; they longed only for the callow boys, a couple of years older than them, who came and went as they did.

Bertie disapproved of their liberty, but wanted it for himself. He had the sensation of having been born too late, of having grown up at the wrong time. He had emerged from adolescence into a war and become an adult overnight, but now there had been some kind of revolution, beyond his comprehension or control, and he knew he was jealous of the youngsters because they seemed to be having so much more fun than he had ever had. He tried to remind himself frequently that the reason he had fought in the war was so that the future's children could enjoy the kind of liberty that he had never had himself. It did not occur to him that much of what they were up to was play-acting and self-delusion; that they were confused, uncomfortable and frightened children, desperate to follow the herd, with no sense that youth's immortality is no immortality at all.

So Bertie walked the streets of Soho, looking at the handwritten scrawls on doorposts that said 'Model Upstairs' but disdaining to ring or knock, or ascend. For no good reason at all he decided to go to Leicester Square.

It was early May and the place had not yet filled up with its summer influx of tourists. He sat on a bench, spreading his arm across the back of it, and spreading his legs, as if in ownership. He watched the pretty girls, imagining what they would look like naked, and then instantly forgetting them. He had never been very faithful to his wife but had always managed to keep his infidelities harmless; now that he was in his fifties he was still tormented by lustfulness, but also in a frequently recurring panic, in case the loss of his potency should set in any time soon. Looking at pretty girls was no infidelity; in his opinion, it was every man's birthright.

A woman approached and sat down at the far end of the bench, beyond the reach of his ownership. She was in her thirties, he guessed, or perhaps her late twenties. She was wide-hipped and large-breasted, and wore her shiny black hair in a bob. She was neatly dressed, neither smart nor casual, and wore a red beret very fetchingly to one side of her head.

She looked dejected, sitting with her elbows on her knees and her chin on her hands. She seemed to be stifling sobs, frequently wiping her eyes with the back of her hand. She riffled through her white handbag, and found only the most pathetic remnant of a tissue with which to dab at her eyes.

Bertie took his handkerchief from his pocket and reached it out to her. She took it from him, inspected it, and said, 'Oh good, it's clean.'

'I wouldn't have given it to you otherwise,' said Bertie.

'OK, so you're a nice man,' said the woman. She had an accent that he found hard to identify, but her voice was soft and melodious.

'Forgive me for asking, and you can tell me to mind my own business, but are you all right? I mean, is there anything I can do?'

'You just did do something. You are wanting to know why I am crying. Isn't that it?' She looked up at him and he saw that the tip of her nose was red, and her large brown eyes were sore.

Bertie held up his hands. 'It's none of my business.'

'I tell you anyway, not that anyone bloody cares in this bloody place.'

She said nothing, however, but stared silently at the pavement, with its strange cohorts of deformed pigeons and perky house sparrows. Bertie looked at her expectantly, but she neither looked up nor said anything at all for what seemed like several minutes.

Then she looked at him and said, 'Everything's fucked up. My whole life. And now the old man's died.'

'The old man? Your father?'

'My father? I don't know. Maybe he's dead and maybe he isn't. He might be by now. I mean *Stari*. The Old Man.'

Bertie remained puzzled and expectant, and finally she said, 'Tito. The leader of my country. Now my country's fucked for good, that's for sure.'

'Oh,' said Bertie, 'I read about it this morning. He was eighty-seven wasn't he? He had a good long life.'

'OK, but now my country's dead too,' said the girl. 'I got nowhere to go back to.'

'It can't be that bad, surely?'

'Just you watch,' she said. 'No one in the Balkan does killing like we do. Not Greek, not Bulgarian. We're the bloody expert. Anyway, I'm Rosa. Who are you?'

'I'm Bertie.'

'So, you want a drink before you go home?'

'I shouldn't.'

'Yes, but even so, you got a nice face, you got sympathy, you feel sorry, you're liking me, you're going to have a drink, don't you think?

'Yes, I think I am.'

52

Bertie and Rosa (2)

'So,' said Rosa, 'do you like my room?'

Bertie looked around at its outrageous shades of puce, and said, 'It's delightful.' The smell of perfume was so strong that it almost stifled him.

'Well, I like it.'

'Can I ask why you always have a cigarette in your hand, but you never light it?'

'It was my old boyfriend. He didn't like the smoking, so I stopped, but I still like the cigarette in my hand.'

'Your old boyfriend?'

'Chris. You know, I loved him but he was a drunk, and I only found out too late. I finished it. And he was married, of course.'

'Of course?'

She drew seductively on her unlit cigarette and said, 'Yes, of course. Rosa seems to have a thing for the married men. I'm crazy like that.' She pulled a wry face, as if in self-deprecation, and Bertie was struck by how sweet she was.

'You're married of course,' she said.

Bertie thought of denying it, but said, 'Yes, I am. I am married.'

'But your beautiful wife isn't beautiful any more, and she has no time for you, and she doesn't love you any more, and there's no passion left, and there's been no blow job for five, maybe ten years, and she loves the dog more than she loves you, but for one reason or another reason you can't leave her.'

'How did you know?'

She looked at him disdainfully. 'All you long-time married men, you are the same. I don't even have to listen. I know it all before you speak. I might as well have a tape and play it so you don't have to give me the explanations.'

'I don't know about other men. I only know what's true for me.'

'I know other men. I used to work in a hostess club. Bergonzi's. You know it? Every night I hear the same thing, and I hear "Rosa, I love you. Come away with me and we'll be happy. I give you everything. La la la la, la la laa."'

'Perhaps I'd better go.'

'No, I like you. You stay.'

'Tell me about yourself, then.'

'Well,' she said, 'did I tell you that my father was partisan? With Tito. When I tell you that my father was partisan, and that I am his daughter, then it explains me.'

'Does it?'

She took another smokeless puff on her cigarette, and he noticed that there was a ring of red lipstick around the filter. 'My father had an eyepatch that made him look like pirate, and he had five bullets still in his body from the war, and every year he went for an X-ray to see where the bullets had got to. My father was like a mountain.'

'My father was an air ace in the Great War,' said Bertie.' I know what it is to have a father who's like a mountain.'

'Oh, Bertie,' she said, 'nobody is like my father. Nobody. You know, once I slept with him, but it was my idea. It fucked him up and I was sorry.'

'I don't know what to say.'

She looked at him unblinkingly, coolly appraising him. 'It's OK, Bertie. You just listen, and I talk, OK?'

53

Bertie and Phoebe

The suicide of Gaskell and Christabel had knocked Daniel sideways. Ever since he had heard the news he had felt numbed, deserted and bereft. Christabel had been his last and longest love, and Gaskell had been like a comrade, or a sibling. On the mantelpiece above his fire he had a large photograph of her that he had taken, one night when the wine had flowed, dancing drunkenly with Puss, the lion towering over her, his paws on her shoulders, his chin on the top of her head. In the background Christabel was raising her glass and laughing. Every day, on his slow progress to his armchair, he would stop and look at it, and then hang his head and carry on. The gramophone had been playing Glenn Miller. It was 'Moonlight Serenade'. It was one of his happiest and most vivid memories. Now all he had to look forward to were letters and visits from his grandchildren, and the daily walk to his son's house at suppertime.

One day the telephone rang, and Daniel picked up the receiver. Now that he was eighty-seven years old, he could not rely on himself to get to the phone quickly, so he had rerouted it to his chairside table. It would rouse him out of his long snoozes, and he would suffer a heart-racing moment of confusion before he realised that it was not the scramble alarm.

It was Phoebe. 'Gramps! Daddy's crying in the downstairs loo. What should I do?'

'Hang on a minute, darling, I've got to switch my hearing aid up.' It squealed painfully in his ear, and he exclaimed, 'Damn the bloody thing! What did you say, darling?'

'Daddy's crying in the loo. It's horrible. What am I supposed to do about it?'

'Are you alone with him?'

'Yes, Mum's gone out to the gardening club and then she's going to the WI.'

'Well, I don't think I'm the right person to talk to him. He's not the kind of man who can cry in front of his father. He'd just get angry and ashamed, and clam up. You'll have to deal with it yourself.'

'But what can I say?'

'Just knock on the door and say, "Are you all right?" Then take it from there.'

'But what can it be?'

'It'll be something to do with a mistress. I don't see what else it could be, really.'

'Gramps! A mistress! I'm only sixteen!'

'Sweetheart, people used to go to war at sixteen. You look after him and I'll look after you. Pop down as soon as you know what it's all about. You're old enough to start learning about life as it really is, and if he's crying loud enough to be heard, it means he wants somebody to hear.'

'OK, Gramps.'

'*Bon courage*, sweetheart. Oh, and something else.'

'Yes, Gramps?'

'You know, sometimes things get reversed, and the child has to become the parent to the parent. It mostly happens in old age, but it can happen at any time. Do you understand?'

'Sort of.'

'Good luck, then.'

Phoebe put the phone down, hesitated, and then, chewing her lower lip, she crept into the corridor that led from the hallway to the side door. She listened quietly to her father's sobbing, and then knocked on the door. It ceased abruptly.

'Daddy, are you all right?'

There was a long silence, and then, 'No, I'm not all right. Not really.'

'Are you coming out?'

There was another long silence, and then Bertie turned the lock and emerged, his eyes bloodshot and his face flushed.

'I'll make you a cup of tea,' said Phoebe.

'Where shall I go?'

'Into the drawing room. I won't be a minute.'

An hour and a half later, barefoot and wearing a tie-dyed purple smock, Phoebe knocked at Daniel's door and entered without waiting for a response. She found her grandfather in the tiny, shabby kitchen, half-heartedly washing the rings out of an old mug, whilst listening to Radio 4, which he obstinately continued to call the Home Service. She was trembling, but she had an excited air of self-satisfaction.

'You should use bleach,' she said.

'Oh no. The aftertaste lingers horribly. So, how did it go?'

'It is a mistress. She's dumped him.'

'Any details?'

'She's Yugoslavian and she lives in Soho, wherever that is. He says he met her in Leicester Square when she was crying because someone had died, and it just grew from there. He said he used to visit her flat and she kept telling him stories about herself and was just completely fascinating, and she liked hearing his stories about the war that he's never even told us. He said they fell in love and it's been very passionate. But now she's decided to go home because she's a poet and she's just had her first book of poems published in Belgrade, so this is her big chance, and she's got to take it.'

'Apparently, she's got black shiny hair and big brown eyes. And a beautiful voice with a sweet accent. And the most fabulous body he's ever seen.'

'He said that? Fancy saying that to your own daughter!'

'He just blurted it all out.'

Daniel wondered whether he could ever have talked to his own daughter in that manner. His relationship with Esther had always been teasing, open and affectionate, and Felicity was sometimes alarmingly straightforward; perhaps he could have. It seemed very strange that his dark and angry son, so much imprisoned inside himself, had been able to say such things to Phoebe.

'Dad said that he's fifty-five and Rosa is much younger, and she's his last great love, and now he's done for, because Mum isn't what she was and doesn't care a fig for him any more. He said, "I've got nothing to look forward to now."'

'It's true that your mother's got very difficult,' said Daniel. 'It's the change of life. She can't really help it. You must have noticed.'

'Not half,' said Phoebe wryly. 'She keeps biting everybody's heads off. She's a nightmare. When she's due for an explosion she puts on her Satan face. That's what we call it.'

'The other thing is, in any relationship the sexual passion nearly always wears off. Sometimes it only lasts six months.'

'Gramps!'

'I'm sorry, darling, but one has to be frank.'

'Mum and Daddy aren't. Or at least Dad hasn't been until now.'

'I don't suppose you can even imagine them in bed together, can you?'

'Oh, Gramps, don't!' She put her hands over her ears.

'Well, you'll just have to take my word for it. Sexual passion wears off, and that's when you find out whether you're actually made for each other or not. And if one of you needs passion more than the other, then that person starts to have affairs. I know it's shocking and unromantic, and you don't want to think about it, but it's true. It's nobody's fault. It's Mother Nature's. Or God's, if you believe in Him. God's probably French, if you think about it.'

'I don't know if I do or not,' said Phoebe.

'Anyway, it's nobody's fault. I don't know if I ever told you, but your great-grandfather, Hamilton, had about twelve mistresses, all at once. Anyway, all you can do is become the head of the family for a while, until it all sorts itself out.'

'But, Gramps, I'm too young to be head of the family.'

'I'll be your hoary-headed adviser. I'll be the secret head. The power behind the throne.'

'It'll never be the same, now. It can't be. Not after what I did.'

'Why? What did you do?'

'I slapped him.'

'Slapped him? Phoebe darling, whatever did you do that for?'

'He deserved it. He said that this Rosa woman was the love of his life, so I slapped him. Twice. Once with each hand. Look!' She held up her hands to show him the palms. 'They're still stinging and a bit red.'

'What made you do that?'

278

'It was when he said that this woman was the love of his life. I slapped him and shouted at him, "How can you say that when you've been with Mum for a million years, and she's given you four children, and given up everything to look after us all, when she's an intelligent woman who could have been anything she liked, and she's cooked you thousands of meals and ironed your shirts and gone to your stupid office parties, and put up with your drinking and your foul moods, and stayed at home while you wafted up and down to London every day and got drunk on the train on the way home?" And he just looked at me with tears pouring down his face, and I slapped him again and came straight down here.'

Daniel looked out of the kitchen window. 'Don't be too hard on him. He had a very difficult war. And a long marriage is even more difficult than a difficult war. It's like an unending SOE mission. Nothing but frustration and disappointment and aborted manoeuvres.'

'You had two difficult wars, Gramps, and you're much nicer than he is.'

'We've got to think about your mother,' said Daniel. 'If he blurted it all out to you, he's bound to confess to her too.'

Before she turned to leave she put her arms around her grandfather and said, 'Thanks, Gramps.'

He patted her back and felt how sweet it was to have her slight body in his arms. He laughed softly. 'You've got all this love business to look forward to,' he said.

'I think I've been put off it already,' she said.

'It's all worth it,' said Daniel. 'In the end it really is. There can't be anything worse than getting to old age and looking back on a life in which none of these things ever happened. It's the overwhelming feelings that you remember. You don't really remember anything else. Can I give you some advice?'

She looked at him wryly. 'You're going to anyway, aren't you?'

'Mmm, yes. My advice is to acquire the knack of learning from other people's mistakes, so you don't have to repeat them too often yourself.'

'I'd better get back to Dad.'

'Good luck, Little Gypsy. Little Gypsy?'

'Yes, Gramps?'

'You remind me terribly of my daughter. Your Aunt Esther. The one who was killed. It's like having her back.'

He stood, trying to hold himself back, his lip trembling. Phoebe put her arms around him again. She laid the side of her head against his chest. 'Oh, Gramps,' she said.

54

Daniel and Kate

Daniel came through the gate they had made in the fence at the bottom of the garden, between his bungalow and the house, and walked up the garden path between the two rose beds. His feet were hurting today, as if recalling for themselves those nightmarish days of interrogation by the Gestapo. Nonetheless he was determined to take the dog for a walk, because it made him both listless and sleepless if he did not stride out at least once every day. He liked to ascend the hill to the top of the common, sit on the Maclachlan bench, and look out across the ocean of trees towards Blackdown and Chanctonbury Ring. In the winter he would go up there, the only adult, and an exceedingly old one at that, to participate in the communal tobogganing of the village children. The snow reminded him of Afghanistan, the bite and chill of it, the strange metallic taste it gave to the air, the way it seemed almost warm at first, and then chilled the toes and fingers to an ache. Here there were no snipers, and the religious fanatics were not jihadis but the nuns in the school behind the crest of the hill, who gratified themselves by making miserable the lives of the abandoned children in their untender care.

The dog greeted him with its customary yelps, caracoles and leaps, and scurried away to find a shoe to present to him as a gift. He found Kate weeping at the kitchen table, and rightly surmised that her husband's infidelity had come out into the open.

She looked up at him with red-rimmed eyes, and said, 'I know you know all about it. Phoebe told me she'd told you. She's told the other children too, even though I asked her not to.'

'I'll make you a cup of tea,' said Daniel.

'I'm full of tea.'

'Well, I'll make myself one.'

'Don't put that shoe on the table. It's bad luck.'

'What bollocks,' he said brightly, but gave it back to the dog anyway.

'Don't touch me!' she said, and he withdrew the arm he had been about to put around her shoulder.

Daniel put the kettle back on the gas, and made himself a weak cup of black tea by dunking in the tea bag, squeezing it once against the side with the teaspoon, and then sliding it out. He sat opposite Kate, and waited for her to speak. Eventually he said, 'I don't mind what you say. There isn't much I've never heard.'

'You can't help,' she said. 'Your son's a bastard, a dirty, disgusting unfaithful bastard, and I've spent twenty-five years cooking for him and ironing his shirts and waiting on him hand and foot, and putting up with his drinking and his shouting and his foul moods and his ignoring the children. Twenty-five years of being nothing but a devoted bloody servant, and I was never unfaithful once! I never even looked at another man!'

'If I know how marriages go, which at my age I do, I would guess that you don't look at him much either.'

Kate raised her head and glared at him. 'Are you taking his side? Bloody men! You're all the bloody same, aren't you?'

'Probably. As you well know, my marriage to Bertie's mother was a failure. If I wanted any intimacy, I had to be unfaithful. As she refused to divorce me I had no choice.' He made a sweeping gesture with his right hand. 'Technically, I've been unfaithful for most of my life. I know a great deal about infidelity.' Daniel stood up and went to the window, looking at the aubretia that was growing in the interstices of the wall outside. 'My mother, who you never met, said there were two kinds of fidelity. She shocked your mother-in-law by telling her so.'

'Two kinds? What are you talking about? Your mother was French, wasn't she?'

'Yes. But I hope that's not a disqualification. She said there was positive fidelity and negative fidelity. Negative fidelity is when you don't go to bed with anyone else. Positive fidelity is when you do go to bed with the one you're supposed to be going to bed with.'

'What do you mean?'

'I think you know what I mean.'

Kate flushed, and said, 'Well, after all these years, what can anyone expect?'

Daniel shrugged. 'I don't know the answer. I've never lived with anyone long enough to know. It's for you and Bertie to sort out. I can't talk to him. He wouldn't take a lecture from me. He'd just call me a bloody hypocrite. Maybe you can. I love my son, but I know he's hard to love, and often not even very likeable. Maybe you should talk to Fairhead. He and Sophie pulled it off beautifully, as far as I can see.'

'I'm not talking to Fairhead! And I'm not talking to Bertie either. He can sleep in the bloody spare room, and go off with Yugoslavian whores half his age, and I'll just see him at supper-time. I don't care any more.'

'That would be one solution,' said Daniel drily. 'But I think Phoebe might be able to sort him out. She's got the bit between her teeth, and she's not the kind of girl who would take any nonsense. From either of you. Why don't you come for a walk? The fresh air will do you good.'

'I might as well,' said Kate. 'I was going to do his washing, but actually I am not bloody well going to. From now on he can do it himself.'

In the lobby Daniel helped her on with her coat, and said, 'You know, I think going on strike might be the best possible thing you can do. He might think about what he stands to lose. And let me just tell you something.'

'Oh yes?'

'Once I dropped a parachutist out of a Hudson, over France, in midwinter. For some reason her harness got caught in the tailwheel. There was absolutely nothing I could do. She almost certainly froze to death, but if not, she was killed when I had to land at Tangmere and drag her along the airstrip. I never knew her real name, only the code. But she was a lovely young woman.'

'Why are you telling me this?'

'Just try to keep a sense of perspective. There are a thousand things worse than what's happened to you.'

55

Daniel's Intervention

In the months following the crisis over Rosa the Serbian poet, the atmosphere within the family had become so tense and poisonous that finally Daniel summoned up his courage and agreed with Phoebe that he would have to assume control of the situation rather than leave it to her. At his age, when all he longed for was the peaceful contemplation of memory, this amounted to a tedious burden.

Nonetheless, he had gone to their house one Sunday evening and summoned his son and daughter-in-law to the dining room, where he told them to sit down. Bertie still resented being 'ordered about' by his father. He had lost a great deal of weight, his hands trembled, and he was as enraged as his wife, although he barely knew why, since the infidelity had been his. Kate sat, pale and indignant, chewing her lip, convinced in advance that Daniel was going to take his son's part.

Daniel went to the drinks cabinet and poured them both a tot of whisky, which he set down before them.

'Do we have to go through with this?' demanded Bertie. 'I don't see the point.'

Daniel sat down at the head of the table. 'Well,' he said, 'the situation has become so bad that I am persuaded – in fact Phoebe has persuaded me – that I've got to try to sort things out, because you two are never going to do it on your own.'

'There's nothing to sort out,' said Kate.

'You have no authority over me,' said Bertie. 'You never did. I don't know why I'm sitting here waiting for orders. Do you think you're the Lord God?'

'I've been thinking,' said Daniel, 'about what my mother would have said. She was very wise. She tried to save my marriage to your mother, Bertie. She gave us both good talkings-to. She always saw things from the perspective of a sophisticated Frenchwoman.'

'So you've been having a séance, have you?'

Daniel regarded him scornfully. 'My mother is built into me in the same way as yours is built into you. Just be quiet and listen. And that applies to both of you.

'You have three choices. One is to reconcile. It would take time and patience, and above all, forgiveness. From both of you.'

'He has nothing to forgive me for,' said Kate.

'I've already talked to you in private about this,' said Daniel. 'I don't have to repeat it in front of Bertie.

'Our marriage is dead,' said Bertie, looking at her coldly. 'Stone dead. It's been nothing but a formality for years and years.'

'The second choice is to separate and divorce. You would have to decide who gets the house and who gets what share of Bertie's income. You would have to break it to the children and cope with their anger and disappointment and distress. You would blame each other and try to get them to take your side. You would have to decide who gets the dog and the cat. Your friends would have to choose between you. Most of your money would go on lawyers who have a vested interest in ratcheting up the acrimony so that they can profit from all the time you'd have to spend arguing about the details.'

'What's the third option?' asked Kate.

'Your marriage remains a formality. You stay together for the sake of habit and convenience, and for the happiness of the children. You do things together, such as going to cocktail parties and the theatre, and the kinds of occasions when it's expected. Otherwise you do exactly what you want to, and you explain nothing to the other except what's necessary for the diary. You become companions, and that's all.'

Bertie and Kate looked at him silently.

'The last suggestion is what my mother would have proposed,' said Daniel at last.

'That's the French solution,' said Kate, folding her arms. 'I'm English.'

'The point is,' said Daniel, 'that you both love the children, you both love this house and the Surrey Hills, you both love the dog and the cat, you both love your neighbours and your mutual friends. All that you don't love is each other. All these other loves … they outweigh the absence of married love. That's all I'm saying. You don't have to throw out half a dozen babies with the bathwater. You live for these other loves, together but separately.'

'That really is too bloody French!' exclaimed Kate. Bertie polished off his dram, and stood up. 'I've had enough of this,' he said. 'I'm going to walk the dog.'

'Before you go,' said Daniel, 'let me tell you something. I have often wished that your mother and I had adopted the "French" solution. If we had, I could have been a proper father to you. And one day we might have come to terms and made a decent fist of our marriage.'

56

Daniel Pitt's Last Dream

In the last summers of his life Daniel still dressed in the manner of the North-West Frontier, in loose trousers and jacket of plain white linen, and more often than not without anything at all on his feet. He liked to sleep in the garden in a deckchair, with his face to the sun so that he felt he was absorbing the essence of life itself. He dreamed of curious things, such as being trapped in a tunnel of chalk, or of a ginger cat having two litters of tabby kittens simultaneously, and the house being overrun with them, and then the ginger cat turning into two cats that were having a fight on the roof.

Sometimes his dreams took him straight back to the cemetery in Peshawar, or to his days in the Royal Flying Corps, or his days with Christabel and Gaskell at Hexham. It was at these times that old age failed to touch him or encroach. It occurred to him that sleeping and dreaming were, as a matter of course, how one travelled in time. More often than not, he was disappointed to have to return to the present when he woke up. 'When I'm asleep I become a Time Lord,' he liked to say.

One of his delights was to show off his missing toes. 'At my age,' he said, 'I'm entitled to do what I bloody well like, and to hell with everyone else. If I want to be odd, I'll be odd. It's only when you don't know you're mad that you really are.'

As he grew ever older, even the events of his early old age receded into the distance and became more beautiful. His ride across North America in his sixties seemed as far away as his learning to fly the Lysander in his forties, or being dressed down by his platoon sergeant as an officer cadet.

'How tall are you, sir?'

'Five foot eleven, staff.'

'Well, I've never seen a stack of shit piled so high, sir. You have an idle belt, sir. You, sir, look like a sack of shit tied up with raffia, sir.'

The years dreamed their way past him. It became customary to say how 'marvellous' the old man was, still living more or less independently, in a state of intellectual clarity, good humour and robust health.

Yet more years dreamed their way past him. He made himself breakfasts of raw oats and cups of tea, and at midday walked very slowly and carefully up to the family house to be fed Welsh rarebit, or ravioli, or tomato soup, by Kate. He would have to struggle against the capricious looseness of his false teeth. Afterwards they would sit side by side on the sofa, doing the crossword in the previous day's *Daily Telegraph*, which they found discarded each morning in Bertie's armchair. In the evenings Daniel often ate nothing at all, and these days half a glass of wine was enough to put him off balance.

Somehow Phoebe turned twenty-three, and he hardly saw her except when she came home for occasional weekends and holidays. She was studying the violin at the Royal Northern College of Music, going back and forth in a third-hand Triumph Herald that he had helped her to choose, and then taught her to maintain. He had once found her trying to replenish the oil through the hole for the dipstick, and it had become a standing joke between them. When he knew that she was coming home, he would sit bolt upright in the kitchen for hours, straining to hear her knock on the door, waiting for his Little Gypsy with the silvery voice singing, 'Gramps? Where are you? Want to hear a sonata?'

Then, one day, Theodore was thirty-two years old, and for six years had not come home from the Andes, where he was living with a wife of Kogi descent, with their four children. In the latest photographs, of his family standing in a row on the scree of a mountainside, flanked by two enormous black cats, he is balding at the forehead, has three days' stubble, and carries a rifle slung across his back. At his belt, clearly visible, is a severe, black Sykes Pickavant commando knife, the parting gift of his grandfather, who had used it last in 1944.

Daniel knew that Phoebe had given him another chance to be a father to a daughter, and Theodore another chance to be the father of a son. For this he was thankful to whatever inscrutable force it is that manoeuvres us into making a hash of our lives and then, as if in afterthought, gives us a shot at redemption.

Daniel had to give up driving his Brough Superior in his eighties, no longer capable of kicking it over, or walking far enough to find someone who could. Moreover, Dr Matthews had told him that it really was time to stop, because his hearing had become too bad and his reaction time too long. He kept it in the shed, covered over with a tarpaulin, but was still conscientious about cleaning the chrome, checking the battery and recharging it. He had plans for its immortality, just as he had none for his own. Nowadays it would take him an hour to do things that had once taken him five minutes.

Every three months or so, Daniel would go to stay with Fairhead for a week, and then Fairhead would come down to Notwithstanding. Daniel enjoyed the prosperous suburban calm of Blackheath, and was reconciled to Fairhead's obsessive search for books on theology and philosophy in the two local second-hand bookshops, and in Charing Cross Road. In his last years Fairhead's obsessive search for ultimate truth was becoming ever more intense; every book he read, he read in the spirit of the explorer who imminently expects to find the source of a river or the last example of a species thought to be extinct. For him it was a matter of deep joy to find the Complete Lectures of Sir William Hamilton, or the original German edition of *The Idea of the Holy* printed in Gothic script so heavy that it was almost illegible. After he and Daniel walked slowly home up the hill from the village, laden with old books, Fairhead would relax with a sigh of contentment into his armchair to peruse his new acquisitions, and fall instantly asleep, his demilune spectacles sliding down to the tip of his nose.

Fairhead had become a miniaturised version of his former self. He had always been slight, and had never seen the point of acquiring new clothes if his old ones were still serviceable. Accordingly, he dressed in old tweed suits that had become too big for him, and a waistcoat with a fob watch and chain, whose gold plating had all but worn away. He had never stopped wearing his dog collar, not least because it saved all the bother of faffing about with ties. These days his hands, their backs covered with wide liver spots, had a noticeable tremor. His tired rheumy eyes only crackled into life when he laughed or suddenly became fired up with interest in some philosophical point.

Without Sophie he had managed but not managed well. He was inclined to live off baked beans on toast and slices of apple, washed down with glasses of milk, and found himself quite frequently aimless and melancholy. Nowadays he wished that he had been a philosopher rather than a clergyman, and written at least one magisterial work on metaphysics. All his life he had wanted to write one final definitive book on Death and Survival, but he knew now that it would never be done. He was, as he said to Daniel, 'Just waiting to do the final bit of research. That should clinch it.'

In summer they sat out in the walled garden, which Fairhead had allowed to revert to jungle. Daniel had thought it was because he no longer had the energy for gardening, until one day Fairhead explained that 'This was our garden, Sophie's and mine. If the weather was good, we could take our clothes off. That's why we asked you to help us build the wall, to make it impossible for the scopophiles. It was Sophie's idea. She said that if she were God she would want us to remake the Garden of Eden. So that's what we did. We recreated Paradise with our fruit trees and flowers and our patch of lawn, and we took off our clothes and lived and walked in the light. But there have to be two of you. Without Sophie there is no Eve, and without Eve I can't be Adam. So I gave our garden back to the world. After I've gone, whoever moves here can make it back into a garden, if that's what they want. People who come here just see nettles and briars and bind-weed, but I see with the eyes of memory. Out in this garden I see it as it was, with Sophie in it, and the dogs, and the rose beds. The thing is, you see Paradise much more clearly when it's passed away.'

In Surrey, Fairhead and Daniel drove the old black A35 to the highest places in the Surrey Hills: Hydon's Ball, Blackdown, Busses Common. Sometimes they drove to Box Hill on the North Downs, or Chanctonbury Ring on the South, until neither of them could manage the walks to the top. Daniel liked to return to Partridge Green, where his mother had lived, and they would eat a ploughman's lunch in the Green Man or the White Hart. Once Daniel took Fairhead to Beachy Head, and told him the story of the strange, tall man who had prevented him from toppling off it after the news of Esther's drowning.

When Daniel was ninety years old the Falklands War broke out, and he found himself deeply surprised, almost shocked, by how detached he was. His whole life had been arranged and disarranged by warfare and his part in it, but this time he felt as if it was all happening in another world. On television he saw aircraft that he did not recognise or know anything about, and warships that looked terribly small and under-armed compared to the ones that he remembered. The soldiers still looked like soldiers, but they were not in battledress and puttees, and their helmets were the wrong shape. Their semi-automatic rifles looked too short to be accurate. It all appeared very amateur, and there were too many cock-ups. Worst of all, even though he had no doubts about the justice of the war, he did not feel any great surge of patriotism. Sitting in front of the television watching grainy images of burning ships with helicopters hovering above them winching off the casualties, he realised that he had become too old even to be an old soldier. He had become Olympian. War was for people who believed they had a future; it was no longer his business, now that he was waiting out his time.

The Commemoration on Remembrance Day was still the only church service he ever attended, in the pinstriped post-war suit that had become vastly too capacious for his shrinking frame, a poppy through the buttonhole, his rows of medals pinned to his chest. Every year in St Peter's he shuffled up the aisle to the lectern to read Binyon's poem, and then as soon as he had intoned '...we will remember them', he could not prevent himself from thinking 'but as a matter of fact almost all of them have been forgotten'. To have your name and rank inscribed on a memorial is not to be remembered.

Every year the congregation would sit and marvel that this little stooped old man had been one of the greatest flying aces of the First World War, and an SOE pilot in the second. It was unimaginable. One by one the other village veterans of the First World War died away, until Daniel was the only one left. There were a general, a major and a colonel left over from the Second World War, and Bertie of course, but the only one who interested him was the postman, whose deeply polished boots and smartly ironed uniform betrayed his personal history. He was one of the few people in the area who still had the old Surrey accent, and most assumed that he must be from some such county as Dorset.

He had served in the 1st Battalion of the West Surreys, firstly in India, and then in Burma, before ending the war as a company sergeant major. He liked to hold back Daniel's letters until last, so he could stop there with the old man, drinking tea and talking about India, preparatory to his daily tryst with Miss Agatha Feakes's reclusive lodger.

When Daniel was ninety-one Kate went to fetch him some food, found a green ham in the fridge, saw that it had broken down, and was horrified to realise that he had been eating rotten food, although without apparent consequence. The doctor said that he had anosmia, and that it was common in extreme age; he had entirely lost his sense of smell. 'I could have told you that,' said Daniel. 'Nothing tastes of anything any more. It takes all the fun out of eating. That's why I've got so thin.'

Evenly and equably the time passed. Molly became a doctor in Warwick. She had neither husband nor children, but Kate liked to reassure Daniel that she was 'perfectly normal' and had 'lots of boyfriends'. 'These days,' Daniel used to say to her, 'it's perfectly normal not to be normal. Even in my day it was quite usual, especially if you had enough money to get away with it, and never talked about in public.'

'Like poor old Oscar Wilde?'

'I think he must have wanted to be caught,' said Daniel. 'No, I mean like Christabel and Gaskell.'

Daniel wished that he was able to tell Kate that her husband had a half-brother and a half-sister by a woman who had loved both women and men, but something made him feel that he could not break his vow of secrecy. The family was complicated and troubled enough already. These days he only heard from Felix and Felicity at Christmas. He was just their 'godfather' and 'uncle', after all, and time and distance had pushed them all ever further apart. He often considered what he might have missed out on, but then again he could not bring himself to regret the very evident happiness they had brought to Christabel and Gaskell. At night he still dreamed of his overwhelming trysts with Christabel, in hotels, or at the estate in Hexham. In truth he dreamed of her more often than he dreamed of Rosie.

Somehow Jemima settled into a little stone house in Northumberland with an unsuccessful poet who was really just an English and drama teacher in a local school. He talked a great deal about 'the kids' in a knowingly affectionate tone of voice, and never admitted to anyone that his real job was to be a futile and anxious combination of babysitter and riot policeman. He was not aware of ever having managed to teach any pupil anything, such was the deeply engrained cultural resistance of his pupils. He was thinking of getting out by looking for work writing advertising copy, so that then he could continue with his poetry in his spare time. For this he believed that he would have to move to London, however, and Jemima was strongly opposed. She loved this wild and rugged region, so different from the cosy and domesticated Surrey where she had grown up. She had a scheme to open a craft shop where she would sell to tourists the handmade knick-knacks produced by the small coterie of super-annuated hippies who had moved to the area in the hope of establishing the kind of utopia where everybody is very relaxed and cooperative and tolerant, and grows their own marijuana on windowsills. She tried in vain for three years, but then gave up. There was never any stock, and her suppliers were always falling out.

On impulse she went to Sri Lanka, where she found cheap supplies of wonderful crafts produced in great volume by people who had no objection to working. Her shop would eventually have white tea and jaggery, masks from Bali, bamboo flutes from Nepal, dreamcatchers from Canada, and panpipes from Chile, alongside stones and crystals which were supposed to have restor- ative powers and be chosen so as to be complementary to one's star sign. She became very expert, but believed none of it, having the same relationship to its mythologies as her Great-Uncle

Fairhead had to his Anglican faith. Eventually, Jemima's husband escaped the bedlam of teaching, and came in on the business, hanging around uselessly for much of the time, but running poetry workshops there on Thursday evenings. He and Jemima would eventually produce children too late for Daniel ever to know them.

57

The Grampians

After all the cats had gone, Margareta realised that her plan to become British had failed, and she left to spend her last days in Germany. The family decided to sell The Grampians, the great house in Eltham that Hamilton McCosh had bought with his first fortune in the 1890s.

It was acquired by a property company that intended to turn it into flats, but failed to perform the conversion before it slid into bankruptcy. For ten years it rotted. Thieves stole the copper wiring, and lead from the roofs and water pipes. The rain entered. Little boys broke the windows with stones, and climbed in. Foxes made dens in the maintenance tunnels and in the room under the conservatory. Pigeons flew in and nested, covering the floors with parti-coloured slime. Bats clung to the walls behind the swags of wallpaper. Mould blossomed from the wet plaster, and small brown toadstools grew in the moss of the window frames.

Out in the garden the lawns and rose beds became engulfed in nettles and brambles. The mortar crumbled from the high walls, and the blue door rotted and fell. The neighbours bricked the doorway up. The trees of the orchard grew gnarled, and every year their fruit was smaller, until finally the great Bramleys were as small and hard as nuts. Beneath them, in their invisible graves, lay the delicate bones of generations of well-loved cats and dogs, their names and endearing characteristics altogether lost to memory.

One day a team of workers arrived and erected signs that read 'UNSAFE BUILDING. DO NOT ENTER'. They left steel barricades behind them, linked by chains and padlocks, which were stolen six months later by totters.

The brick pillars, with THE GRAMPIANS inscribed in a square insert of Portland stone, fell over, tilted too far by the roots of the vast chestnut tree that grew from a conker planted by a squirrel behind the low front wall.

The Grampians stood and sagged, like a weary giant, defeated by the elements, the loss of love, the attrition of time. It was waiting for new life, for resurrection. It was remembering the voices of children, the bustling of servants, the clink of cutlery on plates, the soft padding of cats.

58

After the Grandchildren

After his grandchildren had left home, Daniel understood that the last and most golden era of his life had passed, and that the remainder of his time was to be spent thinking about its meaning. He lived in the manner of one who is getting ready to leave. He was content with this. He was tired now, and expended a great deal of time dozing in his armchair with his mouth open, the upper row of his false teeth falling askew onto the lower, adrift in dreams wherein he was still young and strong, in places bright with novelty and wonder. People would turn up in his memory uninvited, such as the young Greek doctor on the voyage back from Ceylon, or Hans and Fritzl from Dortmund, or Wavey Davey, or Bertrand Russell. Sometimes his reveries took him back to the Western Front, and he was stunting over the lines to amuse the mud-bound troops below, or he was on the North-West Frontier, with its wild fanatics eager for blood and martyrdom.

It took him two hours to get up in the morning, mostly because of the struggle to get his socks on, and it required an hour to get to bed when he retired at half past eight. He was frightened that he would not be able to get out of the bath, or would slip in the shower, so he stood before the basin and performed what they used to call a 'top and tail' back in his military days.

He carried a pink plastic hearing aid the size of a cigarette packet that resided in the breast pocket of his shirt, which would squeal loudly and painfully if it was turned up too high. The plaited wire would often get in his way or become entangled, but when the batteries ran out he would be enveloped in a strange, muffled semi-silence that in truth he quite enjoyed. He would listen to the inconsequential babble of his own thoughts, and wonder if he was losing his sanity or, indeed, whether he had ever been sane at all. Much of his life, in retrospect, made no sense to him; it resembled a drama in which he had been forced to take part without his consent or comprehension. Now he was in a waiting room, which was pleasant enough, and the past was his equivalent of a waiting room's untidy stacks of anachronistic magazines.

Above all, he was determined not to be a burden to anyone else. In his bedside drawer he had hidden his brother's Webley, loaded with six rounds. It was an illegal weapon, but he felt not one twinge of guilt about hanging on to it, and had ignored the occasional amnesties. It had seen Archie through two world wars, and any number of skirmishes in Afghanistan. If necessary it would see Daniel Pitt out of this world, and if necessary he would be prepared to use it on an intruder too. Sometimes he took it out of the drawer to feel the familiar heft in his hand. It was getting heavier by the day. He sometimes took the bullets out and polished the tarnish off the brass cases. He was damned if he was going to be killed by a mucky old round. Sometimes he would unload the gun and pull the trigger, just to make sure that he still had the strength, and that everything was in order.

He began to have a great deal of trouble getting through the winters. Setting fires was too difficult these days, and he made do with a single-bar electric fire in his drawing room, and another in his bedroom. His last winters left him deeply demoralised and listless. He lived in dread of influenza, and even a cold could knock him back so badly that he could hardly walk for several days afterwards. His muscles lost strength the moment he stopped using them, so a period in bed was something that he avoided at all costs. He had suffered pneumonia twice, and been saved by antibiotics. 'I ought to be dead, really,' he said to Kate. 'Sooner or later, everyone's got a right to be dead. Next time, I don't want to be saved. And if I have a stroke and can't look after myself any more, I don't want to be saved then, either.'

'You'll live forever,' said Kate.

It is truly said that for every person who dies, an entire universe dies with them. A human life is a light, but Daniel's was becoming exhausted, guttering, flickering and smoking as it began to drown in what remained of its pool of wax.

All of his old friends and lovers were dead, as far as he knew; Fairhead, found dead at his desk in his pyjamas and dressing gown, a glass of dry sherry in his right hand, his forehead resting on the open pages of *The Fourfold Root of Sufficient Reason* in the original German; Ottilie, dead in her sleep two weeks after a catastrophic stroke; Frederick, horribly destroyed not long afterwards by a prostate cancer that went straight to his bones. They had requested that their ashes be combined in one jar, to be emptied out in the harbour at Bosham, and that was the last that Daniel had seen of them; their intermingled flakes and specks flicking away in the twilight, out across the green, ebbing tide, settling on the gentle swell. Daniel wondered whether they had hoped, like Hindus, that their ashes might drift far enough to mingle somewhere with water from the Ganges.

Daniel had no idea what had happened to Oily Wragge and Millicent, his old comrade Fluke, or to Mary FitzGerald St George, the fraudulent lady maid. One day Bertie drove him to Blackheath to visit Sophie and Fairhead's grave, and they found engraved in italics upon the headstone the words that they had composed for it many years before, on the cusp of middle age:

Nothing is or is not as it seems.
As we are, so you shall be.
As you are, so were we.
As dancing motes of golden dust
We whirled within our beam of light,
And then became, but always were,
This dust that falls from dreams.

He remembered something that Fairhead had once said to him about Spinoza's stone: having been thrown, it thought it was flying. He wondered whether anything could have been other than it was.

The world created by his generation skittered away from him and sank, like a flat pebble flicked across the frozen waters of a lake. How strange it was that he had fought in two world wars against tyrants and totalitarians just so that youngsters in the 1970s could talk in strange argot, throw their hair about to pagan rhythms, and propose impracticable utopias. How strange that this dreamtime should then have been superseded by a new generation of youngsters in the 1980s who were energised only by opportunities to conjure money out of thin air, by means of cleverness alone. Whatever would be next? The latest talk was of a world taken over by autonomous machines.

'I'm the family ghost,' he would repeat to himself as he shuffled to the window with his walking stick. 'I'm the ghost who hasn't died yet.' His past, so vivid to him, so full of faces, places and events, was going to disappear and be utterly lost, would vanish as if it had never been, because his memory was the last place on earth in which it might reside. Now he lived a life that seemed to go on eternally, day after day, in which almost nothing happened. It was like waiting in the antechamber of a lord who has no regard for other people's time.

He was increasingly oppressed by the humiliations of old age. It was becoming almost impossible to defecate or to urinate. He would have to sit for what seemed like hours, or stand before the pedestal gripping the downpipe from the cistern as a dismal, attenuated stream trickled out. Wistfully he remembered his schooldays, when the Pals, he and his brother and friends, would compete to see how high they could piss up the wall by the blue door in the garden of The Grampians. How much laughter there was back then; how immortal they had been.

59

Spero Meliora

J ust as Oily Wragge was granted one last miracle, so was Daniel Pitt.

In the summer of 1988 Amado Daniel da Silva and his son Daniel o Terceiro da Silva stand outside in the porch of Taprobane, the gardener's cottage at the end of Ram Alley Cluns, whence they have been directed by Kate when she found them outside the door of the family house. Both men carry a wooden rosary wended through the fingers of their right hand.

Amado Daniel is a distinguished man in his late sixties, slender and long-legged, but narrow in the shoulders. He is smartly dressed in cavalry twill trousers, carefully polished shoes, tweed jacket, a tailored blue shirt, and the tie of the Nuwara Eliya Golf Club, done up in a Windsor knot. On the tie is embroidered an arm brandishing a club, and the words 'Spero Meliora'. Amado Daniel's face is light golden brown, the hue that is the usual result of the union of a European and a Tamil. One might easily have assumed that he was Singhalese. He wears a disciplined toothbrush moustache, more becoming a retired officer than someone who has risen to become the manager of a tea estate.

His son is an almost exact replica, but with the advantage of being in his late thirties. Although he is off duty, he has decided to come in his Air Lanka uniform, because his grandfather had been a great flying ace, and he likes to think that perhaps he might see his grandson from beyond the grave. He is one of the captains of Air Lanka's first Boeing 747, the King Vijaya. His wife is of Burgher stock, and they have two sons and two daughters. The boys are St Thomas' College in Mount Lavinia, and the girls are at Newstead Girls' College in Negombo. He has high ambitions for all four of them.

Amado Daniel and his son Daniel o Terceiro have at last gathered together the funds and the courage to come to England to look for the missing half of their family.

Daniel is asleep in his chair, and at first the knocking is the sound of the engine of his Sopwith Pup as a piston slams against the head of a damaged valve. The ringing of the doorbell is the telephone in the mess. He wakes and looks around him. There is somebody at the door. Gingerly, his hands and arms trembling with the effort, he rises slowly to his feet. He fumbles for his stick and sets off towards the front door. When he opens it at last he finds Kate, smiling mysteriously, and two smartly dressed brown men, with startlingly blue and completely familiar eyes. Their build and bearing are unmistakable. The younger man looks like Samadara and also like himself.

'Guess who these are,' says Kate.

The ancient man raises his eyebrows, and his mouth falls open. He holds out one trembling hand; Amado Daniel takes it and raises it to his lips. He lowers it, puts his hands together as if in prayer, drops his gaze and says, 'It has taken a very long time to find you. You have no idea how difficult it was. So many letters! So many enquiries! You are not even in *Who's Who*! I thank God that it is not too late. My mother was Samadara da Silva. I believe I have the honour of being your son.'

60

Yellow Birds

In the autumn of 1988 the USSR sent tanks into Yerevan, and in Yugoslavia there were Serbian demonstrations against their oppression by Albanians in Kosovo. Dhaka was flooded, and Hurricane Gilbert struck Mexico twice. The world was carrying on without him.

One morning, in the opulent peace of the Surrey Hills, Daniel rose early, and thought about the brief hiatus he was hoping to enjoy before the bad weather set in. His little garden was sparkling in golden sunlight, and there was dew on the grass. A blackbird sang, as if it were spring. Across the lane the goats of Miss Agatha Feakes were bleating in their paddock, and her hens were clucking in their great wire run. The swallows and swifts had gone. The fallen trees of the previous October's catastrophic hurricane had been tidied up at last, and tiny saplings were breaking through the leaf mould in the broken spaces that they left behind them.

He was fully expecting that by midwinter he would have died of a pneumonia brought on by influenza; he was so convinced of it that it almost amounted to a plan. But today he saw that the weather was good and decided that he would see if he could walk far enough to get to the farm gate. He spent some time there, leaning on the galvanised top bar as he watched the Friesian cows champing on the rich grass. Then he challenged himself to walk the entire length of Ram Alley Cluns to the main road, and back again.

On his return he made himself a cup of black tea, sat exhausted in his armchair, and fell asleep for an hour, his drink turning cold beside him. When he awoke he took one sip of it, and gazed around his living room as if for the first time. He picked up the photograph album on the table at his chairside, and looked through it again, reading the names and gazing at the faces. His son had brought it from Sri Lanka, complete with a complicated tree of who was who, and how they were related. How strange and wonderful it was to have one's family increase in size so immensely in one's last years. In the front was an old black-and-white photograph of Amado Daniel as a five-year-old, holding his mother's hand. How poignant it was to see Samadara again, just as he remembered her, but with all the colours taken out. She had died some ago, of course. Daniel gazed at her young face and said, 'I'll not be long.' He closed the album and put it down. He heaved himself up slowly and carefully, fumbled for his stick, and shuffled from his chair to the window. On the way he looked at the photograph of Gaskell, dancing with Puss to the 'Moonlight Serenade', and Christabel laughing.

On this autumn day, he saw that one of his fruit trees seemed to be full of yellow birds. 'Yellowhammers?' he asked himself. It was enchanting, and he thought he had never seen anything so pretty. He tried to remember if there had been yellow birds like that in Ceylon. Then he fumbled for the glasses that hung around his neck, and said 'Damned old fool!' as he realised it was simply that the quinces were in full fruit. He should have noticed them a long time ago. 'Daniel Crawford Pitt, you're losing your marbles,' he said. He loved the quinces. They were like huge plump pears, and, if you didn't have anosmia, they smelled so enticing that it was a shame they were inedible when raw.

Daniel remembered that both Kate and Miss Agatha Feakes liked to make quince jelly in the autumn. He had little else to do, so he went outside the shed to fetch his stepladder. Whilst he was in there he partially lifted the tarpaulin over his Brough so he could pat its petrol tank affectionately. 'I'm sorry you haven't been out much,' he said. He relied on the two brothers at the garage to take it out for a spin from time to time, and would sit in the sidecar with his flying helmet and goggles on, recalling when he used to put Esther in there, and lift the wheel as they careered around corners.

The stepladder was only made of aluminium, but it was heavier than he remembered. He could walk with it by using it as frame. He managed to get it out under the tree, and then struggled to open it. When he was finally sure that it was steady, he climbed up carefully, holding on to the top of the ladder with his left hand, and picking with his right, tossing the fruit into the long grass as gently as he could manage. Some came away easily, but the rest had to be plucked quite hard. It suddenly occurred to him that it might have been more sensible to wait for the fruit to fall on their own. They always did, and they were never rotten.

The tree was pleasingly symmetrical, like the Tree of Life in old tapestries, and was not particularly tall. Slowly and carefully he worked his way round it, climbing down to move the ladder, and putting his weight onto the bottom step just to make sure that the legs bedded in to the soft turf before he began to climb.

Finally, there was one quince that was too high to reach easily, but it was a particularly large and handsome one, and Daniel stretched out to reach it, finding that he had no choice but to take his left hand off the curved bar at the top of the steps.

The old man fell.

In the tranquil, infinitely protracted dream of his death, Daniel Pitt stands on the edge of the cliff at Beachy Head, looking down at the sea, and at the gulls and choughs that cling to the tiny ledges, or wheel in the updraught. The sun lays down a blinding triangular carpet of light across the waters. Behind him is all the bustle and fuss of soldiers at war. His motorcycle and sidecar wait for him near the entrance of the encampment, and the ATS girls have ceased fire because above him a Spitfire has arrived and is climbing to attack the Junkers 88 from beneath. He watches the fight for a while, and then loses interest. It is a fine day, and he struggles to see France, the other *patrie* that made him so much of what he became. He is not sure whether he can see her or not. '*Je sais que tu es là,*' he says.

He stands nearer to the edge and spreads out his arms. He feels as young and strong as Adam on the day of his creation. As he looks down he feels the same powerful urge to jump that he had felt all those years ago when he had come here in a state of cavernous despair in the aftermath of Esther's death, and the cliff had willed him to go over. This time, however, he feels only a light euphoria, akin to taking a glass of champagne on an empty stomach.

Behind him a soft voice says, 'The wrinkled sea beneath him crawls; he watches from his mountain walls, and like a thunderbolt he falls.'

When he steps back and turns round he expects to see the tall chaplain who had intervened last time, with exactly the same words, except that this voice is completely different. He recognises it even though he has not heard it for more than forty years. 'It's you,' he says. She is exactly as he last saw her, when she was in her Wren's uniform, ready to leave, kissing him on both cheeks and hugging him to her chest before boarding the train. The last smile, the last small wave of the hand, the last kiss blown.

'There's no point in jumping now,' she says, 'you wouldn't even fall.'

'Flying without an engine? That wouldn't be any fun at all.' He waves an arm at the sublime landscape of the Downs behind her and says, 'Look at all these yellow birds.'

'I've brought someone with me,' says Esther, and a small dark woman appears at her side, wearing gold bangles and a red sari, as if she were dressed for a wedding.

'It's you,' says Daniel.

The woman holds out her hand and says, 'A long time ago, in a house on the side of a mountain, I told you I'd be here.'

Samadara becomes Rosie, becomes Christabel, becomes Mary, becomes Samadara, becomes Rosie, becomes Christabel.

Something strange begins to happen to his sense of time, as if one chronology has blossomed out of another, or as if his usual sense of it had, all along, reposed within another, like an embryo within an egg or a closed bud that had not known it was waiting to bloom. Relative time dissolves into absolute time; he feels an eager curiosity rising up within him; he looks up; a sense of imminent explanation carries him onward into mystery.

61

How a Proper Airman Dies

Daniel did not come back to consciousness in the County Hospital, despite the attentions of the doctors, and the rush of people in and out of the small room in which he had been placed.

Agatha Feakes had found him early in the morning, sparkling and glistening with frozen dew, lying amid a beautiful scattering of golden quince. He had lain for twenty-four hours, unable to move, drifting in and out of consciousness. She had run into the house and called 999, and then up to the family house, where she had found Kate in the kitchen, making fudge for the village shop.

Agatha was beyond distress. She saw the ambulance leave, and then went to sit in the filthy chaos of her house, too upset even to put the kettle on or feed the animals. Bertie took the first train down from London, ringing Phoebe from the station, asking her to telephone the others because he had no time to do so before the train departed. Phoebe cried at the other end of the line. Later that morning she cancelled that evening's concert and sent telegrams to Felicity and Felix.

Bertie drove to the hospital with Kate, and listened to the doctor explaining that the old man had broken both his pelvis and the top of his femur, right at the ball of the joint. He felt that Daniel was too old to get through the operation, let alone recover from it, especially now that it was obvious that the hypothermia had brought on a severe attack of pneumonia which was quite capable of killing him on its own.

Kate fell to her knees on the mat beside the bed, and buried her face in her hands, crying 'Oh God, oh God, it's all my fault! It's all my fault!'

Usually she checked up on her father-in-law last thing in the evening, but the previous night she had not. It had seemed so

307

much that the old man would go on and on, vehemently independent until the crack of Doomsday. She felt exactly as Rosie had, when she discovered that Ash had been mortally wounded the day after she had forgotten to pray for him.

The doctor said, 'We can always try our best to bring him back. I leave the decision to you. But I have to say that I think he's reached the end of his journey. If he comes back he'll be so weak and constrained that he'll wish he hadn't.'

Bertie and Kate looked at each other, and Bertie said, 'I really don't think I can condemn my own father to death.'

'We're all condemned to death,' said the doctor softly. 'I do advise you to consider what your father would have wanted.'

'If you think about it,' said Kate, 'this would be a proper airman's death.'

'What do you mean?'

'This is how an airman dies. He falls to earth.'

62

Bertie and Kate

On the same morning that Kate found Christabel's letters to Daniel, Bertie found the Webley Government revolver in the drawer of his father's bedside table.

Kate came in just in time to find him standing bolt upright, wide-eyed and white-faced, his hands quivering, in front of the long mirror, with the barrel at his temple, and the hammer cocked. He saw her horrified face in the mirror and held her gaze for a few moments.

Bertie had been thin and quiet for years now, like a man who knows he is beaten and that further struggle is pointless. In truth, he had just been waiting for the end, hoping that a headache might be a brain cancer or a pain in his arm an impending heart attack. He read the *Daily Telegraph* every day, tutting at how exasperating the world had become, and when he was at home was usually asleep or drunk in his armchair because he had no energy or enthusiasm for anything else. The thought that he might as well be dead revolved in his mind like a mantra.

He watched dispassionately as his wife became ever more grey, distant and misshapen. He dreamed vividly of Point 153 and the deaths of his comrades in burning Sherman tanks. He saw them climbing out and running in flames, collapsing as the snipers picked them off. Otherwise he dreamed of Rosa, fixing him with her intense brown eyes and low hypnotic voice, holding his hand, telling him her shocking stories across the tables of Soho restaurants, before taking him to her stifling pink-walled flat, kneeling before him, and coolly unbuckling his belt. It was crueller by far to have been expelled from Paradise than never to have been in Paradise at all.

'I was just …' said Bertie, lowering the revolver. 'I wanted to see what it was like.'

'Is it loaded?' asked Kate.

'Yes. It has six rounds in it.' He moved to raise the revolver back to his head.

'Please don't.'

'There's nothing left.' He paused, blinked back the welling of his eyes, and said, 'I never realised how much I loved the old man.'

Kate waved the letters in her hand, and proffered them to him. 'It turns out you've got another half-brother and a half-sister. Don't you want to know about it?'

For many years their marriage had been just a case of living long enough to see which of them would die first. They had adopted Daniel's 'French solution' but it had made neither of them any happier. Kate's affections had been poured entirely into her children and grandchildren, her friends, roses and vegetables, her dogs and her cats. She had cooked and washed for him, despised and resented him, and righteously ignored his suffering.

But then there he was, standing before her, his father newly dead, a revolver in his right hand, rigidly at attention, pale and tragic. She realised that he was even thinner than when she had first met him in Germany. She remembered that for a while it had looked as though she had saved him from himself. She hesitated, and then put her arms around him, laying her head against his chest for the first time in seventeen years.

'Oh, Bertie,' she said. 'What have we done? There's so little time left. Let's try and get the last bit right.'

63

The Headstone

BENEATH THIS STONE LIES AT PEACE

SQUADRON LEADER
'CAPTAIN' D. C. PITT

DSO, MC & BAR, DFC
CROIX DE GUERRE, LEGION OF HONOUR
ROYAL FLYING CORPS AND
ROYAL AIR FORCE
1892–1988

BELOVED FATHER AND
GRANDFATHER

SIC ITUR AD ASTRA

TDTFFD

penguin.co.uk/vintage